19x 6/12 ʟᴛ 5/10

P9-EDV-186

MUSE

MUSE

Michael Cecilione

Kensington Books
http://www.kensingtonbooks.com

KENSINGTON BOOKS are published by

Kensington Publishing Corp.
850 Third Avenue
New York, NY 10022

Library of Congress Card Catalog Number: 98-075337
ISBN 1-57566-313-9

First Printing: July, 1999
10 9 8 7 6 5 4 3 2 1

Printed in the United States of America

for Johanna

"The only way to atone for the sin of writing is to annihilate what is written."

—Georges Bataille

I

The week before I met him for the first time, I woke up in the middle of the night with the strongest feeling of being *watched*. There was a man standing in the doorway of my bedroom. He was dressed all in black with some kind of mask or stocking pulled over his face that made his head look smooth and featureless like a black skull. He stood there blotting out the light I always left burning in the living room: a black nightmare shaped like a man.

I wasn't dreaming. I knew it then and I am even surer of it now. I felt myself rising rapidly through layers of sleep, my heart pounding, my throat constricting, until I was wide awake and he was still there. He didn't move; he didn't speak. He must have known I was awake, propped up as I was on one elbow, staring at him in the darkness, but if he knew or cared, he made no sign.

We might have stayed like that for five minutes, maybe more, neither of us moving or speaking. It was as if we were under some kind of magic spell, but one that could be broken by a single word. Had he come to rape me or only to rob me? Had my waking up spoiled his plans and would he now think he had to kill me? If only I could have remained asleep and he could have gone about his business without my knowing. I wanted to tell him he had nothing to fear from me, that he could take whatever he wanted, that there was no need to hurt me, but I was afraid to say a word for fear it would galvanize him into some sudden and violent action.

So we just stayed there, staring at each other across the twilit room, until he finally backed away, turned, and walked swiftly and silently as a shadow down the short hall to the living room, quietly letting himself out the front door.

I lay there paralyzed for a minute or two longer and then I picked up the phone and dialed 911, so nervous that my finger pecked out the wrong number three times before I finally got it right. I climbed out of bed, went to the closet, and threw on a sweatshirt and a pair of jeans. About twenty minutes later the police arrived. They had woken up my landlord, who stood in the hall in his pajamas and robe, hair standing on end, looking worried and asking questions in broken English the cops didn't bother to answer. They checked the windows and the door, took my report, and asked me to look around and make sure that nothing was missing. There wasn't.

"Do you mind telling me what you do for a living?" the cop filling out the report asked.

"I'm an actress," I said.

"Anything we might have seen you in?" his partner asked.

"Do you brush with Electrify?"

"No."

"Then forget it."

"Actress, huh?"

They looked at each other as if that answered everything. One of them suggested that I might have been imagining the whole thing and when I rather sharply told him what I thought of that idea, he merely shrugged his shoulders and advised that I install some better locks.

It was about forty-thirty by the time the police left, along with my landlord: too late to go back to bed, too early to get ready for work, not that I could fall asleep anyway after what had happened. I made my own check of the apartment. There wasn't a lot to check. Just a living room, a small kitchenette, the bedroom, and the bath. The living room was just a little bigger than the bedroom, which was barely big enough for a scarred bureau, a mismatched nightstand, and a rather spartan single bed covered with a matching set of floral sheets and quilt that had been a gift from my best friend, Cindy.

The living room wasn't much better. A run-down sofa with a brown-and-gold print half worn away in the places you'd expect it to be worn away. An end table on either side, each looking more rickety than the other, and a coffee table with so many water rings they looked like part of the design. The wallpaper, unfortunately, looked like it had once been selected to match the sofa, but had begun to take on the indeterminate color of the passing years. The television was a cheap nineteen-inch affair I'd bought at a second-hand shop for seventy-five dollars. It had a busted dial so you had to guess from the show you were watching what channel you were on, and a large piece of aluminum foil wrapped around its antenna that seemed to help the reception, though I still couldn't pick up CBS.

I had taken the place because it was cheap and because it was furnished. It was the best I could do after the money from the toothpaste commercial ran out and I was forced to leave Manhattan. When I signed the lease, I had consoled myself with the thought that I'd only be living here for a while. Before long, I assured myself, things would turn my way. I'd soon be able to move into a better place, afford to buy my own furniture, and decorate the way I wanted. In the meantime, I would just have to make the best of things. That had been nearly three years ago. Still, I stubbornly refused to do anything to make the place my own. As if by doing so, I would be admitting defeat, like those prisoners you see in movies decorating their cells, knowing they're going to spend the rest of their lives there.

Actually, I did try to spruce the place up once. It was after visiting the Museum of Modern Art. I bought a print of Georgia O'Keeffe's red peony and put it in one of those ten-dollar frames they sell in art supply stores. I took down some dreadful yellow-and-gold oil painting of a pair of sailing vessels at dusk that looked as though it had been stolen out of a third-rate motel. I put up the O'Keeffe, but when I stood back to admire it, I broke into tears—it looked so pitifully out of place in this drab hopeless room. I took the print down, slid it facedown under the bed, and returned the ugly oil painting to its rightful place on the wall.

The one good thing about the Queen's apartment—besides its being cheap—was that it was safe. In all the time I lived there no one in the building had ever called the police. In Manhattan I'd had my apartment broken into four times. Of course, this hadn't been a robbery. Whoever had been in my apartment hadn't taken anything. According to the police, he hadn't even forced entry. It wasn't assault, thank God. So what was it? How did he get in? What was it that he wanted?

He had just stood there.

Looking at me.

Once I had checked and rechecked the rooms and the closets until I was satisfied that there was no one in the apartment, I thought about taking a shower. I had to laugh. What kind of idiot would take a shower right after a man had broken into their apartment in the middle of the night? It was the kind of thing they did in every cheap horror movie ever made. I shook my head. Maybe art imitates life after all. Or maybe it was just conditioning. Lord knows, I had auditioned for enough similar parts when my agent sent me out to L.A. for six months, making the rounds of every casting director she knew on the West Coast. I exhausted all her contacts at about the same time I got disgusted with the whole silicone-and-coke scene and decided to come back to the relative sanity of Manhattan, where black-clad men broke into your apartment in the middle of the night and stared at you in your bed.

So instead of the shower, I made myself a cup of instant coffee and curled up on the living room sofa and switched the TV on to the *Home Shopping Network*. They were selling cookware. I didn't care. I just found it comforting that there was someone else up and around at this hour of the morning. I had thought about calling Cindy, and actually picked up the receiver of the phone and punched the first three numbers, and then laid the receiver back in its cradle. There was no sense waking her up at this hour. What could she say anyway? Nothing that couldn't wait until a more decent hour. Besides, I had pretty much calmed down by then. Not that Cindy would have complained about being woken up. I never knew her to complain about anything. I had met a lot of people since I'd come to New York. Cindy was the only one I trusted.

I took a sip of my coffee. It was bitter in spite of the extra sugar I had stirred in. Bittersweet. I thought of Stephen. At one point the cops suggested that my visitor was an old boyfriend I'd given a key to. I'd never given a key to Stephen and he wasn't the type to become obsessive. I'd met him almost two years ago at one of those interminable parties someone was always throwing somewhere for some event or other in this business. I really had no right being there in the first place, but my agent wrangled an invitation from a friend of a friend of a friend of hers. It was infatuation at first sight. On my part anyway. I saw him across the room, holding court before a small group of important-looking people. They were laughing, as if on cue, at everything he said. I started up a conversation with an anorectic-looking artist's model to find out who he was.

"His name's Stephen Kiley," she said dreamily.

It was during the resurgent heyday of heroin chic and I suspected from the marks on the insides of her bony arms that it wasn't the considerable charm of Stephen Kiley that was having an intoxicating effect on her.

Before she drifted off into her own private paradise, I was able to find out that he was considered by many to be one of the most promising up-and-coming young talents in the business. He had already landed a variety of bit parts on various television shows and had even done some movie work. The word was that he had the charisma, good looks, and talent to be the next Harrison Ford.

I couldn't vouch for the latter at the time, but charisma and good looks he had in spades. Before the night was over, I made it a point to find myself talking alone with Stephen Kiley. He was flirtatious in a boyishly irresistible way and, what was worse, he knew it. I was falling for him in the worst possible way. I knew he was trouble. I knew he would hurt me in the end. And yet I went home with him that night.

A woman has two sets of instincts about these kinds of things. One tells her what she wants to do. The other what she'll regret doing.

Unfortunately, all too often the two are one in the same.

No, Stephen wasn't my mysterious visitor in black. I was certain of that. He was far too narcissistic to become obsessed with anyone but himself. Besides, Stephen was history for about two months now. It was a decision that for all the pain it caused me I still didn't regret and one he accepted with little more than a puzzled shrug of the shoulders. I didn't miss him much at all.

I must have dozed off around then because the next thing I knew they were no longer selling cookware on the TV but Hummel collectibles and the coffee table was bathed in light from the window behind me. I felt a jolt of adrenaline kick start my heart and cleared my eyes enough to peer at the clock over the kitchen sink, just visible from where I was sitting. To my utter disbelief, it was almost a quarter to eight. If I didn't hurry, I was going to be late for work.

2

There's an old saying among unemployed actresses: you either have to have a pair of sturdy legs or ten intelligent fingers. I have the latter. I tried waiting tables my first two years in New York and hated it. I could never quite get used to the frenetic pace of most city restaurants and the pay was terrible. On top of that, I was developing varicose veins behind my knees. I switched in a hurry. Luckily, I'd been paying attention in Mrs. Walters's eleventh-grade vocational typing class. I hated it and Mrs. Walters at the time, but I owed her a debt of gratitude now. As it turned out I preferred the regularity of office work to waitressing; dull and repetitive as it often gets, you can at least earn your money sitting down.

And that's a lot better than earning your money lying down, if you know what I mean. Of course, I had heard all the horror stories about young women who came to New York from all over the country, hoping to make it in show business. It was a place and a profession filled with slick predators with pockets full of ill-gotten cash and mouths full of empty promises who preyed on starry-eyed dreamers like myself. I wouldn't last more than six months, the more encouraging of my friends predicted. I was too nice a girl, they all agreed, hardly ruthless or devious enough to protect myself in the cutthroat, dog-eat-dog world of show business. My mother, supportive and optimistic as always, gave me two weeks.

I was determined to prove all of them wrong. Even if it meant proving I wasn't nearly as nice as they thought I was. I had always been the quiet, thoughtful, bookish type in school, the kind of girl who read Keats and Shelley and didn't do a lot of socializing. I could count on the fingers of one hand the number of boys who had asked me out in high school and college and still have enough left over to competently use a pair of chopsticks. The fact of the matter was that I was painfully shy and even more painfully awkward. It wasn't really until my junior year in college that I began to grow into my body.

Even then, I just wasn't the type that guys seemed to gravitate toward. My mother said it was because I acted too aloof and that most guys wanted a girl who looked like she'd be fun. Of course, I didn't have to be fun. I just had to look like I was fun. By then, it would be too late for the poor guy. That has always been my mother's philosophy about men. And to give her her due, she's done pretty well with it. She was always trying to get me to be more outgoing and popular. Popularity is a big issue with my mother. I think it was always the bane of her existence that I wasn't more popular in school.

That's not to say that I didn't have any social life at all. It was in college that I caught the acting bug and I hung out a lot with the school drama club. Needless to say, we didn't exactly represent the in-crowd. Actually, if truth be told, we were all considered something of a gang of misfits. But I found I had more in common with them than I had with any of my other classmates. We were all bound by a single, all-consuming passion: the desire to be someone other than who we really were. Or, at the very least, something more than who we were.

It's something I've always loved about acting. Real life is so limiting. You get up and day after day you have to be the same person. Everyone around you expects it. And so all the wonderful possibilities, the variations of mood and character, all the different voices, the different facets of your personality are smothered, unborn, unlived. To me, that is what acting is all about. That is what makes it such a passion; you might even say, an obsession. It's the chance to be absolutely everything—and everyone—you can possibly be. To live a thousand lifetimes in one.

By that time I'd been dating a boy in my drama class. He was five years older than me, not a boy really. He was working two part-time jobs so he could attend drama classes. He was quiet and even more painfully shy than I was. Like me, he only really seemed to come alive on stage. The highlight of our young lives came when we did a production of *Hamlet* together. He played the lead role and I played mad Ophelia. The local newspapers gave us both good reviews. We were incredibly optimistic and incurably in love, and we shared hopes and dreams everyone outside our intimate circle of two considered completely unrealistic. In the end, our romance turned into every bit the tragedy we had played out onstage. One of Tommy's part-time jobs was as a night-security officer for one of those self-storage places. He was apparently surprised from behind, bludgeoned and stabbed to death while making his rounds one hot summer night. His assailant fled the scene without so much as taking his wallet and had never been caught.

I didn't even go to the funeral.

I dropped out of school a week later, packed two bags of clothes, gathered up my savings and what I could borrow from my reluctant friends, and headed for New York.

I didn't know a soul in the city. It was scary and intimidating and I almost got right back on the bus and headed home. But the die was cast. There was nothing for me to return to at home. Besides, this had always been my dream. Tommy's dream, too. I knew I could never live with myself if I didn't at least give it a chance. I owed it to him. I owed it to myself.

I checked into a fleabag hotel near Times Square for the first several weeks, trying to conserve money as I looked about for work. There was a girl in the building, an aspiring model obviously past her prime, who suggested that I hook up with a temp service. I took her advice and before long I had a fairly steady income. I learned later that the poor woman was found dead in her room of a drug overdose. She would not be the last victim I met in a business whose road to that elusive promised land was strewn with the bodies of those who had died trying.

After a while, I was able to save up enough cash to eventually move out of that rattrap and split the rent of a decent apartment in SoHo with a roommate I met through the classifieds. In the meantime, I checked the trade papers for every available audition and job. I went on photo shoots in the living room "studios" of photographers with dubious credentials and pornographic portfolios, read hack scripts written by wannabe producers who turned out to be out-of-work dishwashers, and answered ads for voice-overs that turned out to be nothing more than phone-sex operations.

After two years in New York, I found myself no closer to an acting career than when I arrived. On top of that, my roommate situation had gone from bad to worse. My first roommate, who turned out to be on medication for paranoid schizophrenia, simply disappeared on me without so much as a note, leaving me stuck to pay the rent by myself. I had to scramble around to find someone fast and what I wound up with was a high-school runaway. Of course, by the time I realized that it was too late and she had all but moved in her considerably older boyfriend who, as it turned out, was selling drugs from the apartment. Only my threat to go to the police persuaded them both to leave.

My next roommate was a clean-cut, preppy-looking, professional woman in her mid-twenties from Connecticut. I thought she would work out fine until I started noticing that things were missing from the apartment. I never did find out why she was stealing from me: whether it was a compulsion or whether she really needed the money. She had a good job as a public defender. Go figure.

She was followed by a singer-songwriter I had met in a club down in the Village. Stacey wasn't crazy, didn't have a boyfriend into drugs, and wasn't a thief. But she was a total slob. She left a mess wherever she went: cartons of half-eaten takeout on the kitchen counters, wet towels and dirty clothes piled up in the bathroom, newspapers spread out on the sofa, you get the idea. I'm not exactly the tidiest person in the world, but I don't like to live in squalor. I was continually cleaning up after her. A person can only take so much of that. Still, if it wasn't for her, I probably would never have met Cindy Dresner.

We were at a downtown club having a drink at the bar when Stacey spotted Cindy sitting at a table with her then-boyfriend, Paul. She invited herself over to Cindy's table and motioned me to join them. I didn't feel comfortable barging in, but I apologetically pulled up a chair. Stacey babbled on about how Cindy was an actress, too, how she had done some modeling work for Georges Marciano and Calvin Klein, and how we should have a lot in common. Then she pulled out a wrinkled piece of paper on which she had written the lyrics to her latest song and turned her attention to a horrified Paul, who had some connection or other to some people in the music industry. As she began singing to Paul in a gratingly high falsetto, Cindy and I looked at each other as if to say "How in the world do you know her?" We both started laughing.

By the end of the evening, Cindy and I were on our way to becoming fast friends. As it turned out, she and Paul were heading in the opposite direction. She had actually welcomed our interruption and credited it for speeding up the inevitable split. The evening had put Paul in such a bad mood that they had a big fight later that all but finished their relationship then and there. All that was left for the breakup were the formalities.

Cindy and I began seeing each other after that. I learned that she had come to New York a couple of years after me. She was naturally modest, or perhaps just sensitive about my feelings, but eventually I came to know that she'd actually done quite well for herself. It was Cindy who helped me find an agent. I knew the importance of a good agent in this business. After all, there were just so many open auditions available. Yet it was almost as tough to get an agent as it was to get a part. It was a real catch-22. To get work in this business you had to have an agent. To get an agent, you had to have worked in the business. Cindy introduced me to her agent, who politely refused to represent me, saying he already had too many clients. But he did suggest an agent who was looking for new talent. That was how I came to know Ruth.

Still, as I was about to find out, having an agent wasn't the same as working regularly. In fact, it wasn't much different than not working at all. It was just that the door opened a little easier, the auditions were a little more on the up-and-up, and people didn't treat you like a complete charity case. It was Ruth who, noticing my perfect teeth, set me up to audition for the Electrify toothpaste commercial. It was good money and by far the biggest break I'd had in the business so far. It enabled me to leave Stacey on amicable terms and move into my own place for the first time since I came to the city. It was a modestly fashionable three-floor walk-up that cost more per month than what a mortgage payment would be on a house in the suburbs. I even bought my own furniture. But I knew it was only one lucky break. Maybe it would lead to something bigger. Maybe it wouldn't. I wasn't about to quit my day job.

Or should I say jobs.

In the last three years I had worked for a dozen companies, including a brokerage firm, an advertising agency, a publisher, and a clothing designer. Working as a temp gave me a certain illusion of freedom, allowed me to choose which days I worked and which days I didn't, and kept me from getting bored. It also exposed me to a vast array of people and personalities, which I figured I could use in my acting. Maybe I was just fooling myself, putting off the inevitable when I would have to take a conventional job with benefits and health insurance and all the rest, giving up the vagabond life for a little security. With thirty looming just around the bend, I was particularly conscious of the fact that I wasn't getting any younger. My mother didn't help. During her periodic calls every three months, she never failed to remind me that it was long past time that I settle down, get married, have kids, and live a normal life. After her divorce from my stepfather years ago, she had moved down to Florida to soak up the sun and the last time I talked to her, she was enjoying the attentions of the most recent in a series of senior citizen romeos.

My latest job was working for Ms. Parker, the vice president of an investment bank on Park Avenue. Fortyish, waspy, a real shark in perfectly tailored suits, she had her cold eyes glued on a corporate headquarters position, determining to break through the glass ceiling if she knocked herself unconscious in the process.

And she just might. She smoked like a maniac, came back from lunch reeking of booze, and several times I caught her popping pills which she claimed were for migraines, but which looked suspiciously like the amphetamines I'd seen certain actors use to psyche themselves up for an audition. She would have been a tough boss to work for on a full-time basis. In fact, I'd heard from the office grapevine that she had gone through six assistants in the last four years, but she was a little less than impossible on me, knowing I suppose that I wasn't going to be around for more than a couple of weeks at most. All in all, it would have been almost comical if it weren't so sad to watch her juggle two or three calls at once, ask for a file at the same time she wanted me to take a letter, bark for a form she had mailed off days ago, and all the while stabbing out and lighting cigarettes like some kind of demented tobacco-testing machine. What was even more tragic was the fact that apparently everyone in the office but her knew that the promotion she wanted was going to a hotshot twenty-four-year-old boy wunderkind who worked down the hall and had only been with the bank for a year and a half.

If the subways had been running on time, I would have made it. As it was, I was only fifteen minutes late. Still that was late enough to find my computer terminal papered over with Post-it notes. From inside her office, Ms. Parker glared at me through a cloud of cigarette smoke as she spoke to an account on the phone. I shook off my coat, plopped down in my chair, and slowly began peeling the notes from the computer. I made a little pile of them on my desk in order of priority and looked back to Ms. Parker's office. She had swiveled around so that she was facing the window. Only a puff of smoke, like a gray flag, was visible over her high-backed chair.

"Tough morning?"

The saving grace of the job was the girl who sat next to me. Judy was a temp who worked at the firm to support her career as a performance artist. She did her act at the famous P.S. 122, where such people as Eric Bogosian, Laurie Anderson, and Spalding Gray had gotten early recognition. Judy did an act with a jar of honey, two snakes, and a handful of pins. She had invited me to come and see her perform, but I politely declined the invitation. I've never been one for pain. How she even got assigned the job as a temp in such a conservative environment as an investment bank, I'll never know. She didn't fit the part. She had short, spiky, bleached hair, a silver nose ring, and a pierced tongue. Half the men in the office were after her; the other half were afraid of her. Neither group needed to concern themselves. Judy had confided to me one afternoon over lunch what I had suspected all along.

I told her about the break-in. She stopped typing and looked over at me, her blue eyes wide. She really had pretty eyes. In fact, if she grew out her hair and lost the creative body piercing, she could be a real beauty.

"You were lucky it wasn't worse," she said.

"I know it."

"What do you think he wanted?"

"I honestly don't know. That's what really creeps me out about the whole thing. I'm sure he was watching me for some time before I woke up. Why didn't he just rob me while I was still asleep and just leave?"

"Maybe he wanted you to see him."

"But why?"

Judy shrugged. "That's the million-dollar question. A lot of sickos running around in this city."

The rest of the day passed fairly uneventfully, for which I was grateful. My boss didn't ask for an explanation for my tardiness; apparently she wasn't interested, so I didn't give her one. I tried to call Cindy around lunch time but I hung up when I got her answering machine. I hated getting her answering machine. I made it about halfway through the stack of Post-it notes before five, rode the elevator down to the lobby with Judy, and said good-bye when we hit the street.

I took the subway to Queens. Like I said, I had to give up my Manhattan apartment and most of my belongings when the residuals stopped coming in from the toothpaste commercial. It turned out that Electrify caused liver tumors in rats. As a result, I was forced to move to cheaper lodgings in the outlying borough. It was tough to move, a kind of admission of defeat, but it was either that or go the roommate route, and I wasn't about to go through that hell again. Either way, I had to face the fact that my career was going in reverse. I figured I might as well have the comfort and privacy of living alone in my misery.

I walked the three blocks from the train station to my building, forcing myself to enjoy the sight of the ice-laden trees. That was one good thing about living outside Manhattan. You got to see a little nature. I said hello to a couple of the neighbors' kids playing on the stoop, pulled open the front door, and got my mail: bills, flyers, and a belated Christmas card from my dead father.

I stopped at the landlord's apartment and knocked on the door. Mr. Kazantzakis came out, dressed in a pair of khaki pants, and a stained T-shirt—a short, squat, Greek man with wiry silver hair, and smelling of onions. He had bright eyes the color of new pennies and he never failed to look me over from head to toe whenever he talked to me. I'm sure it was unconscious. I didn't take it as an insult. In his culture, it was probably perfectly natural. He was still chewing something; I had no doubt interrupted his dinner, for which I apologized and got right to the point. I asked him if he had changed the lock on my door. He swallowed, crooked his finger, and motioned me to follow him up the stairs to my apartment. He pointed proudly to the new lock on the door. It was made of heavy gold metal and looked sturdy enough.

"If you were Fay Wray," he said in a thick Greek accent unscratched after ten years of living in America, "not even King Kong could get in."

He laughed at his own joke. I smiled politely. I had made the mistake of telling him about my acting ambitions. Actually, I didn't have much of a choice. When I applied for the lease, I had to explain why I worked for a temp agency instead of holding down a regular job. He had the annoying habit of teasing me about it every time I saw him.

He reached into his loose-fitting pants, pulled out a heavy, serious-looking key, and handed it to me.

"No problem now," he said meaningfully.

"Thank you."

He nodded. "You good tenant. Quiet. Pay on time."

He turned and made his way back down the stairs. For a moment I tried to picture if the intruder could have been him. No. The man who broke in was taller, thinner. I unlocked the door, then locked it carefully behind me, threw my mail on the table, and checked my answering machine. There was one call from Cindy. There was an open audition for a role on a leading soap opera tomorrow at ten a.m. It was a long shot, but worth the effort. I wrote down the address on a pad I kept by the phone. I would just have to remember to call the agency early enough in the morning to have them schedule another girl to fill in for me at the bank.

I changed into my sweats and did twenty minutes on the Nordic Trak, one of the few possessions I hadn't sold off after I moved from Manhattan. I considered it a professional necessity. I couldn't afford a gym membership and, at my age, I really had to begin watching my figure. I put on the six-thirty news as I walked for a little over a mile; then I stripped off my clothes and took a quick, hot shower. I eased into a bathrobe and slippers, turned the heat up and prayed it would respond, and scuffed my way into the kitchen where I microwaved a

Weight Watchers dinner of rice and beans. The microwave was another necessity: it had cost me only ninety-nine dollars at one of those rip-off discount electronics stores on Forty-fifth Street. It took twice as long as it was supposed to to cook anything, but that was still half the time it took my run-down electric stove.

While I was waiting for my dinner to cook, I called Cindy back. I was certain I'd get her machine. I was glad to hear her pick up the phone.

"Did you get my message about the audition?" she asked.

"Yeah, it sounds great."

"What's the matter, you don't sound like yourself?"

"Well I guess I'm a little on edge. Someone broke into my apartment last night."

"What!" Cindy said. "Why didn't you call me last night?"

"There was no sense in us both being awake."

"Damn, Johanna. Don't you think the situation warranted it?"

"Do you want to hear what happened or not?" I said somewhat crossly.

"I'm sorry," Cindy said. "Of course I do."

I told her the whole story.

"Jesus, Johanna. Do you really think you should stay there alone tonight?"

"Sure. Why not?"

"He may come back."

"If he was going to do something to hurt me, I think he would have already done it."

"A peeping Tom maybe?"

"Maybe."

"Well, you're welcome to stay here overnight if you want."

"Thanks, Cindy. But I'll be all right."

"Are you sure?" Cindy said.

"Yeah, I'm sure."

We talked for a while longer. She asked again if I wanted to stay over, and I finally convinced her I'd be okay alone. I told her not to worry and that I'd meet her tomorrow at the audition. Later I sat on the couch, my feet propped up on the coffee table, and painted my toenails while watching one of those Generation X sitcoms on TV. I couldn't help but compare myself to every actress on the screen.

I was okay until a Jeep commercial came on and I saw Stephen in a flannel shirt, looking unshaven, but rugged as he steered a Grand Cherokee over an impossibly rugged terrain. I had to laugh. Stephen wouldn't be caught dead in either a Jeep or a flannel shirt, but his rugged good looks carried it all off to perfection. It's true we were history, but I couldn't help watching the commercial and remembering all the good times we had shared. Not that there weren't bad times. But that night I was lonely enough and depressed enough that my mind had to be forced to remember the bad times.

He was always too wrapped up in himself to be a very good lover and when he tried, it was all so obviously a performance. But he did have a quick, brilliant mind, a great talent for acting as it turned out, and a fantastic sense of humor, which I guess was enough to keep me interested. I had always suspected he was bisexual and made sure we used protection every time, even when he vehemently protested. I had myself checked for HIV seven times in the six months we saw each other, though I never told him. He would have been crushed. I shrugged. I was glad I had stuck to my convictions and played it safe. Better to be safe than sorry.

I flashed back to the last time I saw him in person. I had come to his apartment one morning with a bag of bagels and some coffee, ready to watch the New York City Marathon. Stephen must have forgotten. He answered the door with a bedsheet wrapped around his waist. He looked completely baffled. When I reminded him of his invitation, his expression changed to apologetic, and then to slight amusement. She came out of the door behind him wearing one of his dress shirts. She took one look at me, a look of shock on her face, and retreated quickly into the bedroom. It was like one of those prototypical scenes from every soap opera you've ever seen.

"This is not what it looks like," he said.

I remember thinking in amazement: *people actually say that.*

Then he tried a different tack.

"So what's the big deal?"

I didn't stick around long enough to explain the concept of fidelity to him. It would have been useless, anyway. I threw the bag of bagels and coffee at him—which he caught deftly—turned away, and slammed the door behind me. I can still picture him taking the bagels and coffee back to the bedroom to share with his lover without the least sense of guilt. From what I hear through mutual acquaintances, he still doesn't understand what I got so upset about.

When the car commercial was over, I slammed the door on my memory like I'd slammed the door of his apartment. I immediately stopped thinking of Stephen and went back to polishing my toes.

I put off going to sleep for as long as possible. I remember thinking that maybe I should have taken Cindy up on her offer to stay with her for the night. I sat through the vapid star interviews on the *Tonight*

Show, vowing I'd never stoop to such inanity if I ever made it to the top, and knowing at the same time I'd give my eyeteeth to be sitting where they were sitting. I followed that up by watching *Late Night* and even more mindless interviews. I finally switched off the television and picked up a novel I had very nearly finished. I read a couple of pages and went to the medicine cabinet in the bathroom and pulled out an old prescription of pills I'd gotten a few years back when I was having crippling bouts of anxiety attacks during auditions. My doctor had prescribed the pills. I'd almost forgotten about them. It was like finding gold.

I struggled with the child-proof lid, finally prying it off by sheer force, and retrieved two small pink pills which had fallen into the sink. I poured myself a paper cup of water and swallowed the pills. Then I picked up the remaining pills that had fallen onto the floor, and put the bottle back in the medicine cabinet. I returned to the living room and my book. I don't remember exactly how many times I rechecked the door to make sure that the new lock was properly engaged, but it was nearly two a.m. before the pills began to take effect. I knew I wouldn't be able to fall asleep in my bedroom, so I moved the alarm clock out to the living room, set it, and then settled back onto the couch with my book. I'd brought the quilt from the bedroom and covered myself while I read. I remember realizing I was dreaming in the middle of a sentence and I took the opportunity to lay the book aside and close my eyes. Somehow I fell asleep with every light in the apartment blazing.

3

---•---

I never failed to go to an audition without getting a fresh perspective on why everyone in the business referred to them as cattle calls. The small, overheated room was filled with actresses of every description, each jostling for position, every one of them giving each other the once-over, sizing up the competition. Even though Cindy had heard about the tryout from an inside source, somehow the word had gotten out. It was hard to keep a secret in the acting business.

I'd woken up early that morning, still groggy from the pills I'd taken the night before, and went straight to the shower. I worked the shampoo into my hair and turned my back on the shower head, letting the hot water work its way over my tired muscles. I shaved my legs standing up, using a Bic razor that had seen better days and wound up nicking myself. I cursed under my breath, staunching the trickle of blood with a washcloth. Reluctantly I stood up and rinsed my hair, turned around, and slowly turned off the hot tap, letting the water turn frigid, shocking my body fully awake. Shivering, I cranked off the water and grabbed two soft and waiting towels, wrapping one around my body and the second in a turban around my soaking hair. Then I dripped a trail of water to the phone where I called the agency. I knew Ms. Parker would be pissed, but that's the nature of the temp business. I figured if she didn't like it, she should consider dropping the boss-from-hell routine and get herself a full-time assistant.

I stood in front of my open closet and tried to decide what to wear. From the living room, I could hear the coanchors on the *Today Show* laughing it up with the weatherman over some lame joke or other, pretending to be enjoying themselves. They could really use some acting lessons. I listened to the weatherman long enough to hear it was going to be a cold day, possibly with some snow flurries, high of around twenty. I stood in front of the closet as if I were hypnotized. I decided to put off choosing an outfit and go back to the bathroom to blow dry my hair. I had no idea what the part was, what they are looking for. A friend who used to be a production assistant for an afternoon talk show before he died of AIDS told me that they often did that on purpose in order to test your range. I finally chose a black dress, black stockings, and heels. I figured you couldn't go wrong with basic black, unless of course they were looking for the innocent type. I looked at myself in the full-length mirror behind my bedroom door and thought, "No good." I changed three times before I settled on a neutral beige suit and skirt with matching flats.

I went back into the bathroom and applied my makeup, but not too much; I didn't want to look like I had anything to hide. Was I already too old for the role? I gazed at myself critically in the mirror: shoulder-length brown hair, darker in winter than summer, full lips, and a heart-shaped face, the chin a little too pointed, though, for my liking. My single most outstanding feature was my eyes: a rich aquamarine the color of nothing else on this earth. Not even Cindy had such eyes. I looked at the clock. I had to hurry. I hesitated long enough to decide whether or not to use perfume and decided against it. What if the director hated the scent? You never knew when something as simple as that would work against you. You really had to think of everything.

I took the train into Manhattan and splurged on a cab to take me to the studio where the audition was being held. I spotted Cindy seated in a gray upholstered armchair by a potted plant that may or may not have been real. She motioned me over with a small nervous wave. She looked stunning: tall, blond, green eyes, and four years younger than I was. She'd already had a short stint on a defunct sitcom, costarred on a pilot that just missed making it to the network, and played a beautiful corpse on an episode of an Emmy–award-winning police drama. It wasn't much, but compared to me she might as well have been Meryl Streep. I asked her if she had heard anything more about the part we would be trying out for. She said no, just that they wanted someone fast. Her friend David, who played a doctor on a rival soap told her about the opening. I thanked her again. "What are friends for?" she said and smiled a movie-star smile that made me want to hate her. If it came down to between me and her, I knew I didn't stand a chance.

As it turned out, Cindy got called in first.

"Wish me luck," she said.

"Luck."

I took her seat and flipped through a copy of *Vogue* that someone had generously left behind. I tried to concentrate on an article about relationships, but it was pointless. I flipped through the magazine a half dozen times, staring dully at the photographs and advertisements. I absently touched one of the impossibly green leaves of the plant. Sure enough, it was fake.

Twenty minutes later, Cindy came out of the audition room and walked over to where I was now standing, waiting for her.

"So how'd you do?" I asked.

"Lousy," Cindy said. "I flubbed a line right at the beginning and my timing was all off. I played the most emotional part of the scene like I was reading a damn grocery order."

"I'm sure it wasn't as bad as you think."

Cindy shrugged. "It couldn't be."

I glanced over her shoulder at the closed door, already mentally gauging my chances now that it looked like Cindy was out of the running.

"So what are they like in there?"

"The usual. A gathering of vultures waiting for you to die so they can pick you apart."

I noticed a girl sitting next to us shift in her seat to get a better angle on our conversation. She pretended to still be reading the copy of *Time* she was holding, but she wasn't fooling me. If that was her idea of acting, I didn't have anything to worry about from her. Still, I wasn't taking any chances. I wasn't about to give up my advantage that easily.

"Come over here," I said to Cindy and walked her over to the corner where a water cooler stood surrounded by an almost convincing pair of fake ficus trees.

"Seriously," I whispered. "What's going on in there?"

"All the big guns are present, but I think it's the director who's calling the shots. My bet is it's him you've got to impress."

"What's he like?"

"A self-important-looking s.o.b., who acts as if his true genius is being wasted. The way he's sitting there you'd think he was Scorsese instead of some schmo directing a damn soap opera. Didn't speak much and then it was all right to the point."

"How's the script?"

"Usual soap opera pap. Nothing out of the ordinary. You could handle it in your sleep. Just don't play the part as Elmer Fudd like I did and you should be fine."

"Thanks."

"No problem," Cindy said. "If you don't mind, I think I'd like to get out of here now. Go some place quiet and lick my wounds a little."

"Don't be so tough on yourself."

"Hey, that's my line, isn't it?"

"Yup."

"Ever work?"

"Nope."

Cindy smiled that smile that made me wonder why she didn't get every part she auditioned for.

"Good luck in there," she said. "If I can't get the part, I hope you do."

"That makes two of us."

"Give me a call and let me know how you did."

"Sure thing," I said.

I poured myself a small paper cup of water and looked around the room after Cindy left and wondered if I would wind up being called last. I watched as girl after girl was called in to the next room. I took a seat. I stared at the pictures in some magazines. I looked at my competitors and wished a case of the Elmer Fudds on all of them. I daydreamed. I panicked. I calmed myself. I must have waited about an hour and a half before my name was finally called.

I was escorted into a gray-carpeted office with two floor-to-ceiling window walls that gave out on a view of the Hudson River. I could feel my heart pounding in my temples. There were three of them sitting there. In the center was a short, heavy-set balding man with a studiously cultivated five o'clock shadow and what little remaining hair he had tied back in a short black ponytail. He was flanked by two dour-faced women, one of whom was introduced as the director of casting and the other as an assistant to the producer. The man in the center was the director. I handed him my resumé, but he pushed it aside without looking at it. Instead the woman on his left, the casting director I think, asked me what I had done before. I could feel myself blushing as I told her my credits: several off-off-Broadway plays and a toothpaste advertisement. The woman scribbled some notes and the director thrust a script at me. I grabbed it and gave it a quick glance. I was so nervous the words seemed to be written in a foreign language.

"Are you familiar with *The Way We Live?*" the director asked.

"I've seen it a few times," I lied. "I temp during the day."

"No matter. You're playing a bitch," the director said brusquely.

"You've come back to town to steal away Cole, one of our heroine's husbands," the casting director said helpfully. "You were his childhood sweetheart. He thought you died in a car crash with his best friend when you were still in high school. You're eventually going to come down with a rare blood disease—"

"You die after six episodes," the director interrupted. "It's a short running part. Is that a problem?"

"No."

"Good."

"So you understand the situation?" the casting director said.

"Yes, I think so."

"All right, I think we're ready then. You'll be reading with Brady. He's going to be playing Cole this afternoon."

For the first time I noticed a thin, familiar-looking man standing off to my right by a large oak desk. He came forward, a script in his hand, and spoke the first words of the scene with a pronounced lisp. I played the part as best I could under the circumstances, finding it hard to connect with my partner, but hoping I was pulling it off all the same. All of a sudden, I felt something click and I felt I was really into the role. It was a magical feeling, something that's impossible to describe, but for a few moments I had stopped being myself and really became this bitch called Jessica. I hadn't gotten halfway through the scene when the director put up his hand.

"Thank you," he said, sounding incredibly bored. "I've heard enough."

"But I'm not done," I said. "There's still—"

"We'll get back to you," he said.

The abrupt interruption left me feeling somewhat disjointed, as if I were caught between my own identity and that of the woman I was portraying. Before I knew what was happening, the casting director was taking the script from my hand and the woman who had escorted me into the room was escorting me out again. I turned to thank them for the chance to read, but they were already looking down at the papers in their hands. Anything I could have said at that point would only have been an unwelcome interruption.

I found myself in the waiting room again, heading for the door, the name of the next girl to audition ringing in my ears.

Needless to say, I didn't feel very confident when I left the studio. It was gray and cold out, a few flakes of snow dancing in the air. It was nearly four-thirty. I walked the six blocks to the train station and got on a car crowded with the beginning of the rush-hour crowds. I managed to get a seat next to a nice-looking businessman, who tried to start up a conversation with me, but I wasn't in the mood to talk. He mercifully got the hint and returned to his *Wall Street Journal*. All I could do was replay the script in my mind over and over and think about how I could have played the role better. If I'd only had enough time to summon the proper motivation, if only they'd given me a better partner to read with.

If only—

I tried to console myself. Maybe I had done better than I thought. Sometimes it was hard to tell. I didn't think I had done that well during the tryouts for the toothpaste advertisement either. The more I thought about the audition, the better I began to feel. I couldn't go by the director. He was just being an ass. Cindy had warned me about him. What had I expected him to do? Leap out of his chair and yell, "Send the rest home, she's the one!" Yeah, that was the fantasy, but it never happened that way. I had been a little stilted in the beginning, but I remembered that moment during the audition where it all came together, where I had lost myself in the part, where the words on the page were the words in my head, as if I weren't reading them but thinking them. That's what acting was all about. That was the secret: to get to that place between fantasy and reality where acting wasn't acting. It was as if you became possessed by the character on the page, as if you lent it your voice, your body, your spirit, your life.

I had experienced that moment of authenticity during the audition. I knew it. There was no fooling myself about that. Surely everyone in the room must have recognized it.

By the time I got home I was jittery with excitement. I ran to the answering machine the moment I got in the door.

The light wasn't blinking.

I wasn't concerned. They were probably just finishing up the auditions. I checked all the rooms before I took off my coat. Then I went back to the door and locked it. I shuffled through my mail, glanced over at the Nordic Trak, and thought, "Not tonight." I glanced again at the phone and thought about my promise to call Cindy. I didn't feel like talking to anyone. Not even Cindy. I was too excited. Besides, I didn't dare take the risk of tying up the phone line in case someone from the audition tried to call.

I changed into a pair of old sweats and thick socks and made myself a bowl of cornflakes for dinner. I ate about five spoonfuls before I put it down. I swallowed half a dozen vitamin pills and went into the bathroom and put cold cream on my face. I tried to finish the last twenty pages of the book I was reading, but could hardly concentrate. I read the same pages over and over again, unable to follow the convoluted ending and finally gave up. I started pacing around the living room like a caged tiger and I thought again about the Nordic Trak. Maybe I could burn off some nervous energy. I got on the machine half-heartedly but found myself too restless to repeat the required motions. I had to relax. As a last resort, I went to the bathroom and took out my bottle of pills. It took a half hour to feel any effect and then it only took the edge off my anxiety. I wound up watching television, one of those real-life crimestopper shows, though I found myself too preoccupied to really pay attention.

The phone rang and my heart gave a leap. I dashed across the room and picked up the receiver, hoping against hope for good news. When I heard Cindy's voice on the other end, I was so disappointed I almost hung up.

"Jo," she said, breathless with excitement, "guess what? They called. They called me back!"

"What?" I said, too stunned to say anything else.

"They called me back."

"The audition?"

"Of course, silly, who else?"

"When, I mean—" I didn't know what to say. I was scrambling for words. I felt sick to my stomach.

"Well, when I left the audition I was kind of depressed. So I just wandered around the streets a while. Did a little shopping. Stopped in a Starbucks. When I finally got home, there was a message on my machine. It was the casting director. They said they want me to come back and read again. Can you believe it? Jo? Are you there?"

"Yes," I said, scrambling to get my emotions under control. "Yes, of course."

"Did you hear me? Isn't this fantastic?"

"It's great," I said, the enthusiasm in my voice surprising me. "It's absolutely wonderful."

"I know it's just a callback. I mean it doesn't mean anything. They probably called back a dozen other girls. I can't allow myself to get too excited. But damn, it's something, isn't it?"

"Yes, it is," I said. "You'll probably get it, too."

Cindy laughed nervously, but when she spoke, I could hear the hope in her voice. "Oh no, Jo. Don't even say it. It's impossible."

"What's so impossible?" I said, the feeling coming over me again, the feeling I'd had during the audition, the sense of losing myself, of playing a role. I was the good friend, the gracious loser, the perennial bridesmaid. "You're just as good as anyone. Better. I think you'll get it. In fact, I'd bet on it."

"You're terrible, Jo, you know that? You're going to make me a basket case. I'm already so excited I can hardly sit still."

"Hey, what are friends for?"

"I'll take you up on that bet, though."

"Yeah. What's the wager?"

"The Peking Duck. If I don't get the part, you can console me, Dutch treat as usual. If I get it, dinner's on me."

"How can I lose?"

"Jeez," she said, sighing, "I can't believe it. And I was so sure I had messed up."

"I tried to tell you it wasn't as bad as you thought."

"I guess you were right. Hey I'm sorry, Jo."

"Sorry about what?"

"Well . . . you know."

That stung. For a moment I thought I would lose it. But I didn't. I remembered the advice of my acting teacher at the Actor's Studio. When a real emotion comes up unexpectedly, use it.

Use it.

"Oh, I really didn't expect to get called back. The character was all wrong for me. I knew that going in. It was good experience, though."

"I'm glad you feel that way. Now I don't have to feel guilty."

"Guilty? Don't be silly. You just go back there and get that damn part. When's the callback?"

"Tomorrow."

"At least that doesn't give you much time to worry over it."

"Are you kidding? It gives me twenty-four hours. I don't think I'm getting any sleep tonight whatsoever."

"Well, I won't be to blame for that," I said. "I'm getting off right now and you're going right to bed."

It was another half hour before our conversation was finished. I don't even remember what else we said before I finally hung up the phone. I only remember it was nearly midnight by then. I felt numb and empty, as if someone had vacuumed out my insides. I knew I needed to get to sleep myself: it was back to work the next morning. I went through the usual routine of getting ready for bed, but I might as well have been a zombie. I set the clock and made up the couch again. I crawled under the covers with the lights on and in full sight of the bolted door. I closed my eyes. I opened my eyes. It didn't seem to make a difference.

I felt like crying. I wanted to cry.

But I didn't.

I had no tears left. They had been sucked out of me, along with the rest of my emotions.

I thought of the pills in the medicine cabinet and wondered if I could take another on top of the one I'd already taken.

I decided against it.

Instead, I did the next best thing to drugging myself into oblivion. I stared at the television until the inane monotony of it bored me to sleep.

4

———————•———————

The next day at work was a total nightmare.

I had barely taken off my coat and booted up my computer when Ms. Parker called me into her office.

"Please shut the door," she said.

She looked even more stressed out than usual.

"What's up?" I said, trying to sound casual. I was certain she was going to give me grief for being out the day before and nearly twenty minutes late again this morning. I decided to try a preemptive apology. "I'm sorry I was late. I'm not really feeling all that well and the trains were a mess this morning coming in from Queens."

Ms. Parker waved away my excuses.

"Never mind that," she rasped. It wasn't even nine-thirty yet and her ashtray was already overflowing with cigarette butts. She was taking a pull from a cigarette even now, inhaling so hard the orange ring moved visibly toward the filter. I could feel the nervous energy radiating off her from all the way across her large, glass-topped desk. "I've got an important project for you."

"Shoot."

Ms. Parker looked warily at me. "This is important, Johanna. I can't afford any screw-ups. Do you understand?"

"Yes," I said, feeling a little put off by her implication. I'd never screwed up before.

"Good. This concerns the Rothman Group."

The Rothman Group was one of the bank's most important clients. They had decided to restructure a sizable loan. The company was not one of Ms. Parker's accounts, but she had been chosen to do the legwork in preparing the initial proposal. It would be submitted to the bank's president and CEO for modification and then presented at a preliminary meeting with representatives of the multimillion-dollar company the following week. Ms. Parker obviously saw it as just the opportunity she needed to prove herself worthy of that long-awaited promotion.

"Do you want a record of their overseas transactions?" I asked.

"Everything. I want everything. Go downstairs to the microfiche files for whatever they took off the network. This report has to be right."

"I understand, Ms. Parker. Should I see what Mr. Traynor has on the account?"

"Yes," she said. "Good thinking. Get his input."

Charles Traynor was the young hotshot destined to get the job Ms. Parker hoped this project would cinch her.

The personal line on her phone rang twice and she checked the LCD display before picking it up. "Yes, Mr. Henderson," she said, "I'll bring them up personally. No, sir. Yes, sir. No problem at all."

She hung up the phone, took another drag of her cigarette, and hardly needed to crush out what little was left in the ashtray. She immediately replaced it in her mouth with another, which she lit with a black, matte-finish, Dunhill lighter.

"Jesus. That was Henderson. He wants to know where the Severese Construction papers are."

"Severese Construction?"

"Yes. I'm sure I told you about it two weeks ago."

"I'm afraid not, Ms. Parker."

"You mean you haven't sent them?"

"I didn't know I was supposed to. Should I pull them together this morning?"

"No, Henderson will have to wait. This takes priority."

"But you told him you'd be bringing the papers."

"Dammit," Ms. Parker said, rubbing her brow. "All right. Pull together the Severese material as fast as you can. But don't waste too much time. Eleven o'clock at the latest. Then get on that Rothman project."

I spent the rest of the day staring into computer screens and scanning microfiche records. I worked straight through lunch—a diet Coke and a pretzel, which I ate at my desk, downed along with three Tylenol—and was still hard at it when quitting time rolled around.

"Time to go," Judy said, shucking on an old army fatigue jacket.

"I'm almost done," I said. "I just have to finish gathering this information. Ms. Parker wants to work on it over the weekend."

"A temp working overtime?" Judy said. "I should report you. You're setting a dangerous precedent. What are you trying to do, go legit and get a job in this hellhole?"

"Not a chance," I said, indicating Ms. Parker's closed door. It had been closed most of the afternoon. "I'm just trying to help her out."

"Why?" Judy asked. "She's a complete psycho."

"I know," I said. "But I kind of feel sorry for her. I know what it's like to want something so bad."

"Yeah," Judy said. "I guess so. Still, I wouldn't burst a blood vessel over her."

"Don't worry. I'm just trying to give her a fighting chance. We all deserve at least that much."

"See you Monday."

It was nearly seven o'clock before I delivered the completed file to Ms. Parker. I knocked on the door and entered her office. She had the phone propped between her shoulder and jaw, a cigarette still clamped between her teeth, while checking stock quotations on the computer behind her desk.

"Excuse me," I whispered.

She whirled around in her chair, reached across the desk, and grabbed the file from my hand, waving me impatiently out of the room.

So much for gratitude.

It was long after rush hour and the train was nearly half empty. I took a seat by the window and stared out at the drab scenery shuttling past. It was a Friday night. TGIF and all that. It was that in-between time in the city when the frenzy of the business day ended and the fever of the nightlife began. You could almost sense people taking a collective breath, winding down from the nine-to-five grind, and gearing themselves up for the excitement that lay ahead. Soon the hunt would be on: girls looking for boys, boys looking for girls, boys looking for boys, girls looking for girls, and all of them looking for booze, sex, parties, drugs, entertainment, and fun, fun, fun.

There were others, too, the lucky ones, who had already found someone with whom to spend their lives. I imagined them sharing quiet evenings, no longer desperately hunting for fun, but having found something even better: satisfaction in each other's company. It wasn't so long ago that I, too, lived for Friday and Saturday nights. Now I was old enough to see them not as a boundless opportunity for unlimited excitement, but as a nagging reminder of the lasting satisfaction I sorely lacked.

I bought a salad at a Korean deli a few blocks from my building and ran up the stairs to my apartment. In spite of the hectic day and the lousy sleep I'd had the night before, I wasn't the least bit tired. I changed into my sweats and hit the Nordic Trak, doing about thirty minutes while watching one of those Hollywood tabloid shows. I climbed off, toweled down, and got an Evian bottle from the nearly empty fridge. Of course, the water in the bottle wasn't Evian. I couldn't afford to pay two bucks for water anymore. I merely used the bottle and filled it with good old New York City tap water, which, surprisingly, was supposed to be one of the cleanest supplies of city water in the country. I carried my salad into the living room and finished watching a story on the latest scandal involving Kathie Lee when the phone rang.

"Jo, you're finally home. I've been trying to call you. I didn't want to leave a message. Where've you been?"

"Work."

"Work?"

"Yeah. I had an unprecedented attack of conscientiousness. It's a long story."

I couldn't help feeling annoyed that Cindy expected me home directly after work. What if I went out for a drink? Or maybe, God forbid, I had a date? After all, it was Friday night. On the other hand, what did I expect? Cindy knew me better than anyone. She knew I had virtually no social life lately. If anything, she often encouraged me to go out more often. She'd even tried to set me up a few times, much to my chagrin. Of course, she knew I'd be home. Where else would I be?

"I went to the callback today," she said.

"How'd it go?"

"Well, I don't want to jinx myself Jo, but—"

"Yeah?"

I could hear her struggling with barely suppressed excitement to find the words that wouldn't offend the theatrical gods. Actresses are a decidedly superstitious lot.

"I think I was pretty convincing."

"That's great, Cindy."

"I mean, at least I didn't fumble through my lines like last time. Naturally, I was so nervous I could've puked. They kept me waiting and waiting until I was about ready to go crazy. I was actually praying. Praying. Can you believe that? I don't think I've prayed since I was a junior in high school and I was waiting for the results of a home pregnancy test. But then right before it was my turn, I just had this great calm come over me. It was like I said to myself, 'The hell with it, whatever happens, happens.' If they wanted me, they wanted me.

If not, no amount of worrying was going to get me the part. So I just went in there and read, and it all just kind of flowed out of me. I did better than I ever did. At least I was better than last time. You know something, Jo? I think I found the secret of auditioning. Not giving a shit if you get the part or not." Cindy laughed. "Really, Jo, you should try it next time."

Next time. I felt something twist inside me. "So what did they say?"

"Oh, nothing, of course. The usual. We'll let you know. But the director did look up at me and smile."

Yeah, I thought. He probably wants to boff you. I felt guilty even as the thought flashed through my mind.

"That sounds great, Cindy," I said, trying to make amends with my conscience. "I'll bet you get it."

"Nah, I really doubt it. But maybe they'll keep me in mind for something else. You never know. Anyway"—she laughed—"the hell with it. Whatever happens, happens."

"Well, whatever you say, I think you're going to get it. Remember, you heard it from me first."

Was I being encouraging or trying to jinx her?

"So the bet's still on?"

"Yup. And I already know what you're buying me for dinner."

Cindy laughed again. In the background I heard a doorbell.

"Oh, that's Brad. We're going to the movies and then to grab a bite. It'll take my mind off the audition. Do you want to meet us?"

"No thanks."

"Are you sure?"

"I'm sure."

"You know Brad. He wouldn't mind. The more the merrier."

I did know Brad. He was an insurance executive with all the unctuous charm of a used-car salesman. I never knew if his overly solicitous manner was an attempt at flirtation or a habit left over from his days selling death and dismemberment policies. Cindy met him when he had offered to share a cab they simultaneously laid claim to during a sudden torrential rainstorm. A classic New York moment. He was good looking enough, but I was certain he wasn't Cindy's type. Flavor-of-the-month material, no more. But I didn't mention that to Cindy. She always thought she was in love.

"Thanks anyway, but I have to get up early tomorrow. Acting class."

"Right, I forgot. But if you change your mind—"

In the background I heard the doorbell again. Twice this time.

"I won't. You'd better get that."

"Oh, Brad doesn't mind ringing doorbells. He's still really good at it. Besides, it's like a trip down memory lane for him."

We both laughed at that, but when I hung up the phone the bad feelings started. It wasn't fair. I had nailed that part, I knew it. By her own admission, Cindy had screwed up at the first audition. If anyone should have gotten a callback it was me. Yeah, Cindy was younger, prettier. But I was the better actress. Didn't that count for anything in this lousy business? Maybe I wasn't so far off the mark. Maybe the director did want to screw her. I no longer felt guilty thinking that. Instead, I felt anger. Pure hot anger. I realized now that if I didn't get the part, I didn't want her to get it either. It wasn't pleasant to realize how small-minded I could be, but there was no sense fooling myself any longer. I wasn't that good an actress.

It was half past nine. Cindy's call had left me wired. I thought of going out, but decided against it. Considering the mood I was in, I would only be courting trouble. At least I had that much sense left. I was still dressed in my sweats so I hit the Nordic Trak again to bum off the excess energy. I was still going at it nearly an hour later. Finally I stopped, my lungs sucking air, my heart pounding, my clothes drenched with sweat. I never knew I could go that far. I was impressed. I knew I would pay for it the next morning, but the Nordic Trak had done its job. I was exhausted. I stripped off my soggy sweats, threw them in the laundry hamper, and stood under a hot shower until what was left of the tension drained from my body.

I set the clock for early next morning.

I hardly needed to bother. In spite of my exhaustion, I don't think I got more than half an hour's sleep all night.

5

---•---

I usually hate to get out of bed in the morning. Even more so, I hate to get up early on the weekends. But that is the only time I can make it to the Actor's Studio and so no matter how tough the week has been, or how much I'd rather sleep in on my day off, I manage to drag myself out of bed, throw on a pair of jeans and a sweatshirt, and hop the train back into Manhattan.

It was even tougher that morning than usual. Like I said, I didn't get more than half an hour's sleep the night before, but that wasn't what made it tough to get going. In fact, I'd been up since four in the morning, staring out the window, watching the empty street below, and waiting for the sky to brighten over the building across the street. No, it wasn't lack of sleep that bothered me. I had been wide awake for hours. I had spent the time staring into the long tunnel to nowhere that seemed to be my future.

Maybe my mother was right. Maybe it was time I settled down to a regular job, found a man, even had a baby. I had been chasing my dream long enough. It was time to wake up. If I wasn't careful I'd end up like the middle-aged waitresses I saw serving coffee to tourists in the theater district, their once pretty faces, hardened by years of disappointment, petrified into masks painted to recapture their prime, their tired eyes staring out the window at marquees on which their names would never appear.

I guess it was sheer force of habit, or the fact that I had already paid for the classes, or that somewhere deep down inside I still hadn't given up hope, but somehow I found myself dressed and on the train, a paper cup of hot tea in my hand as the train hurtled into the city. If you didn't realize it by now, I can get kind of dramatic. My mother always said that about me. If I fell down in the yard and scraped my knee, it was like the death scene from *Madame Butterfly*. If I broke up with a boy, even if I didn't really like him that much, it was like *West Side Story*. Nothing could ever be just ordinary. I guess that's what attracts me to acting. Everything in acting is bigger than life. If I don't have a role to play on stage or in front of a camera, then my life becomes a sort of role.

I slurped at my tea contentedly.

I was just feeling sorry for myself. It was a pretty good performance if I had to say so myself. I smiled. Too bad the audition hadn't called for a self-pitying would-be actress. Cindy wouldn't have stood a chance. I would have won the part hands down. I thought about my reaction to Cindy's success. Really, I shouldn't have been so upset. There would be other chances. I found myself hoping Cindy hadn't picked up on my resentment. I felt like calling her back immediately and giving her my sincere congratulations, not to mention my best wishes. I really did hope she landed the part. I decided I'd call her the first thing when I got home that afternoon.

I got off the train on the Lower East Side and climbed the stairs to the street. I could smell the cold air whipping off the river as it snaked its way up the sleeves and under the collar of my coat. I shivered, pulled the coat closer around me, bent my head, and hurried off down the street.

The Actor's Studio was located on the sixth floor of an old warehouse down near the piers. There was no elevator and the stairs were warped and covered with splitting linoleum. The studio itself was a long, narrow room with a bare wood floor, one large square of which was covered with a tattered remnant of rug that someone had obtained from somewhere. It was there where my class was held. The room was empty except for a few metal folding chairs, but these were used for props. Everyone sat on the floor. A handful of students had already arrived. Some were sipping coffee, a few were smoking, others were either reading the paper or talking quietly. I sat cross-legged at the back of the group as far away as possible from the draft blowing through one of the boarded-over windows. A skinny, intense-looking young guy with a carefully cultivated look I could swear was consciously borrowed from Robert DeNiro in *Taxi Driver* turned around and nodded hello.

I nodded back, quickly averting my eyes to the front of the room, where the instructor had fortuitously decided to get the class underway.

Adam Drake was tall and thin, his iron-gray hair brushed straight back from a face that looked as if it had been chiseled in granite. His eyes were the color of blue ice and just as cold and uncompromising. They were the eyes of a perfectionist. He was somewhere between fifty and sixty and was said to have done quite a bit of stagework in his younger years, though no one dared to ask him exactly what he'd played in or why he had given up acting for teaching.

He had studied with both Strasberg and Hagen, inheriting from the latter an intense dislike of both film and television. I'll never forget the look I got when I told him about the Electrify commercial I'd done. It was as if I'd admitted to keeping the heads of kidnapped poodles in my freezer. Those hypnotic eyes froze me like a mouse in front of a snake. I was afraid he was going to throw me out of class then and there. For Drake the only true outlet for acting was the theater. It was a conviction that I'm sure not a single one of his students shared; but no one was about to tell him that.

He was dressed in a pair of black jeans and a black turtleneck, his boots echoing through the huge, drafty room as he strode to the front of the class. He was holding a sheaf of papers which he handed to one of the girls sitting in the front row.

"Take one and pass them on," he said.

The Travis Bickle clone in front of me handed one back. I scanned it quickly. It was a page xeroxed out of the *Better Homes and Gardens Cookbook*.

"We're going to try something a little different today," Drake said. "I'm sure you've heard it said that a good actor can read the phone book and make it sound interesting. Well, it's true. It's not the words so much that are important to a good actor. It's the emotional power that's released. Sometimes a bad actor can hide behind emotional words. But only a good actor can convey emotion through neutral words. Who'd like to go first?"

The class was dead silent.

"Well?" Drake demanded, hands on hips, his gaze raking the room as mercilessly as a scythe.

I suddenly feigned an intense interest in the scuff mark on the tip of my left shoe.

"How about you?"

He never recognized any of us by name. It was always "you" or "him over there" or "the girl with the yellow sweater." I redoubled the attention I was giving my shoe.

"Yes, you!"

I could feel every hair on my scalp prickling. I could sense the heads of every student in the class turn in my direction. I looked up, trying to appear surprised, but Drake only looked annoyed at the delay.

"Me?" I pointed to myself.

Drake didn't answer. He just stood there glowering.

I stood up and walked to the front of the room, the xeroxed sheet clutched in my suddenly clammy hand. I knew everyone was thinking the same thing: thank God it wasn't me.

"The exercise is simple. Simple, but that doesn't make it easy. You'll learn that the simplest things in acting are the hardest. I will give you an emotion and you will bring it to life through the words on that page."

"But these are just recipes—"

"Anger!" Drake shouted, cutting me off.

I stared down at the paper in my hand. My eyes came to rest on the second recipe on the page.

"Anger!" Drake shouted again.

I let the anger I felt toward him at that moment pour through the meaningless words.

"Buckwheat griddle cakes," I snapped back. "Combine flour and salt. Soften yeast in warm water; stir in one tablespoon brown sugar."

"Sadness!"

Easy. I had been in a self-pitying mood all morning. "Stir in dry ingredients. Mix well. Cover; let stand overnight at room temperature." My voice broke.

"Malice."

I could feel the transformation immediately. My face twisted into a mask of spite and disgust. The emotion flowed out effortlessly. "The next morning stir batter; add remaining sugar, soda, and oil, mix well."

I was shocked to realize I'd still had such strong feelings about Stephen.

"Orgasm."

Suddenly the spell was broken. The word woke me up like the snap of a hypnotist's fingers.

"Excuse me?"

"You heard me," Drake growled.

"I don't know—"

"Orgasm!" he demanded.

"This is really . . . I mean . . ."

I stared down at the paper, my hands trembling, but the flow was gone. I started to read nevertheless, hoping something would come through as I read the meaningless words, trying desperately to reconnect to some deeply rooted feeling.

"Refrigerate one cup batter—"

"Enough," Drake snapped. "Sit down."

I felt the warmth crawling up my face, the wad of embarrassment choking my throat. I hadn't even turned away before he called the next sacrifice to the front of the room. Behind me, I could hear Drake shouting out his first command as the would-be actor slipped into character, reading his recipe for Buckwheat Griddle Cakes with snarling intensity. I considered heading straight out the back door and down the stairs to the street, but I meekly took my seat in the back of the room. To my relief, no one so much as dared to glance my way for fear of appearing inattentive and thus incurring Drake's implacable wrath.

The class seemed to drag on forever. The longer I sat there, the more angry I became. I hardly even heard the students who came after me. Who the hell did Drake think he was? He might be a brilliant teacher, but he had no right to treat people the way he did. He wasn't Sir Laurence Olivier, for crissakes.

I waited until the class was over and made my way to the front of the room. Usually a few students would try to get a personal word or two from the great man, only to be answered with a brusque economy of words. Today was no different. I hung around in the background until the last of my classmates departed before I approached him. He was putting the xeroxed recipes in a battered leather briefcase.

"Excuse me, Mr. Drake?"

"What is it?" he said, without looking up.

"I just wanted to explain something. You caught me off balance before. Ordinarily . . ."

He looked up at me, his eyes sharp, fierce, and totally without understanding.

"There is no such thing as being caught off balance. In life, you can get away with it. On the stage, you cannot. On the stage, there are no second chances. If the actor you're working with improvises and you aren't ready, the moment is lost forever. It cannot be repeated. Even in a movie, when you can do take after take, the spontaneity, the creativity, the genius of that one particular, irretrievable moment is lost and what you are left with is something lifeless, practiced, *rehearsed*. Do you understand the difference between reading and being?"

"Yes," I said tightly.

"Good. Because if you don't, then you don't understand acting. In which case, you're wasting your time and mine. The former I can excuse. The latter I cannot."

I was so stunned by his words I turned away without a word. All I wanted was to be out of that room, away from those cold eyes now piercing me between the shoulder blades.

"One more thing, Miss Brady."

I was shocked as much by the fact that he knew my name as that he had stopped me.

I turned around. "Yes?" I managed.

"Have you ever actually had an orgasm?"

"What do you mean?"

"Can there be two ways to interpret such a question?"

"I don't know . . . I'm not sure I understand . . ."

"You didn't seem thrown off by any of the other emotions I asked you to bring forth. Why that one?"

"It was embarrassing."

"Embarrassing? No human experience is taboo to an actor. Besides, I didn't ask you to have an orgasm—only to act as if you'd had one."

"To me, it's almost the same thing."

"Not almost. It *is* the same thing. Now I'll ask you only one more time. Have you ever had an orgasm?"

"I don't think it's any of your business—" I started and saw the darkening look on his face. "Of course," I blurted out. "What the hell do you think?"

"I think you should consult a therapist. Perhaps you need to work through some psychosexual block or other. Are you sure you've had an orgasm?"

"I think I'd know," I said, anger rising in my voice.

He seemed to note the tone. Something changed in his eyes. The arctic gaze was gone, replaced by a feverish intensity. His sharply drawn, ascetic face suddenly morphed into a leering, wolfish mask.

"Because if you haven't, I'd be glad to help you out."

"This is totally inappropriate, Mr. Drake," I stammered, anger replaced by shock and fright.

"Is it?" he asked.

"I don't have to listen to this."

"No, you don't. You can leave right now."

I stood there, rooted to the spot, unable to move.

As suddenly as before, his expression changed back again. The ice was once more back in his eyes, his face angular and as severe as an Old Testament prophet.

"That," he said, "is acting. I'm afraid you failed again, Miss Brady. Now go home. You've wasted enough of my time."

I raced for the door, trying to beat the tears that were burning in my eyes. I made it to the street just before the tears started running down my cheeks. I was walking against the wind and the cold air felt good on my face. I suddenly noticed that someone was walking beside me. I turned to see the Travis Bickle clone from class matching me stride for stride. His hands were thrust deeply into the pockets of his army surplus jacket and he was smiling a crooked DeNiro smile. He took a hand from his pocket and jerked a thumb over his shoulder toward the warehouse.

"Don't let him get to you," he said in a rough Brooklyn street accent he was either cultivating or couldn't suppress. "He's riding you cause you got potential."

"What the hell makes you think that?"

"I can tell," he said. "I see it myself. Of everybody in there, me and you got the goods."

"I see."

He stopped walking, and since he was still talking, I felt compelled to stop, too. He glanced up the street, then back at me.

"Say, I was thinking. Maybe we could go some place for coffee or something?"

"Thanks, but I'd rather be alone now."

"Yeah. Okay, that's cool. Sometimes I like to be alone, too. Johanna, right?"

"Yes."

He smiled again. "Harry. Harry Krinkle."

He held out his hand and I shook it.

"Maybe some other time, huh?"

"Yeah, maybe."

"Good. I'll look forward to it."

He smiled his crooked smile and stood there staring at me.

I turned away and headed quickly up the street, afraid he'd call out after me, but I made the corner, certain he'd been watching me the whole time.

What the hell, I thought, as I sat in a coffee shop and picked at a stale croissant. Harry Krinkle. Was it all an act? Or did the guy really think he was the next DeNiro? Was Drake acting, too, as he'd said, or was he just using that as an excuse? I thought about his suggestion that I go into psychotherapy. Maybe he was right. Not about a sexual problem, damn him. But perhaps I did have some emotional blocks that needed to be cleared. I had been in therapy for a while once; hell, every actor and actress I knew was seeing a shrink. But once the money stopped coming in, I realized that therapy was more a luxury than a necessity.

I was beginning to think it was time to get out of this business. It was all too damn weird.

6

It was a little after two by the time I got home. The red light was blinking on the answering machine.

I didn't play the message. I knew who it was.

I waited two hours before I called her back. She answered on the first ring.

"Did you get my message, Jo? Can you believe it?"

"I knew you'd get it. Congratulations, Cindy."

"I mean I just keep thinking it's some kind of mistake. That they're gonna call me back and tell me they really meant to give it to someone else. I've been afraid to pick up the phone ever since they called. I thought this might be them right now. God, Jo, what if it is all a mistake?"

"Don't be silly," I said. "They don't make those kind of mistakes."

"I hope not, Jo. If they do, I'll just die."

"Try to calm down."

"I can't. I'm a nervous wreck. I tell you this is worse than not getting a part. That I can handle. Success? Forget it."

"You'll get used to it. Tell me, what did they say?"

"I can hardly remember. I was on my hands and knees scrubbing the kitchen floor when the phone rang. I never expected it would be them. Like, who calls on a Saturday, right? Some woman came on telling me to hold for Mr. Donovan. He's the director. Anyway, I figure they just want to inform me of another audition or something, so I think okay, maybe this is going to be pretty cool. Then Mr. Donovan comes on and he's telling me how much he liked my reading and how much presence I have and before I know it, he's telling me I've got the part."

"You must have been excited." I was smiling, but I could feel the smile frozen on my face. I could only imagine the excitement she must have felt.

"I tell you I thought I was going to have a heart attack then and there. If he could have seen me! I'm standing there in a pair of rolled-up sweats, my hair pulled up in a bandana, rubber gloves on, stinking of ammonia and he's going on about my cool sensuality and erotic glamour. To make matters worse, I started babbling like some kind of idiot, telling him how much I liked the show, how I looked forward to working with him. I don't even know what I was saying. I just remembered wishing the phone would go dead, anything, just to get me to stop talking before I screwed the whole thing up. I'm sure he thought I was the biggest airhead on the East Coast."

"I wouldn't worry about it. I'm sure he's used to people being excited."

"I hope so, Jo. This is it. My first really big break."

"You deserve it, Cindy."

"So do you. That's the one thing that's keeping this from being perfect. I wish it was you, too."

"It'll happen for me. Don't worry. Just enjoy it. I promise I'll enjoy it when I get the chance."

"You're a doll, Jo. Thank you. You're right, too. You will make it. You're a much better actress than me."

"Not today." I laughed, feeling a little sick to my stomach.

"Hey, you did beat me at something, though."

"What's that?"

"Our bet. Remember? If I got the part I was supposed to treat you to Chinese."

"Oh yeah. But you don't have to—"

"No, a bet's a bet. Besides, it can be a kind of celebration dinner."

"You mean tonight?"

"Sure, why not?"

"What about Brad? Wouldn't you rather celebrate with him?"

"No."

I knew that tone.

"Trouble?"

Cindy sighed. "Not exactly. We had a bit of a fight the other night."

"The night I called?"

"Yeah. It was one of those really stupid fights you can't even remember how it started but somehow changes everything. You know what I mean? Anyway, he's out of town for a couple of days. Setting up some corporate life-insurance deal in Minnesota. Can you imagine me spending the rest of my life with some spook who shakes down folks by putting the fear of death in them?"

"I'm sorry," I said. "About things not working out."

"It's no big deal. Besides, I'd rather spend the evening with you."

"Do you think we could do it another night? I'm kind of tired—"

"Oh please, Jo. I can't stay here tonight. I'm too wired. And there's really no one else in the city who means as much to me as you."

"Well if you put it that way . . ."

"Great. I'll meet you at the restaurant at eight."

"It's a date," I said and heard Cindy's call waiting clicking. "You'd better get that. It's probably another one of your admirers."

Cindy laughed. "You're the best, Jo. Talk to you later."

I put the phone down in its cradle. If only Mr. Drake had been here to see that performance. I stripped off my clothes, put on an old sweat suit, and slipped a Rolling Stones CD on my decrepit boom box. I set the program so Mick Jagger kept on singing "Can't get no satisfaction" and worked out for nearly an hour on the Nordic Trak, trying to sweat away my frustration. It didn't work. When I stopped, I only felt frustrated *and* exhausted. I took a quick shower, dressed, and headed into Manhattan to meet Cindy.

The Peking Duck was one of those hole-in-the-wall New York places you had to be a native to know about. They had the best mu shu shrimp in the city. For years Cindy and I had made it a ritual to go there every New Year's Eve to recount our failures of the past year and our hopes for the new, and every time one of us lost a part or a boyfriend we would meet there to commiserate and cheer each other up. The restaurant had become a kind of clearinghouse for our emotional lives. There was a lot of past history between us soaked into the old plaster walls. I looked around the dim restaurant, still decorated with tinsel and Christmas lights, and picked out Cindy among the sparse crowd. She was sitting at our usual table, a large bottle of champagne in front of her. She looked even more stunning than usual. Was it only my imagination or was she emitting an aura of exhilaration that separated her from the rest of the humdrum Saturday evening crowd? She stood up as I approached and we hugged.

"I'm so happy for you," I said, and for the first time since I had heard the news, I really meant it.

"Thank you," Cindy said. "That means so much to me. I only wish somehow it could be you, too."

You and me both, I thought.

We sat down and opened our menus. I had brought two bottles of champagne and when the waiter came over, I asked him for a pair of wineglasses. I'd been a vegetarian for the last two years and had recently included fish on my Thou Shalt Not Eat list, so I ordered the Buddhist's Delight, a combination of steamed vegetables in a tasty Szechuan sauce. Cindy ordered the shrimp.

"What you girls celebrate?" our waiter asked as he opened the champagne. He was a short, handsome, unfailingly friendly Chinese man who was thirty-seven, but looked young enough to be fifteen. He always seemed to be working whenever we came in and always made a point of waiting on us. He was saving his money to bring his fiancée, whom he hadn't seen in five years, over from China. When we had the money, we always tried to leave him an extra big tip.

Cindy told him about her role on the show and I noticed a couple glancing over at her. Again I felt a pang of jealousy. Why her and not me? The waiter grinned, bobbed his head up and down, and pointed to the small black-and-white television behind the cash register.

"I watch show ever afternoon. Boss watch it really. She love it. But I watch sometime, too. Very good for you. You make lot of money now, become big star."

Cindy laughed.

"We haven't discussed that yet. It's a small part. But it's a start."

"Well, good luck to you."

He poured our champagne into the glasses and carried our orders back to the kitchen.

"Congratulations," I said as sincerely as I could as we touched our glasses of champagne.

"Thanks," Cindy said and sipped. I'd never seen her so happy. "I can't believe this is really happening. I keep expecting them to call up and tell me it was all some kind of mistake."

"It's no mistake. You're beautiful and talented. It was bound to happen sooner or later. You deserve the part."

"I know it's a minor role, but I can't help but fantasize. Do you know how many stars were discovered off soap operas?"

"A lot," I ventured.

"Not that I think I'm going to be a star. It's just that . . . oh I don't know what I'm saying, Johanna. I'm just so damn happy. I've never been so happy in my whole damn life."

"You have the right," I said, smiling. Her enthusiasm was infectious.

"And it'll happen for you. I just know it. It's only a matter of time."

"Thanks," I said. "But let's not talk about me. Tonight's your night."

The food came, but Cindy could hardly stop talking long enough to take a bite. I barely touched my own food, but for quite different reasons. As she talked about the script, the tight shooting schedule, the fact that she could be on the air as soon as the following week, I looked over at her lovely, perfect face in the dim light of the paper lantern overhead and couldn't help feel an overwhelming sense of sadness. I was no longer jealous that she'd gotten the part and not me, but rather what her success meant to our friendship. I somehow knew that tonight marked the end of our friendship. She was moving on to bigger and better things and I was being left behind. I couldn't have told her my fears and she wouldn't have accepted them, but I knew it to be true all the same. It was unavoidable. She couldn't have stopped the wheels of fate if she tried. The waiter came by, noticed our half-empty plates, and offered to wrap our food for us. A few minutes later, he returned to the table with two neat little white cardboard boxes.

I poured myself another glass of champagne. I don't remember how many I'd had at that point, except that we had nearly finished the bottle and Cindy wasn't drinking much. I didn't usually drink and the champagne was going straight to my head. By the time Cindy settled the bill and we stood to leave, I felt a little unsteady on my feet. Cindy left our waiter an even larger tip than usual. I offered to chip in on the tip as usual, but Cindy wouldn't hear of it.

"A deal's a deal," she said.

Cindy, no doubt, was feeling expansive out of the expectation of bigger things to come. I simply felt a new sense of kinship with the waiter struggling to bring his fiancée over from China. Outside the restaurant, I gave Cindy a rather sloppy kiss on the mouth and she stepped back and looked at me a little strangely.

"Are you okay getting home on your own?" she asked. "You can come home with me if you want."

"No, I'm okay," I slurred. "Just a little too much bubbly. It'll wear off on the train."

"Are you sure?" Cindy asked, concern furrowing her normally flawless brow.

"Sure."

"All right," she said uncertainly. "I'll call you. Let you know how the first day of rehearsals went."

"Great," I said, hardly knowing what I was saying, just knowing I suddenly wanted to be alone.

We hugged again, and then we went our separate ways down the cold, dark windswept street to our respective subway entrances. In my drunken, maudlin state, I was certain that it was probably the last time I would ever see Cindy—at least the Cindy I knew—ever again.

I got on an empty car and stared out the windows at the shuttling lights. At Forty-fifth Street a young black man in a bulky Timberland jacket and a stocking cap, with the word "Killer" stenciled across the front, got on and took the seat opposite me. I felt his eyes on me. Normally I would have made a move to a more populated car, but tonight I didn't care. I looked at him in the irregular light of the train and for a moment caught his angry, hostile eyes. Instead of being afraid, I somehow wanted to tell him how much alike we were, how both our dreams were stifled, how we were both going nowhere, how he wasn't alone. No doubt he would have just taken me for some drunken white lush who deserved to be mugged. As it was, he looked as though he was trying to decide whether or not it was worth his while to hassle me. I dropped my eyes before he could interpret my gaze as either an invitation or a challenge. He kept on looking me over and didn't take his eyes off me, even as he got off the train two stops down the line.

I got home about a half hour later. I checked my answering machine. There were four messages. I didn't feel like answering back. I put my container of leftover Chinese food into the refrigerator, went to the bathroom, and ran the hot water for a bath. I stripped off my clothes, slipped into a terry-cloth bathrobe, and went to the kitchen to pour myself a glass of chardonnay.

I carried the glass and the half-full bottle back into the bathroom, pinned up my hair, shed the robe, and stepped into the steaming tub. I sank my body up to my chin in the hot water, feeling the warmth loosen my tight muscles. I took a sip of wine. As I did I spotted the razor at the corner of the tub and for a brief moment had one of those morbid thoughts everyone has once in a while about what it would be like to slash my wrists. Too squeamish. I could never do it. Besides, my greatest fault is an undying hope. I always think something good is going to happen right around the corner. Besides, it was one of the plastic Bic disposable razors, and the blade was dull at that.

The envelope containing the Christmas card from my father was sitting on the edge of the tub beside the glass of wine. I know I said he was dead, but he really wasn't, at least not biologically. I hadn't seen or talked to him since he'd gotten divorced from my mother when I was twelve years' old. That was three stepfathers ago. He left for California to work in the computer industry just then burgeoning in what would later come to be known as Silicon Valley. I didn't even visit him when I was out in Hollywood, though I had an open invitation. In the past few years he had been expressing an interest in seeing me. After all these years, I had no idea why. Maybe now that he was growing older he was feeling the tug of nostalgia. Maybe now that I was on my own, he could see me without having to see my mother. In any event, ever since he left, he'd always made sure to send me a card on Christmas or my birthday. In spite of myself, I'd saved them all in a shoebox I kept at the back of my closet. A hundred times I meant to go down to the incinerator in the basement and throw the damn collection into the flames, and a hundred times I couldn't bring myself to do it.

Go figure.

I took another sip of wine and fingered the edge of the envelope. Then I tore it open and pulled out the card.

When I opened the card, a photograph tumbled out. I caught it before it hit the water. It was of my father with his new family. He had six kids, my half brothers and sisters, I reflected, with a sense of unreality. I didn't want to, but I glanced at his wife, and felt a glimmer of satisfaction at the signs of age creeping up on her. She had been only twenty-three when my father married her sixteen years ago.

My father stood in the center, his already fine blond hair noticably thinning since last year's photo, a beard grown in to compensate. Beside the cheery Christmas greetings my father penned a note that started "Dear Joey." It was the name he had for me as a kid. It always made me feel like he'd have rather had a boy. It made me cringe even now. I read through the note quickly. It was another invitation to come down and see him, how he missed me, how he hoped all was well with me, how he hoped my acting career was going well, all that blather.

I knew he still talked occasionally to my mother. How else could he have gotten my address and learn about what I was doing? I made a mental note to tell my mother not to tell him any of my business. I'd told her before, but she never listened. He informed me that his wife was pregnant with their seventh child, as if I cared. He was almost sixty—what was he doing having more kids?

Attached to the card with a paper clip was a check for five hundred dollars. My first impulse was to tear it up, but necessity got the better of me. I could certainly use the extra money. I put the card aside and settled back into the water until it cooled. By that time I had nearly killed the bottle of chardonnay. I was pretty toasted when I climbed out of the cold soapy water.

That night, for the first time since the break-in, I slept in my bed.

7

Like I said, I met him for the first time a week after the break-in. I had just finished my typical lunch of yogurt, granola, and a diet Coke at my desk and decided to spend the rest of my lunch hour getting a little fresh air. I walked along, looking in casually at the shop windows, daydreaming about the day when I might be able to afford the dresses in the windows of Saks. It was an unseasonably warm day for mid-January, and I unbuttoned my coat, enjoying the feel of the sun.

A display of books caught my eye in the window of the Barnes & Noble on Fifth Avenue. I walked through the revolving doors and went over to the new arrival table and a display of the red-and-gold books. It was a hardcover book by an author I'd never heard of before, Matthew Lang. I was reading the flap copy when I heard a man's voice over my shoulder.

"Take it from me, that's a great book. The copywriter who wrote those flaps didn't do it justice."

I turned to the voice and had to move my eyes a couple of inches upward to see his face. He was tall, good looking, with a strong jaw. He had a thick mane of dark hair, professionally clipped, graying slightly and attractively at the temples. To top it off, he had a dimple in his chin. He was wearing a sports coat made of an expensive-looking tweed, perfectly faded blue jeans, and a pair of comfortably worn brown loafers. There was a look of amusement in his gray eyes.

"Did you read it?" I asked, one half of my brain frantically trying to think of what to say next, the other half chiding me for such a lame opening. Of course, he read it, you idiot, I heard a voice inside my head say, how else would he know it was a great book?

"Well, I didn't exactly read it—"

I remember thinking that the man was trying to pick me up. I was unattached at the time. Of course, I'd had a few dates since Stephen, but nothing serious. The fact of the matter was that I wasn't really looking for a relationship. Did I really want this? Around me, businessmen were rushing to the racks to grab their copies of the latest Tom Clancy or John Grisham novels to begin on the evening commute home, but for a moment it was as if we were the only two people in the store. I could feel my heart pounding and my palms sweating. Had I heard him correctly? Did he say he hadn't read the book? Maybe my question wasn't so stupid, after all.

"You didn't read it," I said, smiling, flirting in spite of myself. "Then how do you know it's a good book?"

"I wrote it."

"You wrote it?"

"I'm afraid so." He smiled.

I thought he must be joking, but I flipped the book over. Sure enough, there was his photograph on the back jacket. I looked from the book to his face and back again.

"It is you."

He laughed. It was a nice laugh—strong, clean, masculine.

He reached into his sports coat and pulled out a slim, alligator-skin billfold. He plucked out two twenty-dollar bills and handed them to me.

"My treat," he said, indicating the book.

"I couldn't."

"Please take it," he said. "I put you on the spot, coming up to you like that. But I just couldn't resist. Now you'll feel obliged to buy a book you had no intention of buying. Please . . ."

He pressed the money into my hand. "I'll consider it an investment," he said, smiling again, a killer smile. He could have been an actor. "If you like the book, you might consider buying my backlist."

"All right," I said, relenting. "On one condition."

He arched an eyebrow and I blushed. I wondered what he thought I was going to ask him.

"And that is?"

"Would you sign it?"

"Certainly," he said, an expression of amusement playing about his full, sensual lips. He took the book from me and reached back into his coat. He uncapped a burgundy Mont Blanc fountain pen and started writing on the title page. He looked up from the book.

"What's your name?"

"Johanna. Johanna Brady."

He looked back down to the book and wrote quickly, the sharp nib of the pen scratching across the book's crisp paper, and snapped the book closed before I could read what he'd written. He handed the book back, capped the pen, and returned it to his inside pocket.

"Perhaps we might run into each other again and you can tell me what you think of the book," he said.

"Yes," I said, trying in vain to control the rush of blood to my face. "Yes, I would like that. In the meantime, I can start your book."

He laughed. "Maybe you should wait. You might hate it."

"I doubt it."

"Will you be honest?"

"Can you take it?"

"I've been panned by some of the best."

"Then I'll be honest. Brutally."

"Well, then it's a deal. Can I have your number?"

"Yes," I stammered. "Of course."

He wrote it down on a pad covered with scrawls that I figured might be ideas for future books.

"Do you normally do this kind of thing to meet women?"

This time it was he who blushed.

"It's a first for me, I promise. . . ."

"I'll take that as a compliment."

"It was meant to be."

"Well, in any event I'm glad you came over."

"Me, too. I'll be in touch."

"Good."

We shook hands. His grip was warm, firm, and soft. I walked to the register, conscious of his gaze on my back, and paid for the book. But when I turned to look for him by the stacks, he was gone.

By the time I returned to the office, I was fifteen minutes late. Ms. Parker had plastered three urgent Post-its on my computer terminal. I shucked off my coat and sat down to read them. There were two faxes to send out and a couple of client files to retrieve from the records department. At the bottom of a stack of phone messages was one from my agent.

"Nice lunch?" Judy asked, without taking her eyes off her computer terminal.

"Yes, as a matter of fact," I said. "I met a guy. An author." I showed her the book and flipped it over so she could see his picture.

"Good looking," she said.

"His name is Matthew Lang."

"Matthew who?"

"Lang. Writes psychological suspense novels."

Judy shrugged. "Never heard of him."

I peeled the Post-its off my computer, arranged them in order of importance, went to the records department for the files Ms. Parker had requested, and then decided I could wait no longer. I sat down and dialed the number of my agent.

"Good as Gold Talent Agency. Ms. Gold isn't in right now—"

"Hello, Ruth, it's Johanna."

"Hey, Johanna. How are you?"

Ruth Gold wasn't exactly the cream of New York's agents. I suppose that was how I'd managed to convince her to handle me in the first place. She had a small office in her apartment down in the Village. Most anyone who was anyone in the business had real offices in Midtown. But Ruth had probably been in the business as long as anyone and never having made a big success of it, she knew the secrets of survival. At bottom, she held out the unrealistic hope of all struggling agents that she would somehow snare the big talent everyone else had overlooked. For a while I held that designation. But the honeymoon period was over. I was now just another wannabe she was hoping might be good enough to pay a few bills.

She had a niece who worked part-time answering the phone for her when not attending classes at N.Y.U. The rest of the time Ruth answered it herself, pretending to be a secretary, and usually telling callers that Ms. Gold was busy with a client or "doing" lunch. I had seen her pull that trick on more than one occasion while sitting across the desk from her. I also recognized her cigarette-cracked voice, no matter how she tried to disguise it.

"I'm doing fine. I got your message."

"Yes. Listen, I have something on the burner that could be just right for you. Can you make it downtown in an hour?"

I looked at the clock. "I just got back from my lunch. I'm kind of stuck here till five."

I heard her sigh on the other end.

"All right. Do you think you can make it by three-thirty? I have to sit shiva at my sister-in-law's funeral tonight."

"I'm sorry."

"Sorry?"

"About your sister-in-law."

"Ech. God made her let Him keep her."

I looked up and saw Ms. Parker standing at the door to her office.

"Look, I've got to go. I'll see you at three-thirty."

"Don't be late. If I don't get uptown by sundown, my brother Marty will never let me hear the end of it. He could hardly stand Sheila himself, but he's a real stickler for tradition."

"Don't worry. See you then."

I hung up the phone, found out what Ms. Parker wanted, and headed for the xerox room to send out the two faxes on my desk. While I was waiting for them to go through, I thought about Ruth's call. She hadn't so much as hinted at what she had lined up. Obviously it was something that had come up on the spur of the moment or time wouldn't be of such importance. Maybe someone had fallen ill or gotten fired from a part. Or perhaps they had left to take a better role somewhere else. Maybe it was some inside connection that Ruth had to some production or other. No doubt it wasn't anything big. Probably just a bit role in some commercial or off-off-Broadway play. Or a voice-over for a radio spot. It could even be someone who needed a pair of hands or legs to model some product or other for television. No doubt it was a bone some friend had thrown Ruth out of courtesy or pity.

No matter.

I'd take it. When you were in my position, you pulled at every string offered. You never knew where it might lead.

I just had to think of some way to get out of the office and over to Ruth's by three-thirty.

I stood outside Ms. Parker's office and knocked on her half-closed door.

"Excuse me, Ms. Parker. Can I have a word with you?"

"Do you have those files I asked for?"

"I brought them to you already," I said. "Right there under your coffee cup."

Ms. Parker scanned her desk, located her coffee cup, and saw the files underneath.

"Good," she said, trying not to appear nonplussed. "Did you get those faxes off and call back the accounting department?"

"Yes and yes. I'd like to ask you a favor. I know this is a bad time, but could I leave a little early today?"

"Early?"

"Yes. It's—well, my doctor called. Something suspicious came up on my mammogram and he wants me to come in for further tests. He's pretty sure it's nothing to worry about. Just a shadow or something. But he wants to make sure."

Ms. Parker rubbed her eyes.

"I see." She sighed, as if my request were all part of some monumental conspiracy to destroy her. "I guess you really have no choice then, do you?"

"I'll stay later tomorrow to make up the time, I promise."

"Yes. That would be good. For now, try to clear your desk. I'll need all the information I asked for before you leave today."

"Yes, ma'am." I turned to leave.

"And Johanna."

"Yes, Ms. Parker?"

I looked around and for the first time noticed the heavy bags cracking the foundation makeup applied heavily under her eyes.

"Good luck."

"Thank you."

When I got back to my desk, Judy whirled around from her computer monitor. She leaned forward, winked, and whispered, "For Best Performance by an Employee Trying to Shirk Her Responsibility, the Academy Award goes to . . ."

"Sssh," I whispered back.

Judy started laughing. "You're shameless, you know that?"

"I had no choice. The only way Simone LeGree would let me go is if it were a matter of life or cancer."

"Yeah. Besides, you have been busting your hump for her."

"Not that she seems to notice. After all, I am just a temp."

"If you covered yourself in gasoline and immolated yourself outside her office I don't think she'd notice. Unless, of course, you hadn't gotten her the latest printout on the Rothman Group."

"Stop it," I said, stifling a laugh. "I'm supposed to be worrying about whether I have cancer or not."

"Well, you know what they say: laughter is the best medicine."

I worked frantically, gathering everything together Ms. Parker wanted, and waited until she was safely on the phone before grabbing my coat and sneaking off to the elevators. I caught a subway down to the Village and made it to Ruth's brownstone with about fifteen minutes to spare.

Ruth ushered me into her apartment. She had somehow managed to successfully graft together living room and office into one dual-purpose area. The furniture had that dark, drab, slightly out-of-date look that either marked it as having been rescued from a secondhand shop or as a legacy from some older relative. Of course, Ruth herself was old enough to have been the original owner. I didn't know her age exactly, and she was not the kind of woman to whom the years had been kind, but from references she made to her experience in the business, whether they were true or not, she looked to be at least in her late sixties. If anything, you had to admire the sheer moxie of the woman.

"Please sit down," she said, pointing the end of an unfiltered cigarette at a red leather chair in front of her desk. The seat was faded from many a hopeful prospect and patched in the center with a strip of black tape. "I'm literally racing the sun here, so I'll get to the point."

"I just want to say thanks for thinking of me."

"No need to thank me. You're the first person I thought of for this. I think it's a great opportunity for you. I just hope you haven't set your goals too high."

"I'm really eager for work, Ruth, you know that. I'm up for anything."

"I heard about the audition for *The Way We Live.*"

"How did you know?"

"Word gets around. I heard your friend got the part."

"Yes," I said. "It's a wonderful opportunity for her. She deserves it."

"I'm sure," Ruth said, with just the barest trace of a sardonic smile. "Anyway, here's the deal. An old acquaintance of mine is coming into town sometime next week. His name is Sol Silverstein. He's a producer. I'd like you to meet him."

"Does he have something for me?"

"Not exactly. But it wouldn't be a bad idea for you to get to know him."

"I don't understand. Is he in the process of putting something together?"

"Not at the moment. You might say he's between projects."

"I don't think I've ever heard his name. What has he done?"

"It's been awhile since he's done anything really substantial. Some low-budget sexploitation stuff in the late seventies. Some softcore porn. But he's got some interesting plans. He's definitely a player. He has potential. And he's a good man to get to know."

"I still don't get it. What would he want with me?"

Ruth leaned forward and stubbed out her cigarette. "He just wants to get to know you. That's all."

"Wait a minute. I think I get the gist of this."

"Don't take this the wrong way, Johanna."

"Don't take this the wrong way?" I shouted. "What other way is there to take it? I'm an actress, not a call girl. If he wants someone to keep him company, why doesn't he call a goddamn escort service?"

Ruth calmly pulled out another cigarette, placed it between her thickly painted pink lips, and picked up a silver lighter engraved with someone else's initials. She closed her eyes, drew deeply from the cigarette, and exhaled slowly. She opened her eyes even more slowly, the look in them shrewd and merciless. Her face, a road map of lost journeys, looked every bit its six-plus decades in the business.

"No one is asking you to do anything you don't want to do, Johanna. But you have to face facts. You aren't getting any younger. For a woman in this business, you're already past your prime. If I'm being blunt with you, it's for your own good. Someone has to be. Besides, it's my job. If you don't succeed, I don't succeed. You have to start playing the game, Johanna. Give a little, get a little."

"I got an agent so I wouldn't have to play the game."

"You always have to play the game, Johanna. You got an agent so you could be put in touch with the right players. Sol Silverstein is one of the right players. On top of that, he is an old acquaintance of mine and a perfect gentleman. Now if you want to meet him, fine. If not, I'll just call up someone else. There are plenty of girls who would jump at the opportunity. I thought of you first because I like you. I want to see you make it. I still believe in you. But time is running out."

She measured my reaction through a blue haze of cigarette smoke, the fingers of her right hand resting meaningfully on her overstuffed Rolodex.

"All right, dammit," I said. "I'll take it."

"Good. I'll arrange it all with Sol and get back to you. Keep the last week of January open. He's a busy man. I'm not sure when he'll be free. You're making the right choice, Johanna. Sol has some interesting plans. If you play your cards right, you can be part of them."

"That would be nice," I muttered.

"Good. Now if you'll excuse me, I really must be getting over to my brother's. He's all the way out in Flushing."

"Yes. I'm sorry. I won't keep you waiting."

Ruth stood up, came around her desk, and hugged me. Her dyed blond hair, fine as cotton candy and done up in a fluffy flip, tickled my face. Her wrinkled cheek was surprisingly soft.

She patted me between the shoulder blades, stepped back, and put the cigarette back between her lips.

"You're doing the right thing, Johanna. You'll see."

"Yes, I suppose so."

I sat on the subway, thinking about what Ruth had said. It was hard medicine to swallow, but sometimes the truth was bitter. I was at a dead end. My career was going nowhere. I was getting older. I was even taking grief in acting class. I'd meet Sol Silverstein. I'd be an ornament on his arm for a night or two. If that's what it took to get a break, then I would just grin and bear it. I'd put on the performance of my life. Besides, as mercenary as Ruth was, I trusted her judgment of character. She would never have suggested that I meet him if she didn't believe him harmless.

How bad could it be?

I let my thoughts drift to my encounter with the man in the bookstore that afternoon. Was it only this afternoon? It already seemed like a thousand years ago. He sure was handsome. And charming, too. With my sudden change in spirits, I decided a little celebration was in order. I stopped off at Midtown and went into an exclusive boutique and bought a little party dress and a pair of shoes way out of my price range. I knew I would regret it when I got my credit card bill later that month, but for the time being I didn't give a damn. Besides, I still had that five-hundred-dollar check from my father folded inside my wallet.

That night after dinner I turned the television down, made myself a cup of tea, and curled up on the couch with Matthew's book. I turned the book over to his picture. I felt a familiar tingling at the base of my spine. Had I really fallen for the guy already? I opened the book to page one, hoping I liked it, not knowing what I would say to him if I didn't. Of course, I was making the gigantic assumption that he was going to call me in the first place.

At least I didn't need to worry about liking his book. I was hooked from the first page. The story was about a lonely woman who meets a man on a computer bulletin board and ends up being stalked by a killer. It was riveting reading. It was told from the woman's point of view and I was surprised at how well the author had captured what a woman would think and feel. The book didn't seem written by a man at all.

I must have read about a hundred pages before I grew too tired to read anymore and laid the book on the coffee table. To my surprise, it was already close to midnight. I had completely lost track of the time. I put my empty teacup in the sink and carried the book with me as I walked down the hall to the bedroom. There I undressed in the half-light coming in from the street lamps outside and climbed into bed, setting the alarm for the next morning.

It was then that I remembered the inscription he'd written and opened the book to the title page.

Johanna
To a woman with such beautiful eyes
One must tell everything.
            —Matt Lang

Three hours later I woke up and knew he was back. I remember looking calmly at the clock by my bed and seeing the bright red display reading 3:00 A.M. I don't know why I wasn't more scared. Maybe it was because he had come before and done nothing. I'm not sure. But instinctively I seemed to sense that he wasn't here to harm me. I turned slowly, raising myself on one elbow, brushing the hair from my eyes.

Sure enough, the dark outline of a man was standing in the lit doorway.

"What are you doing here?"

I was almost surprised that he answered.

"I came to see you."

His voice was soft, intimate, not threatening. Under any other circumstances, it might almost be called comforting.

"Why?"

"I find you interesting."

"How did you get in? I just had a new lock put on the door."

"Locks are no problem for me."

"Who are you?"

"That question is off base."

"Okay," I said. "Do I know you?"

"No."

"Well, what do you want from me?"

"Just to talk."

"What do you want to talk about?"

"Whatever's on your mind."

I reached toward the nightstand. "Can I turn on the light?"

"Lights are off base."

I took my hand away from the lamp and settled back on the bed. I could hardly believe I was having this conversation, but in a strange way it all seemed so natural.

"If I could see you it would make this easier," I reasoned.

"Lights are off base," he repeated flatly.

"Okay," I said, not wanting to make him angry. "I have to admit, I find this whole situation a little frightening."

"There's nothing to be frightened about."

"Well, it's not the usual thing to have a total stranger break into your apartment in the middle of the night."

"It is my hope that you won't think of me as a stranger."

"What should I think of you as?"

"The man of your dreams."

With that, he turned away and walked quickly and without a sound to the front door. I heard the door shut quietly behind him, the heavy lock engaging, the lock that should have kept him out in the first place.

I gave him a good minute or two to change his mind and come back, before getting out of bed and padding barefoot down the hall to the front door. Sure enough, the lock was bolted tight, the living room undisturbed, not so much as a footprint left on the carpet. I thought about calling the police, but realized there would be no point in it. They'd be no more help to me than they were the last time. Besides, they would probably think I was crazy. Who breaks into someone's house in the middle of the night twice just to talk?

Maybe I *was* crazy.

The fact of the matter was that, loss of sleep aside, my unwelcomed visitor hadn't done me any harm and didn't seem likely to. He was more a nuisance than anything else. I almost felt a kind of sympathy for him. Funny what living in the city long enough could do to your psyche. With that thought I returned to my bedroom, slipped under the covers, and fell back to sleep, sure I wouldn't be interrupted again that night.

The next day at work I didn't even bother to tell Judy about my mysterious visitor's return.

8

---•---

It was a Thursday night.

I had just gotten home about a half hour earlier. I had changed into my sweat clothes planning to do a half hour on the Nordic Trak, but one look at the machine and I knew it just wasn't going to happen. I was totally wrung out. Ms. Parker had been called in to see the chief financial officer that morning and when she got back to her office, she looked like she was ready to chew nails. She began barking orders like a drill sergeant, but underneath it I could sense her desperation. She was in over her head and losing it fast.

I stayed close to my desk and tried my best to get her what she needed as fast as possible. I plied her with coffee, files, and computer printouts. I ordered lunch for her, which she hardly touched, and dinner, which she insisted I eat instead. I didn't leave the building until nearly eight o'clock. She was still at it, poring over a pile of statements when I finally decided I'd done enough for one day. After all, I was only a temp.

So instead of the Nordic Trak, I grabbed a package of Milano cookies from the kitchen and a can of Coke—not the diet kind either, the real stuff, chockful of caffeine and sugar—and crashed in front of the television. At least, I thought, it was Thursday night. Only one more day to go before the weekend. If only I could get through another day . . .

That was when the phone rang.

I thought about letting the answering machine get it, but for some reason I hoisted myself off the floor from in front of the couch and picked it up myself.

"Hello?" I said.

"Er, hello. Johanna?"

"Yes?"

"I hope I'm not disturbing you. This is Matt Lang."

I felt my heart do a back flip. Instinctively my hand began brushing away the cookie crumbs from the front of my sweatshirt.

"Matt," I said stupidly.

I gave myself a mental kick in the backside. What a stupid thing to say. I tried to think of something a little more clever than just repeating his name, but time was ticking by uncomfortably. No doubt he was already thinking what a colossal mistake he had made. He mercifully filled the silence.

"We met the other day at Barnes and Noble?"

"Of course. Matthew Lang, the author."

Johanna, you idiot, can't you get it through your head? He knows who he is.

"Is this a bad time?"

"No, not at all."

Too desperate. Try to act cool. "I mean I was just sitting around. Doing nothing. Relaxing."

Great, I thought. Now I sounded like a complete dolt.

Just sitting there. Doing nothing.

Yeah, like a potted plant.

Well, what was I supposed to say? "Oh, I was just recalculating the equations behind Einstein's theory of relativity and I think I found a mistake." Okay, maybe not. But I could have thought of something a little more interesting. Couldn't I have said I was reading a book? Or, at the very least, watching a program on the Discovery Channel. Of course, I didn't get cable. But he didn't know that.

"I really enjoyed meeting you," he said. "I realize we don't know each other, so I'll understand if you decline, but under the circumstances, there's really no other way we could get to know each other." He paused, then sighed. "I'm afraid I'm making an awful mess of this. If my editor were here, she'd be whipping her red pencil out right about now. To make a long story short, I was just wondering if you'd like to go out with me sometime."

I felt a semicircle of sweat around my hairline.

"Y-y-yes," I stammered. "I think that would be nice."

"Great." I could hear the relief in his voice. I couldn't imagine him being so uncomfortable about asking a woman out. I had expected somone a little more worldly-wise. It was rather disarming.

"How about dinner?" he asked.

"I like dinner."

OH GOD NO!

I like dinner? Did I really say that? Was there no way to stop my voice from traveling over the telephone line? Could I pretend someone else had broken into our conversation? Would it be worse if I claimed I had Tourette's Syndrome and couldn't be responsible for what I said? Should I say my shoes had caught fire and I had to run to the sink and put them out, just to get off the phone? I felt myself blush, and blush an even darker shade when he laughed.

"Good," he said, softly, without the slightest trace of irony in his voice. "I like it, too. I know it's awfully short notice, but are you free Saturday night?"

"Yes, as a matter of fact, I am."

Naturally I should have paused a little, acted as if I had to juggle things around a bit, or at least think about it. Oh well, if he hadn't hung up on me by now, he had to be damn intent on going out with me.

"What kind of food do you like?"

Okay, I thought. So now here's the part where I tell him I don't eat meat. He's going to peg me for some crystal-gazing, new age woo-woo nut for sure.

"Well, I'm a vegetarian. Everyone tells me what a pain in the neck I am to eat with. . . ."

The truth is, ethics be damned, if you gave me a knife and fork at that moment you could have barbecued the animal of your choice and I'd have partaken with carnivorous gusto if it meant having dinner with him.

"That's no problem. I've dined successfully with lots of vegetarians. Do you know Carmine's?"

"Yes. I love that place."

"It's one of my favorites. A little heavy on the garlic, but so long as you're both eating it, you don't notice."

Don't notice? Was he talking about kissing? I felt a little weak in the knees.

"So how does eight sound?"

"Eight's good."

"Okay. I'll meet you there. I'll give you my number if anything comes up."

I wrote it with my index finger on the air. Nothing would come up.

"You know," he said, "I'm so glad I called you. Like I said in the bookstore, I just don't do this sort of thing."

"Well, I'm glad to hear that."

"What I mean is that . . . well . . . you seemed like someone special. Someone I just couldn't let go out of my life without getting to know. Do you know what I mean?"

I looked down at myself, dressed in a baggy gray sweat suit, and a pair of broken-down sneakers. If only he could see me now.

I couldn't help myself. I started to laugh.

On the other end, Matt laughed nervously. "I sounded like an idiot, huh?"

"No, not at all. I know exactly what you mean. I felt the same way about you. It was just something on television."

"Oh? What are you watching?"

"One of those hospital dramas."

"I didn't know they were supposed to be funny."

"Well, you know how hilarious heart failure can be."

I felt like my own heart was going to fail right then and there.

"I guess it's all in the writing. So, Saturday night, eight o'clock at Carmine's?"

"I'll see you there."

"Good night, Johanna."

"Good night, Matt."

I hung up the phone. I just stood there in a kind of shock. I had barely allowed myself to think about Matt since our meeting in the bookstore earlier that week. It was partly superstition, partly logic. My superstitious side was convinced that if I allowed myself to think too much about it, I'd jinx any possibility he'd call. My logical side was all too ready to offer up any number of reasoned arguments why a successful, handsome author would have little interest in pursuing a woman he'd only bumped into in a bookstore. So I pretty much forced the matter from my mind, though from time to time over the last three days I found myself wondering in spite of myself if he'd ever call. And, suddenly, when I'd least expected it, he had.

I knew I had to get up early the next morning to be at the office. Ms. Parker would need me. But I just couldn't settle down. A thousand scenarios were running through my head. I called Cindy, got her machine, left a brief message, and hung up. I went to the medicine cabinet and took out my bottle of Xanax. I shook two free, swallowed one, broke the other in half, and swallowed that one as well. I sat through *David Letterman*, *Tom Snyder*, an old war movie with John Wayne, and an infomercial for some kind of car wax. In between, I went from bedroom to couch, trying to force myself to sleep. Finally, a little after four I realized it was hopeless. I would have to get up in less than three hours anyway. If I fell asleep, I would feel worse trying to wake myself up than if I just stayed up all night. So I took a shower, dressed, and took an early train into the city.

Ms. Parker was already at her desk. I took off my coat and went to the door of her office.

"Good morning," I said.

She looked up at me bleary-eyed, grunted softly, and returned to the printout on her desk. Her expensive blue serge suit was rumpled. Her eye makeup was smudged. Her usually impeccably coiffed hair looked finger combed. I tried to remember what she had worn the day before because I was certain that she was wearing the same outfit. I glanced over at the couch beneath the modern art print on the far wall and wondered if she had spent the night in the office.

"I'm going to the pantry to get some coffee," I said. "Do you want some?"

Ms. Parker looked up as if out of a dream.

"What?"

"Would you like some coffee?"

She looked to the left of her blotter where her personalized corporate coffee mug sat. She stared into it uncomprehendingly for a few seconds and then looked back at me without saying a word.

"I'll get you some more," I suggested.

She didn't object, so I grabbed her mug and headed for the pantry. Someone had already started the coffeemaker. The only other person I'd seen on the floor this early was Wendy and she was a confirmed tea drinker, so I suspected Ms. Parker herself had made the first batch of morning coffee. I poured the steaming black liquid into her mug and grabbed a paper cup for myself.

As a temp, I traveled light. I didn't want the burden of carrying so much as a coffee mug home with me when I left. Unlike Judy, who had personalized her space with avant-garde postcards, playbills, cartoons, family photographs, and the like, I maintained a monk's simplicity that was often the butt of her jokes.

"Jeez," she'd complained on more than one occasion, "can't you buy a calendar with pictures so I can look at something different at least once a month? How can you stand looking at those same four walls day after day?"

I put the paper cup of coffee down on my desk, looked around me, and shrugged my shoulders. The bare walls didn't bother me at all. If anything, I drew a kind of satisfaction in the idea that when the time came to leave, the only thing I'd have to remove from my cubicle would be me.

I carried Ms. Parker's mug into her office. She didn't bother to look up from the printout on her blotter. I noticed the stale smell of cigarette smoke and saw the ashtray next to the phone filled with crushed, lipstick-stained butts. Underneath the stench of burnt tobacco there was another smell: the musty, intimate scent of a body cooped up too long in one room. No doubt she had spent the night in the office.

"If you need me . . ."

I decided to just leave her alone. Besides, I had little desire to do much more than sit quietly at my desk anyway. I turned on my computer, opened up a file at random, and sat staring at it. Every once in a while I moved the mouse to keep the screen saver from kicking in.

Judy arrived about an hour and a half later.

"You're early this morning," she said.

"Couldn't sleep last night. Big news," I said.

"Yeah? What is it?"

"He called."

"Who?"

"Matt."

She wrinkled her brow.

"Matt? Who's Matt?"

"The guy from the bookstore. Remember? The author?"

"Oh right. The author. So are you going out with him?"

"Saturday night."

"Hey, I've got a show scheduled at P.S. 122 this Saturday. I'm debuting my new performance piece. I've got a couple of tickets. How about taking your author friend?"

"Well . . ."

"Afraid he's too square?"

"No. It's just that it's a first date."

"And you don't want him thinking you're some kind of freak?"

"It's not that. It's just—"

"I promise: no snakes or body piercing. At least not in my act. Of course, I can't vouch for the other performers."

"No snakes or body piercing?"

"I promise."

"Okay then," I said, taking the tickets from her hand. "I'll suggest it."

The rest of the day passed fairly uneventfully. Ms. Parker shut her door at lunch hour, telling me she didn't want to be disturbed, and didn't emerge from her office until nearly three hours later. I suspected she had probably fallen asleep. Unfortunately, I didn't have the same luxury. By three, it was all I could do to keep my eyes pried open. The only thing keeping my head off the desk was the steady stream of caffeine I kept pouring into my body. That and Matt's book, which I read surreptitiously a few pages at a time.

I intended to go straight to sleep the moment I got home. Instead, I found I'd gotten a second wind from somewhere. I was also hungry. I went into the kitchen and rummaged around in the cabinets until I found something to eat. I was boiling some pasta on the stove and had just opened a jar of tomato sauce when the phone rang.

"Hi, Jo, it's me."

"Hey, Cindy."

"I'm sorry I couldn't call yesterday, but I didn't get in until after one and figured you'd be asleep. What's up?"

I told her about Matt and how we met in the bookstore earlier that week, how I never really thought he'd call, even though he asked for my number, and how he had called just last night and asked me out for tomorrow evening. By the time I was done talking, I was out of breath.

"Wow," Cindy said. "That's a great story. It's like something out of a movie."

"I know. It's almost too good to be true."

"What's he like anyway?"

"He's smart, witty, sexy. And he's a writer, too—did I mention that?"

"About ten times." Cindy laughed. "What's he written? Anything I've heard of?"

"I meant writer as in books."

"Very funny. I read books."

"Yeah. Jackie Collins and Harold Robbins."

"Hey. I read Stephen King."

"Only the books that were turned into movies."

"So? I like to know what I'm getting into before I start a book that's seven hundred pages long. Give me a chance. Maybe I've heard of him."

"Okay," I said. "His latest book is *Forbidden Truths*."

I could almost hear her forehead scrunching in concentration.

"See, I told you."

"Okay, okay. So I never heard of it. Maybe I'll buy a copy tomorrow. Give the poor guy some extra royalties so he can afford to treat you right. Hey, you didn't tell me. Who would play him in the movie version?"

It was a long-standing game Cindy and I played. Whenever we met a new guy, we would describe him by picking the actor who would best portray him if our relationship was turned into a film. Sometimes the casting changed as the relationship changed. Cindy's current boyfriend, Brad the insurance ghoul, was a case in point. William Hurt had originally been cast in the starring role. Lately, it was Ed Begley, Jr.

"Well I haven't given it much thought," I said. "Everything's been happening so fast."

"Come on," Cindy teased. "Give it up."

"All right. I suppose if I had to cast right now I'd be looking at a cross between George Clooney and Tom Berenger."

"Whooey," Cindy squealed. "It sounds like you're in love."

I heard a sizzling sound from the kitchen and saw the foam roiling over the pot.

"Hold on a minute! My pasta's boiling over!"

I ran to the stove and turned off the burner. Then I returned to the living room and picked up the phone.

"Nice save," Cindy said.

"No, really. The pasta was boiling over."

"Well, whatever. I'm really happy for you, Jo. I hope it works out. He really does sound terrific. Promise you'll call me with all the details."

"I will."

I thought about asking her what was going on with *The Way We Live,* but decided against it. I didn't really want to hear about it. Not tonight anyway. Tonight was my night to crow a little. I didn't want to spoil it by stirring up my feelings of resentment and jealousy. Not that they weren't bubbling right under the surface anyway. I'd hear about it all soon enough. Instead, I wished her a good night and hung up the phone.

I ate my dinner in front of the television and then headed for the bedroom. I had to decide what to wear to dinner. I pulled out the little black party dress I'd bought earlier that week after my meeting with Ruth. I held it up in front of me and looked in the mirror.

No way.

Completely inappropriate for a quiet dinner for two. The last thing I wanted to do was to look like I was trying too hard. Why had I bought the dress, anyway? Not only was it expensive, but it was impractical. It was the kind of thing the society set wore to highbrow charity functions or actresses modeled in the audiences of award shows. I supposed it would stay in my closet forever.

I rifled through the rest of my clothes, pulling out dresses and suits at random, until my room looked like the site of a Salvation Army clothing drop-off. After two and a half hours of searching, mixing, and matching, I finally conceded: I didn't have a thing to wear.

It was nearly midnight and the long day and lack of sleep were catching up with me. I decided I'd go shopping the next day. I had deposited my father's check and the credit card bill, when it came, could wait. With that settled, I climbed into bed and let myself fantasize about where my relationship with Matt might lead. Before I realized it my fantasies had become dreams and I was fast asleep.

9

———•———

I got up late the next morning.

I needed the sleep and to hell with Drake and his damn acting class. I'd probably go back next week, especially since I was already paid up until the end of the month, but after last Saturday's class I was in no mood to see him again this morning. No doubt he would take my absence as proof of his critical acuity. Truth hurts and all that. But the fact of the matter was that I was in no mood for thespian psychobabble. Besides, I had some shopping for a hot date to do.

I took the train to Midtown and hit the stores. I must have tried on two dozen outfits before I settled on a dark green bolero-style jacket and matching skirt.

"That outfit is sooo you," the salesgirl cooed. She couldn't have been older than twenty.

"Do you really think so?" I said, staring at myself in a tryptich of mirrors that reflected my image from virtually every angle.

"Oh yes," she enthused.

I looked at myself critically.

"You don't think the jacket makes me look a little high-waisted?"

"You have the perfect waist for that jacket," the salesgirl stated, as if it were an incontrovertible fact. "Not every woman can wear a jacket like that. You have the perfect figure for it. And I'm not just saying that," she assured me.

I could have looked like a bratwurst tied in the middle and she probably would have said the same thing. After all, she was working on commission. I turned to the side, examining the fit of the jacket from a different angle, studying the outline of my butt, and had to admit it did look pretty good. Of course, the mirrors in department stores always seemed to make the clothes look like they fit better than they did in the mirrors at home. Or maybe it was the lighting. In any event, it was close enough. Besides, it was getting late and I had to get home and start getting ready.

"So you'll take it?" the salesgirl said.

"Yes. I think I will."

"Great. Let me show you some accesssories."

By the time I got home it was nearly five o'clock and I was nearly three hundred dollars poorer than when I left that morning. Still, I figured if Matt was every bit as good as he seemed to be, it was an investment well worth making.

As I was getting ready, it struck me how much preparing for a date was like getting ready for an audition. There was the same excruciating attention to detail. Everything had to be just right: hair, makeup, nails, clothes, jewelry, perfume. The least little thing could lose you the role. Finally, after nearly two hours of fussing and deliberating I took a final look in the mirror. The salesgirl was right. I did look good.

I smiled nervously at my reflection.

"Good luck," I said.

Just to calm down my racing heart I swallowed a Xanax. I didn't want to have a panic attack in the middle of dinner.

God, this was even worse than an audition.

This was real life.

Carmine's was an Italian restaurant on Forty-fourth Street, right in the heart of the theater district. I'd been there two or three times with friends after a show, but it was normally out of my price range. It was large and comfortable, a popular spot with tourists, but not a tourist trap, and for that reason it drew a mixed crowd of out-of-towners and business people. There was a large bar off to the right when you walked in, which always seemed to be well-patronized by men in suits. The lighting was muted, but not so dark as to be pretentious and the tables plentiful, but ingeniously placed.

I walked up to a mahogany podium behind which stood the hostess. She was a tall, exotic-looking brunette with pouty, collagen-inflated lips and boobs to match. She had "would-be actress" written all over her.

"Reservations?"

"I'm here to meet Matthew Lang."

"Lang, Lang," she said, running a chartreuse-painted nail over the ledger lit by a brass lamp.

"There he is," I said.

He was sitting at the bar. He had already seen me and greeted me with a smile.

"I'm sorry I'm late," I said, as I walked over to him.

"I thought you were going to stand me up." He laughed.

"I had trouble with the trains," I lied.

The fact was that except for auditions, I usually ran late for appointments. And I always kept my men waiting. It was one of the few bits of wisdom I had retained from my mother. I took off my coat.

"You look terrific," he said.

"Thank you."

"Can I buy you a drink?"

I looked down at his glass.

"What are you having?"

"Just tonic water with lemon. I don't drink."

Alarm bells went off in my head. My mother was an alcoholic and so were several of my ex-boyfriends. I had no intention of going down that rocky road again. "Are you recovering?"

"No. I just don't drink."

"I'm sorry. That could have been a potentially embarrassing question. It's just that I meet so many people these days who are recovering from something or other. Sometimes I'm a little too direct for my own good."

"That's okay," he said. "I like honesty."

"I'll have a wine spritzer."

He ordered the drink and we made our way back to the hostess. She called a waiter over to lead us to a table by the window across from a dominating portrait of a well-fed, Italian-looking man who was undoubtedly the restaurant's namesake. I stared across the immaculately set table at Matt.

He was wearing a different sports coat, but it was just as impeccably cut and made, and a dark turtleneck that made his gray eyes appear almost blue. I caught a whiff of his aftershave, something clean and masculine. He was freshly shaved, but the evidence of beard was still visible along the strong line of his jaw, and especially in the dimple in his chin.

If anything, he was even more handsome than I remembered. I placed him at about forty, though it was hard to judge his age—his graying hair might be premature. In any event, he was a well-preserved forty, his body showing not the least trace of flab. I decided he must work out regularly.

The restaurant was only half full. It was an off time. It would get crowded after ten-thirty when the post-theater crowd hit the streets. Carmine's served up its vittles family-style, so I had to remind Matt that I was a vegetarian.

"No problem," he said. "Is that an ethical choice or for health reasons?"

"A little bit of both," I answered. "But I'm not one of those militant fanatics."

"So you won't hold being a carnivore against me?"

"No. Just so long as you don't try to force a Big Mac down my throat."

Matt laughed. "It's a deal."

Our waiter returned, his pad open, pen at the ready.

"My name is Antoine," he said, looking directly at Matt, glancing only briefly at me, "and I'll be serving you tonight."

He was a good-looking young guy with shiny black hair carefully pulled back in a ponytail and the perfect features of an Apache. He spoke with a French accent that I was certain was fake. Was the whole place staffed by aspiring actors?

"We have several specials tonight. Would you like to hear them?"

"Yes, please," Matt said.

The waiter smiled, his black eyes glinting. He put his hands behind his back and recited the specials from memory.

"Did I say anything to tantalize you?" he asked Matt.

Matt looked at me. "Anything tantalize you?" he said.

I shook my head no.

"Sorry," Matt said. "I think we'll just order off the menu."

"Sure I can't tempt you?"

"I'm sure," Matt said.

"Too bad." The waiter pouted.

Matt ordered. He chose the fettucine alfredo with almonds and the gnocchi with broccoli and sundried tomatoes.

"You have excellent taste, sir," the waiter said, touching Matt briefly on the shoulder.

"Thank you," Matt said. He ordered another tonic water.

"Right away, sir. And for the lady?" the waiter said, turning to me for the first time.

"Diet Sprite."

"Of course," he said, looking positively scandalized.

"It seems you have an admirer," I said after the waiter left.

"What do you mean?" Matt asked.

"I mean that waiter was all but sitting in your lap."

It took awhile to process and then Matt blushed.

"Oh come on."

"It was pretty obvious."

"Not to me."

"That's because you're straight. Most straight guys don't realize they're being flirted with, even when it's a woman doing the flirting."

"Why do you think that is?"

"Because straight men aren't culturally trained to pick up on the signals, that's why. And because the signals women send out are a lot different from the signals men send out."

"That's an interesting theory. Kind of makes me wonder what I've been missing out on all these years. You know, it occurs to me that I don't know anything about you."

I played with my fork. "What would you like to know?"

"How about what you do for a living?"

I told him about the temp jobs and the pursuit of an acting career. I was sure he would think the whole thing was terribly predictable, if not pitiful. Instead, he seemed to find it interesting.

"Have I seen you in anything?"

I told him about the toothpaste commercial, but he just furrowed his brow and shook his head.

"You know, you mustn't give up your dream. I can't tell you how many times my first book was rejected before I finally found a publisher. I had quit law school to become a novelist. My father was a lawyer and his father before him. Naturally I was expected to follow in the family footsteps, maybe even get a job in the government. It was a terrible scandal when I chucked it all for writing. My father threatened to cut me off completely and made good on the threat. I didn't care. I was young and foolish. Being a fool is a luxury of being young. I moved to the city, thinking it all very romantic. I wound up living in a walk-up in Hell's Kitchen and working as a dishwasher for a rib joint two blocks away from here.

"I used to write in notebooks on my lunch break and type it all up on a rented typewriter when I got home at night. For ten years I lived like a monk. I was just about to give it all up and go back to law school like my father wanted when my agent wrote me a letter telling me he'd sold my book. He couldn't even call me because I didn't own a phone.

"I'll tell you a secret. Though you may not believe it, I look back on those days and think of them as among the happiest of my life. The struggle to get where you're going is more than half the fun of getting there. It might not seem like it at the time, but it's true."

"I've heard people say that before, but somehow it's difficult to believe."

"You just need the perspective of success."

"I guess so."

"Don't worry. You'll get there. You just have to keep believing in yourself."

Our food came and we started eating, making small talk, comparing notes, getting to know each other better, the usual thing. We stared out the window at passersby. At one point a homeless man shuffled past, stopped, and stared in at the window.

"The one bad thing about window seats," I said. "I always feel like Marie Antoinette or something."

"Yes," Matt agreed. "It's a terrible shame. There's so much food here, more than we can eat at one sitting, and only a plate of glass separates us from a man who is cold and hungry and living on the street."

"If he's still there when we leave," I suggested, "maybe we can give him the leftovers."

"That would be a nice idea."

I was glad to hear the genuine sympathy in his voice. There were so many people in the city, good people, liberal people, many of them my own friends, who had grown tired of the whole problem and dismissed the homeless as a bunch of lunatics, or worse, simply a nuisance that wouldn't conveniently go away. I told Matt how I felt and how I appreciated his compassion.

"When you come up the hard way, you don't forget."

"So many of my friends just think they're crazy, not poor."

"Poor or crazy, what's the difference? Since when don't we have an obligation to the mentally ill?"

The homeless man spit on the window and walked away.

"Poor soul," Matt whispered.

It wasn't until espresso and tiramisu that I brought up the topic of his book.

"I loved *Forbidden Truths*," I said.

"Ah," he said, smiling, and putting down his cup. "I wondered when you were going to come around to that."

"Well," I said, "I didn't want to gush. I'm sure you get enough of that."

"An author can never get enough of that."

"Well, I did love it."

"I hope I can trust your honesty and that you're not just being polite."

"No, I really loved it. I finished it at work yesterday afternoon on lunch break. In fact, I kept sneaking it out of my desk drawer whenever my supervisor had her office door closed. The climax was unbelievably suspenseful."

"Thank you." He nodded.

The truth was that I had enjoyed the book more than I could ever have hoped. I was afraid that I wouldn't like it and have to act as if I did. But the book had everything: love, violence, sex, a resolute heroine, a twisted male lead, and a surprise ending. I was mesmerized from the first page.

"Honestly," I said, "I couldn't put it down."

"I hope you become famous real soon," he joked. "I could use your review on a book jacket."

"How do you get your ideas, anyway?"

"I just think of situations where people are vulnerable, where danger could intrude in everyday life. I guess you could say I'm a little paranoid. I suppose all suspense writers are the same way. They're sensitive to the ways in which ordinary people can be exposed to evil."

"It was so realistic, though. I felt like I was the heroine."

"The ultimate compliment. Thank you."

"The woman was so convincing. Strong, yet vulnerable. You didn't write down to her like so many men do with women characters. How do you do it?"

"I'm not sure. I always seem to write from a woman's point of view. I read somewhere the theory that writing as a woman is the best way for a man to step out from behind his macho posturing and feel the true vulnerability of the human condition. Perhaps that's the answer. I suppose it's not that much different from acting. You find a character, in this case a voice, and you inhabit it."

"I'd like to play the role myself."

"If I'm ever fortunate enough to have the book produced as a movie. I'll be sure to suggest you for the part. Unfortunately, writers get so little say once their books are bought for the screen."

"Have you ever had one of your books turned into a movie?"

"No. I've been close. I've had a couple of books optioned for the movies, which means the studios have bought the rights to the story and just have to decide whether or not to actually make a movie out of it, but so far none of my books have made it to the screen."

"I'm sorry for being so nosy," I said. "It sounds like I'm fishing for a job. An old actress's habit, I guess. I really didn't mean it to sound like it did."

"Don't worry about it. I didn't take it that way."

I stared out the window for a couple of seconds and looked back across the table. "Can I ask you a personal question?"

"Sure."

"How old are you?"

Matt laughed. "Forty-five." He took a sip of his coffee, and put his cup down carefully on his saucer. "Is that a problem?"

"In your case, no."

"Good. Anything else?"

"No," I said, feeling embarrassed to have even asked the question. "It's really none of my business. After all, we've just met."

"So? Isn't that what this is all about? Trying to learn about each other?"

"Yes," I said. "But usually people try to be a little more subtle about it."

"Subtlety just wastes time. Are you sure there's nothing else you'd like to ask?"

"I'm sure."

"Your hands say differently."

"My hands?"

Matt looked down and I followed his gaze. I had torn at least three empty sugar packets into pink confetti.

"I can't. . . ." I protested, but inside I felt the press of curiosity. If I didn't ask him now, when I had the chance, I knew I'd regret it later. On the other hand, I was almost afraid to hear the answer.

Matt threw out his arms. "Fire away."

I cringed inside, barely able to get the words out. "You're not married, are you?"

Matt laughed heartily. "Is that what you've been worried about?"

"Kind of."

"Well, I can assure you that I'm not married."

I felt a huge sense of relief. I decided to press my luck. "Have you ever been married?"

"Never. Would that have disqualified me?"

"No. I just wondered. You know, if you like had an ex-wife hanging around or kids from a former marriage. Sometimes that can be sticky."

"Only if two people are serious."

I felt myself blush. This conversation was veering into dangerous territory. I was seriously tipping my hand and that was something I didn't want to do. I tried to recover my composure, hoping Matt couldn't read through my awkward bluff.

"I mean, it just seems like you'd have been married by now."

Matt smiled wryly. "Because I'm so old?"

Jeezus. Why didn't I just keep my mouth shut? Because I had to know where I stood right off the bat. I didn't want to play the game again and be disappointed.

"I didn't mean it that way! I guess I just don't know how you avoided it."

"Half my adult life I've been too poor and the other half too busy. It's not a good combination for attracting women."

"Look," I said, figuring if he was sticking with me this long I had nothing left to lose, "I know it's just a first date and you don't have to answer. I mean I can't expect . . . it's just that I'd kind of like to know where things stand. . . ."

I was rambling like an idiot. Mercifully, he cut me off.

"I'm not involved with anyone."

"Really?" I said, a note of doubt in my voice.

"Scout's honor," he said.

"Were you ever a scout?"

"No."

I grinned. It had been rather embarrassing to question him like that, but now that it was over, it seemed to clear the air. Better to find out now than later when it was too late and I'd already fallen for the guy.

"Anything else you'd like to know?"

"No," I said. "Cross-examination over."

"How'd I do?"

"So far you're batting a thousand. Is there anything you'd like to know about me?"

"No," he said. "I kind of like the unknown. It makes things more interesting."

Just then the waiter returned with our check. "I hope everything was satisfactory," he said.

"Everything was fine," Matt said.

"Excellent. Come back real soon," he said. I could swear I saw him wink. Good God, I thought. The guy was completely shameless. He looked briefly at me and I couldn't resist giving him a smug smile.

All mine, pal.

I took a sip of my coffee. It was ice cold.

It was time to go.

Matt settled the bill with a platinum Amex card and we left the restaurant with a doggie bag. Our homeless friend wasn't around, so we grabbed a cab and made our way down to P.S. 122, or as it was also known, Performance Space 122.

We sat through three acts before Judy came on: one an androgynous creature, with a mauve mohawk, expounding on the dangers of being a city bicycle messenger; a tattooed man wearing nothing but a loin-cloth, a crown of thorns, and with hundreds of purple lesions, loudly proclaiming President Reagan's complicity in the AIDS epidemic; and a middle-aged transexual delivering a monologue on the glories of lesbian masochism.

Matt seemed to take it all in good humor. By the time Judy came on, I was a bit apprehensive. She was doing a piece on Joan of Arc. She appeared dressed in a simple white tunic, tied to a stake, her bleached hair dyed pitch black in contrast to her face, which in the stark white stage lights took on a spooky, unearthly beauty. She spoke in a clear, heartbreaking voice to her God, her faith undestroyed despite her calamitous turn of fortune. In the background a recording of what sounded like medieval chanting played over dirgelike music.

More than just a piece commemorating the martyrdom of a saint, it was a testament to every woman who had suffered for daring to rise above her station. I found myself with tears in my eyes, genuinely moved by the sheer poetry of her monologue, and awed by her acting talent. I never knew she was so good. My own bias aside, I thought hers was the most effective performance of the evening. Judging from his enthusiastic applause, Matt seemed to agree.

Later we met Judy backstage, where I congratulated her and intro-duced her to Matt. We both told her how much we'd enjoyed the show. She seemed appreciative, if somewhat shy of Matt. We invited her out to a local coffeehouse, but she politely declined, saying she had already accepted an invitation to meet a group of the other players for a late dinner. As far as I was concerned, it was just as well.

I wanted Matt to myself.

We found a small coffeehouse around the corner. It was one of those well-meaning arty little establishments that grow up like mush-rooms and vanish just as quickly due to soaring real-estate prices, too much competition, and owners with bigger dreams than bankbooks. It was even darker inside than it was outside and it took several seconds for my eyes to adjust enough to take in the decor.

There was a counter to the side, behind which stood large, old-fashioned copper coffee urns. What I at first took to be a dwarf standing next to the window turned out to be a papier-mâché caricature of a 1920s newspaper boy. As my eyes grew more used to the gloom, I noticed several of these rather grotesque sculptures stationed at various places throughout the restaurant. The walls were stuccoed and covered with framed photographs of famous Beat writers. Among those I recog-nized were Jack Kerouac, Lawrence Ferlinghetti, Allen Ginsburg, and the expressionless face of William Burroughs.

An androgynous young girl with a shaved head and piercings in her nostril and eyebrow led us to a small wooden table, where we both ordered decaf cappuccino and listened to some bad pseudo-beatnik poetry. It must have been open mike night, because some long-haired, bearded guy was standing on the steps leading to the men's room that served as a makeshift stage and reciting some kind of diatribe about dry sticks. He was followed by an anorectic-looking woman mumbling something about her cycle that no one could hear. She was succeeded by a sporadic parade of volunteers who were variously inspired to read from notes scrawled on cocktail napkins, pieces of newspapers and, in some cases, the palms of their hands.

"Not exactly the *New Yorker*," I ventured.

"Just as well," Matt said. "I'm not a great fan of the poetry in the *New Yorker*. I find it rather intellectually pretentious. But then again, I may just be bitter. They rejected enough of my stuff."

"You write poetry?"

"Wrote poetry. It was my first love. Unfortunately, it was an unrequited passion."

"I'll bet it was beautiful."

Matt smiled and I felt my heart flip-flop. His hand reached over and touched mine. The contact was brief. Just a touch and it was gone. It was the first real physical contact between us. But it sent an electric shock through me that rendered me completely flustered. I sat there staring across the table into his eyes. Up until now, our attraction had been almost theoretical. Now, with that one touch, there was no doubt in my mind about the chemistry between us.

All it needed was one little spark.

I wondered what it would be like to have him hold me in his arms, to feel the curve of his sensual lips as they covered mine, to have his hands, so warm and alive, undressing me. What kind of lover would he be? Slow and gentle? Hungry and passionate? Suddenly the atmosphere in the coffeehouse seemed too close, too hot. I could hear nothing but the sound of my own heart pounding in my ears. Impulsively, I reached out and stroked his thick, curly hair. He grabbed my wrist, turned it over, and kissed the place where the pulse throbbed just beneath my pale flesh.

"It's been a wonderful evening," he said. "I can't remember when I've had such a good time."

"Me either," I said in a small voice.

"It's getting late. I should see you home."

"Yes—" I said, trying not to reveal the disappointment in my voice.

"Yes." I looked at my wrist and realized I wasn't wearing a watch. "I really should be getting home."

"I've got an early morning engagement tomorrow. A publicity thing. An interview on a local radio station for the book."

"What station?" I said numbly. "Maybe I'll tune in."

"I don't even remember. But you wouldn't want to listen anyway. They're all terribly boring. But necessary, I'm afraid. At least that's what my publisher and agent say. I'm sure you know about agents."

For the first time in days I thought about Ruth and the "engagement" she had set up for me with that producer—what was his name?

Matt walked me to the street, where he hailed a cab, and paid the driver. He leaned inside, smiled, and gave me a modest kiss good night.

The cab driver wanted to talk. But after a couple of monosyllabic answers from me he finally got the hint. On the long ride home I stared out the window, feeling a mixture of elation and disappointment. It wasn't that I was in the habit of going to bed with men on the first date, but I did like to be the one who ruled it out. In spite of my attraction to Matt, I wasn't certain by any means that even if he had asked me back to his place I wouldn't have made an excuse not to go.

That night as I undressed for bed I couldn't help going over the date in my mind. I picked apart everything I said, everything he said. Did I get the role? Had he liked my performance? Did I at least merit a callback? Or did he have someone else better suited in mind? Someone who fit the part better? Would I lose out again?

I should have pressed him for that radio station to find out if he really did have an early interview or if that was just an excuse. Of course, that would have been kind of obvious. In any event, I decided the next morning I'd scan the dial and see if I could find him on the radio.

I had to laugh. I sounded like a teenager.

Not only that, I felt like a teenager.

By the time I climbed into bed I had convinced myself that it was just as well that he didn't invite me back to his place. I probably would have gone and that would probably have been a mistake. It always struck me as a little sleazy, not to mention desperate, sleeping with someone on a first date. If nothing else, at least I had left him with a reason to call me back. Besides, abstinence added a little anticipation to a relationship.

Still, there was that nagging question at the back of my mind: he did want me, didn't he?

I gazed at his photograph on the book on my nightstand, told him what he missed, and turned off the light. I fell asleep only to be awakened two hours later by my dark visitor. He had come the night before last, skipped a night, and now he was back again. By now I had lost all fear of him.

"You're late tonight," he said. "You had a date."

"Do you spy on me?" I asked, annoyance in my voice. All things considered, I should have been terrified talking to a black-clad intruder standing in my bedroom doorway in the middle of the night. I should have been even more afraid of saying something that could get him angry. Strange, what we can get used to.

Instead of being angry, he ducked his head, laughing softly. "No. I can just tell."

"So what is it?" I said, sarcasm replacing annoyance in my tone. "Don't you approve of my seeing someone else?"

He'd stopped laughing, but I could still hear the amusement in his tone. "Do you like him?"

We were starting to sound like an old married couple, for crissakes.

"Yes, I do," I said defensively.

"What's he like?"

"Bright, sensitive, handsome, every woman's dream."

"He sounds perfect for you."

"So I have your blessing? What a relief. You don't know how worried I was."

What was the matter with me? Was I crazy or something, talking to him like this? I should be trying to placate him, not antagonize him. On the other hand, I'd read somewhere that the worst thing you could do when faced with a stalker or rapist was to act terrified. They got off on that. Suddenly I did feel terrified. I had never really considered—

"Sarcasm," he said, sounding disappointed, "doesn't become you."

"I'm sorry," I said. "I was trying for wit. It must be the hour."

He nodded his black-cowled head. "Forgiven."

"What if I had brought him back here tonight?" I asked quietly.

He shrugged. "I would have respected your privacy, of course."

"I appreciate that."

"Do you think it will come to that?"

"What?"

"Sex."

The atmosphere in the air suddenly grew almost palpable, electric. I was afraid the wrong answer could change the whole dynamic between us in a disastrous way.

"Does that make you jealous?" I asked gently, hoping to carefully feel him out.

He cut me off. "That question is off base."

"I see," I said, anger once again taking over. "But breaking in here in the middle of the night and disturbing my sleep isn't."

"You didn't answer my question."

"Which was?" I asked, stalling.

"Do you think it will lead to sex?"

He'd know if I were lying. And what was the use of lying anyway? He'd find out sooner or later. I decided it was better to be honest.

"Probably. If he calls again."

"I see," he said thoughtfully. He stood in the doorway, staring down at the floor for a long while, as if pondering what I had just said.

"Look, I've had a long night. Could we talk about this some other time? I could really use some sleep."

He looked up, his featureless face raising goose bumps on the flesh of my arms. "You should have thought of that earlier."

"Are you my conscience now?"

"Maybe."

"Strange manifestation of a conscience," I said shakily.

"I'm only trying to look out for you."

"I appreciate it."

"Sarcasm again."

My heart gave a little flip. Did I catch a note of displeasure in his voice? "I can't help it," I said apologetically. "I'm tired."

"Okay, I can take a hint," he said good-naturedly. "Good night, my angel."

"Good night."

As usual, he walked quickly and quietly down the hall. My heart was still beating erratically, and the sweat was just beginning to dry on my brow long after he carefully locked the door behind him.

10

Even though I hadn't set the alarm, I woke up early Sunday morning, forgetting what day it was. I turned to the clock radio beside the bed, heard the wind driving an icy rain against the windows, and was just about to get up when I realized it was the weekend.

I settled snugly back under the covers. Outside, the wind hurled a fresh load of frozen pellets against the panes. I imagined how I'd ordinarily have to get up and start preparing for work, and tried to savor the fact that I had nowhere to go and nothing to do.

It was nearly ten o'clock before I woke up too much to force myself back to sleep. I lay there, happy and content under my warm blankets, again going over the details of the night before. As dates went, I thought it had all gone pretty well. There was always a little awkwardness, things you wish you had said, and even worse, things you wish you hadn't. I still couldn't help but feel a nagging sense of doubt over the lack of physical affection Matt had displayed. Not that I enjoyed a man pawing all over me on a first date or anything. But, in Matt's case, I wouldn't have minded him being a *little more* aggressive. I mean, even his kiss good night had seemed somewhat reluctant.

Maybe he wasn't attracted to me, after all? No, I thought. He wouldn't have asked me out in the first place. Well, maybe I'd done something to turn him off during the date. But what? Had I missed a piece of broccoli caught between my teeth or something? I had checked in the lady's room at Carmine's after dinner. It was sheer torture to think that a whole relationship could turn on so little. But it could. Like I said, it was just like an audition. The least little slip and the director moved on to the next actress. There was no room for error because there was no end to the competition.

Christ, dating was hell.

I knew I'd go crazy if I kept on thinking like this. I'd been on enough auditions to know whether I had done well or not. Better to just go with my gut feeling. We'd had a good time. Matt seemed interested. Maybe he was just being cautious. I didn't really know much about his romantic history, except that he wasn't married. Or maybe he was just being respectful. My gut feeling told me things had gone well. Of course, my gut feeling had told me I'd nailed that audition for the role on *The Way We Live*.

Oh no, I thought, here we go again.

I reached over and turned on the radio. I remembered Matt had said he was being interviewed on one of the stations this morning. Even if he didn't remember the station, I should have asked him the time. I tried NPR, but they were blasting some right-winger or other over his plan to end public welfare. I moved the red needle up and down the dial several times without success. I tried FM without any better luck.

I got up and went to the kitchenette. I turned on the old taped-together RCA boom box left by the previous tenant and brewed myself a pot of coffee. While the coffee was dripping into the pot, I searched the shelves for something to eat. I was surprisingly hungry. I pulled out a box of cereal, stared inside, and put it back. I opened the refrigerator, scanned the nearly bare wire shelves, and swung the door shut. Then I went back into the bedroom and threw on a pair of old jeans, a sweatshirt, and a pair of rubber duckboots. I shucked on my hooded parka, grabbed an umbrella, and headed downstairs to the corner market to get some donuts and a paper.

On the way to the street I saw Mr. Kazantzakis heading up the stairs. He was wearing a pair of baggy old overalls and a thermal T-shirt opened at the collar exposing a thatch of wiry white hairs. In his right hand he was carrying an old-fashioned wooden toolbox filled with wrenches, pliers, hammers, and such.

"Good morning, good morning," he said, waving a red kerchief he'd pulled from his back pocket to wipe his sweaty face. His eyes gave me the customary once-over.

"Good morning Mr. K. How are you?"

"Ech." He waved the red kerchief in his hand disgustedly. "Mrs. Brody in 3C complaining about the heat. First she says it's too cold. Now she says it's too hot. I been up and down to the furnace room three times already. I tell you. I sell this place to the first person who gives me enough to break even. Then I move back to Greece. Here, regulations every time you turn around. Inspectors of everything. Everyone needs to be paid. In Greece you can live on pennies. Bread, sun, olives, pretty women, and wine. What else you need to be happy?"

"Sounds nice."

"You bet it sounds nice."

"But I think you'd get bored."

"Yeah, yeah. How that new lock working out?"

"Great," I lied.

Mr. Kazantzakis shook his head. "Crazy city. People break into your home and stare at you when you sleep. What kind of crazy people do that?"

"I don't know," I said, feeling kind of guilty. He was the only one with a key to my apartment. I was certain it wasn't his silhouette I'd seen in the doorway or, for that matter, his voice I had heard. But could it have been someone he knew? One of his many nephews, perhaps, who often visited the building?

"Well, I better not catch him," he said, stuffing the red kerchief into his pocket, pulling out a large monkey wrench, and shaking it. "I tighten the screw loose in his head real good." He lowered his voice conspiratorially. "Unless, of course, he pay a visit to Mrs. Brody."

I could still hear his gruff laughter as I reached the outside door.

The frozen rain was hitting me like handfuls of dried peas thrown by some unseen instigator. I used my umbrella as a shield as I made my way down the treacherous sidewalk, but I was frozen and soaked by the time I reached the corner. Usually, most of the good donuts would be gone by now, but the weather had encouraged most of the neighborhood to forage their breakfasts from their own shelves. I chose a crumb bun, an old-fashioned, and, my favorite, a jelly donut covered with powdered sugar. I grabbed a *New York Post* bearing yet another lurid headline about our president, paid for my selections, took a deep breath, and headed back out into the storm.

The trip back to my apartment was even tougher. Halfway there, I miscalculated the direction of the wind and my umbrella turned inside out. I tried to fix it, but the delicate metal undercarriage was bent beyond repair. Between the broken umbrella, the pelting rain, and the driving wind, it was all I could do to hang on to the newspaper and my bag of donuts. I finally reached my building, discarded the broken umbrella in the trash, and rushed up the slippery stairs into the comforting warmth of the hall.

Inside my apartment, I carried my wet jacket into the bathroom and hung it up over the tub. I took my boots off there, too, and placed them by the heating vent. Then I padded through the living area into the kitchenette, took down a thick ceramic mug, poured out some coffee, grabbed a paper plate from the cabinet under the sink, and headed back to where I'd left the bag of donuts and the newspaper. I had just sat down when I heard the radio. I retrieved it from its place on the windowsill, brought it back into the living area, and unplugged a lamp to make room for it in the outlet closest to the table.

The old radio was too far away from the window to get decent reception. Even when it was close to the window, the broadcasts sounded like they were coming from Beirut. But as I ate my donuts and read the paper, I absently flipped through the channels. I knew there was little chance of stumbling upon Matt's interview, but I figured I'd try anyway.

I finished the paper, and was on my third cup of coffee when I decided to give Cindy a call.

I thought I was going to get her machine, but she answered on the fourth ring.

"Huh? Hello?"

"Cindy, it's me, Johanna." I looked up at the clock. It was already after twelve. "I didn't wake you up, did I?"

"No," she said hesitantly. "Not exactly."

I heard an impatient voice in the background say "Who the hell is it?" and then complete silence as Cindy must have put her hand over the receiver. She came back on a moment later.

"Look, Jo, can I call you back?"

"I'm sorry, Cindy I didn't mean—"

"Don't worry about it," Cindy said. I heard a toilet flushing in the background. She lowered her voice. "I wasn't having much fun anyway. Listen, this should all be over in about three minutes. I'll call you back, okay?"

"Okay," I said. "But don't rush on my account."

"No problem with quick-draw here."

Well, either Brad was putting on the performance of his life or they had found something else to amuse each other because I was still waiting for Cindy's call an hour and a half later. I was getting restless and anxious and the real reason wasn't that Cindy hadn't called back, but that Matt hadn't called at all. I understood that he had the radio interview that morning, but surely he could have found a spare minute or two to call during the course of the day. I mean, it didn't have to be an hour-long conversation, just a short hello to tell me he had had a good time or he'd like to see me again.

Something.

To tell the truth, I was beginning to rerun all the earlier feelings of doubt through my brain. Maybe my worst fears were true. Maybe Matt hadn't really liked me, after all.

I turned on the television. The rain had stopped and the wind had died down. Outside the window the day had turned flat and bleak. I resisted the urge to call Cindy back. I went to the kitchenette to make myself something to eat. But when I got there, I realized I wasn't really hungry and returned to the living area, only to decide that what I really wanted was something to drink. So I returned to the kitchenette and poured myself a glass of grapefruit juice. I forced myself to take a sip before pouring the juice back into the container. I had to get out of the house. I couldn't sit still. I was driving myself crazy. This was even worse than waiting for a callback after an audition.

I grabbed the *Post* off the table and scanned the movie section. There was a small artsy theater down in the Village that was running a couple of Garbo movies. I decided it would be good to get as far away from the apartment as possible for a few hours and my compulsive hovering around the phone.

The theater was small, shabby, and reeked with the musty smell of old, wet coats. I bought a tub of popcorn, a Coke, and chose my seat from the dozens available in the nearly empty theater. The first movie was *Ninotchka,* which I'd seen at least ten times before. As always, I was mesmerized by the sultry perfection of Garbo's performance, how she was able to convey so much with just a gesture or an expression, how when she spoke, you always felt as if there were some deeper and profound hidden meaning in what she said. The second feature was *Mata Hari.* I had seen this movie several times as well—not as many times as *Ninotchka,* but enough times to know entire sections of dialogue by heart. I sat there, slouched in my movie seat, munching popcorn, and mouthing the words along with the great Garbo.

Ever since I was a young girl, I had always found Garbo fascinating. I had come across her films by chance on a classic movie station. It was love at first sight. To me, she was a model for everything a woman should be: beautiful, intelligent, enigmatic, untouchable. There was an invulnerability about her that made you want to worship her. And I did. She was my first schoolgirl crush.

Her real life was as fascinating as her on-screen persona. She had a relatively short career, becoming one of the most famous stars in the world, and then all but voluntarily giving up her film career before she was forty. And yet, in that short time, she had become a legend. And not the way someone like Marilyn became a legend: with her sexpot roles, failed marriages, scandalous affairs, and untimely, sordid, and mysterious death. Garbo had simply vanished from the movie scene to live out her life in obscurity in an apartment in Manhattan. I couldn't imagine any of today's female stars following her example. Just the opposite. Today they hung on as long as possible with their collagen injections, breast implants, face-lifts, and liposuction treatments, continuing to play the sexy siren long after they were old enough to be grandmothers.

I remembered a time only about a month after I came to the city. I was walking through Central Park and I saw her. I don't know how I recognized her. It was a warm day. She was wearing a wide hat and a large pair of dark glasses. Her long gray hair hung loose, clean, and combed, but as if it hadn't been touched by hands other than her own in the last fifty years. Later, I'd heard that walking was perhaps her greatest pleasure in life and that although people often recognized her on her jaunts, except for the occasional shameless paparazzi, her self-imposed exile was universally respected. Her naturally regal bearing kept even the crassest of celebrity hounds at a respectful distance. I was young and foolish and I suppose I took it to be some kind of omen that our paths had crossed and I started toward her.

She was walking beside a well-dressed man who looked to be a good thirty years younger than herself, but old enough to be my father. He tried to intercept me, but her voice stopped him—that same sexy, sultry, hypnotic voice from the films that I had watched over and over again.

"What is it, my dear?" she said.

"I just wanted to tell you how much I love your work. What an inspiration you've been to me. You're why I came to the city to become an actress."

"I'm sorry," she muttered. "I truly am. Please forgive me."

I stood there too stunned to say anything. The well-dressed man beside her took her arm and shot me a withering look as he guided her away.

Years later, after her death, I read an article in *Vanity Fair* that described her last years. It told how she had become a virtual recluse, of her tedious obsession with her diet, of her compulsive deliberations over the most insignificant details of life from buying a lamp to choosing a pair of shoes, of her increasing hatred of publicity and, most of all, her reluctance to discuss her film career. But most interesting of all was a quote the author attributed to Garbo that perhaps explained in part her peculiar reticence. Once, commenting on the passing of time, Garbo supposedly said that one day one looks at one's face in the mirror and it is beautiful, and then it's as if a hand passes over it and when one looks again, it's like a withered apple.

Maybe, for Garbo, her image in those famous movies was nothing more than a reminder of a woman who no longer existed. As she changed, grew older, and began to reveal the frailties of mortality, the image stayed the same: cool, poised, untouchable in its perfection. It became a beautiful ghost that haunted her, mocked her, tormented her with the idea of everything she had lost, of all she could never recover. As I sat there, I couldn't help but realize that in a few years I would be the age at which Greta Garbo had retired.

When I left the theater, it was almost as dark outside as it had been inside. I shouldn't have gone to the movies to see Garbo. It never failed to depress me. Yet as I sat on the train back to Queens, my mood unexpectedly started to brighten. Maybe Matt had called while I was out. By the time I turned the corner and walked down the block to my building I was almost certain that he had.

Sure enough, when I unlocked the door to my apartment, I saw the familiar red light blinking on my answering machine. Even though I was a little short on funds, the answering machine was one of the first things I had bought when I moved in. In my line of work, it wasn't a luxury: it was a necessity. Casting directors didn't spend a lot of time calling back actors who didn't answer their phones. They just went to the next name on the list.

I ran across the room and hit the playback button.

"Hi, Jo, it's Cindy. I'm sorry I didn't get right back to you, but Brad was being such a prick. We wound up having a big argument. Then he insisted on making up. Anyway, he's finally gone. Call me back. I want to hear all about you and Mr. Berenger Clooney."

"All right, all right," I said aloud. "Next message."

Cindy finally said good-bye. The machine beeped, clicked, and beeped again.

The red light came back on.

There were no more messages.

He hadn't called after all.

"Bastard!"

11

He sent a dozen roses to the office the next day.

Judy arched a pierced eyebrow. "Nice touch. A little conventional, but nice."

"It's not what you think," I said.

"Sure," Judy deadpanned and resumed typing.

"Really, nothing happened. Though I kind of wish it did."

I read the card accompanying the flowers. *Thanks for a wonderful evening. Matt.*

Ms. Parker came out of her office with an armful of folders, looked with mild distaste at the bouquet on my desk as if it were taking up valuable room where work might be done, and hurried off down the hall.

"What's with her?" I asked.

"Where have you been?" Judy said. "The Rothman people are here."

"Oh," I said, looking after Ms. Parker's well-tailored back.

That afternoon I ate lunch with Judy at a health-food restaurant down the block and we walked down to the Barnes & Noble on Fifth Avenue. While Judy went downstairs and browsed the theater racks, I looked through the fiction section for the rest of Matt's books. They only had two of his titles in paperback—*Dangerous Fantasies* and *One Hand Clapping*. I grabbed both and paid for them at the register.

Judy came up the escalator with an anthology of monologues by some of her peers at P.S. 122. I waited by the revolving doors while she stood in line, took out one of Matt's books, and read the back cover. I remembered how we'd met only a few days ago in exactly the same circumstances and couldn't help looking around the store as if I might actually see him.

I wasn't much good at work the rest of the day. Fortunately, Ms. Parker didn't have much use for me. She was in meetings the entire day. I had done all I could for her over the past week or so. It was in her hands now. I typed up some letters, made some copies in the xerox room, shot off a few faxes, but all the time my mind was on Matt. I couldn't help but wonder whether he would call me again. Of course he would, I told myself, don't be foolish. I looked at the roses as if to convince myself. But when would he call? Would he call tonight?

"Watching the clock isn't going to make it go any faster," Judy said.

"I'm just trying to make sure that hour hand is moving. Is it my imagination, or was it three o'clock an hour ago?" I whined. "I swear this is the longest day of my life."

"Well, I hope he calls you soon," Judy said, "because I sure as hell can't take much more of this."

At last five o'clock rolled around. I rewrapped the roses, said good-bye to Judy, and beat it to the elevators just in case Ms. Parker was on her way back to the office. I had to stand most of the way on the train, hanging on to a pole with one hand, the flowers cradled in my other arm. When I got home, I put the roses in an old Oriental vase I had bought from a secondhand store years ago. I set them on the center of the kitchen table, shook myself out of my coat, and went to check my messages.

I would usually have gone to the machine first thing when I walked through the door. But somehow I didn't want to jinx things. I wanted to savor the hope that one of the voices on the tape belonged to Matt. So long as I didn't listen, I couldn't be disappointed. Hope remained alive. With crossed fingers, I reached out and touched the playback button. It turned out I didn't have long to wait for Matt's call after all. His was the first message that greeted me.

He wanted to know if I'd mind meeting him at an uptown B. Dalton's, where he had a book signing at eight and afterward catch a late supper. I scarcely listened to the rest of the messages: a call from Cindy, saying they were starting shooting Monday; a call from my dentist's office reminding me I was due for a cleaning; and a call from a collection agency hired by the Nordic Trak people. Like the answering machine, the Nordic Trak was a necessity in my line of work. I had to stay in shape. So I had bought it, even though it was completely beyond my budget. I paid whenever I could, but lately that wasn't frequently enough.

I glanced at my mail on the way to the bedroom, where I threw the assorted envelopes and flyers on the bed and stripped off my work clothes. I folded myself in my robe and padded to the bathroom where I took a long hot shower. I washed my hair, shaved my legs, even though they didn't need it, stretched, and rinsed myself off under the pulsating water. I could feel the butterflies fluttering in my stomach. I couldn't remember being so nervous on a date. I stepped out of the shower, wrapped my hair in a towel, and let the bathrobe absorb the water from my warm, damp flesh. I went into the kitchen and pulled open the refrigerator, looking for something to calm my nerves, and filled a glass with the last of the chardonnay I'd drunk the night I learned Cindy had gotten the part.

I took the glass into the living room and watched the news. By the time I was finished, I felt a little better. I took the glass back into the kitchen. Why was I so nervous? I wasn't even this nervous on our first date. But then again that was before I'd really gotten a chance to know him. Suddenly I realized why I was such a basket case. This was the callback. I had passed the initial audition. If I did well tonight, I could get the part.

It was a long time since I had felt this way about a guy. I didn't want to admit it, not even to myself, because if it didn't work out, I would have to face the disappointment of failure all over again. But the fact was that I really liked him. There was something special about Matt.

Could he be the One?

I took a long time getting dressed, trying to figure out just what outfit to wear. I finally decided on the little black party dress I had bought after my meeting with Ruth. I had ruled it out for our first date, but now I figured it was time to turn up the heat a little. It was while I was slipping into my underwear, a nearly transparent push-up Wonder-Bra from Victoria's Secret and a pair of lacy black slingshot briefs that I had to laugh at myself.

I remembered something a girlfriend of mine once said about getting dressed to get undressed. There was no doubt that that was what I was doing. As I put on the black dress, rolled up the black stockings, slipped my feet into the high-heel pumps, my fantasy mind was rolling the tape in reverse, picturing Matt removing my clothes one item at a time. I puckered up in the mirror, put on my lipstick, and was ready to go. I caught the train into Manhattan and walked three blocks to the bookstore, making it there at about eight-twenty.

There was a sign in the window next to a display of Matt's books announcing the signing, which was supposed to run from five to eight.

Inside, they had a section of the store cordoned off with velvet ropes and a table behind which Matt sat, a stack of his books on either side of him. The ropes were unnecessary. There were only a handful of people on line, some of them holding copies of *Forbidden Truths,* but most with copies of his cheaper paperbacks. He was signing a book when I came in, looking up to exchange pleasantries with a large middle-aged woman, when I caught his eye. He smiled, gave a small wave, and turned his attention politely, if reluctantly, back to the large woman all but blocking the table. I browsed the sale tables and casually made my way over to the display of Matt's book.

He looked rather forlorn sitting there with his life's work piled around him. Most of the people in the store looked curiously at him as they passed by. They paused only long enough to confirm in their minds that they didn't know him from Adam before turning away. He was like an exhibit: The Author with His Books. A few found him interesting enough to stop and look at the titles of his book before they moved on.

Two people actually picked up a book and one got in line to have it signed. Matt nodded cordially at everyone who passed his table, making a studied effort not to appear pushy. Nonetheless, I could feel his discomfort. He looked like a man forced to sell some deeply personal and private part of himself against his better judgment. I could tell that this signing was not his idea.

Fortunately, the people who were in line were rather enthusiastic fans of his work. They were clearly excited to have a captive audience with one of their favorite authors. And they had decided to take advantage of the opportunity. From where I stood, I could hear them going on at great length about the characters of Matt's novels as if they were real people. They asked for clarification of plot points and ambiguous endings and not a single one of them left the table without asking Matt where in the world did he get his ideas.

Matt suffered their questions patiently and as a result there was always someone at the table.

I could feel his eyes sneaking glances at me as I made my way around the store. I think he was afraid I would get bored and leave.

It was nearly nine by the time he had finished with everyone. The manager came over to shake his hand and thank him for coming. Matt was polite, but I could see his eyes over the manager's shoulders, searching the store for me. There was a certain desperation in them that I found satisfying. His expression relaxed when he finally spotted me in the true-crime section. He made short shrift of the manager and came over to me, a look of apology on his handsome face.

"I'm sorry," he said, reaching for my shoulders and kissing me on the cheek. "The signing was only supposed to last until eight. I had no idea it would drag on the way it did."

"I didn't mind. I've never been to a signing where I knew the author."

"I'm glad you came. I know it was short notice. But I just had to see you. You look fantastic."

"Thank you."

He looked around the store and then lowered his voice. "I'm going to kill my editor. She insists this is a good way to generate publicity. God, I hate these things."

"Your editor is right. It never hurts to get your face out there."

"I feel like a damn prostitute. Did I look as awkward as I felt?"

"You looked great. And your fans seemed to love you."

"So you're not angry?"

"Of course not. After all, you can't turn your public away."

"Thanks for being so understanding. I promise you I'll try to be the same when you're signing autographs outside your stage door. Though I'm not sure I could stand to wait."

This time he took me in his arms and his mouth hungrily found mine. It was the first time he had kissed me, *really* kissed me, and I felt a fevered electricity run straight down to my toes.

Maybe this guy truly was the One.

"Let's get out of here and have dinner. You must be starving."

The temperature had dropped and there were some snowflakes dancing in the air. Matt held me close against the wind and I watched as the snow landed in his thick hair and winked out.

We found a small French restaurant two blocks away and ducked inside. It was a quaint little place with real stone walls, handwritten menus, and Edith Piaf playing on the stereo. I stared across the table at Matt and felt a pleasant dizziness that had nothing to do with the fine French wine Matt had ordered. The whole setting was all too perfect to be true.

"I didn't get a chance to thank you for the roses," I said. "They were beautiful."

"I hope you didn't mind me sending them to the office. I didn't want to be discreet. I just wanted to make sure you got them before I called."

"You don't know much about women and flowers, do you?"

Matt smiled shyly. It was an expression that suited him well, endearing on a man who otherwise seemed so worldly and certain of himself.

"What do you mean?"

"I'll tell you a secret, but you've got to promise not to tell one of your kind. If it falls into the wrong hands, it could be dangerous."

"Promise," Matt said with mock solemnity.

I leaned forward as if to whisper.

"All women like to get flowers at work. There's nothing we enjoy more than having everyone see someone's thinking about us. We've come a long way in many areas, but when it comes to relationships, I guess we're still pretty vain. We all want to be worshipped."

"In your case, that is no problem."

Our eyes locked, and my mouth hung open. Luckily, the waitress came. She was petite, blond, and looked like a thirteen-year-old Olympic gymnast. I was prepared for the usual pretentious accent, but she surprised me by speaking perfectly ordinary English. I stared down at the handwritten menu again, realizing for the first time that it was in French.

"Perhaps you better order," I said, having regained my composure. "I took only two semesters of French in high school and since then I've used it even less than trigonometry."

Matt glanced at the menu, asked the waitress a few questions in French, and ordered something of which the only word I could make out was "crepe."

"I'm impressed," I said.

"What do you mean?"

"Your French seemed to pass muster. I didn't so much as hear a single sniff of derision."

Matt laughed. "I spent some time in France. That was my bohemian period. I thought I would be the next Rimbaud."

"I'm glad you didn't become him."

"No. Things didn't exactly end well for him, did they? He died in the desert, his leg amputated, slowly consumed by infection at the age of thirty-nine. He'd spent the last years of his life trying to make a fortune running guns. He didn't write a poem after the age of twenty-one."

"I was thinking more along the lines of him being gay."

"Yeah. That, too. You know, I've been meaning to tell you that I was sorry I didn't call you on Sunday."

I took a sip of my wine, waving my hand dismissively. "Don't worry about it. I know you were busy."

"I wanted to tell you what a good time I had. But things got really hectic. The folks at the radio station were completely disorganized. We didn't get on the air with my interview until nearly noon. Then I had to meet with my agent for lunch, who reminded me I had an appearance at a bookstore in Lenox, Massachusetts. I had completely forgotten. I had to hop a shuttle flight that afternoon. By the time I got done, it was close to midnight. I wanted to call, but by then I figured you were probably asleep . . . or out."

"It's okay. You didn't have to call."

"Were you?"

"Was I what?"

Matt looked down. He was wearing an expensive-looking wool suit that appeared to be custom-made. I noticed he was nervously fingering his Armani tie. "Were you out?"

I toyed with the idea of torturing him a little. It was one of Mother's little strategies. The fish always bites harder if you play with it a little, she always said. But I didn't want to play games with Matt. Besides, I didn't know much about fishing, but I did know that if you play with the fish, there was a chance that you'd lose it. I didn't want to take any chances on losing Matt, especially not by playing games.

"No," I said quietly.

He looked momentarily relieved, but then a small crease of worry appeared between his knit brows.

"You know, you asked me a lot of questions on our first date, but I didn't get to ask you too many. I really don't know much about you."

"What do you want to know?"

"Well, I realize it's none of my business—"

"Hey, I all but gave you the fifth the other night. I think you're entitled to a few questions."

"Okay." Matt smiled, looking relieved. "I mainly just wanted to know if you're involved right now."

"Involved?"

"Look, like I said, I know it's none of my business."

"Matt, I wouldn't be here if I were involved. I'm not that kind of woman."

"I'm sorry. I didn't mean to offend you. It's just that I want to know where I stand before things go too far. I sound like an idiot, right?"

"No," I said. "You sound honest and sweet. It's rather refreshing, really."

It was true. I hadn't run into many men who gave a damn about a woman's situation. They didn't think any further ahead than the end of their penis.

"I just don't want to sound too"—Matt made a face—"too sensitive."

"Sensitivity is an underrated turn-on," I said.

"What about your work?"

"Right now, you don't have to worry about my work. I'm in-between parts, as they say in the business. Translation: I don't have a prospect in the world. As I told you, I'm working as a gofor for a psycho investment broker who could double for Lady Macbeth. I'm taking acting classes from a teacher who makes the Marquis de Sade look like Richard Simmons, and unless the FDA takes the ban off Electrify toothpaste, you're not likely to see me on television anytime soon. So you see, you're getting involved with a complete and utter failure."

"You're too young to sound so bleak about the future."

"Bleak is chic among us Gen-Xers, haven't you heard?"

"Hey, don't make me feel any older than I already do," Matt joked. "I guess I just have more confidence in you. I see the potential. You never know when something is going to land in your lap."

"Well, even if it does, I'm not the kind of girl who forgets the little people who believed in her."

"I'm glad to hear that," Matt said. "But if you become famous, I suspect you'd drop me in a minute for that fellow, what's his name? DiCaprio?"

"Leonardo DiCaprio? Not likely. I don't go for any guy who'd look prettier than me in this dress."

Our food came: the delicate crepes were beautifully arranged on fine china, sprinkled with spices and surrounded by artfully placed wedges of brightly colored fruit. Each crepe was filled with a delicious mixture of chopped green vegetables and a kind of lightly whipped cheese. Poured over the top of both crepes was a rich creamy sauce. In spite of my protestations on behalf of my waistline, Matt insisted on dessert. He ordered the specialty of the house: a sinfully wonderful fruit flambé for two.

Afterward we walked a little in the thickening snow, talking and laughing about nothing in particular, as if we had known each other for years. When we finally got too cold, Matt hailed a cab. He gave an address on the Upper East Side and casually turned to me.

"My place," he said matter-of-factly.

"Okay," I answered without batting an eye.

His building had a uniformed doorman. If I had any doubts left over that Matt had given up the starving artist role and traveled in a different economic stratosphere than I did, they were instantly dispelled upon entering his building. I just never expected that he did *this* well. The doorman greeted Matt with a "Hello, Mr. Lang, bit nippy out tonight I'd say," and a discreet but not impolite nod to me. Matt returned his friendly greeting and we crossed a worn but expensive-looking rug in the well-appointed lobby to the elevators, one of which appeared promptly, with another uniformed attendant on duty.

"Good evening, Mr. Lang," he said with an English accent and pressed the button to Matt's floor. "Did the signing go well?"

"Well enough, as those things go."

"Yes"—the man nodded, no doubt meaning me—"I can see that."

"I'll take that as a compliment," I said.

"Then you take it correctly," the elevator operator said.

"Good evening, Joseph," Matt said as we climbed off at our floor. "Rather cheeky fellow, wouldn't you say?" Matt said, imitating the man's accent perfectly after the door shut behind us and the elevator headed back downstairs.

"I didn't mind."

Matt hugged me tightly to him.

We walked down a long hall to Matt's door. He took out a card-key, inserted it into the door, and the lock sprang open.

"After you," he said.

He turned on the lights behind me and I tried not to sound too gauche when I asked him, "Do you live here?"

The apartment looked like something out of one of those pricey fantasy decorating magazines, all cream and gold. The room was spacious without being barren, furnished in minimalist sparsity, the latest in chic, each piece selected for comfort and practicality. The paintings on the wall were all contemporary and looked to be original.

"Part of the year," he answered. "When I'm not writing. Can I get you something? Would you care for some merlot?"

"Yes, please," I said, suddenly feeling a little out of my element.

I walked to a series of three windows opening on a view of the river, the lights of the Triborough Bridge twinkling like an earthbound constellation on the horizon.

Matt returned with a glass of wine and his usual tonic water.

"Please have a seat," he said.

I sat down on the couch and Matt sat across from me in an oversize armchair. We each sipped our drinks.

"It's a beautiful view," I said, looking out the window.

"Yes. Although without someone to enjoy it with I'm afraid you start taking it for granted."

I looked for a place to put my glass down. He must have read my mind.

"You can just put it down on the table."

"But it'll make a ring."

"Don't worry. Someone comes in once a day to clean up the place."

"I see," I said. Something about the way he said that struck me the wrong way. He didn't have to care about such things as rings on the table; apparently it was somebody else's job to clean up after him. I'm sure he didn't mean it that way, but still—

I held the glass in my lap.

"I had a nice time tonight," he said.

"Me, too." I took another sip of my wine, the red liquid trembling like mercury in the fancy wineglass.

What was I doing here? I was just a failed actress living hand-to-mouth, wearing a dress I couldn't afford, and working a temp job that just kept my chin above the ever-rising poverty level in this city. What could this man possibly see in me? I was little better than the faceless, nameless "someone" who came in once a day to clean the rings off the glass of his fancy imported coffee table. I could very well be that someone.

"Do you believe in destiny, Johanna?"

"Destiny?"

"Yes, destiny," he said.

"I don't know what you mean."

"I mean when two people meet. Don't you think there's more to it than chance?"

"I don't know. Sometimes it just seems like coincidence."

"The way we met. I don't think that was a coincidence. I think it was meant to happen."

"People meet all the time. Mostly it doesn't work out. Is that fate?"

"We all meet for a reason. Even if it doesn't work out. I truly believe that. I don't think it was just a coincidence that led me to that bookstore, that led you to pick up my book, that brought us together. It was something more. Something incredibly special."

He was looking at me with a seriousness that made me uneasy. I was falling for him, it was true, but I had fallen for men before and it had always turned out badly. Whatever he thought I was, I was certain I would disappoint him. It was a strange thought. Usually, I feared that the man would disappoint me. But something about Matt brought out all my feelings of inadequacy. I was certain that whatever he saw in me, or thought he saw in me, was just a facade, an act. I had put on too good a performance. I was an actress after all. But sooner or later I would have to take off the mask. When I did, he would see me for who I truly was and I didn't think I could bear the pain of that.

"I think," I stammered, "maybe I should be going. I have work tomorrow and all—"

He laid his hand on my wrist. "Please don't."

I looked up and saw a pain in his gray eyes that I couldn't identify—or resist. I stayed for what I promised myself would be just one more glass of merlot. He moved beside me on the couch and before I quite knew what was happening, his hands were on my body, undressing me, just as they had in my fantasy, his lips on my eyes, my mouth, my throat, my breasts. I made a weak show of protest and then sighed and pulled him closer.

We ended up in his Jacuzzi bathtub, our bodies still locked together, the hot water bubbling all around us, as if our passion alone were heating it to the boiling point. He took me for the first time right there in the tub, his hand separating my thighs, his hard urgency penetrating me, pulsing blood even hotter than the steaming water, his flesh filling mine.

I reached around and grabbed his slippery buttocks as he kneeled between my legs, forcing him deeper inside me, his face in my sweat-damp hair, his lips moving from my ear to my mouth, locking there, his tongue pushing between my parting lips. I came with a soft shudder and he followed my lead, his hardness breaking inside me, his hips bucking wildly, pushing me up the side of the slick tub, a moment of unbearable suspense, and then the surrender of his scalding need firing in short, soul-shuddering spasms.

We stayed locked in each other's embrace, our mouths gently exploring each other's unspoken words, the only sound that of the hot water bubbling all around us. Finally he stood up, the water around his thighs, and I stared up at him, the thatch of dark hair on his chest, his flat stomach, incredible for a man of forty-five, the even more incredible fact that his penis was already half hard, floating on the waves only inches from my face. I moved forward and covered it with my mouth, kneeling in the water as his hands kneaded my hair.

I licked and teased him, pumping him gently with my hand as I tongued the swollen head of his cock, hearing the satisfying evidence of my efficacy as he groaned above me. I could sense him nearing his crisis as he lifted me out of the water and held me close to him, kissing me full on the mouth, and then grabbing me under the knees, lifting me easily, and climbing the steps out of the Jacuzzi.

He laid me on the warm wet tiles surrounding the tub and took me again, this time not putting off his own need, but satisfying himself with selfish abandon. He pushed my slick breasts together and kissed my nipples as he plunged inside me, coming again almost immediately, holding me close as the spasms once again wracked his body.

He left me lying there on the soapy tiles, spent, satiated, while he retrieved an armful of towels. He slowly and carefully dried my body and then his own and led me to his bedroom. He laid me down on the rich quilt comforter and spread my legs, but this time not to spend his own lust, which was quieted, but to give me pleasure.

He traced a line of kisses from my mouth to my breasts to my belly to my pubic bone. There he stopped and teased me with his tongue until I was squirming and moaning, surprised that I still had that much sexual tension left in my body. I grabbed his broad shoulders, lifting myself away and then gently lowering myself onto his face.

I locked my hands behind his head and held him close between my thighs as his mouth went to work, expertly speaking the language of ecstasy, his thumbs squeezing my erect nipples as I came with a delighted cry, my eyes shut tight on the vision of him down between my thighs. When it was all over, he came up to lie beside me and we kissed gently, our bodies both spent, words no longer necessary.

He held me in his arms, his breath growing deep and heavy, his chest rising and falling rhythmically.

"Well," I whispered, "did I get the part?"

"What?" he murmured.

"Nothing," I said. "Go to sleep."

I snuggled closer to his chest. Just before drifting off to sleep myself, I thought with satisfaction of my midnight visitor and how if he came to my apartment tonight, he would be disappointed to find I wasn't at home.

12

———•———

The next morning we ate breakfast at the American Café in Rockefeller Center, its floor-to-ceiling glass windows overlooking the famous ice-skating rink, where expert skaters whizzed effortlessly past those wobbling less confidently on their blades. One woman in particular, tall and svelte in black ski-tights, her hair pulled back from an overly madeup face, cut elaborate arabesques in the ice, occasionally moving to the center of the rink where she crossed her arms tightly over her chest, stood on the toe of one skate, and spun in a dizzying blur.

"Do you think she's a member of Disney on Ice or just showing off?" Matt asked.

The skater passed by our window, her hands on her hips, her heels together, her face frozen in an expression of almost religious beatitude.

"I don't know," I said, sipping my two-dollar glass of orange juice and pouting. "But if she's showing off, I'd swear it was for you."

"You, my dear, have nothing to be jealous of."

I had woken up late, the sun streaming in off the river and into the window, bathing Matt's king-size bed in golden light. I took a look at the clock and felt a surge of panic rush through me. I tugged off the covers and swung my legs off the bed.

Matt rose up on one elbow, his hair mussed, looking confused.

"What's the matter?"

"I have to go to work," I said, grabbing a towel and slipping it around my naked body. "I'm going to be late."

Matt reached for his watch on the nightstand.

"You're already late."

I rushed into the living room and began a frantic search for my clothes. I couldn't find my dress anywhere. Instead, I found one of my pumps under an antique chair in the corner.

Matt had slipped on a robe and followed me into the living room.

"Christ, do you know where my other shoe is?"

Matt laughed.

"What's so funny?"

"Why not just call in sick?"

"It's a bad time. My boss is going to go bonkers."

I found my stockings rolled up in a ball between the cushions of the couch.

"What's one day? Surely she can manage. Besides, you said you hated that job anyway."

"I hate it but I need it."

"So, you're not entitled to get sick? We can spend the day together."

"I can't. I just can't. You don't understand."

"The whole day. Just me and you. We'll have breakfast, take a walk in the park, maybe pick up where we left off last night. . . ."

"What are you, the devil?"

Matt grinned. "Why don't you come back into the bedroom and find out for yourself? That is, if you dare."

He turned back to the bedroom. I stared at him for a moment, then looked down at the silly sight I must have presented, and had to smile. There was no way I was going to make it on time anyway. I dropped my shoe and followed him into the bedroom.

I ducked playfully beneath the covers and roused his already stirring penis. It didn't take much cajoling to have it standing flat against his stomach. I placed my mouth over it and felt Matt's warm body grow rigid and then waken, his hands finding my arms and pulling me up until our bodies lay pressed tightly against each other, our mouths sealed together. We made slow, lazy morning love, and then luxuriated in the sunlight warming the black silk sheets.

Matt showed me to the shower and climbed in after me, taking me again, this time from behind, after soaping my back and buttocks. He thrust into me as I held my palms against the tiles, tossing my head back to the rush of the shower spray, his strong hands on my hips, all but holding me up as my legs turned to jelly when we both came.

Can't have an orgasm? Take that, Mr. Drake!

Now we sat across from each other, basking in the sweet afterglow of sex, staring into each other's eyes as if we were the only two people in the crowded restaurant, as if we were the only two people in the world. It was like a scene out of a movie. Only I wasn't playing a part—I was actually living it. For the first time in days I didn't feel a pang of envy when I thought of Cindy. Matt and I had both attacked our breakfasts ravenously, our passion fueling our appetites, and had quickly devoured our stacks of pancakes dripping with butter and syrup in what I'm sure was record time. Our waiter came over to refill our coffee cups and I was just thinking how perfect life could be when Matt dropped his bombshell.

"I'm leaving tonight for Chicago and then L.A. It's a book tour. I loathe the damn things, but my publisher demands I go. It's in my contract and besides, it helps sell books. When I get back, I'm leaving for Maine to begin work on my next novel. I should have told you sooner, but everything happened so fast. There was no time."

"No time!" I said, my voice rising higher than I'd intended, causing several nearby patrons to turn in our direction.

"Please," Matt said.

"Of course, anything but make a scene," I said, lowering my voice anyway. "We wouldn't want this situation to be an inconvenience to you. What do you mean there was no time? No time to explain you were just using me?"

"It's not like that, Johanna."

"Then what is it like, Matt? There was plenty of time for us to get involved. Or was I mistaken in believing this meant something more than just a night in the sack? Maybe this is just something you do all the time."

"I told you it wasn't."

"Well, forgive me if I don't believe you."

The fact was I didn't know what to believe. I couldn't deny the chemistry between us last night. It had been a long time since a man had made me feel like Matt had made me feel. No, that wasn't quite right. It was worse than that. No man had ever made me feel the way he made me feel. Last night had been the most romantic night of my life. I had given the performance of a lifetime in the role I was supposed to play. Now, almost as an afterthought, he was telling me he was leaving. It was over. Cut. Finished. Just like that. I had gotten the callback and I'd blown it.

"What was it? What did I do wrong?"

"Nothing, Johanna. It's not like that."

"Tell me, dammit. I can take it. You owe me at least that much."

Just then the skater swooped dramatically close to our window, thrusting her perfect breasts out from her tight bodysuit, spreading her arms behind her like some great bird of prey.

"I can tell you're upset," he said. "But believe me, I didn't plan on it happening this way."

Upset didn't begin to describe what I was feeling. I felt like throwing the rest of my orange juice in his face and walking out of the restaurant. I wasn't worried about creating a scene. After all, I was an actress dammit. Even if I couldn't get a role. I was beginning to realize that my life was the biggest role I was ever likely to get. Why the hell not make it dramatic? I should have thrown that juice in his face. But I didn't. I'm still not sure what held me back. I could almost hear Mr. Drake's mocking voice in the back of my head. *Spontaneity, Ms. Brady, spontaneity is the heart of acting.* Damn Mr. Drake, too. The moment had passed. The glass of orange juice remained where it was.

"So it's wham, bam, thank you, ma'am," I said, my voice empty even of sarcasm.

"No," he said. "This is difficult for me. You've got to believe that."

"Sorry. But I can't seem to drum up a lot of sympathy for you."

"You don't understand. I don't want this to be over with."

"So what am I supposed to do, wait around until you come back?"

"No," he said. "Come with me to Maine. The book tour should last a week, enough time for you to tie up any loose ends. When I get back, you can fly with me out to my chalet for the winter."

I felt like I was on the end of a yo-yo string. One moment I was as low as I could get; the next moment I was being pulled all the way back to the top. I must have looked dazed, because he was still talking, trying to explain. I only heard his last words.

"I know what I'm asking is unfair, selfish. I know it's going to be difficult for you to leave everything behind here in New York. You've got your own ambitions to pursue. But I really need you. I don't think I can write without you by my side. I love you, Johanna. There, I said it. I love you. It'll only be for a few months and you can come back whenever you like. Please tell me you'll come."

He was wrong about only one thing. It wouldn't be difficult for me to leave New York. After my last audition, the last in a long string of disappointments, I needed a break, a chance to reassess my life. There was nothing holding me to New York but a quickly fading dream and an unending series of temp jobs that had been growing increasingly unbearable. Maybe what I needed was a change of scenery.

I had never been to Maine before. The idea of spending the winter there seemed strangely appealing. I had heard about how beautiful the country was and had always longed to visit. In winter, I imagined it would be spectacular.

But the real reason I'd even consider leaving New York was Matt.

There was no denying that. I hadn't been wrong, after all. Something had happened between us. Something beautiful, something wonderful. He had felt it, too. I hadn't been fooling myself, after all. He had said the magic words: *I love you, Johanna.* I wanted to replay the scene, have him repeat the line, repeat it over and over. It was the scene I had been waiting for all my life. And now that it was finally being played out, I wanted it to last forever.

"It's kind of short notice," I said. "I'd have to find someone to sublet the apartment."

"Please?" he pleaded. "I'll pay the rent on the damn apartment if you can't find a sublet."

"It's okay. I have someone in mind."

"Then you'll come," he said hopefully.

I waited a heartbeat and a half, studying his earnest face, and the hunger in his eyes I'd first seen in the bookstore when he looked for me among the stacks, uncertain whether I'd given up and gone home. I enjoyed his discomfort immensely.

"I'll think about it," I said.

The line etched deep between his eyebrows suddenly disappeared. His face broke out in a smile.

"You mean it?" he said. "You'll really think about it?"

"Yes."

"Great," he said, "that's just great. I hardly dared to even hope you'd say yes. I can hardly believe it."

He grabbed my hand from across the table.

"You'll love it at the chalet. I had it built myself. It's perfectly private. Miles from the nearest town. It's the one place on earth where I can really let my hair down. You'll find it the perfect place to relax and recharge your batteries."

His face was beaming, like a man who couldn't believe his good luck.

"Whoa, I didn't say yes, remember? I just said I'd think about it."

"Okay, okay," he said. "I won't pressure you. In fact, I won't even call you. I'll give you the whole week to think things over. You can give me your answer when I get back."

I wanted to tell him I didn't need to think about it. I wanted to tell him I'd follow him anywhere. But something inside me told me it was better to let him wait. I toyed with the idea of telling him about my date with the producer, but decided against it. That might be too much. In any event, I decided to reserve the right to be angry, or at least to make him think I was still angry. It gave me the upper hand. Mother always told me it was best to take the upper hand. I never believed her. I was always too honest. But honesty had never gotten me anywhere up to now. Maybe she was right.

We finished our coffee, walked outside, looked down at the skaters, and then walked back to his apartment in the winter cold, where we had sex again, this time not making it to the bedroom or the Jacuzzi, but shedding our clothes in the living room and doing it right on the floor in front of the gas fireplace.

We lay together until the sun began falling on the other side of the building and rush hour traffic started creeping across the bridge. I didn't wait until he told me it was time for him to get going. I got up and dressed quietly, my back to him. He pulled on his trousers and shirt. He threw on his topcoat and walked me down to the street, where he hailed a cab and paid the driver to take me home.

On the sidewalk in front of his building he gave me a passionate kiss and hugged me tightly to the warmth of his chest. I finally relented, kissing him on the cleft of his chin, and he kissed me again, deeply, passionately, momentarily chasing away the late afternoon chill.

"One week and we'll be off together for Maine," he said.

"Maybe," I reminded him and climbed into the cab.

"Maybe." He smiled, as if there were no maybes about the matter.

I didn't turn around, but I could see him in the rearview mirror, standing on the curb until my cab rounded the corner and disappeared from sight.

I had a lot of excess energy to burn when I got home, so I changed into my leotard and hit the Nordic Trak. Forty minutes later, I was physically exhausted and soaked with sweat, but my insides were still churning. I took a hot shower, wrapped myself in a towel, and headed for the kitchen. I heated up the leftovers from Carmine's from a couple of nights before and sat down to eat in front of the television, flicking the channels until I came to *Jeopardy*.

None of the categories were familiar—subjects like geography, science, and the 1600s—and I did miserably by my own reckoning, but the game seemed to take my mind off Matt for a good thirty minutes. I half-watched some lame TV movie-of-the-week starring Morgan Fairchild for another hour before I decided to give up trying not to think about Matt. His plane would be on its way to Chicago by now. He'd be back in a week. How could I wait that long?

I saw the two new paperbacks I had bought on the end table. I picked up *Dangerous Fantasies*. If I couldn't have him, I could at least have the next best thing. I turned to the first page and began reading, almost immediately engrossed in the story. When I looked up from the book, I was surprised to find it was after midnight. Almost three hours had slipped by.

I went to the kitchen for a glass of water and stared out the window. The streets below were empty, dusted with unmarked snow. I thought about going to bed, even changed into my flannel nightgown, but I knew I'd be unable to sleep. I returned to the couch and Matt's book, picking up the heroine's harrowing tale right where I left off.

When I at last put the book down, it was after two a.m. I could feel the grainy sensation under my eyelids telling me that I had read too long. I was overtired. I knew I would never be able to fall asleep. I thought of the old Xanax prescription in the medicine cabinet, but decided against the pills. Instead I made my way to the bedroom, pulled the covers to my chin, and waited for the sandman to come.

He didn't.

I lay awake staring at the ceiling, my mind whirling with the events of the past forty-eight hours. It wasn't long before I kicked off the covers and decided to take one of the pills after all. I returned to bed and waited for it to work. The digital clock on the bedstand switched over to three a.m. I turned and looked at the doorway. My dark visitor had not come. I realized with something of a shock that I almost wished he had come tonight. I had so much to tell him.

13

I had every intention of getting to work early the following morning, but an electrical problem on the train kept me stuck for nearly forty-five minutes. By the time I hit the street, I tried to make up some of the time by catching a cab, only to find that it had started raining and everyone more or less had the same idea. I didn't have an umbrella, my old one having been wrecked beyond repair after Sunday's downpour, and naturally the weatherman hadn't whispered a word about rain, so nearly everyone seemed caught unprepared.

After jumping in and out of the shelter of an awning for nearly twenty minutes, I finally decided to give up on a cab and bought a five-dollar umbrella from a poorly dressed but good-looking black man fortuitously standing about fifty feet away on the corner.

"Good morning, ma'am," he said with a pleasant Jamaican accent. "You need umbrella?"

"Yes, I'm afraid so."

"Only ten dollars," he said. "Very fine umbrella. Gucci."

He smiled broadly at the name. He twirled the umbrella in his hand, blurring the distinctive design, no doubt a knockoff.

"No thanks," I said, pointing to a bucket of short-handled, Tote-style umbrellas. "How much are those?"

"Five dollars," he said, as if he had expected better of me.

"I'll take one."

I fished through my purse, gave him a soggy five, and he handed me an umbrella.

"Have a good day, ma'am," he said, grinning.

"Thanks," I said, struggling to open the cheaply made umbrella. "You, too."

He laughed.

"As long as it keeps raining, ma'am. As long as it keeps raining."

By the time I got to the office, I was half-drenched, cold, bedraggled, and a good two hours late. I peeled off my wet things in the coatroom and headed for my desk, expecting to find at least a dozen urgent messages from Ms. Parker demanding my immediate presence, if not the woman herself waiting impatiently for me. I felt badly enough about abandoning her the day before on such short notice—the second time I'd called in sick in a matter of two weeks—and especially when she obviously needed my support. I could hardly blame her if she laid into me. I'd earned it. But I was still on an emotional seesaw over the whole situation with Matt. I didn't need a verbal harangue. Nevertheless, I mentally prepared my list of excuses and steeled myself for the worst.

I never expected what I found when I got to my desk.

There were no messages posted on my computer. Ms. Parker was nowhere to be seen. And a group of uniformed men were in the process of filling up boxes with her personal effects.

"What's going on?" I asked Judy.

She was looking over her computer at the men in Ms. Parker's office and had stopped pretending to type when I walked up. The only thing I could think of was that against all odds Ms. Parker had somehow gotten the promotion and they were moving her into the corner office.

"She's been sacked," Judy said, not moving her lips, as if she were trying out a new ventriloquist's act.

"Fired? Ms. Parker's been fired?"

"Security came up and escorted her out of the building about an hour ago."

"But why? What happened?"

Judy shrugged. "No one's sure exactly. But word is she screwed up that Rothman project big time. So bad, in fact, that Rothman took his business elsewhere. They've been looking for you—"

"Me?"

I no sooner got the word out of my mouth than a security guard came up behind me.

"Ms. Brady?"

"Yes."

"Please gather your things and come with me."

"But why?"

"Just come with me, please."

"I have to get my coat."

"I'll come with you."

I didn't even get a chance to say good-bye to Judy. The guard whisked me down a secured elevator to the personnel department where I spent a half hour being interviewed by the director of human resources. He asked me a lot of questions about Ms. Parker, about the Rothman project, and about company business in general. When he had satisfied himself that I knew almost nothing of importance and had convinced himself that I understood my obligation to keep even that confidential, he wished me good luck in my future endeavors and entrusted me to the care of the security guard, who promptly delivered me to the front of the building.

I was still in a state of shock when I got back to my apartment. I fixed myself something to eat and sat in front of the television. Two hours later, I realized I hadn't touched my lunch or been paying attention to what I had been watching. I knew I should call the temp service and let them know what was going on, but somehow I just couldn't bring myself to do it. I thought about going out, but there was nowhere to go, and besides, without the temp job, money was going to be even more of a problem than it was already.

I thought about calling Cindy, but I was tired of playing the catastrophic friend. Naturally, my thoughts drifted to Matt. He was in Chicago by now, doing whatever it was authors did to promote their book, and then on to L.A. I would dearly have liked to hear his voice about now, but I knew he wouldn't call, and I wasn't sure I really wanted him to. He had left me with a lot to think about and having him call would only keep me from thinking things through clearly. Still, I was glad he hadn't given me a number at which to reach him. I would have been sorely tempted to use it.

Just then the phone rang.

I crossed the room and picked it up. Her hoarse, cracked voice wasted no time on pleasantries, let alone introductions. Ruth got right to the point, picking up the conversation of a week ago without missing a beat, as if we'd never stopped talking. It was something I had grown used to by now.

"Sol Silverstein is in town. Are you available at the end of this week?"

I almost told her that with Matt away and the loss of my job, I didn't have much of anything to do, but decided to spare details that to her would be irrelevant.

"I'm available," I said.

"Good. Sol will be in touch with you to set things up. I told him all about you and he's looking forward to meeting you."

"Okay."

"He'll only be in town for a couple of days. He's an old friend. Do me a favor and make him feel at home."

"I'll do my best."

"Remember, Johanna, he can make things happen for you."

"I will, Ruth."

"This could be your break, kid. It might not be the way you dreamed it would be, but for most of us, it never is. Good luck, I gotta go."

"Ruth?"

"Yeah?"

"Thanks."

"Don't mention it," she said and rung off.

14

Sol Silverstein called two days later.

I had just gotten off the phone with the temp agency. They told me that they had nothing available at the time and to try them back the following Monday. The woman on the phone seemed rather cold and standoffish. I wondered if the personnel director who conducted my exit interview had said something about me. I had to admit that temping for a high-level executive who gets canned for incompetence wasn't the best reference in the world. Maybe I was just being paranoid. Still, I was feeling kind of desperate when Mr. Silverstein called.

"Is this Joanne Brady?"

"Jo-hanna."

"What?"

"Johanna Brady."

"Let me put it this way, you the broad Ruth Gold set me up with?"

"Yes."

"Then you know who I am."

"Yes, sir."

"Jesus Christ, I had a hell of a time getting through. The line's been busy for an hour."

I must have been on the phone for ten minutes at the most, but I didn't want to contradict him.

"I'm sorry. I was calling work."

"Getting the gossip on who's shtupping who? Jesus Christ with a boner. You can never call a broad without getting a busy signal. Don't you have call waiting?"

"No."

"Well, get it, sweetheart. You almost lost out on the time of your life tonight. Can you be ready by eight?"

"Yes."

"Don't bullshit me. You got something to wear? Your shoes match? Your hair in good shape? I don't want to hear you were all ready and couldn't find the right shade of lipstick."

"I'll be ready," I said tightly, my throat choking down the words *Go to hell.*

"Good. Be ready about eight. We'll have dinner and then head out to a party uptown. I'll send a car for you."

I exercised enough self-control to wait for him to hang up before slamming down the phone. Ruth said he'd been out of circulation for a while, but didn't he know that the Rat Pack were all dead and buried? Who the hell did he think he was anyway? Oliver Stone? What had Ruth said? For most of us it's never the way we dreamed it would be. Well, that was the understatement of the year. Still, I knew she was right. I wouldn't be the first one in this business who had to swallow her pride.

I looked at the clock.

It was already half-past six. That didn't give me much time to get ready, but damned if I was going to be late and give that chauvinistic son-of-a-bitch the smug satisfaction of being right. It didn't take me long to choose what to wear. I pulled a simple black wool dress from the closet. It fit close enough in the right places to look chic, but not so close as to give anyone—especially Mr. Silverstein—the wrong idea. I thought about how I had dressed for Matt on our second date. Dressed to be undressed. Well, tonight I was dressed to stay dressed. I slipped on a pair of modest black pumps and a strand of faux pearls and went into the bathroom to put the finishing touches on my hair and apply a little makeup.

I studied my reflection in the mirror.

I changed my lipstick twice before I remembered what Mr. Silverstein had said. I had to laugh.

Almost in defiance I chose the reddest lipstick I had. I blew a kiss in the mirror before turning off the light.

That's the last kiss I'll be giving out tonight.

Eat your heart out, Sol.

The car pulled up to the curb at eight sharp. For some reason I had expected a limousine, but what came instead was one of those large black town cars with New York livery plates. The driver lowered the passenger window.

"Silverstein party?"

"Yes."

"Get in."

I opened the door and slid into the empty backseat.

"Mr. Silverstein had some business to attend to. He will meet you at the restaurant."

That was fine by me. I was in no great hurry to meet this moth-ridden giant of sixties celluloid sleaze. In fact, I was beginning to feel a little jittery. I could use the time to settle down. I stared out the window, wondering if this was all a big mistake, as we crossed the bridge, leaving the twinkling lights of Queens behind for the brighter, far more numerous, twinkling lights of Manhattan.

The driver pulled up in front of a fancy steakhouse whose name seemed vaguely familiar to me, though I was certain I'd never dined there before. I couldn't help but be impressed. The place had all the attitude of the kind of restaurant where even a hamburger cost twenty-five dollars. Maybe Ruth was right. Maybe Mr. Silverstein had something going for him after all.

The maitre d' pointed him out to me.

Sol Silverstein was at a table near the back of the restaurant. He was wearing a polyester suit with the kind of pattern that usually only hurt the eyes when seen on a television set. As I approached, he took a fat green cigar out of his mouth and let his pale watery eyes roam over my body.

"You must be Joanna."

"Jo-hanna," I corrected him.

"Have a seat," he said. "Something to drink?"

"Yes," I said, almost too quickly. "Please."

He snapped his fingers and a waiter came by to take our order.

"Chardonnay please," I said.

"Another," Mr. Silverstein said, shaking the ice around in his empty tumbler.

The first three buttons of his yellow shirt were undone, revealing wiry white hair, and a chain from which dangled a gold charm signifying the zodiac sign for Libra. His mouth was framed by an untrimmed goatee. He turned with undisguised interest to watch a blond woman on her way to the ladies' room. At the back of his head, a dirty elastic band collected what was left of his oily gray hair ring in a sparse ponytail.

My first instinct was to get up from the table and leave right then and there. But something stopped me. It was what Ruth had said. Repulsive as he was, Sol Silverstein might be able to help my career. I should at least see what he had to offer. He was a connection and connections were hard to come by in this business. I couldn't afford to be picky. This man just might be my last best chance.

"It's a pleasure to meet you, Mr. Silverstein," I forced myself to say.

"What's this 'Mr. Silverstein' crap?" he said. "Call me Sol. I may be old enough to be your grandfather, but I sure don't intend to behave that way. Unless, of course, you have some interesting childhood memories you'd like to share?"

"No, I'm afraid not."

"Too bad," he said, looking around the restaurant. "You ever been here?"

"No, but it seems familiar."

"You probably read about the mob hit they had outside a few years back. Well, I guess more than a few years back now. Happened right out front. Big boss in the Gambino family. Whacked him right on the sidewalk as he was getting into his limo. Something like that gives an establishment a kind of aura all the fucking stars in *Zagat's* and *The New York Times* put together can't give it."

The waiter came back with our drinks and took our food order. Mr. Silverstein ordered the extra thick prime rib, blood rare, cold inside. I had already looked at the menu and the only concession they made for non-meat eaters was a steamed vegetable platter.

"What the hell are you, a goddamn rabbit? Or one of them fucking health nuts? Shit. I had quadruple bypass two years ago." He thumped his chest. "Put in all new tubing. Doc said I had the cardiovascular system of a twenty-year-old. I intend to take advantage of it. Figure I've got another sixty years on the old ticker. Had colon cancer six years ago. For nearly a year I had to crap out of a hose in my side. Talk about having a hard time getting laid. I'd have had better luck if I had to tell a broad I had AIDS."

"Mr. Silverstein—"

He shot me a look.

"Sol," I corrected myself, trying to change the subject. "Ruth told me you had some interesting projects planned."

"Yeah. Ruth is a great old gal. Not bad in the sack either, about two hundred years ago. She recommended you highly."

"That was nice of her," I said uncertainly, given the context.

"Do you know my work?"

"I'm not sure—"

"You ever hear of *Vampire Vixens from Venus?*"

"No—I—"

"How about the *Necromaniac* series?"

"It sounds sort of familiar," I lied.

"You're too damn young. Can't blame you for that. Before all that Jason and Michael Myers shit, I was doing *Necromaniac*. Where do you think they stole the idea from? I was decades ahead of my time. Me, Russ Meyer, Herschel Gordon Lewis, we were the pioneers. Today a punk like Tarantino makes one fucking movie that breaks even and every major studio in Hollywood is falling all over themselves to give him money.

"It wasn't like that in my day. You scratched and you scrambled and you sold your soul to make a movie and when it was over, you got screwed up the asshole. And then you waited for the bleeding to stop, picked yourself up, and you started all over again. Nudie films, biker flicks, you did what you could to make a buck and survive. Let me tell you something, sweetheart, if one of those young faggots like Tarantino needed mouth-to-mouth resuscitation I wouldn't so much as squeeze a fart out of my ass to save his miserable life."

I had never seen Mr. Silverstein's work, but I was a huge fan of Quentin Tarantino. I was reasonably certain that—breaks or no breaks—Mr. Silverstein was no Quentin Tarantino.

Our food arrived and Mr. Silverstein fell to his bloody steak like a lion on the grasslands of Africa. He guzzled another scotch while I politely declined a second glass of chardonnay. Not that I couldn't use the drink to help me get through dinner. I only wanted to make sure I had all my wits about me. It was going to take the diplomacy of a Kissinger to get what I wanted from him without giving him what he wanted.

Mr. Silverstein leaned forward, jabbing toward me with his fork. "I'll tell you something, though, sweetheart," he said, his cheek stretched taut over an overlarge chunk of steak. "The VCR is going to be the salvation of poor schmucks like me. Home video. That's where the money is coming from now. It's the kids, the kids who never got to see *Ten Thousand Maniacs* or *The Corpse Grinders* or *Bloodsucking Freaks*. They weren't even born yet when that stuff came out. They grew up on *Halloween* and *Scream* and Marilyn Manson. But now they can get the real thing in their local video store. Or they can order through the horror mags and fanzines, even over the Internet. We're reaching a whole new generation. What we didn't get the first time around, we're gonna get back in spades now. Sex and blood sells, baby, and we have the genuine article. Kids today see nothing but that slick, anesthetized Hollywood crap. When they see what we've done, it'll blow their fucking minds."

"And that's a good thing?" I couldn't help but say.

"It's all about freedom, baby."

"It's nice to know someone's looking out for the youth of America."

Mr. Silverstein laughed, choking on the chunk of steak he was chewing. He held up a finger, brought his glass to his lips with the other hand, and took a swig of scotch to wash down the meat.

He cleared his throat.

"Only one person I'm looking out for now, sweetheart," he said, his voice raspy. "That's Sol Silverstein."

He sawed off another piece of steak, a huge purplish-red chunk dripping from his fork. "You ever do porn?"

"No," I said, a little more indignantly than I'd intended.

"Come on," he said, wiping blood from his beard. "I never met an actress who didn't have a little blue film of her somewhere."

"Not me."

He popped the steak into his mouth. "Maybe that's why you aren't getting anywhere in this business. Ruth told me you were a bit of a tight ass. I can see that by looking at you. You want to make it, you've got to broaden your horizons. There's plenty of opportunities. You don't even have to get fucked. You can do a little lickety-lick with some pretty bitch. Hell, I see that shit and sometimes I wish I were a woman. Christ, you don't even have to do that. There's plenty of chicks turning a good buck filming that crap where they just tie you up and smack your ass a little bit."

"I don't want to be a porn star."

"Who's talking about being a porn star? You don't have a porn star's body anyway."

"Thanks," I said dryly.

"It's a compliment, honey. Those broads can't get jobs outside the industry. They look too much like sex toys. For you, on the other hand, it could be a way to get your face out there."

"I'd prefer to do it the legit way."

Mr. Silverstein laughed. "There ain't no legit way. You sell your ass, plain and simple. Otherwise, you sit in the theater seat and watch someone else who sold theirs."

"Is that what you would have told Greta Garbo?"

"Reality check, honey. You're not Greta Garbo. I'm not Cecil B. DeMille. I've told you what I've done in this business. You tell me what you've done so far, Joan."

"Jo-hanna."

"Joan, Joanie, Joanna, whatever. Until your name is on a marquee, it don't mean a damn thing."

"I've been in a toothpaste commercial that ran from coast to coast. I've also done some off-Broadway work."

"Yeah? How far off-Broadway?"

I felt myself blush.

"Let me guess. It would probably have cost you fifty bucks by cab to get to Broadway if you could have found a cab passing through such a rathole neighborhood."

I didn't say anything.

"You know what you just gave me, sweetheart? The resumé of a wannabe. You know how many girls like you are out there? Tens of thousands. You know what separates the one successful one out of the tens of thousands? Luck. And you're one of the lucky ones. We're going to a party tonight. You're probably going to meet some of the most important people you've ever met in this business. They might not be named Speilberg or Lucas, but they're the guys whose backs those sons-of-a-bitches stand on. You just stick with old Sol tonight. You play your cards right, you'll get further by morning than you have since you came to this city."

I didn't like the sound of that, but again I thought of what Ruth had said. Mr. Silverstein could be my ticket into the show. Sure, the ticket may cost more than I'd like and the seat might be awful, but at least I'd get through the door. Mr. Silverstein was crude and chauvinistic, but I was certain I could handle him. I would play him along, get what I wanted, and promise more than I had any intention of delivering.

We stood on the curb outside the restaurant and Mr. Silverstein punched a few numbers on his cellular phone. A minute or so later the car that had brought me into the city pulled up to the curb.

"This is where he fell," he said.

"Who?"

"Big Paul Castellano," Mr. Silverstein said. "Shot dead by one of John Gotti's henchmen."

"Oh."

He gazed at the sidewalk with a kind of reverence.

"You can still feel the magic. It's better than the Hollywood walk of fame."

As we drove uptown, I expected him to make his move. He was more than a little drunk, the smell of scotch reeking on his breath, filling the back of the car, but to my surprise he behaved like a perfect gentleman. He talked almost incessantly, small talk about his experiences in the movies, but not the embittered diatribe he'd indulged in at dinner. Instead, these were nostalgic tales of the early days of the independent moviemaker. The kinds of stories all film buffs loved:

funny, zany, touching. They were stories of men who loved to make movies and did it with a single-minded devotion that often destroyed them.

"Ed Wood," he said. "Now there was a character. A drunk, a faggot, and the worst director ever to shout 'action,' but I loved that bastard. You ever see any of his movies?"

"I rented one after I saw Johnny Depp play him in *Ed Wood.*"

"Terrible, wasn't it? But you know something? Ed never knew how awful his movies were. He really thought he was creating art. And you know something? He did. In his own way, he did. His passion shows through every piece of garbage he ever made. It was that passion that was his art. Total, blind, unquestioning passion. He died drunk and destitute. But he got what he wanted. Immortality. You know I almost worked with Nicholson?"

"Really?"

"Yeah. He was a nobody back then. Just some guy from some small seaside town in Jersey. But Roger Corman snapped him up to star in some piece of crap called *The Tower* and that was that. Oh well. That's the way this business is."

Mr. Silverstein turned up his palms, shrugged, and smiled sadly. I began to wonder if his vulgar exterior was all part of some kind of act. A defense against more decades of disappointment than I could even dream of at this point. I felt a kind of pity for him. He was just an aging old man still following his dream of making it big in a business that had all but passed him by. He had one last sprint left in him and he was determined to give it a shot. Maybe Ruth knew what she was talking about in setting up this meeting, after all. Perhaps, if I played my cards right, I could tag along with him. Even if he fell short, failed, I might still get the exposure I needed to go on. I was still young enough. I didn't need a success, just a shot.

"By the way," I said, "whose party are we going to?"

"Jack Kauffmann. He's an old pal of mine. Did a couple of biker flicks back in the sixties. A helluva guy. He's got some backers interested in a production company. He used his own money to put together a montage of work by all us old bastards, called it *The Masters of Gore.* It's already made back the money he invested ten times over just on catalogue sales alone. He's got some big players interested. If it goes down, we'll be back in business again. Only this time we'll be able to do things right."

"Well, good luck."

"You be a good girl tonight. If old Sol gets what he wants, maybe you get what you want."

I wasn't sure what he meant by that. Did he simply mean that if things worked out well, he'd consider me for a part? Or did it mean something far less appetizing? I felt like clearing the air with him once and for all. He didn't seem to be an unreasonable man. On the other hand, what could I have said that wouldn't sound either incredibly naive or downright insulting? I decided to stick to my original plan and just take things as they came. It wasn't like I hadn't been in similar situations before. I was certain I could handle Mr. Sol Silverstein if it came to that. Like I said, my mother had taught me a trick or two about stringing a man along.

15

The party was in a building down near Second Avenue, a few blocks away from Dag Hammarskjöld Plaza. The revelry was already in full swing as we exited the elevator onto the sixth floor and walked into the apartment. We were greeted by two huge Irish wolfhounds who sniffed at us curiously for a moment or two and then followed us expectantly, as if hoping to be taken for a walk. Sol took off his coat, handed it to a woman who appeared miraculously out of nowhere to take it, and left me behind as he drifted into the melee of party goers cramming the small living room.

"Hey, Sol," a man yelled over the blaring music, some kind of industrial rock. He raised a glass of coppery liquid over the head of the crowd. He was wearing an improbably bad hairpiece of golden curls that made no attempt to match the thin graying hair at his temples. "You sonovabitch. You're still alive!"

"Fucking doctors did their best to kill me, but I lived anyway. They had me laid open like that bitch in *Bloodfeast!*"

"Dammit. You could at least have given me permission to film it."

"And let you take the credit, Jack, you two-timing opportunistic piece of shit? I'd have rather died."

"What an ungrateful prick. To think, I had such a touching eulogy planned for you. I still have it right here," the man said, touching the back pocket of his pants. "Just in case you keel over tonight."

There was laughter all around and the two men hugged, sloppily kissing each other on the cheek.

Meanwhile, I took off my coat and held it awkwardly over my arm, looking for the refreshment table. I found it against the wall outside the kitchen. Among the usual munchies, there were bottles of booze of every kind, a candy bowl full of multicolored capsules, and a dinner plate on which lay a couple of rolled joints. A girl who looked to be around sixteen, her red hair sticking up messily from her head, her gown slipping off her immature frame was carefully laying down a line of coke with a spoon from a large gravy boat filled with the white powder. She leaned down over the table on which a mirror had been provided for just that purpose and with a small cocktail straw sniffed the drug expertly into each nostril. She stood up shakily on a pair of scarlet high-heeled strap sandals.

"Good stuff," she muttered, her eyes red-rimmed and bleary. "Try some?"

"No thanks," I said.

"Great party, huh?" she said.

I looked around. "Yeah," I said. "Great."

I didn't want to burst her bubble, but I'd been to dozens of these kinds of parties before, especially during my stay in L.A. If anything, this was a poor man's version of those marathon debauches. I looked at the poor girl, her lips and boobs already cosmetically altered, looking more freakish than sexy on a girl her age, and wanted to tell her that she was wasting her time, that nothing ever good came of attending such parties, not at her age anyway. She would just be someone's easy lay, tossed out in the street by morning, wobbling her way home with a broken heel and nothing but a handbag full of broken promises, and maybe enough cab fare to get her home safely if the scumbag who laid her had any class whatsoever.

"How old are you anyway?" I asked.

"Twenty-one," she said defensively.

"Twenty-one, huh?"

"Yeah. I'm going to be an actress."

"Really?"

"Yeah. Royce, my manager, he says I've got real potential."

"You ever done any work?"

"No. But I've done some live performance. Dancing and stuff, you know."

"Yeah, I know. Good luck."

"Thanks," she said.

I saved her the sermon and saved myself the breath. She wouldn't have listened to me anyway. I heard a fresh round of boisterous laughter and turned around to see Sol pulling up his shirt to show his bypass and colostomy scars.

I poured myself a glass of wine from a bottle that had been sealed, to ensure that no one had spiked it with something hallucinatory, found a relatively quiet place to sit down, and laid my coat over the arm of the sofa. One of the Irish wolfhounds walked over, looked at me apologetically, and then squatted down to pee on an expensive-looking throw rug.

No one noticed.

I nursed the wine and watched the swirl of activity around me like a bystander watching a merry-go-round. I knew I should be up, working the crowd, throwing my line out for nibbles, but somehow my heart just wasn't in it.

As if for the first time I saw the desperation behind the too-wide smiles, the shrewdness in each earnest glance, the death grip of even the most casual touch. Every word, every laugh, every move was carefully calculated. I felt like I was in the middle of a real-life play and everyone in it was an unsympathetic character. I got up and asked a woman I took to be the hostess where the bathroom was.

She had the eyes of a fifty-year-old, but the kind of uneasy beauty of a woman whose face looked as if it had been stretched with hooks hidden in her bottle-blond hair and dipped in plastic. She was wearing a red pants suit with low cleavage, showing off more plastic than a pair of beach balls, and a butt that not even the miracle of modern science could quite turn back the clock on.

She pointed me down a short hall.

"Third door on the left."

There was laughter and cursing coming from the rooms along the hallway, squeals and shouts of mock outrage. The door to the bathroom was half open. I knocked, heard nothing, and pushed it open.

A woman was sitting on the toilet, her top open, another woman kneeling between her legs.

The woman on the toilet looked up, her makeup smeared, her hair a mess. She took a joint from between her lips.

"What's up?" she said.

"I wanted to use the bathroom."

"We'll be done soon," she said. "But if it's an emergency, you can go in there." She pointed at the bathtub. Inside of the tub a naked man was lying on his back. He had a bloated fish-white belly and saggy old man's breasts. He was passed out, snoring. "He won't mind. In fact, if you wake him up, he'll pay you fifty bucks."

"No thanks," I said, "I think I'll wait."

"Suit yourself," the woman said.

I went back into the living room. Someone had replaced the industrial rock blaring on the stereo with Billy Idol. At one point or another, some man or other would come up to me and start up the kind of inane conversation that had no purpose but as a prelude to sex. I was just polite enough not to be offensive and to let him know I wasn't interested. They had nothing to offer me. For better or worse, my fate tonight was entwined with Mr. Silverstein's. I hoped, for both our sakes, he was doing better than I.

It must have been nearly three in the morning when the party began breaking up. The Irish wolfhounds were asleep in the corner, two guys in tuxedos were trying to slap awake some woman with a needle hanging from inside her elbow, and someone was vomiting in the kitchen sink. Mr. Silverstein and Jack were embracing again, kissing each other, promising each other the future. I was searching around for my coat, which wasn't where I had left it, when Mr. Silverstein came to collect me. It was the first time he had paid attention to me since we arrived at the party.

"Let's go," he said brusquely.

"I can't find my coat."

"Fuck your coat. We're taking the car. It's right downstairs."

"But I need my coat. It's my good winter coat."

"I said fuck your coat. I'll buy you another one."

I gave up looking for the coat. Someone had probably taken it by mistake anyway.

Damn.

I didn't have the money to throw away on a new coat.

"So what did you think of the party?" Mr. Silverstein asked as we were settled back in the car.

"It was fine," I said, hugging myself, teeth chattering, waiting for the heat from the car to chase away the chill I'd gotten walking from the building.

"Better than fine," Mr. Silverstein said. "Jack and I, we're gonna get this thing off the ground yet. Still cold?"

"Yeah."

"Move over. Let me warm you up."

Here it comes, I thought.

"Come on," Mr. Silverstein said. "I won't bite. Well—"

He started laughing.

I moved over on the seat and he put his arm around me, drawing me closer to his body, his cheap cologne failing, unable to mask the unappealing stench of alcohol, smoke, body odor, and flatulence trapped in his clothes.

"I'd like to go home now," I said.

"In a little while. I just want to take a drive around. It's been so long since I've been in the city. Times Square," he said to the driver.

I saw the empty streets pass by the window as I lay stiff and unmoving against Mr. Silverstein's side. He did nothing more than keep his arm around my shoulders, as if he were really only trying to keep me warm. I still couldn't figure him out. Maybe, in his own way, he was a nice guy, after all. Whatever his intentions, he had me off balance and that was not good. I had to be careful. This was going to be even trickier than I thought.

"Look at this," he said, letting me go.

I sat upright in my seat. Outside the window Forty-second Street flashed by.

"I remember when this was the sex mecca of the world. You could buy anything out on these streets. Now look at it. Guiliani came in and the bastard tore it all down just like he said he would. Now Disney owns it all. Jesus Christ. They turned Sodom and Gomorrah over to a bunch of fucking mouseketeers. They told me all about it. But I still wouldn't have believed it if I didn't see it with my own eyes."

We were driving west now, toward the wharves, when Mr. Silverstein called out to the driver.

"Slow down."

Up ahead I saw a group of women standing near an empty parking lot. We pulled up alongside the women, who began strutting back and forth on high heels, letting their asses twitch in skirts impossibly short for the season.

"That one," Mr. Silverstein said.

The driver followed Mr. Silverstein's finger to a woman with teased platinum hair and a short, white fake fur. As the car pulled up beside her, she turned her face, hollow and wasted in the headlights, her taut pale skin looking even more deathlike for the black and blue makeup around her huge eyes. She let her fake white mini fur fall open to reveal two pointy little breasts beneath a spangled tank top. Mr. Silverstein let down his window and she leaned into the car.

"What are you doing?" I said.

He ignored me. "Want to party?"

The woman looked at him and then at me.

"Sure," she said. "Why not? Cost you double, though."

"No problem. You make it memorable, I'll pay you triple. Get in."

"Mr. Silverstein—"

He opened up the door and the woman climbed into the car. We pulled away from the curb.

"Let's see some green," the woman said.

It was only after she'd settled into the seat and I got a closer look at her face that I saw the slight shadow on her cheeks, the bulge in her throat, the skinny but bony oversized hands.

"Mr. Silverstein, I want to go home."

The transvestite looked at me with undisguised hostility.

"Is she going to be a problem?" h/she said.

"No," Mr. Silverstein said. "Not if she knows what's good for her."

"Mr. Silverstein I want to go home right now."

"You're making a big mistake, Joan."

"Goddammit my name is Johanna and you're the one whose made the big mistake, you fucking sleazebag pervert."

"This isn't the way the game is played."

"This isn't the game I want to play. Now you take me home right now or I'm pressing charges."

The prostitute lit up a cigarette and looked bored.

"Look," h/she said, "I've got a few more hours of work left. Either you let her out of the fucking car or me. If not, you better intend on paying me to listen to this little lovers' squabble."

"You stupid cunt." Mr. Silverstein screamed at me. "You're nothing. Do you realize that? You're absolutely nothing."

"You're nothing!" I thundered. "Nothing but a washed-up hack. You're every stereotype in the book. I'd rather never make it in this business then end up like you."

"Well, you've got your fucking wish. Stop the car."

"Here?"

"Yeah, here. Stop the fucking car."

"You can't let me off here," I protested.

"Get out," Mr. Silverstein said.

"I don't even have a coat. You made me leave it—"

"Get the fuck out of my car. Now!"

"You bastard!" I shouted back, yanking open the door. "You fucking bastard."

He reached into his pocket and threw a couple of dollar bills onto the sidewalk after me.

"That's for the subway. Don't let anyone ever say that Sol Silverstein is not a fucking gentleman."

16

The car screeched away from the curb and I stood there in a cloud of exhaust, tears stinging my eyes. It was still dark. I was freezing. I was scared.

I bent down and picked up the money he'd thrown after me. *Bastard.*

Even with the money in my purse, I didn't have enough for a cab all the way back to Queens, not that I could have found one in that neighborhood at that hour anyway. I walked shivering down the street, looking for a subway entrance. I had never been in this part of town before. Of course not. Why would I be? There was nothing here. Not even a subway entrance, apparently. No way to get in. No way to get out.

A cat yelled from somewhere and my heart doubled its rhythm.

Somehow our popular mayor's plan for urban renewal had completely missed this area. On either side of me rose abandoned buildings slowly crumbling under the force of gravity and neglect. At least they looked abandoned. Surely no one would pay to live in them. Unfortunately, that didn't necessarily mean they were empty. The walls were splashed with graffitti, the violent alphabet of the dispossessed, whose language I didn't understand, but whose message was clear. I wasn't welcome here. I looked up nervously at the broken windows, jagged edges glistening in the moonlight, feeling unseen eyes crawling over me.

In a space between two buildings there was an opening the size of a man. I held my breath and hurried past it, staring sideways down an alley so black it seemed to stretch to the black heart of hell itself. I felt a cold wind blow down the back of my neck. I hurried my pace, not daring to look behind me, as if staring straight ahead could keep the footsteps in my imagination from becoming a reality. I could almost feel my head being yanked back by the hair, the edge of the knife sliding across my throat, cutting off my cry for help as it spilled my life.

I crossed the street, heels clacking in the silence, sounding all too vulnerable. I was heading vaguely in the direction of Grand Central Station. It was too cold and too far to make it there on foot, but it was the closest place to where I was that I knew of that offered any hope of warmth and safety. I also figured that there was a better chance of finding a subway entrance the closer I got to the station. I was hugging myself against the cold, teeth chattering, walking as fast as I could, trying to outpace the irrational, dreamlike fear that I would never find my way home. It was all I could do not to give in to the overwhelming urge to just sit on the shattered steps of one of the crumbling buildings that lined my path and weep.

I turned a corner and nearly let out a shout of joy.

Just ahead I saw the sign over the steps leading to the shadowy underground of the subway.

I was never so happy to see a subway entrance in my life. But that happiness was short-lived. I was halfway toward it when I saw that the stairs were blocked off, a dented sign, its letters all but worn away, announcing that the entrance was under repair.

No. No. No.

The words echoed in my head and now I really did feel tears stinging around the rims of my eyes.

"What's matter, lady? Missed your train?"

There was laughter, mocking, humorless.

I had lived in the city enough years to have imagined this scenario a hundred times. Each time I imagined what I would do under the circumstances. But what I did now wasn't what I had so carefully planned.

I just stood there, frozen.

Even my heart seemed to have stopped.

The only thing that was still going was my brain. It was racing a million miles a minute. *Scream,* it said. But my voice was gone. *Run,* it said. But my knees had turned to jelly. I remembered the small can of pepper spray I carried in my purse. Stephen had given it to me years ago. He'd shown me how to use it, testing it, over my objections, on a dog which someone had let off its leash in the park. The dog had gone running off blindly into the bushes, yelping in pain. It all seemed so simple. You took out the can, sprayed it at your attackers, and ran away.

It made you feel safe.

Like a lucky charm.

And just about as effective.

I stood there paralyzed, feeling a hand on my shoulder.

"I talkin' to you, lady."

I was roughly spun around, off balance, nearly falling.

There were two of them. One was wearing a bulky parka, a black stocking cap peaked high on his head. The taller one was wearing a padded nylon jacket with the logo of some sports team or other, his head framed by a black hood. They were young, probably no more than twenty, their faces handsome, but their eyes were hard and cold and absolutely without mercy.

"Whatsa matter, you lost?" the short one said, not even his bulky parka able to hide his well-built body.

"Yes," I said quietly.

"This ain't no place to be lost in," he said. "Lots of people get lost here. Never get found."

The taller one started laughing again, but this time his laughter was clearly faked. He eyed me carefully, other things on his mind. "Why ain't you wearing any clothes?" he said.

"It's a long story."

"We got a place to keep you warm."

"No, thank you. I really just want to get to a subway."

"Ain't no subway round here," the taller one said. He turned to his friend. "You see a subway around here?"

They both turned their heads around in pantomime.

"Nope. But I know a place we can keep you warm."

"Please, I'd just like to go home."

"You sure is lookin' fine tonight, ain't she, Jug?" the heavy-set one said.

"Sure is."

"Know what I'm thinkin'?"

"What's that?"

"Lady like this shouldn't be out unescorted. Could be dangerous. I'm thinkin' she be safer with us."

"I think you right," the taller one said.

"I don't think—"

"You rejectin' my kind offer, bitch?" the boy in the parka said. "I don't think you wanna do that." He turned to his friend. "She don't wanna do that, do she?"

"Nope. She don't wanna do that."

They grabbed me by the arms and started dragging me down the street.

This is it, I thought, a strange, almost impersonal calm descending over me, even as I struggled in their grip. *This is it. I'm going to be killed.*

With that certainty came a renewed clarity. I was no longer paralyzed by fear. I might get killed, but I wouldn't go down without a fight.

All of a sudden our three shadows were thrown against a brick wall as a pair of headlights swung behind us. We all turned at once. I felt my two assailants drop my arms, backing away from me, trying to get out of range of the lights.

"Hey," the taller one said. "It's just a fuckin' cabbie. What the fuck you want, man?" he yelled at the lights. "Nobody called you. Go on up to Fifth Avenue. This ain't none of your business."

"I'm making it my business."

"Get the fuck out of here before we fuck you up."

"Ain't nobody going to fuck nobody up," the voice from the car said. "You're gonna let her go and get gone."

"Shee-it," the heavy-set boy in the parka said to his friend. "It's the Lone fucking Ranger. What makes you think you giving the rules here, Lone Ranger?"

"I got a radio in this car and I seen your faces."

"You get your ass out of here, you dumb motherfucker," he said derisively. "So you got a radio in your fucking car. And you seen our faces. That the best you got?"

The door to the cab swung open and I felt the boys beside me tense with excitement. But for the first time there was a sense of uncertainty about them.

The man climbed out of the cab, walked around the front, and stood between the two headlights.

"That's it, motherfucker, you're fucked."

The boys started forward and the man raised his arm with a mechanical ratcheting sound. Suddenly a gun appeared in his right hand.

"No," the cabbie said. "That's not all I've got. I got this."

"Okay, motherfucker okay." The two boys stepped back, hands in the air, their faces smiling, their eyes filled with hatred. "No problem. You take the bitch home."

"Come on," the cabbie said. "Let's go."

I stood there for a second, too stunned to move.

"Hurry up!"

I shook myself from my trance and staggered forward to the cab. The cabbie walked carefully around to the driver's side, his gun aimed steadily at the two boys, and climbed into the car. He jammed it into reverse, did a 180, and left a trail of screeching rubber on the road.

"That was close," he said.

"Thank you," I said, trembling, but no longer from the cold.

"No problem."

For the first time I looked at the side of his face in the light of the intermittent street lamps.

"Harry. Harry Krinkle."

He looked away from the street for a moment, gave me a DeNiro-like grin, and stared back out the windshield.

"I didn't know you drove a cab."

"Makes ends meet," he said. "You look cold. There's an all-night place not far from here. It's a filthy little hole-in-the-wall, but it's always open. Would you like to stop for a cup of coffee?"

"I don't know," I said. "It's been kind of a rough night. I'd really just like to get home."

"Look at you," he said. "You're shivering. You need something to warm you up. Besides, you look like you can use somebody to talk to."

I didn't want this night to last any longer than it already had, but considering what Harry had done, I could hardly refuse him a cup of coffee.

"All right," I said reluctantly.

He hadn't exaggerated. The place he stopped at was a dive. The walls were the combined color of smoke, age, and regret. This was a place where the sleepless came: prostitutes, hustlers, con men, alcoholics, and mad poets, all of society's outcasts.

Including out-of-work actors.

We took two seats at the end of the counter. Harry ordered two coffees. I stared into my cup. The coffee looked thicker than used motor oil, but it was piping hot. I put my hands around the cup to warm them. Beside me, Harry tore open packet after packet of sugar and stirred them into his coffee.

"You're still shivering," he said. "Here."

He took off his coat, some kind of drab, olive-green army surplus jacket.

"No, I'm all right, really."

He didn't listen. He held the coat out until I slipped my arms into the sleeves. The coat was warm from the heat of his body and felt good.

"Thank you," I said.

"No problem."

"I mean thank you for everything. Back there. That was really fantastic."

"That," he said. "That was nothing."

"What do you mean? It was like something out of a movie."

He smiled, waved me off, and slurped at his coffee.

"What were you even doing in that area? I didn't see another cab anywhere. You can't pick up a lot of fares there."

"I like going places no one else goes. You get to see a lot of things no one else sees. You meet some interesting people."

"Like those two guys?"

"They were just punks."

"Is it like research? You know. For acting?"

"You might say that."

He slurped at his coffee again.

"It's a dangerous way to do research."

Harry didn't say anything for a while. Then he swiveled on his stool and faced me. "What were you doing down there?"

I stared down into the black hole of my coffee. "Oh, please, I'd rather not even say."

"Come on," he said.

"It's embarrassing."

"You don't have to be embarrassed in front of me."

I looked into his eyes, even blacker than the coffee, but without the least trace of bitterness. They were kind eyes. Eyes that had seen some of the ugliness and disappointment of the world, but had retained their humanity in spite of it. I was tired, drained, and depressed. I looked into his eyes and knew I would find no judgment there, no matter what I did.

He didn't speak for a long time after I was finished recounting the events of an evening that now seemed like it began a thousand years ago. He only opened another three packets of sugar and stirred them into his now cold coffee.

"You know," he said at last, "you don't have to do stuff like that. Why do you want to do stuff like that?"

"I didn't want to." I took a small sip of my coffee. Not only was it cold, but it tasted like it was about two days old. I put the cup down carefully on the saucer. "My agent said it might be good for my career."

He moved forward so quickly on his stool that I instinctively drew back.

"Your agent don't know shit," he said, a little too loud. Some of the patrons at the counter turned their heads lazily in our direction. "What the fuck are you looking at?" Harry said angrily. No one said anything. "Mind your coffee, will you? We're trying to have a private conversation here."

Fortunately, everyone looked too tired and beaten down to rise to the occasion of a confrontation. Or maybe they just didn't give a damn. Slowly, one by one, they turned away, resuming their meditation into the black holes of their own coffee cups.

He waited until every last one had swiveled around.

"Jesus Christ," Harry muttered. "People have no manners anymore. Nobody can mind their own fucking business."

"It's okay, Harry," I said, trying to calm him down.

"Look at you," he said, lowering his voice and looking over his shoulder. No one dared to look in our direction. He turned back to me, his eyes dark and earnest. "You're beautiful, you're intelligent, you're talented. That kind of stuff, that's not for someone like you."

"That's kind of you to say."

"No, I mean it," he said, finishing his coffee. "You've got to believe in yourself. You can't listen to people like that. They aren't going to help you. They're only going to use you."

"It's just that I've been in this business a long time and nothing much seems to be happening for me."

"Maybe it's not meant to be." Harry stopped talking as the waitress came by with the pot of coffee. He watched her closely, almost suspiciously as she refilled it, and waited for her to walk back toward the grill before talking again. "I'm not saying it won't happen. But even if you don't make it, you can do other things with your life. You don't want to do that. You'd never respect yourself. You've got to be able to respect yourself."

"I guess you're right."

"You know I'm right. You think about it."

"I will."

"You promise?"

"I promise."

I would have promised anything right then. I was so tired I could have fallen asleep perched on that stool.

Mercifully, a few minutes later we were back in the cab, approaching Grand Central Station.

"You can let me off here," I said, the lights and hubub of the station forcing me to squint. Even at this hour, people were coming and going. "I'll catch a train the rest of the way."

"It's okay," Harry said, his eyes flicking up in the rearview. "I'll drive you. Where do you live?"

He sped passed the station and headed down a sidestreet for the bridge.

"You don't understand. I don't have enough money to pay you."

He reached over and shut off the meter.

"Don't worry about it." He smiled that DeNiro smile again. "The ride's on me."

I appreciated what he'd done for me. I'd even trusted him to tell him what had happened tonight, even if it was under duress. But the whole *Taxi Driver* thing was a little too weird for me. I really didn't want him knowing where I lived. Still, I could think of no way of refusing his offer that wouldn't be insulting.

"Queens," I said.

We drove the rest of the way almost in silence. He asked me the name of my street and I considered giving him an address a couple of blocks away and then walking the rest of the way after he drove off, but I figured he'd probably insist on sitting at the curb until I got into the building.

"What floor do you live on?"

I told him.

"I'll wait until I see the light come on."

"That's not necessary."

He shrugged. "I got you this far. I want to make sure you get in safely."

I didn't argue. "Thanks again," I said.

"Don't mention it."

I pushed open the door.

"Johanna?"

"Yes?"

He looked out the windshield, smiled, looked at me, and looked back out the window. He shook his head, turned, and looked at me again.

"I was just thinking. I mean if you're not too busy. Maybe sometime you'd like to see a movie with me or something."

"Oh I'm sorry, Harry. I'm kind of involved right now."

"I understand," he said, smiling again. DeNiro trying to be gallant, tough and vulnerable at the same time. He wasn't my type—he was nobody's type. Yeah, he'd heard the line a million times before. Go ahead, I understand. Let me just put the car in gear and I'll drive off alone into the night where I belong.

He was wearing that kind of DeNiro smile.

The fact was I would have blown him off even if what I'd said wasn't true. But it was true and I wanted him to know it.

"Really. It kind of just happened. In fact, we're going away in a few days. I'm really sorry."

He lifted his hand. The lie, the truth, it didn't matter to him. His eyes were already on the dark road ahead, the street lamps sparkling in his half-amused eyes.

"There's no need to be sorry. It's nice to have someone. I hope you have a good time."

"Good night, Harry."

"Good night, Johanna. You remember what I said."

"I will."

"You promised." He smiled.

I barely had the strength to climb the stairs to my apartment. I opened the heavy lock, turned on the lights, and went to the window.

Sure enough, Harry's cab was sitting at the curb. I gave him a little wave and he slowly pulled away.

I stripped off my clothes and threw them in the trash, stockings, underwear, shoes, and all. I then took a scalding shower, wrapped myself up in my thickest terrycloth bathrobe, slipped my feet into a fluffy pair of slippers, and made myself a cup of chamomile tea.

I sat on the sofa and watched an infomercial about an improbable new exercise machine that you only had to use for four minutes a day.

I gathered the robe around me, sinking back against the cushion, trying to warm my hands around the hot teacup. My teeth were still chattering. The cold was in my bones. I finally got up and turned up the heat as high as it would go. I put my hand near the vent, but felt just the barest hint of warmth coming out. I cursed Mr. Kazantzakis. He advertised free heat for a good reason. The building didn't have much heat.

I grabbed the quilt from the bed, went back to the living room, and covered myself with it as I sat on the sofa. Still, no matter what I did, I couldn't seem to keep warm. I thought about what had happened. Jesus, what a disaster. I began to shake uncontrollably and the tears flowed down my cheeks. It was then I realized that the cold I felt had nothing to do with the temperature.

I must have fallen asleep, because the next thing I knew I heard the phone ringing and the sun was streaming in through the windows.

I kicked off the quilt and scuffed my way groggily toward the phone. The apartment felt like an oven.

"Hello?"

"You blew it, Johanna. I went out on a limb for you. And this is how you repay me?"

"Ruth," I said.

"You made me look like a fool. I told Sol you understood. That you knew your way around. And you pull this princess shit. He is a friend of mine. You know what friends are worth in this business?"

"Ruth, you don't understand. Do you know what he wanted me to do?"

"All I know is that you embarrassed me. I have a reputation to maintain in this business."

"A reputation? A reputation as what, may I ask?"

"Don't play the ingenue with me, Johanna. We both know the score. At least I thought we did. I thought you were smart enough to play the game. I was wrong."

"If you thought I was playing that kind of game, you're damn right you were wrong."

"When you're ready to stop waiting for that fairy-tale ending and live in the real world, call me."

"Don't hold your breath."

I slammed the phone down.

Well, that was that.

No job. No money. No agent. No future.

I'd had a decision to make. It seemed like events had made that decision for me. To be honest, it was a decision I had wanted to make all along.

Sorry, Ruth.

I wasn't giving up on that fairy-tale ending just yet.

17

---•---

"People just don't pick up and leave everything behind for someone they only met two weeks ago."

Cindy and I were walking along the footpaths through Central Park. We had stopped at a vendor and bought a couple of big warm pretzels, the kind studded with salt you'd swear the sanitation department used on the streets during a winter storm. The cold weather had given the city a reprieve and the mercury had climbed all the way into the low forties. It was lunch hour and the park was crowded with workers from the surrounding office buildings, looking for a few minutes of fresh air and sunshine. Cindy had a day off from shooting and I had taken the afternoon off from packing.

"Why not?" I said. "Nothing's happening for me in New York right now. It'll be nice to get away."

"It's just not a good idea," Cindy said stubbornly.

"You still haven't given me one good reason why I shouldn't go."

"I've given you the most important. You hardly know the guy."

"What's to know? He's brilliant, good looking, and sexy."

"That's not enough."

"Are you telling me you've never gone away with a man after only a few dates?"

I took a bite of my pretzel. I knew I had her there.

"That was different. I only left for a weekend, a week at the most. You're planning to go away for the entire winter."

"What will I be missing? Another date with some sleazeball producer and a threesome by the wharves with a transvestite prostitute? No thanks." I had already told Cindy about my disastrous meeting with Sol Silverstein and its nearly deadly aftermath. "Besides, Ruth has written me off. She doesn't see me as anything more than a piece of meat to dangle in front of some desperate bottom-feeders. She won't take me back until I accept that. She calls it being realistic. She was really pissed off about the way I handled the whole affair with Silverstein."

Cindy frowned. "Jesus. I'm sorry, Jo."

"Sorry for what?"

"Ruth. I'm responsible for you getting hooked up with her in the first place. I had no idea that was how she operated. I thought she was strictly on the up and up."

"It's not your fault. No other agent was willing to touch me anyway."

"You deserve better."

"But I'm not getting anything better. Can't you see, Cindy? It's just not happening for me here."

"You never know," Cindy offered. "A part could come up."

"A part hasn't come up in three years. Besides, you're on the inside now. You can keep me posted."

We walked past a bronze statue that someone had erected of a sled dog. I always thought it was an incongruous place for a statue of a sled dog. It must have done something really important, like save a life or something. I had always meant to read the plaque bolted into the stone beneath the statue, but never did. We turned the corner and headed in the direction of the zoo.

"I don't know," Cindy said, chewing her pretzel thoughtfully. "You still haven't told me what his intentions are."

I burst out laughing.

"What the hell is so funny?" Cindy wanted to know.

"His intentions," I managed to blurt out. "Who are you, my father?"

"I'm just wondering what he intends to do with you all alone in a cabin in the Maine woods. Are you supposed to be his concubine, his entertainment, someone to keep him warm through the long cold months, or what? And what happens when the winter is over? Does he just drop you back off in the city and say thanks and you never see him again?"

I'd finally stopped laughing. I had to admit I had thought of those very same questions myself. I shrugged, and gave Cindy the same answer I'd given myself.

"Whatever happens happens. Who knows, maybe after a couple of months alone I'll be sick of him."

* * *

It had been a hectic couple of days. Matt had returned on schedule and we'd gone out that very night. He took me to the theater, then to Sardi's, and afterward to a romantic little piano bar I'd never even known existed. He looked handsomer than ever in a dark blue sweater and blue wool sports jacket. We met in front of the theater and I liked the way his eyes lit up when he saw me approaching.

"I missed you," he said. "God, I've missed you."

He hugged me tight and kissed me with a hunger that told me more about the way he felt than any words he could have spoken.

"You should have worn something warmer," he said, looking at my coat. "You must be cold."

He took my arm, pulling me close, and I leaned against him as we walked down the street, taking a sensual pleasure in his warm, masculine strength and in the curiously pleasant feeling of being claimed by this powerful, handsome, and charismatic man.

All evening I waited for him to ask the question, but he didn't say a word. It hung over us like a cloud. I kept hoping he would just bring the subject up and get it out of the way so we could enjoy the rest of the evening. But, maddeningly, we talked of everything but Maine. I was beginning to wonder if he had forgotten his offer or had simply changed his mind. Maybe, I wondered, he was just playing with me. Had I somehow given myself away? Had he sensed my desperation? I hadn't said a word about my experience with Sol Silverstein. Or about my experience with Ms. Parker.

It was driving me crazy. There was no way, of course, that I could bring it up. I was tempted. Sorely tempted. After all, we were living in the age of liberation, an age when a woman could ask a man out and all that. Still, there was something about the game—pursuer and pursued—that seemed thrown off when the traditional roles were reversed. I didn't think Matt was the type that played games. But once again my mother's voice spoke in the back of my head. And even if I didn't agree with the way she ran her life, one thing I did have to admit: Mother knew how to attract a man.

So I kept quiet, made polite chitchat, smiled pleasantly, and all the while burned inside with impatience and growing resentment. Finally, with a bashfulness that made me regret all my earlier doubts and misgivings about him, Matt asked me if I'd come to a decision about Maine.

"I was wondering when you were going to get around to that," I said.

"I didn't want to pressure you. And I didn't want to ruin the evening if you said no. I wanted tonight to be special either way."

"It would have been more special if you'd asked earlier," I said, smiling.

"Do you mean . . . ?"

He stiffened a little in his chair, his eyes filled with an endearing mix of expectancy and vulnerability.

"Yes," I said. "Yes."

He nearly knocked over our coffee cups reaching across the table.

"God, Johanna, I'd hardly dared to get my hopes up. This is fantastic. You're going to have a great time. We're going to have a great time."

He signaled for the waiter.

"A bottle of champagne please. The best you have."

"I thought you didn't drink," I said, as he poured the bubbling amber liquid from a bottle bearing an expensive-looking label that wasn't Dom Perignon.

"Tonight I'm making an exception."

He touched his champagne flute to mine, his eyes sparkling in the candlelight.

"Thank you," he said. "You've made me the happiest man in the world."

We nearly finished the magnum of champagne, chatting excitedly about what lay ahead, not even realizing that the piano had long since stopped playing, the other patrons had left, and the help was putting the chairs up on the empty tables all around us. Finally, our tired-looking waiter came up to apologize, but explained that we would have to leave. We apologized ourselves and thanked him for his patience. I noticed that Matt left him a fifty-percent tip.

Out on the street we stood and necked like teenagers until not even our happiness and passion could stave off the cold. Matt suggested we go back to his place.

"I'd love to," I said. "But I have so much to do."

"Can't it wait for tomorrow? I really want to be with you tonight. It's been so long."

I kissed Matt playfully on the cheek.

"Pretty soon we'll have all the time in the world."

Matt smiled. "You're right."

He hailed a cab, kissed me again, and this time there was nothing playful in my response.

"Just a little preview," I said as I ducked into the cab.

"I can't wait for the show to begin."

"Me either," I said.

I started packing that night. The next morning I started scrambling around for someone to sublet my apartment. It didn't turn out to be as hard as I'd thought. A friend of a friend of Stephen's knew a struggling model who couldn't afford Manhattan anymore and was looking for a place in the outlying burroughs. She came, took a look at the place, and declared it perfectly suited to her needs. I took her down to meet Mr. Kazantzakis and we worked out the arrangements. He wasn't thrilled with the prospect of a sublet, but I managed to assure him that Gloria would be a perfect tenant even though I didn't know a thing about her. In the end, I handed a thankful Gloria an extra set of keys. Of course I made no mention of my three a.m. visitor.

I spent the rest of the week packing, unpacking, and shopping for things I'd need. It was costly and time consuming, but I couldn't help but feel an overwhelming feeling of excitement. I thought about calling my mother and telling her what I was up to, but I didn't have the time or patience it would require to tell her the whole story. Besides, she had lately developed the annoying habit of interrupting whatever I was saying to launch into some long and often pointless tale of her own. I figured I would be gone and back before she even knew it.

My father, as I've said, was dead to me. I wouldn't have told him if I were getting married.

The only person I told was Cindy and she was still trying to talk me out of going.

"What if he turns out to be some kind of psycho?"

"His face is on the back of about forty thousand books," I said. "I'd say he was pretty harmless."

"All right. But what if he turns out to be a real creep? I mean writers can be real weirdos. I auditioned for a play once and the playwright demanded to see my feet. He rejected me outright. He said my big toes were too long."

"Hey, it may be your only fault, but your big toes are too long."

Cindy looked down at her feet, encased in a pair of size ten-and-a-half soft leather boots. "Yeah, you're right."

"If I don't like the situation, I can always get on a plane and fly home."

"Did you forget? You don't have a home. You've sublet your apartment. That's what I'm trying to say, you've turned your entire life upside down."

"Then I'll stay with you. How about that? Surely you can put up with me for a couple of months."

Cindy threw up her hands in resignation. "I give up. Do what you want. Whoever he is, I hope he makes you happy."

"Thanks," I said.

"By the way, I've been meaning to ask you. Where in the world did you ever get that ratty jacket?"

I looked at the bulky army surplus jacket I was wearing.

"It's Harry Krinkle's. You know, the guy from my acting class who rescued me on the street. He lent it to me because I lost my coat at the party. I forgot to give it back to him."

"Is he a Vietnam vet or something?"

"I don't know what he is," I said. "But thank God he was there when I needed him."

We were passing by the zoo, where there was a long line, mainly women and children, an occasional businessman with an hour or two to kill between appointments, waiting to get inside. There was a small snack bar outside the gates that catered to the zoo crowd, selling hot dogs, hamburgers, and soft drinks. I suggested to Cindy we go inside for a soda. The salt from the pretzel had made me terribly thirsty. We took a small table near the window and watched the people pass.

"So you're going to Maine?" Cindy said, taking the wrapper from her straw.

I pulled the end of the wrapper off mine, blew into the straw, and let the paper shoot across the table and hit her square in the forehead.

Cindy scrunched up her face. "Very mature."

"Yes, I'm going, silly."

"And there's nothing I can do to talk you out of it?"

"Nothing."

Cindy worked her straw through the plastic lid of her soda.

"So where exactly in Maine are you going?"

"I don't know. Some place like Green Cove or Green Hill. Something like that."

"I never even got to meet him," she said.

I took a swig of my Sprite.

"Maybe that's a good thing."

"That's not fair, Jo."

"Sorry. I don't think he's your type anyway."

"Probably not. I just want the best for you."

"I know. And I appreciate that, Cindy. I really do. But enough about me. How's the show going?"

"Pretty good. The director isn't as much of a prick as I thought he was. It's not quite what I'm used to, not that I've had enough experience to really get used to anything. But it's a daily show, so there's not much time for rehearsal. You pretty much have to act on the fly. It's kind of like the stage. Right now I'm just standing around watching. They've been working with me a little on the side to get me ready."

"When do they work in your story line?" I slid my straw in and out of the plastic lid, making a kind of squeaking, honking noise.

"I think I make my first appearance next week. You know the writers are already talking about expanding my part."

"That's great. So what's it like to work with real actors?"

"Some of them are really nice," Cindy said, sucking the last bit of soda through her straw. "But most of them wouldn't give you the time of day. And the stars, God, what prima donnas. You think you're watching a soap opera in front of the cameras—you should see the soap opera going on behind the cameras. Still, all in all, let me tell you, they're a hell of a lot better than workshop students."

"What about your costar? You're supposed to try to steal him away, if I remember correctly."

"His wife can have him as far as I'm concerned. He's the most obnoxious prick you can imagine. Unfortunately, he's the show's biggest draw."

I pushed my paper cup, still half-filled with soda across the table. "Like they say, that's why they call it acting."

We didn't talk any more about Matt or about me leaving for Maine. We left the snack bar and for a while watched the seals sunning themselves on their cement islands, occasionally slipping into the water to frolic. Finally we made our way out of the park, standing on Central Park South across the street from the Plaza Hotel and about a hundred yards from the spectacular equestrian statue of General William Tecumseh Sherman.

"I guess this is it," Cindy said.

"It's just for a couple of months. I'll call."

"So you say."

"I promise."

"Still, it won't be the same. I'm really going to miss you, Jo."

"You'll be so busy, you'll hardly know I'm gone."

"That's not true. Who am I going to call every time I want to complain about Brad?"

"Or whoever."

"Yeah," Cindy laughed. "Or whoever. Who am I going to go to the Peking Duck with?"

I could see tears forming in Cindy's eyes.

"Hey, don't get all emotional on me."

"I'm sorry, I can't help it."

"I know," I said, tears stinging my own eyes.

We threw our arms around each other and I no longer felt the need to hide my tears. They flowed freely down my cheeks, blotted out in the thick material of her camel's hair coat. We pulled away, sniffling.

"You'd think this was a scene from *Fried Green Tomatoes* or something." Cindy smiled, dabbing her cheeks.

"Well, we are actresses," I said, feeling a sudden stab of embarrassment. *She* was an actress.

"Good luck, Jo."

"You, too," I said.

We turned and walked away in separate directions. Cindy headed back to Midtown, I headed to Queens.

I spent the rest of the afternoon and early evening clearing out the closets for the sublet. I packed up the clothes I definitely wasn't taking with me and, with Mr. Kazantzakis's help, hauled them down to the storage area in the basement. After I was done, I went back upstairs and once again checked through the clothes I had decided to bring. I had bought all-new luggage to replace the tattered suitcases I'd first brought with me to New York what seemed like ages ago.

In the last few days, I had used my credit cards to refurbish my wardrobe. I wasn't sure what I was going to do when I got back. I wasn't thinking that far ahead. I suppose Cindy was right. I was being foolish. But I didn't care. I stopped my obsessive baggage rooting long enough to bake myself a vegiburger and heat up a can of soup, and then I continued packing, unpacking, and repacking items in my new Samsonite bags. Finally, I gave it all up, turned the television on low, and picked up one of Matt's books.

I read until I felt tired and headed for the bedroom where I changed and slipped under the covers. Before I turned out the light, I checked the clock.

Nearly one a.m.

My dark visitor hadn't come in days, not since I'd agreed to go to Maine with Matt. I almost wished he would show up. I felt I had unfinished business with him. It's strange how you can get used to the most bizarre circumstances. Somehow I felt I owed it to him to tell him that I was going away.

I wasn't disappointed. I woke up to the familiar sense of his presence in the bedroom doorway. I opened my eyes and there he was, no different than the first time, all dressed in black, a dark stocking or nylon ski mask pulled down over his face. He could have been anyone.

"You haven't been around for a while," I said.

"Miss me?"

"Not exactly. I've been sleeping better."

He gave a soft chuckle.

"Where've you been?"

"I've been busy."

"Breaking into other women's apartments?"

"That question is off base."

"Sorry. I forgot how touchy you are about breaking in here."

"Are you jealous?"

"That you might be interrupting the sleep of some other poor woman? I don't think so."

"You're being sarcastic again."

"I've got something to tell you."

"What is it?"

"I'm going to be leaving for a couple of months. Going out of town."

"With your man-friend."

He said it matter-of-factly and for a moment I felt a tingle of fear. What if my leaving became the catalyst for some kind of violence on his part? The end of our relationship might trigger his need for a climactic catharsis: rape, or even worse. Funny, how I hadn't thought of that until this moment.

"Yes," I almost whispered.

I saw him nod. "It was inevitable, I guess."

"You're not mad?"

"Why should I be mad?"

He seemed sincere, but I still wasn't relaxing. I was prepared to scream bloody murder if he set foot into the room.

"I don't know," I said. "I just thought you might be, that's all."

"I wish you luck."

"Thank you." I was still tense under the sheets, ready to bolt at the least threatening movement on his part. "Can I ask you a favor?"

"It depends."

"I have someone subletting the apartment. She's a model. Well, she's trying to be. I didn't tell her about you. I was kind of hoping you'd not break in here anymore. I don't think she'd understand."

"That's not a problem. I'm not interested in her. Only you."

"Can I ask you why me?"

"That question is off-base."

"I see."

"So I guess this is good-bye."

"I guess so. Unless you decide to come in the next two nights."

"No. We might as well say good-bye now. There's no sense in drawing it out."

"Good-bye then."

He nodded his sleek black head and turned on his heel. For the last time I heard him walk down the hall, open the door, and lock it carefully behind him.

I stayed awake for a long time after that. It was with a strange mixture of relief and sadness that I finally fell asleep.

18

———•———

We left LaGuardia on a cold, clear, sunny winter morning. It took a little less than two hours to reach the airport in Bangor, Maine. On the way, I pulled Matt's book out of my carry-on bag. Matt took one look at the book and blanched.

"Please," he said. "Don't read that now."

"Why not?"

"It's embarrassing. I'll be watching every expression on your face. Please, put it away."

I laughed. "Okay. If it's going to bother you that much. But you're being unfair. I'm dying to know how it turns out."

"I'll tell you."

"Don't you dare," I teased, stuffing the book back into my bag. Instead I pulled out a copy of *Variety* and listlessly thumbed through the announcements.

At the airport I received the unwelcome news that my luggage was missing. I tried to keep my calm as I filled out the papers at the desk across from the luggage carousel. I had over six hundred dollars worth of new clothes inside that luggage, not to mention the cost of the brand-new suitcases themselves. The only thing that wasn't lost was the new winter coat I had bought.

The woman behind the desk tried to reassure me that my luggage would probably come in on the next flight from New York, but that wasn't due in for another four hours. Matt suggested that we head for the chalet as we had a long drive ahead of us. He said we could always come back for my luggage the next day. When I argued that I had all of my clothes in the lost bags, he bade me not to worry. He had taken the liberty to buy me some things and had them delivered to the chalet.

"I'm sure you'll find something to suit your taste," he said.

"Okay," I said, still reluctant to leave my lost bags to fate. "Let's go."

His wood-paneled Jeep Grand Cherokee was parked in the airport lot where he said a friend had left it the night before. It was about fifteen degrees colder in Maine than it had been in New York and I rubbed my gloved hands together for warmth. Matt unlocked the passenger side door. As he put his own bags into the back, I climbed into the comfortable front seat, using my carry-on as a footrest.

Matt came around the side of the Jeep, slid into the driver's seat, and started the car, letting it warm up. He put on the heat and I felt a welcome blast of warm air fan my face and hands. He had bought me a hot cocoa back at the airport while I was filling out the papers at the luggage claim desk, even though I said I didn't want one. Now, as I pulled back the little tab on the plastic lid I was glad he had ignored my grouchiness.

A small cloud of steam rose from the hole in the lid and filled the car with the rich aroma of chocolate. The cup warmed my hands and I blew into the lid before carefully taking a small sip of the scalding cocoa.

"How is it?" Matt asked.

"Delicious. Thank you."

Matt smiled. He put the Jeep into gear and we crunched over dirty old rinds of snow as we made our way to the airport exit.

For the next two and a half hours we drove northwest into the dark pine-forested heart of Maine. The farther we drove, the higher the snow rose on either side of the cleared roadways. I saw road signs for towns like Dover-Foxcroft, Guilford, Dead Meadows. The last sign I remembered seeing was for a place called Green Hollow.

The warmth of the car, the airplane trip, the drink I'd had to steady my nerves before boarding the plane, and the smooth hum of the tires on the road soon made me drowsy and I fell asleep. When I woke up, a darkness like fine gray ash was sifting down over the road outside the window and we were passing a large lake, whose flat, semifrozen expanse stretched out as far as the eye could see. We drove for miles along the winding road into the mountains, without seeing so much as a sign announcing the presence of a town.

At one point, I looked out the side window and saw a doe standing tentatively by the side of the road among a stand of barren trees.

"Look," I said, "deer."

Matt glanced briefly. "You don't get out of the city much do you?"

"No, I guess not," I said, somewhat embarrassed. "But she is beautiful."

"Yes. You see a lot of deer this time of day. Unfortunately, twilight is dangerous for them. They lose a sense of the boundary between woods and road. A lot of them get run down that way. You see them scattered all along the side of this road, especially in the spring."

I turned and looked back to see if the doe had strayed out into the road, but she hadn't. I watched until the road veered off to the left and I lost sight of her.

Matt switched on his headlights as the darkness deepened. We drove another half hour, during which time I didn't see another road sign.

"This is it. We're home," he said.

"Home?" I said, sitting up in my seat and peering out at the impenetrable snowy woods. "I don't see anything."

"Exactly."

He turned off the main highway onto a narrow, single-lane road that hadn't been plowed, but whose covering of snow was well packed down with tire tracks. Matt switched the Jeep into four-wheel drive.

"Hang on," he said. "It gets a little bumpy."

The chalet was located in a secluded clearing about a mile up the road. I could see it mainly by the glow of the moon, which had risen large and full behind the house. It was a large, improvised A-frame structure of redwood and glass, set so naturally into the surrounding woods that it looked as if it were a part of the forest.

"It's beautiful," I whispered.

"I designed it myself," Matt said. "Drew up the blueprints and everything. Had a contractor come in and made certain he followed them to the letter. He argued with me almost every step of the way, but I knew what I wanted. He said it was impossible. I wouldn't listen. If I hadn't become a writer, I would have been an architect. I have to admit, I'm inordinately proud of the place."

He took me by the arm, my carry-on bag in the other hand, and led me down the path to the front door. I looked around into the dark pine forest surrounding the chalet.

"Do you have any neighbors?"

"That's the best part. Not a neighbor for miles. I own about ten acres of the surrounding land and the state owns the rest. It's held in trust by the Environmental Protection Agency. No one can build on it. I made sure of that before I bought the lot. I wanted privacy. Here I can be sure I won't be disturbed."

The path we walked down was clear of snow, two rounded burrows piled on each side, bluish in the moonlight. Obviously Matt had hired someone to shovel him out. From somewhere off in the woods to my left I could have sworn I'd actually heard an owl hoot. Not wanting to risk another city-girl crack, I kept my wonderment to myself.

Inside, the chalet was large and airy, the main living space dominated by a cathedral ceiling and the huge glass windows that afforded a perfect view of the thick blue-green pine trees. Along the side wall was a big flagstone fireplace. The furniture was about what one might expect from a man living alone in the woods: pine, with rough-textured cushions, an overstuffed easy chair, a large-screen television, and several tables that looked hand-made of highly polished wood. An Oriental rug that must have cost a fortune covered the hardwood floor.

And books.

In addition to the books stuffed into the shelves built into the walls, there were books on every available surface. On the tables, on the mantel, in a tall, precipitously leaning tower beside the easy chair. Inside nearly every book were sheets of paper, tags, and markers of various kinds, as if he were in the process of reading them all at once.

In the corner, by the kitchen, obscured by yet more piles of books, stood a computer on a small, unassuming wooden desk.

"I'm sorry it's a bit of a mess, but—" He shrugged. "I was going to make an excuse, but to be perfectly honest with you, it's always like this."

I sniffed the air; it smelled of something wet and burnt.

"That's the flue," he explained, walking over to the fireplace. "I'm afraid I forgot to shut it before I left last fall. No doubt the snow came down the chimney. That's why it's so damp and cold in here. Not to worry, though. I'll turn on the furnace and build us a big fire. We'll be warm and cozy in no time. Shall I show you upstairs?"

I followed him up a spiral staircase to a loft that overlooked the living room. There were two bedrooms separated by a small sitting area decorated simply with two overstuffed armchairs and a small table on which sat three more volumes of the seemingly omnipresent books.

Matt pointed to the room on the left and led me toward it.

"This will be your room."

My room, I thought, somewhat disappointed. I had just assumed that after what had already occurred between us, we'd be sharing a bed. Well, at least he wasn't pushy. And it would be nice to have a little privacy.

"What do you think?" he asked, as he opened the door on a room decorated in Victorian fashion, including lacy curtains and a canopied four-poster bed. If the rest of the house looked like it was decorated by a literary lumberjack, this room looked as if it were torn right out of the pages of *Victorian Digest*.

"It's lovely," I said. "Did you decorate it yourself?"

Matt laughed. "Right down to the last doily."

"What's in there?" I asked, pointing to the closed door of the room at the other end of the loft.

"That's my bedroom," he said. "It's not much to look at."

I followed him into my room. He put my bag down on the bed and opened the door to my own private bathroom. The bathroom was also decorated in a Victorian motif, including a luxuriously deep claw-footed bathtub. I decided I rather liked the setup of separate rooms after all. Matt pointed to a panel of folding doors.

"Your new wardrobe is in there. You can freshen up, pick out something to wear, and in the meantime I'll get the furnace up and running and rustle up some dinner. Take your time."

I walked around the room, looked out the window, tested out the bed, and waited until I heard the furnace kick on and the room begin filling with warm air. Then I undressed and headed for the bathroom. I ran the water, waiting for the icy flow to slowly turn hot before plugging the drain and letting the tub fill. I settled into the steamy water letting my body relax after the plane ride and the three-hour drive. I soaked until the water turned tepid, and then I climbed out of the tub and wrapped myself in a thick, thirsty towel.

I walked to the closet doors and pulled them open. Inside I found a variety of diaphanous gowns of varying lengths and delicacy. I shuffled through the hangers. There was absolutely nothing practical among the whole lot. What had he been thinking? I couldn't wear any of this stuff outside. How would I leave the house?

I was tempted to leave on the clothes I had worn from New York, but they were stale and travel worn, so I pulled out the most modest gown I could find, slipped it on over my naked skin, and examined myself in the mirror. If nothing else, it was a perfect fit.

I looked around for some shoes, found none, and since neither the boots I'd worn on the trip, nor the sneakers in my bag were appropriate for the delicacy of the gown I was wearing, I decided to go barefoot downstairs to dinner.

19

———•———

Matt turned from where he was kneeling by the fireplace, an orange tongue of flame licking the snow-covered pile of logs on the grate, and smiled up at me.

"I see you found something you liked."

I came down the stairs.

"Your tastes all seem to run in one direction," I quipped. "I don't know what I'm going to wear out of the house."

"Don't worry about that," Matt answered. "I'm sure your bags will turn up at the airport. If not, we can get you something in town."

He coaxed the fire by waving a couple of sheets of newspaper at it and then threw the paper onto the logs, where they burst into a sudden flash of orange light.

Matt stood up. He, too, had changed from his airplane clothes into a pair of thick corduroy pants and a dark blue velour pullover. His handsome face bore the not unflattering traces of a five o'clock shadow.

"I hope pasta with red pesto sauce is okay with you. It was all I could find in the cupboard. I'll have to go pick up some supplies tomorrow. The radio reported a big storm on its way tomorrow night. We might be snowed in for a couple of days."

"It smells delicious," I said.

"Great. Have a seat."

Matt went into the area designated as the kitchen: a wall of cabinets over a generous counter space interrupted only by a large refrigerator and range. He donned an apron and set about preparing two plates of pasta. As I sat down on one of the chairs at the large wooden dining table, I could smell the delicious aroma of the sauce bubbling on the stove.

"I'm afraid I didn't have my secret ingredient on hand. A half cup of burgundy," Matt said, "so I apologize in advance."

"I'm sure it'll be just fine," I assured him.

He set down a plate of pasta in front of me, the thin linguine covered with a rich, dark red sauce. He went back into the kitchen and pulled down a bottle of Chianti from a rack above the cabinet over the stove. He worked the cork and poured me a glass of the dark red wine.

"To warmth, discovery, and love," he said, lifting his glass, which was filled with mineral water, to mine.

I touched mine to his and took a sip of the wine, feeling it color my skin. I saw his eyes drift down the front of my gown to my breasts, which I knew were only barely hidden by the gauzy fabric, the aureoles of my nipples almost visible through the flimsy material. I suddenly felt naked before him. I could feel myself blushing and this time not from the wine. As if by force of will he tore his eyes away just before his gaze became impolite, put down his glass, and laughed good-naturedly to cover both our embarrassment.

"Dig in," he said.

The moment passed, we both set in to eat. I didn't realize how hungry I was. By the time I was finished, I'd had two helpings of Matt's pasta and three glasses of Chianti. I was feeling pleasantly warm and full when we settled into the couch in front of the fire, my feet tucked up under me, Matt's arm circling cozily around my shoulders. I laid my cheek against the soft material covering his broad chest, breathing in the pleasant smell of his Drakkar Noir cologne.

We sat like that for a long time, not saying anything, perfectly content, watching the flames lick the large gray logs, occasionally popping and snapping, sending a shower of orange sparks up the chimney like fireworks.

Finally I broke the silence.

"Have you lived out here a long time?"

"I split my time between here and the city. Personally, I've found New York is a good place to share art, not to create it."

"So you go back to the woods to write?"

"I don't think I've ever written one decent sentence in the city. I've tried, but I just can't seem to find the Muse on Fifty-seventh Street. Just businesswomen with briefcases and Reeboks."

"The muse?"

"The muses, actually. The ancient Greeks believed they were nine sisters: Calliope, Clio, Euterpe, Thalia, Melpomene, Terpsichore, Erato,

Polyhymnia, and Urania. They were the daughters of Zeus and Mnemosyne, the goddess of memory. Their presence was necessary if one was going to write even one inspired word. But I prefer Robert Graves's decidedly unclassical description of the Muse. She is a beautiful maiden with leprotic white skin and bloodred lips who inspires nothing less than an erotically charged life-and-death terror that makes the hair stand up on your skin."

"Is that what you feel when you write? Terror?"

"When I'm lucky. It's as if a deadly snake were slithering unseen somewhere in the room and all that stands between us is the written word."

I involuntarily looked around the baseboard of the cabin and shivered in spite of the warmth of the fire.

"Why do you do it if it's so painful?"

"That's the paradox. It may be painful, but I've never found anything as fulfilling."

"Well, one thing is for sure, I'll bet you don't have many distractions up here."

"No," Matt said. "That's one of the reasons I come up here to write. No visitors to take my mind off the work in progress. In fact, no one knows about this cabin except for my editor and she's sworn to secrecy."

"Boy, you really are protective about your privacy."

"One has to be. If you're not careful, there's no place you can get away from it all and create. What with computers and e-mail and faxes, the world's getting smaller and smaller. You might say privacy is a fetish of mine. An obsession, really. Without privacy, the Muse doesn't come."

"How long does it usually take you to write a book?"

"About six months. Five, if the Muse is particularly cooperative."

I calculated five months in my mind. I really didn't plan on being here until June, but there was still plenty of time to decide about that later, especially when I saw how things between Matt and me were working out. Right then I was more concerned with the effect of the synergy between the warmth of the fire, the smell of his cologne, and the proximity his body was working on my libido.

I looked up at his strong, darkly shadowed jaw and gave him a kiss. He smiled, turned his head, and kissed me back, a deep, lingering kiss, his hands going to my breasts where they seemed to have wanted to go all along. I slid my own hand to the front of his soft corduroy pants and felt him as stiff as the poker on the brass stand beside the fireplace. I rubbed him through his pants with one hand while I grabbed the curls of his dark hair with my other, pressing his sensual lips closer to mine, tasting his tongue in my mouth.

I increased the speed of my hand on the front of his pants until I could feel the warmth build up beneath my hand and then I fumbled for his zipper. But before I could free him, he pulled away suddenly, his eyes glowing in the firelight.

"Not tonight," he rasped, trying to catch his breath. "Work. I have to begin work. I have so many notes to transcribe."

"Can't it wait?" I said. "After all, we just got in tonight."

"I wish it could, darling," he said, glancing down once again at my breasts, now starkly visible under the gown. "But if I don't get started, I'll fall behind. Besides, you must be tired."

"Okay," I said reluctantly, if somewhat put off. I wasn't used to being the one turned down. I decided to make him pay for his unnatural masculine self-control with a good-night kiss I was sure would keep him thinking of me instead of his precious work.

He smiled a perfectly maddening smile. "Good try. I almost fell for it. You are an effective little muse after all. But believe me, you'll thank me for the extra sleep in the morning."

"Have a good time with your computer," I said coquettishly, and did my best sashay up the spiral staircase to my bedroom. I looked back down from the top of the stairs, but my effort was evidently wasted. Matt was already standing in front of his desk, booting up his computer.

I walked indignantly to my room, shut the door, and slid under the covers of the bed. Matt was right after all. I was exhausted. It was probably better that I went to bed early, even if I'd have preferred to fall asleep in his embrace. I stared out the window at a pine bough gently brushing the pane, its soft, hypnotic movement lulling the passion still coursing in my blood. In the end, the wine, the food, the travel won out. It was only a matter of minutes before I fell asleep.

Whether it was a matter of habit or the sound of Matt's voice, I woke a couple of hours later. The clock by my bedside wasn't illuminated, but an old-fashioned analog model. I picked it up and pulled it closer where I could read its face by the light of the full moon. It was three o'clock on the button.

I pulled off the covers and went to the door, but Matt's voice was still muffled. I opened the door a crack in order to hear better.

"What the hell do you mean I'm late? I can't help it if you need . . . Listen, I just got here, goddamn it. You can't expect me to work miracles."

I stepped out into the shadows of the landing where I was sure he couldn't see me. He was still sitting in front of the computer, his ruggedly handsome face blue in the light of the screen, the phone pressed to his ear. He was speaking in a harsh, strained voice into the receiver, obviously trying to keep his tone down.

"Money? How can that be? You've gotten more money than you could possibly ever have hoped to get. What have you been doing with it, anyway?"

I crouched down and crept closer to the railing. Matt had turned toward the window beside his desk, his back to me.

Who could he be talking to? His editor? His agent? It definitely seemed like a business call of one kind or another. Had he been talking about his next book when whoever it was on the other end intimated he was late?

"Listen, that's not my problem," Matt said coldly. "If you can't handle your own affairs, I'm not taking the responsibility. I'm not your baby-sitter."

He turned from the window and I jumped back from the railing into the shadows on the landing.

"Don't threaten me. I won't be threatened."

Whoever it was, they were definitely playing hardball. But Matt wasn't giving an inch.

"Oh no? It sure as hell sounds like a threat to me."

He reached back and ran his hands through his thick hair.

"All right, if you must know, I just met someone."

I felt the hairs on the back of my neck prickle. He was talking about me. How was I involved in this? Was I somehow to blame for whatever deadline trouble Matt seemed to be in with his publisher?

"Yeah, yeah," Matt said, "spare me the false congratulations. You can cut the crap."

I could still see Matt's profile from where I crouched. His jaw jutted forward, his teeth were clenched.

"That's none of your business."

Matt had turned again, this time directly toward the landing, and for a split second I felt my heart stop in mid-beat as he seemed to be looking directly at me. I knew that if I moved, not even the shadows would shield me. I stayed as still as a statue, the only thing moving was the pulse in my throat.

"Sure, you never mean any offense," Matt said sarcastically. He turned toward his computer, his finger pressing idly on a key, making row after row of a single character. I let out the breath I didn't even realize I was holding.

"It'll take as long as it takes and that's all there is to it," he said.

Whoever it was on the other end must have changed their tune because suddenly it was Matt who was on the offensive.

"You bet that's okay because that's the way it's going to be." His voice dropped an octave. "And if you do anything to fuck things up, you're going to be sorry."

Matt didn't wait for a reply.

He slammed down the phone, stared up at the computer screen for a moment, and cursed something inaudible under his breath. He switched off the machine, rubbed his face, and started toward the stairs.

I quickly scrambled back to my room, softly closed the door behind me, even as I heard Matt's footsteps at the bottom of the stairs leading to the landing. I slipped back into bed as quietly as possible, hoping the creaking springs of the boxspring beneath me didn't give me away as I pulled the quilt up to my chin and forced my eyes shut.

I caught my breath again as Matt paused at the head of the steps. I wondered if he suspected I'd been awakened by his argument and might come in to check on me. If so, I would have to be prepared to act as if I'd just awakened. He seemed to stand there for a long time before his heavy, tired-sounding steps proceeded down the hall to his room.

I could have sworn I heard the jangle of keys before he opened his door, but there was no mistaking the sound of the lock engaging as he softly eased the door closed.

20

That first morning I opened my eyes with the unpleasant sensation of not knowing where I was.

For a moment I just lay there, paralyzed by fright, staring at the unfamiliar ceiling until I slowly remembered the events that had brought me to this room. All at once I began breathing easier. I lay there for a few moments more, until the last of the panic had drained from my body, and then I shoved myself up on one elbow to look at the clock on the nightstand.

It was a small ornate Victorian clock—an antique or a facsimile made to look antique—which produced an audible *ticktock* I hadn't noticed upon retiring to bed the night before. Its rose-decorated face and fancy black hands were incomprehensible to me at first, accustomed as I was to the bold digital display of my clock radio, and it took me several moments to register the fact that it was nearly eleven o'clock. I was rather shocked for having slept so late, but the shock was replaced by curiosity at the small piece of paper that lay folded beside the clock.

It was a note from Matt.

I read it quickly. He had gone into town for supplies to prepare for the coming storm, didn't want to disturb me, hoped I didn't mind him stealing into the room, etc. Coffee was brewing downstairs and he'd be back with breakfast. P.S. I looked like an angel when I was asleep.

I appreciated that last observation. From the moment I realized he'd been in my bedroom I had an uncomplimentary vision of how I might have looked: my head thrown back, my mouth open and, God forbid, snoring.

I climbed out of bed, sat in front of the mirror at the vanity table beside the armoire, and combed the tangles out of my hair with an embossed silver brush. I went into the bathroom and rinsed my face off, rummaged around in my carry-on, and brushed my teeth with the toothbrush I had brought with me, one of the few possessions salvaged from my lost luggage.

I went downstairs and followed the scent of freshly brewed coffee to the kitchen area, where I poured myself a cup, taking it hot and black. There were still the remains of a fire glowing under the grate and Matt's computer was on, a glowing blue square in the corner by one of the windows. I walked over, knowing I shouldn't invade his privacy, but was too curious to resist. I hit the page-up button, but found the new screen still blank. Unless he had downloaded the night's work to a disk or printed it out, he hadn't had a very productive night. I remembered his phone conversation in the middle of the night and wondered if he might already be under pressure to finish his next book.

I leaned over his leather office chair and looked out the window by his desk. The patch of sky that I could see over the firs was gray and ominous. I turned away from the window and walked to the opposite end of the room, where a group of overstuffed easy chairs were arranged in a cozy horseshoe around a large-screen television. I took the remote from the top of the television and pressed the power button.

The television came on in a blast of sound and color. I fumbled with the controls before I found the volume and surfed the channels until I found one of those sleazy talk shows. This one was about girls who slept with their best friends' boyfriends. I watched until the commercial break and then went back into the kitchen for more coffee.

When I came back, I saw a small strip of text scrolling across the bottom of the television screen from the national weather service issuing a severe winter storm warning for all of upper New England. I walked over to the window again and peeked outside at the gray unyielding sky, looked at the clock, and anxiously waited for Matt to return.

He came back around noon. I heard the Jeep crunching over the old snow and gravel as it made its way up the long drive to the chateau. I watched him from the window as he wrestled plastic grocery bags from the back of the 4x4 and greeted him at the door with a kiss.

"I missed you," I said. "You should have woken me. I would have gone into town with you."

"I'm sorry. I didn't want to disturb you. You were sound asleep."

"You look like you bought enough food for an army."

"Got to get hunkered down. They say the storm is going to be a doozy. Up to forty-eight inches."

I nodded toward the television. "I saw."

I shivered as a chill blast of air sliced through my thin gown.

"You better get back inside," he said. "Before you catch your death of cold."

"Let me throw on my clothes from yesterday and I'll help you with the rest of those bags."

Matt shook his head. "I took them into town with me and brought them to the laundry."

"You did what?" I said, staring at him in disbelief.

"I took them to the laundry."

"What the hell did you do that for?"

"Well, you'd worn them all the way up on the flight. I thought you'd like them freshened up."

Matt started hauling the bags of groceries into the kitchen. I followed him, trying to control my anger.

"But Matt, when the airport lost my luggage, those were the only clothes I had."

He returned to the living room, grabbed another two bags, and headed back to the kitchen. I trailed after him, feeling like a kid trying to get her father's attention. Matt started emptying the bags on the kitchen counter, putting cans up into the cabinets.

"Matt, didn't you hear me? Those were the only clothes I had."

"I'm sorry," he said, turning back. "I guess I wasn't thinking."

"Weren't thinking?" This wasn't the way I wanted to start out our first day together in the wilderness. Still, in spite of my attempts to control my anger, his off-handed attitude to the whole situation was enough to make me want to pick up one of the cans of tomato sauce on the table and hurl it across the room. How could he be so damn dense? I took a deep breath. It didn't seem to help much, but at least I didn't reach for the can of tomato sauce. "How," I said, struggling to keep my voice from rising, "could you not be thinking?"

"I don't know, honey," he said. "It's no big deal. Can you hand me those boxes of pasta?"

"No big deal!" I shouted. "Dammit, Matt, what the hell am I supposed to wear?"

"What you have on looks nice," he said, smiling disarmingly.

I stared down at the sheer robe I was wearing.

"You mean I'm supposed to wear these all the time?"

Matt nodded his head toward the window through which we could see the threatening gray sky. "Chances are we're not going to be getting out much anyway."

"That's not the point."

"Then what is?"

"So I'm supposed to traipse around here in these harem outfits for the next few days?"

Matt's smile widened.

"Matt, I don't find this the least bit funny," I said, already softening. "Why are you laughing? I'm serious."

"I know you're serious," he said, trying to keep a straight face.

"You're an idiot," I said, shaking my head, smiling.

"Yeah," he said, winking. "But a lucky idiot."

We ate a late breakfast together in front of the television, watching the midday news and the increasingly frantic reports on the coming storm. I cleaned up the breakfast plates as Matt went back to work on the computer. I called the airport in Bangor, but they still hadn't found my bags—not that there was any way we would be able to drive out there now to pick them up, with a blizzard on its way.

Around three o'clock the first flakes of snow began to fall. The wind picked up and whistled through against the edges of the chalet. The pines tossed back and forth like grieving widows. I put down the book I was reading and watched the gathering storm. Inside of an hour the snow began falling in earnest, driving almost horizontally past the windows, quickly covering the path to the road and inching its way up the large wheels of the Jeep parked outside.

By four it was almost impossible to see the pines surrounding the chalet and I saw the wisdom of Matt's prudence in stocking up on extra supplies. There was no telling how long it would take us to dig out of what was shaping up to be a monster storm. I spent the rest of the afternoon between the window and the television, each telling me the same story: we were going to be snowbound for quite some time. In fact, the reporters covering the storm were already predicting it could shape up to be the worst storm in New England history.

Before dinner I went upstairs and changed into a short, sheer teddy I was certain would have the desired effect on Matt. I'd make him pay after all for taking my only clothes to the laundry. If he thought it was amusing to keep me dressed like a harem girl, then I'd play along with his little game and see how much he really liked it. I'd take his mind off his work for the night and maybe, just maybe, when I had him good and distracted, I'd leave him down here with nothing to play with but his mouse. That, I thought, with a self-satisfied smirk, would serve him right.

Sure enough, Matt gave a low whistle when I came down.

"See," he said triumphantly, "this is exactly why I took your clothes to the laundry."

I smiled sarcastically. "You'll get yours," I said playfully.

"I can't wait," Matt said.

"Oh you'll wait."

We snuggled on the couch after supper in front of the fire and Matt read to me from Dante's *Divine Comedy,* the cantos in which the poet describes his breathless awe for his beloved Beatrice, who leads him to Paradise.

"She was born a year before Dante himself," Matt explained, "and he loved her from afar ever since boyhood. She died in 1290 when Dante was only twenty-four. But he never forgot her. Nearly twenty years later he wrote these verses honoring her as an angel sent from heaven to lead him through the purgatory of this life."

"He must have loved her an awful lot."

"Yes," Matt said. "He eventually married, but never forgot his devotion to his true muse."

21

Matt read until nearly midnight.

He was a marvelous reader, his voice deep and melodic, full of power and passion. He could have been a fine stage actor. I listened to the rich, captivating flow of Dante's poetry, sipping a glass of brandy, snuggling close to Matt, watching the dancing flames.

At last Matt put the book aside and kissed me full on the lips, his hand stroking the inside of my warmed thigh. I moaned and threw my arms around his shoulders, reaching under his shirt to run my hand over the muscles of his chest.

He lowered his head and placed his lips on my throat as his hand slipped under my teddy. I gave a little gasp and opened myself to him, letting him feel my warmth and moisture. His hand moved gently against me and I pressed myself urgently forward, my carefully wrought plans of revenge melting along with the rest of me, as I sought nothing more than the feeling of him inside me. I reached down, hands shaking, to undo his belt. He groaned and my heart began racing. But what I had excitedly thought was an expression of his growing lust I found to my disappointment to be merely an expression of regret.

He pulled away, and when I reached out to pull his head back to my lips, he caught my wrist, shaking his head.

"I have to get back to work," he said. "I'm sorry."

"But—" I couldn't find the words to continue, the words I wanted to say.

"It won't last forever."

"Couldn't you make an exception just this one night?"

Matt shrugged as if to say it was out of his control. "I really have to get to work. If I don't get started—"

"But you've been working all day."

"Garbage. The whole lot of it. Not a page worth keeping."

"But it seemed to be going well."

"There was no inspiration."

"Why don't you just wait until tomorrow? You can get a fresh start in the morning."

"No," Matt said, his eyes shining. "You don't understand. I needed inspiration."

"Inspiration?"

"Yes. You gave it to me."

"I'd have rather given you something else," I said dryly.

"I'll take a rain check. Now come on, up to bed with you."

I stood up and he patted me playfully on the backside.

I could hardly believe the turn of events that had just occurred. I had planned to seduce him and leave him in the lurch, and instead it was me who was going to bed with my hormones churning.

"Aren't you at least going to kiss me good night," I said, as he headed for his computer.

"I'm sorry," he said. He turned around and walked back to where I stood. He gripped my upper arms in his strong hands and pulled me toward him. "Good night, darling," he said.

"Good night," I whispered.

I gave him a long lingering kiss, my hands running over his back, once again moving inexorably downward.

He held me away with a wry smile.

"Nice try," he said.

"Just trying to be extra inspiring," I said lamely.

"It worked."

"Writers," I said, trying to hide my real feelings behind a mask of mock exasperation.

Matt held up a finger. "We're a rather weird lot. Perhaps I should have warned you."

"Perhaps."

"Please don't be too angry. We'll have time."

"I'm not angry," I lied.

He was still holding me by the arms. "Are you sure?"

"I'm sure."

"Then give me a smile."

I smiled.

"That doesn't look like a smile to me."

"Matt, please."

"Come on. Give me a smile so I know you're really not mad. I can't work if I think you're mad."

I gave him my best Electrify! smile.

"That's better. I couldn't bear to have you angry at me."

He gave me a quick peck on the cheek, strode quickly to his desk, and turned on his computer.

I turned off my smile and slowly walked upstairs to my bedroom.

I stared out the window for a couple of minutes. In the spotlights surrounding the house I saw a thick curtain of snow falling straight down between the house and the woods. The snow showed no signs of letting up. I thought about what had happened downstairs and felt a mixture of frustration, embarrassment, and anger. For the second night in a row Matt had turned me down. I was determined not to let it happen a third time. I had my pride. I'd inspired him, so he said, as if I were supposed to take that as a compliment. If he thought he could just turn me on, then stop things every time an idea popped into his head, he had another think coming. The next time I'd get him so damn hot he'd be inspired enough to write an *Iliad*, an *Odyssey,* and a whole New Testament, and I'd turn him down.

I stood by the window and watched the relentlessly falling snow for a couple of minutes before I finally calmed down enough to crawl into bed. I figured on being awake for a while, but I fell asleep almost the minute my head hit the pillow. I woke up only once, hearing Matt's angry voice on the phone downstairs again, but I was too tired to get out of bed and eavesdrop. Instead, I turned over and fell back to sleep, my dreams taking on a decidedly erotic character.

It was still snowing when I woke up the next morning.

I brushed my teeth and hair, washed my face, and went to the closet to pick out the warmest thing I could find. My selection was very limited. I settled for a relatively concealing red silk robe with a rather fanciful trim of black lace. I glanced quickly in the mirror before I went downstairs, decided against makeup, and turned off the bathroom light.

The wooden stairs were cold under my bare feet. Outside I could hear the wind howling in the pines surrounding the chalet.

Matt was sitting at his desk in front of the computer. He was staring bleary eyed at the screen, his face bathed in electric blue light. Next to the keyboard sat an untouched cup of cold black coffee.

"Good morning," I ventured, but received no answer, so I headed for the remote control on top of the television set.

"Cable's down," Matt called from across the room, his eyes still glued to the computer screen.

In the background I could hear the radio going: a no-nonsense voice giving the latest storm updates.

"I called the guys who usually plow me out," Matt said. "But they can't get to us for the next several days. It looks like we're snowed in."

In spite of the romantic implications, I didn't accept the news with a great deal of enthusiasm.

"What do you mean? Can't we use the Jeep to get to the road?"

I was thinking of Stephen and those damn advertisements, the ones where the Jeeps are rising from beds of quicksand and plowing through walls of snow like Sherman tanks.

"Take a look out the window," Matt suggested laconically.

I did and was not heartened by what I saw: a thick curtain of white falling flakes occasionally pushed horizontal by a northern wind that bent the pines nearly double.

"Coffee's on in the kitchen," Matt said without further comment.

I nodded and went to fetch myself a cup, only to find nothing but a burnt horseshoe of thick black resin in the bottom of the glass coffee carafe. I washed the carafe thoroughly with a piece of steel wool I found in the soap depression on the sink and set about refilling the automatic coffeemaker. As I waited for the coffee to drip through the filter, I added last night's dirty dishes to those already in the dishwasher and searched the cabinet for the last two clean coffee mugs.

When I brought Matt his mug, he was still staring at his computer screen. He gave a little start as I approached and quickly hit a key that wiped away whatever he was doing and activated his screen saver.

"Here," I said, a little disturbed at his secretiveness. "I made you some fresh coffee."

I took the mug of cold black brew sitting beside his mouse pad and replaced it with the fresh, steaming one.

"Thanks." Matt nodded, still staring straight ahead at the screen, which now showed a simulation star storm.

I turned back to the room, determined not to show my annoyance, and walked over to the sophisticated radio tuner set on one of the built-in shelves lining the wall.

"Do you mind if I change this?" I said, referring to the monotonous and repetitive storm broadcast.

Matt waved his hand. "Go ahead," he said. "Just so long as it isn't one of those damn classic rock stations with those screaming, hooting,

imbecilic hosts that keep playing silly sound effects and shouting 'TGIF.'
What do they call them?"

"Zookeepers?"

"Yeah, zookeepers."

It took me a while to find something suitable: a low-key station
playing easy music pop standards. As it was, they kept breaking in
with storm updates every fifteen minutes, which was a little hard to
bear. The last thing I wanted to hear about right then was the storm
raging right outside the window.

Luckily, Matt had brought in enough wood to last what looked like
a couple of days, the logs stacked neatly by the side of the fireplace,
and more downstairs in the basement. I picked up one of the dry logs
and added it to those burning low on the grate. The new log caused
the old ones underneath to collapse into an angry red and white powder,
the hungry flames licking up underneath, as if eager for fresh wood. I
felt the immediate yellow warmth on my face with gratitude, holding
up my palms to the fireplace, until I couldn't stand it anymore.

I found a copy of *Great American Plays* on the bookshelf and curled
up on the couch, rereading Eugene O'Neill's *The Hairy Ape*, and sipping
my mug of coffee. It had been a long time since I'd read one of O'Neill's
plays. The last time was probably in college when I had the lead role
in a production of *Mourning Becomes Electra*. I enjoyed O'Neill's
fevered intensity and welcomed the chance to rediscover his work after
all these years. It reawoke in me the old passion I had to someday do
work in serious theater.

By noon it had finally stopped snowing.

The Jeep was nothing more than a barely defined mound of snow
in the middle of an uninterrupted sea of white that had risen to alarming
heights between the house and the woods. Looking at the view through
the picture window, I could hardly imagine us ever getting out. The
snow, in places, had blown in drifts that threatened to bury a full-
grown person standing up. Matt had finally turned off the computer
and was dressing in a fur-lined parka, L. L. Bean rubber boots, gloves,
yellow overalls, and one of those big hats made of rabbit fur with
earflaps. Beneath his hood he wore a black-knit ski mask to protect
him from the slashing wind.

"Where are you going?" I asked.

"To clear the door," he said.

"The door?"

It didn't take long for me to find out what he was talking about.
After struggling several minutes, he managed to pull open the front
door to reveal a bank of snow nearly as tall as he was.

"Stand away from the draft," he called back.

I didn't have to be told. The cold air rushing into the cabin tore through my satin robe and nightgown like a hurricane of knives.

I retreated to the kitchen while Matt, armed with a pointy shovel he kept by the door, attacked the wall of snow. After nearly an hour and a half of work, broken up by short intervals to fortify himself with hot coffee and regain his warmth by the fire, Matt had at least cleared away a narrow path to the buried front stairs.

Beyond that we were trapped.

22

———•———

"It's hopeless," Matt said.

He'd set the shovel outside the door, banged his feet against the door frame, and come inside. He had just removed his parka, and was in the process of picking at the frozen laces of his boots with stiff red fingers.

I came out of the kitchen with a plate of grilled-cheese sandwiches and a fresh pot of hot coffee.

"I did my best," Matt explained. "But we're just going to have to wait until the guys can come with some heavy-duty equipment. There must be at least thirty-six inches of snow out there, and I'm not counting the drifts. You saw the one against the door. It must have been at least six feet high. I just hope we don't have any leaks."

"Great," I said, trying not to sound too upset. "So we're snow-bound?"

Matt removed his heavy boots and set them on the mat just inside the door. The snow still clinging to the rubber had begun to melt. He stood up and began pulling down the special waterproof overalls he had put on over his regular pants.

"For the time being, I'm afraid so."

We sat at the living room table and ate the sandwiches I'd made and sipped the black coffee. Matt, his appetite inspired by his recent exertion, ate three sandwiches and gulped down four cups of the coffee. I nibbled on half of a sandwich and nursed a cup of mint tea. I watched him across the table. The stocking mask had left his dark hair ruffled, a few stray curls falling on his forehead, giving him a sweet, boyish look that was belied by the breadth of his shoulders beneath his black, cableknit turtleneck sweater.

He finished his coffee, put the cup down, and carefully wiped his lips with a napkin.

"I hope you're not already having second thoughts about coming up here."

"No," I sort of lied. "Not anything like that. I guess I'm just feeling a little antsy is all. I'm a city girl. Even in the worst blizzard, they get things up and moving the next day. I'm just not used to being at the mercy of the elements."

"It's good for the soul. Helps you realize your true importance in the scheme of things. Besides"—he grinned—"I think you'll find that there are worse things than a man and a woman being snowbound together."

I forced a smile, which I obscured behind my mug of tea. So far there had been nothing romantic about it.

Matt spied the book of plays that I had laid on the table.

"You like O'Neill?"

"Yes, though it's been some time since I last read him. College, I'm sure."

"Me, too," he said, opening the book and letting the pages flip rapidly under his thumb. "Sad to say, once you start writing commercial fiction, you have less and less time to read the sort of things you once read that inspired you to write in the first place. You have to keep up with the trends, the competition, and all that."

Outside, the wind howled through the pines. Matt pushed his chair back and went to the fireplace to poke at the dying fire.

"I noticed you have nothing but classics on the shelves," I said.

Matt threw another log on the grate and twisted around, crouched in front of the now rejuvenated flames.

"I keep all the popular junk in the apartment back in the city. And that includes my own work. Out here, I keep only the books that really matter to me. Not that I have a chance to read them. When I get here, I have to pretty much buckle down and work. But I fantasize about rereading the classics in my old age. You know, there was a time I wanted to be a poet."

"Really. What stopped you?"

Matt stood up, placed the poker back in the little stand by the fireplace, and thrust his hands in his pockets.

"Rejection letters." He laughed easily, softly, and turned back to look out the window at the snow. "That and the fact that I realized that poetry would never pay the bills. Even the most successful poets are forced to teach somewhere if they want to eat."

"So you switched to novels instead?"

"Yes," Matt said, walking back to the table, picking up the book of O'Neill plays and staring at the cover. "But even there I found I had to compromise. I was so naive. I thought I was going to become the next Samuel Beckett or Robbe-Grillet. Needless to say, no one was inspired by my attempts at the next great innovation in the American novel. And I was growing tired, old, and broke waiting on tables.

"So I hit the bookstores, spent my last fifty dollars buying the worst trash I could lay my hands on, and read each and every wretched one of those lousy novels. Three months later, I finished my first suspense novel. I sent the manuscript off to an agent I picked at random from *Writer's Market*."

He looked up from the book, tossed it casually onto the table, and smiled. "And the rest is pulp-fiction history."

"I thought you told me never to compromise my dreams."

"I did."

"What about you?"

Matt shrugged. "I lied."

That evening we were curled up on the sofa by the fire. I was sipping brandy. Matt had a cup of coffee. Outside, the wind was blowing dry veils of snow against the windows. I was lying back against his warm chest, his strong heart beating in my ear, his free hand playing idly with my hair. It was then that he asked me about my childhood. The question had come out of nowhere, and he must have felt me stiffen because his fingers stopped what they were doing to my hair and he asked me if anything was the matter.

"It's kind of a painful subject to me," I said.

"Your childhood?"

"Yes."

"I'm sorry. You don't have to talk about it if you don't want to," he offered.

"It's no big deal."

"It really isn't any of my business. I'm sorry. I didn't mean to pry."

"You weren't prying," I said. "It's a common enough question. After all, it's natural we should get to know each other."

"But if you aren't comfortable."

"Maybe it's time to get comfortable."

I hadn't exaggerated. My childhood was a painful subject to me, but nonetheless I found myself telling him things I hadn't talked about to anyone in years, and then only to my therapist in the months shortly after the residuals came in for the toothpaste spot I did.

It was Stephen who had encouraged me to go for "help," as he put it. He thought it would help me work out the problems he claimed were standing in the way of our intimacy. The bastard. What was standing in the way of our intimacy was the fact that he was screwing around and I was too dumb to accuse him of it or even so much as admit it to myself.

"My mother"—I exhaled deeply, feeling a great sadness—"my mother has always been a bit—"

I took a large swallow of brandy, feeling it warm my insides.

"She's always been a bit unstable. She was five when the Nazis took her away, along with her parents, my grandparents, to Bergen-Belsen. There they were separated. My mother and grandmother were loaded on one train, and my grandfather on another. She never saw her father again."

"Johanna, I had no idea. You really don't have to—"

I hardly heard him, his voice sounded so distant. The words came from my mouth as if from the mouth of another person. Words I hardly knew were inside me until they came pouring out. My mother's words. Her mother's words. Not even the voice was mine. It was the story of our family's legacy of pain and tragedy told by the ghost of my ancestors.

"The Nazis sent my mother and grandmother to a work camp in Poland. It was some kind of bureaucratic mixup. My mother should never have been sent there. She was too young to work. They were going to send her away. My grandmother begged one of the officers to let her stay. She told him that she had already been separated from her husband, that she couldn't bear to lose her daughter. The officer wasn't impressed. It was out of sheer desperation that she convinced him my mother could work. So my mother was allowed to stay, she wasn't sent off."

I gulped down the rest of the brandy and stared into the bottom of the glass.

"The Nazis were very accommodating. They gave my mother a job even a five-year-old could handle. Did you ever see those old films and photographs, the ones with the piles of teeth the Nazis pulled from dead Jews to get the gold fillings?"

"Yes," Matt said quietly.

"That was my mom's job. To pack the teeth into boxes to be shipped off to Berlin. One day my grandmother was marched off and shot in the woods outside of the camp. She'd grown too sick to work. To this day my mother doesn't know if one of those precious teeth she boxed—"

"Oh God, Johanna. I'm so sorry."

I leaned forward and put the delicate snifter on the table, my hand trembling. Matt reached over, took it in his, and kissed it.

"So you see," I said hollowly, "my mother had a good excuse to do the things she did. She could hardly sleep at night. She'd pace the house for hours. And when she did finally pass out from sheer exhaustion, she'd have these nightmares, terrible ones, where she'd wake up screaming as if someone were murdering her. My father and I would search the house for her. We never knew where we'd find her. In the closet, crouched in a corner of the cellar, up in the attic."

I shivered at the memory. The screams in the night. The flashlight peering into every dark corner. The sudden sight of my mother cowering and whimpering.

"She drank too much. She took pills. This was before the days of shrinks and posttraumatic stress disorder. Now, who knows? Maybe things would have been different. I guess by today's standards you would say we were a dysfunctional family. We didn't know any better. We just did the best we could. My father was patient, as patient and understanding as any man could be. Even about the other men—"

My breath caught. I wasn't sure I could go on with this, but I had gone so far already.

"And then—then my father was driving back from a business meeting in Tennessee. It was raining, teeming. He should have stayed over, but he didn't like to leave my mother alone at night. The police said it looked like he'd fallen asleep at the wheel. There were no skidmarks on the road, no evidence that he'd ever tried to stop, that he'd ever seen the telephone pole. They said he died on impact. That he wouldn't have felt any pain. I guess they thought that made it better. It's the kind of things people say. As if there's any death without pain. What about my pain? About my mother's pain? There's always pain."

I felt the tears overflow my eyes and roll down my cheeks. I closed my eyes and the tears came faster. I felt Matt trying to wipe them away with his finger, as if by doing so he could somehow erase the hurt. I thought of my father alive and well in California, remarried, with a new brood of kids and cursed him. I'd given him a far more noble death than he'd deserved. Besides, like I said before, he was dead to me anyway.

"I'm sorry," I said. "I didn't mean to cry. It's stupid of me. It all happened a long time ago."

"I don't think it's stupid," Matt said gently. "That must have been devastating."

The tears had dried, the emotion had passed, and I felt only embarrassment.

I shrugged, staring steely eyed into the merrily dancing flames. "I'm sure I'm not the only one in the world who's lost a parent."

"Johanna," Matt said, stroking the side of my face. "You don't have to play tough. I'm not going to be frightened off. You can be yourself with me. You're safe here."

I turned to look at his rugged face, softened by the light of the flames, his eyes gentle with compassion.

"Thank you," I said softly. "It's just that it all seems so silly and self-indulgent. We all have baggage to carry. I just don't want to be one of those people who are always complaining of the weight."

"I don't think you have to be worried about that." Matt smiled. "But you could let someone help you carry it."

"I guess that's always been kind of hard for me. I've pretty much been on my own all my life in one way or another. I guess that's one of the reasons I wanted to be an actress. When you're on stage, you're never alone."

"You aren't alone here," he said.

Matt leaned forward and kissed me.

I must have looked surprised because he sat back and mumbled an apology.

"I'm sorry—I shouldn't have. This isn't the time."

"No," I whispered, "it's okay, really."

He didn't seem convinced. His eyes looked sad and pained.

"I mean it. It's okay."

I reached out, my hand behind his head, and pulled his face toward mine to convince him. His lips were stiff and reluctant at first, as if he were forcing back his desire by sheer strength of will. It was a battle I was determined he would lose. In spite of himself I could feel him opening to me, his tongue pushing softly but insistently into my mouth, his hands moving over my body. I didn't resist.

"Oh, Johanna . . ."

"You talk too much," I said.

"You're right." He grinned crookedly.

I smothered whatever he was about to say next with a kiss.

He had exposed my breasts and was firmly cupping them, his thumbs toying with my nipples. A moment later his mouth replaced his hands on my breasts and I could feel his hot breath on my bare flesh. Any guilt he may have felt only moments ago had apparently vanished in the flames of a passion too long pent up.

He moved upward, tracing burning kisses along the side of my throat, his strong hands mashing my breasts almost painfully. I gave a startled cry and he sealed his lips to mine, pressing the length of his hard-muscled body against me, all pretense of gentle seduction over, overpowered by a raw need for release that was as frightening as it was intoxicating.

He sat up just long enough to fumble with the button on his pants and that gave me the opportunity I needed.

"Matt, I don't think we should . . ."

He froze, his hands still at his waist, staring down at me as if he didn't believe his ears.

"You're going to hate me," I went on, enjoying the look of confusion on his face. "But I just can't."

"I thought . . ."

"I thought so, too. But you were right. This isn't the time."

I covered my breasts and Matt climbed off me, politely averting his eyes.

Got you, I thought. *Just like I said I would.*

I looked at the bulge in his pants.

Use that for inspiration.

"You're mad aren't you?" I said, standing up. "I don't blame you."

"No, I'm not mad," Matt said and from the sound of his voice I could almost believe him. "We would have regretted it."

Now it was my turn to look confused.

He held me lightly by the shoulders and kissed my cheek like a mother might.

"Go to sleep," he said. "Don't worry about me. I have a lot of work to take my mind off—things."

Later, as I stood outside the door to my bedroom, I heard him furiously typing at his keyboard.

23

—————•—————

"Do you want to play a game?"

It had been three days since the blizzard, three days holed up in the chalet. The television was still knocked out, the car still buried beneath the snow. The phone had stopped working some time during the night of the first day. Matt speculated that ice had downed the lines. The radio was our only link with the world beyond the white void outside the windows.

I was developing a serious case of cabin fever. There wasn't a lot for me to do but read, listen to the radio, and putter around the house while Matt wrote. The VCR still worked and Matt had a pretty comprehensive if somewhat disorganized selection of videotapes and I spent a large portion of the day watching films. It wasn't altogether a bad pastime for an aspiring actress.

I guess as a writer of psychological suspense it wasn't unusual to find that Matt's tastes seemed to run to such films as, *Sleeping with the Enemy, Silence of the Lambs,* and *Fatal Attraction,* as well as such classics as *Gaslight* and *Hush . . . Hush, Sweet Charlotte.* I studied the performances of Julia Roberts and Jodie Foster, and especially Bette Davis and Olivia de Havilland, trying to isolate the techniques, the subtleties of character that made them stars. I don't think I ever watched films so closely. I had hardly anything else to do. It was a good education.

That afternoon I was scanning Matt's video collection when I came upon *Taxi Driver.* Although I had seen clips of it before, especially that famous scene when DeNiro talks to the mirror—"You talking to me?"—I'd never actually sat through the whole thing. I had just been a kid when it first came out and though I'd been a fan of Scorsese's recent work, I'd never seen the film that pretty much made him a household name.

I popped the cassette into the VCR and sat back on the couch. There was DeNiro as Travis Bickle, young, angry, on the edge, cruising the streets of the city in his cab. There he was watching the prostitutes, the pimps, the X-rated movie marquees that seemed to have taken over society. There he was in his run-down apartment, writing in his diary, doing push-ups, honing his body for what he believed to be his duty: to clean up the mess and corruption around him and save what was left of the innocence of the world personified by an underaged prostitute played by Jodie Foster.

And then, right about in the middle of the movie, there he was standing in a park watching a rally for a presidential candidate. He was asking questions of a secret service agent, who was obviously growing suspicious of him. DeNiro was talking about how he thought he'd make a fine secret service agent and was asking how one might go about applying. The agent asked for DeNiro's name and just when you thought he would give it, you could see the light go on in DeNiro's eyes and instead of saying "Travis Bickle," he made up a name which the secret service agent wrote down on his pad.

"Harry Krinkle," DeNiro said.

"Goddamn!" I shouted.

"What is it?" Matt said, turning from his computer.

"Nothing," I said. "I'm sorry. I was just watching *Taxi Driver*. I didn't mean to disturb you."

Matt muttered something and returned to work. Meanwhile I jumped off the sofa and rewound the tape to the place just before the secret service agent asked DeNiro his name.

There it was again as clear as day.

"Harry Krinkle."

"Hot damn," I said, this time low enough not to interrupt Matt. The guy drove a cab like DeNiro, tried to look like DeNiro, even wore the same clothes like DeNiro. He hadn't used the name Travis Bickle because that would have been too obvious. But how many people would have remembered Bickle's off-handed alias in *Taxi Driver*? Did he really think he was DeNiro? Or Travis Bickle? As far as I knew, Harry Krinkle was the only name he went by. Was his life some kind of bizarre homage to DeNiro? Or was it just an extreme exercise in method acting? Was Harry Krinkle—or whoever he really was—an aspiring actor or just insane?

I began to wonder if he had targeted me as his love interest the way Bickle targeted Cybill Shepherd in the movie. I thought about how he had miraculously appeared from out of nowhere the night I was stranded on the streets. Could that have really been a coincidence? Maybe he'd been following me. I thought about how he'd asked me out. I thought about my dark visitor. Could it have been him?

"Are you okay?" Matt said.

I nearly jumped out of my skin. "Damn it, Matt, you nearly gave me a heart attack."

I'd been so absorbed in the movie I hadn't seen or heard him coming across the room.

"I'm sorry," he said. "I didn't mean to frighten you. You look like you've seen a ghost."

"It's okay," I said. "I guess I just lost myself in the movie."

"*Taxi Driver*," he said, looking at the screen. "Fantastic film. DeNiro's great in it, isn't he?"

"Yes," I said. "Yes, he is."

"Come on," he said. "It's almost dinner time. I think we both could use a break."

The highlight of the day was sitting by the fire with Matt after dinner, talking about any number of topics. Somehow, the subject he always seemed most interested in was me. Whatever we were discussing, he managed to steer the conversation around to my thoughts, my dreams, my fantasies. It was kind of flattering, if not a little embarrassing, and I found myself competing with myself to stay interesting so as not to disappoint him. The last thing I wanted to do was to bore him.

As a result, I wound up telling him a lot more about my personal life than I had ever told anyone.

Or would ever dream of telling anyone.

All too soon, however, our evenings together were over as Matt always returned to his computer by midnight, leaving me to wander off upstairs to bed, bored, frustrated, and alone. As far as I knew, he spent the rest of the night writing, for when I got up the next morning, he'd still be at the keyboard. I began to wonder if and when he ever got any sleep. Needless to say, after days of this routine, I was up for just about anything.

"Well, it's not so much a game really," he explained. "It's more a way you can help me with my work."

"Great. But how can I help you? I'm no writer."

"But you are an actress."

"Yes," I said, not sure at all what he was getting at.

Matt had risen from the sofa and was pacing the small rug in front of the fireplace, rubbing the back of his neck.

"I'm kind of stuck in my narrative. You can help me figure out what one of my characters might do in a certain situation by acting out her part."

"I see. Sounds like fun. Of course, I'll need a little background first. What's this character like?"

Matt paused, collecting his thoughts.

"Well, she's bright, pretty, twenty-something, very driven, but deeply troubled. She's got a dark secret in her past. A deep hurt. A trauma. Something that makes it difficult for her to allow herself to be vulnerable. Especially to love. Something she's never told anyone before. The problem is I'm not sure what it is."

"Sexual assault? Rape?"

"No. Nothing so obvious as that." Matt began pacing again, his words speeding up with his pace. "It's got to be something a little subtler, but way left of center. Something done to her by someone she trusted deeply. Maybe something in childhood. But not incest. That's too obvious. I don't want a cliché. Still, it's a betrayal by someone she cares about deeply. I see it as something she probably suspected was wrong at the time, but being so young she didn't understand the full ramifications of."

"But something sexual?"

"Yes. I think so. But definitely in a very twisted, offbeat sort of way."

"Okay. What about the situation?"

Matt stopped dead in his tracks. "The situation?"

"The plot of the story."

Matt's brow furrowed. "I don't like to talk about the plots of my books before they're done. . . ."

"I don't need to know how it turns out. Just a general idea of what the story is about."

"I can't—"

"Oh come on. What do you think I'm going to do? Steal your idea?"

"It's not that. I'm just a little insecure I guess. I don't like to show my work to anyone until I have it just right."

I sighed. I had had no idea writers were even more temperamental than actors. "All right," I said. "But you've got to give me something to work with. How about this. You just tell me in general about the scene, the motivation of the characters, and just the barest background of what's going on in the story."

He hesitated.

"If you can't," I said, "I really don't see how I can help you."

He looked me deeply in the eyes as if he were sure he would regret what he was about to do.

"All right," he said finally. "I'll tell you. Can you keep a secret?"

I tried my best to sound reassuring. "Of course," I said.

Matt was about as vague as he could be about the novel.

He sketched out the plot in the broadest possible strokes and in the fewest possible words. I tried to allay his creative paranoia by asking questions only about the scene I was about to play out and only in the most general of terms. He still seemed decidedly uneasy.

"She's with her lover," he said reluctantly, as if with each word he was beginning some deeply personal and painful confession instead of just a story he'd made up in his head. "He's an authority figure of some sort. I haven't decided exactly what kind yet. He could be a cop, or an ex-detective. Maybe a private investigator. He could even be a psychiatrist who's gotten too close and broken the rules separating doctor and patient. In any event, our hero has crossed some ethical line or other. He has committed a taboo. He is compromised."

"Sounds like a dangerous situation," I said.

"It is," he said, his voice lowering. He knelt down in front of me as if we might be overheard. "There's been a series of murders. Our heroine may be the next victim. She wants to trust the hero, but something holds her back. Some nagging suspicion. Something very unsettling about his behavior. If she gives in and trusts this man, she may find herself at the mercy of a cold-blooded murderer. But at the same time I want to leave open the suspicion that she may be the killer herself. So you see, her secret is very important. It should lead the reader to see her vulnerability and her potential for psychotic behavior."

"Interesting," I said. "Very complex. So she suspects him. Does he suspect her?"

Matt stood up and nodded. "They both suspect each other."

"I see. Where do we begin?"

Matt looked around the room. "On the couch. They're making out—"

"How convenient," I said wryly.

"No," Matt said with dead seriousness. "It's not like that. They're making out and something breaks inside her and she pulls away."

Matt sat down close beside me, pushing away the spaghetti strap of the shiny silk gown I was wearing. He leaned foward and suddenly his lips were on mine. I felt my body stiffen with surprise, but he was heedlessly insistent. Soon I was responding, my lips parting, inviting the taste of him inside me. He pressed his mouth harder against mine, hungry, urgent, his left hand cupping my breast, his right hand on the back of my neck, firmly holding my head in place. I allowed myself to feel trapped, desperate, full of fear and repugnance as he covered my body with his.

"Get off!" I screamed, beating on his shoulders with my fists. "Get off, I said. I mean it!"

He only held me closer, one hand dropping boldy down between my legs, the other pulling down the front of my gown, freeing one breast. The taste of him in my mouth drove me wild. I pulled the hair at the back of his head, forcing some space between us, and then worked my hands between our bodies, pushing him roughly away.

"Stop fighting it," he said, his voice hoarse. "This is what you want. This is what you've wanted since you came up here."

He started forward again and I raked my hand down the left side of his face, leaving five ragged scratches in the flesh running from his cheekbone to his chin. He backed away, touching his face gingerly, looking at me with astonishment.

"What the hell—"

"I told you to stop," I said, pulling the gown over my exposed breast. "I told you, dammit!"

"What's wrong?" he said, a look of bewilderment on his face. "I thought—"

"You thought wrong," I said, abruptly standing up, moving away from his hand, which sought to comfort me, but now hung suspended awkwardly in midair.

"I didn't mean to scare you," he said, sounding frightened himself.

"You didn't scare me," I spat back.

"Please," he said. "I want to help you."

He stood up and reached for me again. I twisted away from his touch as if it were white-hot iron. I felt nothing for him but disgust now.

"You can't leave things like this," he said.

"Just keep away from me," I said warningly. "Keep away or you'll be sorry."

"Okay, okay," Matt said. "Just settle down."

"Don't touch me or I swear, snow or no snow, I'm getting out of here."

"I won't touch you. I promise. Look, I'm just going to sit down."

Matt sat down slowly on the sofa as if afraid that the least quick move would have me bolting for the door. "Just tell me what it is," he said. "Please."

I watched him as if he were a dangerous snake. Behind me I could hear the flickering fire, the flames licking the logs piled on the grate. Of course, I knew he was right. I couldn't leave things like this. I had kept the secret for far too long. I hadn't felt about a man as I felt about him for a long time and now I was threatening to drive him away. I had to tell him, had to tell someone. I couldn't allow this secret to taint my entire life.

"It's hard," I said, my voice catching. "It's so hard. I don't even know where to begin."

"It's okay," he said softly, so softly his voice was barely audible above the crack and whistle of the flames.

He didn't try to reach for me again and for that I was thankful. Though part of me longed to be buried in his arms, I knew that now that I was so close to telling him—to telling anyone—I would never allow myself such intimate comfort from him or any man until I had told him what I had kept to myself all these years.

"He said it was a game," I started. "He called it by a dozen different names. But it was always the same. He captured me and I was his prisoner. When I was little, it seemed just like any other game. I didn't understand why he tied my wrists and ankles. Or why he placed the cloth over my mouth and eyes. I didn't understand why I was usually naked. It was all just part of the game."

I turned away, unable to look Matt in the eyes. Instead, I stared into the roaring flames.

"Later, when I was a little older, he told me it was just like what they did on television. On television women were always getting tied up. Even on the cartoons and kids' adventure shows. Like he said, it was just a game. It all seemed to make sense. I never thought of it as bad. Besides, he seemed to like the games so much. I must have been eight or nine when we stopped playing our games. I guess he thought I was too old by then, or that I was old enough to start putting two and two together."

The fire was growing uncomfortably warm against my body, but still I didn't move away, as if I was symbolically immolating myself, hoping to burn away whatever impurities led him to do what he did to me. Like all victims, I somehow blamed myself.

"Anyway, it was all over by then and I pretty much forgot the whole thing. Until one day years later when I was about to turn eighteen. It was shortly before I was set to go off to college. I was rooting around in the attic and I came upon a box. Inside were literally hundreds of photographs. Hundreds of crude old Polaroids of me nude and tied in various seductive poses. It all came back to me in a flash and I doubled over and vomited on the floor. I couldn't stop vomiting. It just seemed to go on forever."

I suddenly felt terribly cold in spite of the heat of the fire. I hugged my body. I was so cold I longed to jump into the orange tongues of flame. It seemed only they could warm me. Only the flames, or the embrace of a man I wouldn't let touch me.

"I never told my mother. She thought I was pregnant. She even made me go to the doctor for a blood test. One day, when she was out, I took the box of pictures outside and burned them one by one in a garbage can. I guess it never occurred to him that he might die like he did and someone would find them. Jesus, in the earliest of those pictures I couldn't have been more than two years old. And do you know what the worst part is?"

I turned around to face Matt. I was no longer ashamed. I was no longer scared. I was a woman full of anger and defiance.

"The worst fucking part is that I blamed myself. Somehow I thought I was responsible for his accident. That I had led him into temptation and he had paid for it with his life."

Matt was sitting with his face in his hands. When he looked up, his expression was one of intense pain and sadness. I felt an undeniable sense of vindication, of triumph. He was silent for a very long time.

When he spoke, his voice registered shock and outrage.

"My God. It was your father."

I didn't say anything. I merely stared at him, eyes burning, but not with tears.

"That bastard. That sick bastard. It's not your fault, Johanna. It's not your fault. You've got to realize that."

He stood up and came toward me. I took a step away.

"Please. No."

He came anyway. He put his hands on my shoulders. It was only then that I realized that I was still trembling.

Trembling violently.

"You can't run away forever," he murmured.

He pulled me toward his broad strong chest, the hairs tickling my cheek from where they emerged from the v-shaped collar of his dark sweater. I could smell the warmth of his body, the slightest hint of cologne, something woody and masculine.

As he held me, he began stroking my hair and rocking me back and forth. There was nothing sexual about the embrace. It might have been one a mother might give to a hurt child.

Or a father.

A good father.

"I'm so sorry, Johanna. So sorry for putting you through that. It was unnecessary. It was selfish."

"Matt," I said, deciding enough was enough, "I was just acting."

"What?" he said, his expression a jumble of confusion.

"I was acting. You asked me to play a part. Remember?"

"I don't believe this."

I laughed. I had the same feeling I used to have when I feigned an illness on a school morning just to see if I could fool my mother: a feeling of elation and guilt.

Matt held me at arm's length, his eyes searching mine.

"You don't have to look at me like that, Matt," I said. "I'm an actress, not an alien."

"I'm not sure exactly what you are."

"You're not angry, are you?"

"No, it's just that . . . I don't know. I guess I believed you."

"I'm sorry. I thought you understood. It was improv. We do it all the time at the Actor's Studio. You set up a scene and just go with it. I didn't mean to upset you."

"I'm not upset," he said, a little too quickly. "I was just worried."

"Then I didn't mean to worry you. I should have explained things before we started. I have to admit I'm glad you found it convincing."

Matt gingerly touched the scratches on the side of his face.

"Did you have to be quite so convincing?"

"I apologize. I guess I just got a little carried away."

Matt stared at the blood staining his fingertips and winced.

"Does it hurt much?" I offered.

"Stings some. It'll sting more when I put some peroxide on it. I guess it's a good thing I can't get out of the house even if I wanted to. People tend to look askance at a man with female clawmarks on his face."

"Matt, I don't know what to say."

"Let's drop it."

His tone was abrupt and matter-of-fact. Suddenly I was taking no pleasure whatsoever in having so successfully fooled him. He had turned back to his desk and was arranging some papers on the shelf above the printer.

"Was I at least of any help?" I asked, hoping something positive could be salvaged from the evening.

"Yes," he said, without turning. "I think so."

"Good," I said brightly. "Maybe we can—"

"If you don't mind, I think I should get to work now."

"Okay," I said, his back still turned to me, as implacable as a mountain.

"Maybe you should get to bed. It's kind of late."

I looked at the clock. It was a little past midnight. But I knew it wasn't the time he cared about. He wanted to be left alone.

"Sure," I said. I felt badly leaving things like this between us, but I figured there'd be plenty of time to put things aright. "I guess so. Good night."

I turned toward the loft when Matt called out.

"Johanna."

"Yes, Matt," I said hopefully.

Matt turned slowly from his desk, his hands in his pockets, his eyes riveted to mine. "The story you told me about your mother and grandmother," he said, his voice full of mocking sarcasm, "was that true or was that all an act, too?"

I felt the blood rush to my face; my hands clenched at my sides. Whatever feelings of guilt I'd had before vanished in a flash fire of righteous indignation.

"You bastard!" I shouted. "You miserable bastard! Do you think I'd make up such a story? Do you think I'm capable of making up such a thing? Did you think I was acting?"

Matt shrugged, standing there casually, hands still in his pockets. "How would I know?"

"Just what the hell kind of person do you think I am?"

"That's what I'm trying to find out," he said evenly.

I felt like crossing the room and smashing my fist right into the middle of his smug face. Instead, I stood rooted to the spot, too angry to move, too outraged to even speak. Matt waited a moment and then did the one thing I'd least expected. He burst out laughing.

"What's so funny?" I asked, taken aback.

Matt pulled his right hand from his pocket, pointed his forefinger at me, and cocked his thumb.

"Got you," he said, dropping his thumb to "shoot" me. "This time it was me who was just acting."

It took a moment or two for what he'd said to sink in and another moment for the adrenaline to start draining away. Still, I couldn't quite bring myself to join his laughter. Especially since the joke was on me.

"Now we're even," Matt said, almost triumphantly. "I've always found there's nothing like a little taste of your own medicine from time to time to keep you healthy."

"Yes," I said. "I guess you're right. What's fair is fair."

"No hard feelings?"

"No," I said, my heart still pounding hard behind my sternum.

Matt chuckled. Whatever anger or outrage he'd felt before had seemingly vanished.

"Good. I'll see you tomorrow morning. Have a good night's sleep."

Upstairs I washed and changed into another, warmer nightgown. I sat down in the antique rocking chair by the window and thumbed through an old issue of *Architectural Digest* that I'd pulled out from the magazine basket on the floor. I stared at the pictures, but saw instead a movie of the night's proceedings. I saw again the look on Matt's face when I'd told him I'd been acting. I froze the frame in my memory. It was not quite the way I'd seen it the first time. The expression on his face was not quite hurt or even anger. It was more like disappointment.

I put the magazine down in my lap and stared at my hands. For the first time I'd noticed the tiny white half-moons dug in the flesh of my palms from where I'd clenched my fists. Matt had gotten me back good all right. But the story wasn't over.

I was already plotting my revenge.

24

It wasn't until two days later that the telephone was working again. I had taken to checking it every half hour or so. There is no silence more absolute than that of a dead telephone line. I had grown so used to it that my heart gave a little jolt when I heard what seemed to me the cheerily sweet melody of the dial tone.

"The phone's come back," I shouted to Matt, who'd been hunched over his computer since breakfast.

"Great," he said, not taking his eyes off the screen. He wasn't in a very good mood. The writing didn't seem to be going particularly well. He hadn't shaved that morning and his eyes had the bleary look of someone who'd had too little sleep.

Or none at all.

"Listen," I said, taking the risk of bothering him further. "Why don't we call those snowplow guys? Maybe we can get them up here to dig us out. They've got to be free by now."

"Yeah sure," he said. "I'll do it after lunch. I'm just trying to get through this chapter."

I had gotten somewhat used to his black moods by now and attributed them to the pressure he must be under to complete his book. I knew how difficult it could be to be creative on demand. When the director shouts, "Action," you have to deliver, ready or not. I supposed it must be the same way when writing a book. Sometimes the inspiration is just not there. Still, understanding his emotional ups and downs did not make living with them any easier.

After lunch I had to remind him again to call the snow removal service. He dialled the number off a small card pinned to the wall next to other essential numbers. He talked for a little while, explaining the situation, thanked whoever it was on the other side, and rung off. He then explained to me that they would send a truck as soon as they could.

"When will that be?" I asked.

Matt shrugged noncommittally. "As soon as they can."

"Can't you call someone else? Someone must be able to get us out of here."

"They're the closest outfit within a hundred miles. A little inconvenience is the price you have to pay for privacy nowadays. You've got to expect that when you live so far off the beaten path."

"But this is ridiculous. We've been stranded here for nearly a week."

"I don't know what to tell you," Matt snapped. "That's just the way it is in the country. This isn't the city anymore."

I was more than a little annoyed myself and didn't mind showing it. I'd been trapped here without my clothes and with only the most tenuous connection to the outside world. No doubt I was coming down with a touch of cabin fever. As I watched Matt settle back in front of his computer for an afternoon writing session, I could feel my blood pressure rising. I was about to say something nasty, but I held back. If we were going to be trapped here together it wasn't going to make things any more pleasant by fighting.

Instead, I busied myself in the kitchen, cleaning up and foraging in the cupboard among our dwindling supplies of food to find something to fix for dinner. Around three o'clock, I made myself a cup of tea and checked in on Matt to see if he'd want a cup. Hunched over the computer monitor, a look of intense concentration on his handsome features, he was tapping out words on his keyboard. I decided not to bother him.

I was about to leave the kitchen when I saw the card for the snow removal service taped to the wall. Taking a peek at Matt, who was still occupied at his computer, I pecked out the numbers, waited three rings, and heard a voice with a heavy New England accent pick up on the other end.

I explained that Matt and I had been snowbound for nearly a week and asked him if it was possible to plow us out immediately.

The man on the other end seemed surprised.

"A week?" he said. "Why didn't you call sooner?"

"The lines were down. The phone just came back on."

"I see. Don't you have a cellular? Most folks in these parts have cellular phones for cases like this."

"I don't know," I said, trying to keep my voice down so as not to disturb Matt.

"You don't know if you have a cellular phone?"

"No. I mean . . . The thing is that I'm a guest here and I don't know if the person I'm staying with has one."

"Why didn't you ask?"

"It didn't occur to me."

"Well, I guess whoever it is you're staying with would have used it if they had it. I'd seriously suggest they get one."

I peeked around the corner at Matt. He was still typing away.

"I will," I said. "Look, the thing is we really need you to come right now and dig us out. I know you're busy. My boyfriend called earlier and he said you'd try to get here as soon as possible, but we've been trapped here—"

"What are you talking about? No one called here for a residential plow."

"Are you sure? I heard him talking to someone on the phone. . . . "

"Not me, lady, and I've been here all day. Maybe it was another outfit."

"Another outfit?" I said, feeling a sinking unease. "There are other places to call?"

"Are you kidding?" The man laughed. "Every other cowboy with a four-by-four and a plow runs jobs around this time of year. A fella can barely keep himself in beer money running plows up here, with all the competition. You know what I think? I think maybe your boyfriend was just selling you the second oldest line in the book outside of 'Honey, the car ran out of gas.' "

I felt myself flush with embarrassment.

"Can you get us out of here?" I said sharply, cutting off the man's laughter. "Now. Today?"

The man cleared his throat. "No problem. Just tell me where you live. The main roads are all clear. I can probably be there within the hour."

"It's—"

I stared blankly out the kitchen window.

"Yes," the man on the other end said.

"It's . . . I'm going to have to call you back."

I hung up the phone.

For the first time it occurred to me that I had no idea where I was.

I stood there in the kitchen, staring at the phone as if it had somehow betrayed me.

Could there have been some mistake? The man said no one had called him. He also said there were lots of other plowing services. Perhaps Matt had called someone else. Yet Matt had said that there were no other plowing services within a hundred miles. Had Matt only pretended to call? And if so, why?

Perhaps he didn't want to be disturbed; perhaps he preferred another couple of days of enforced isolation to help motivate him to get on with his novel. I peered in at him again, bent at his desk. His fingers were no longer playing over the keyboard and he was staring at the screen as if it presented some mind-bending puzzle.

I decided that the first order of business was to find out the address of the chalet. Padding out of the kitchen, I quietly went upstairs to my bedroom and pulled out the copy of *Architectural Digest* I had looked at a couple of nights ago. There was a tacky spot on the front cover where the mailing label used to be. I pulled out the other magazines in the wicker basket beside the antique rocking chair and spread them over the quilt. The mailing labels had been carefully removed from each and every one.

What's the big deal? I asked myself. Sometimes I did the same thing myself with magazines. Often the labels covered a piece of the art or the title of an article. But on every single magazine? Maybe Matt was just compulsive about the labels. He was a writer, after all, and writers were a bit eccentric. There had to be some perfectly logical explanation for his having removed those labels. I was sure of it.

Yet I couldn't deny the nagging sense of unease I felt in the pit of my stomach.

That evening Matt surprised me by making a special romantic dinner. I had already decided not to say anything, either about the magazines or the call to the plowing service. I didn't want him to think I was snooping around behind his back—or that I was some kind of paranoid nutcase. Besides, I was certain that my misgivings were all unfounded. It wouldn't be the first time that I was the victim of nothing more than an overactive imagination.

Plus, Matt was being so sweet and he had gone through an awful lot of trouble to prepare dinner. When I tried to help, he gently but emphatically pushed me out of the kitchen.

"What should I do?" I asked.

He grinned.

"Go upstairs and put on something special."

The playful look in his eyes instantly chased away any remnants of the questions and concerns from the hours before. I resigned myself to the undeniable fact that I'd heard long ago: writers were indeed strange animals.

I curtsied. "As you say."

Upstairs, I searched the closet until I came upon a peach chiffon gown so delicate it looked as though it could have been made by fairy folk. Over it I drew a short peach satin robe that barely covered my thighs. I found a pair of totally impractical but sexy high-heeled mules to match and returned downstairs.

As we sat at the heavy oak dining table, immaculately dressed and lit by candlelight, I asked him what the occasion was.

"Occasion? Can't a man just cook a special dinner in honor of his muse?"

"His muse?"

"Yes. You've been such an inspiration to me. I've really made some headway into my novel."

"Me? What have I done?"

"Just your presence has made all the difference in the world to me," he said. He reached across the table and grabbed my wrists. "I know I've been kind of difficult to live with at times over the past week, but things are going to change. I promise. I just had to get over that initial hump. It's always like that. Then things go smoothly. You'll see. Everything will be different."

He poured me some more wine, a delicious white Chardonnay he had bought especially for me during his trip to the grocery.

"So tell me. How did such a nice girl end up in such a cutthroat business like acting?"

"Maybe that explains it."

"Explains what?"

"Why I haven't had any success. I'm just too good."

Matt began clearing away the plates. When I stood to help, he told me just to have a seat in the living room and relax. I objected at first, insisting on helping out, but Matt was even more insistent, and I gave up graciously. I took my wineglass into the living room and sat down on the couch in front of the fire.

"Seriously," he called out, "what made you want to become an actress?"

"I'm not sure exactly. I always liked makeup ever since I was a little girl. I would think up long, involved games and force my poor friends to play along. It wasn't just plain old cowboys and Indians. They were epics. The plots were so intricate I'd have to explain them over and over again. I was a five-year-old Cecil B. DeMille without the budget or the cast of thousands."

Matt laughed. "But every bit as determined I'll bet."

"Sometimes I would have to take on two or three of the parts all by myself. Poor me, huh? I loved it. When the other kids got bored and ran off to play ball, or when no one was around who would play, I'd play by myself, talking to characters the same way I'm talking to you. I'm sure everyone thought I was quite a nutty little kid."

"Imagination can be a misunderstood thing," he said, carrying a large salad bowl and two glasses into the kitchen. "You said you began acting in college?"

"I was kind of an awkward gawky kid in high school. A real late bloomer. It wasn't until my first year in college that I . . . blossomed, you might say. Anyway, I met a boy who was in the drama club and though I was still a little too insecure to appear on stage, I worked on sets and costumes, things like that. Eventually, I took the part of Ophelia in an adaptation of *Hamlet*. I caught the bug for good after that."

"Where did you graduate school?"

"A small private college in New Jersey. You never heard of it. Besides, I didn't graduate. I left after my junior year to go to New York and become an actress."

I didn't tell Matt the real reason I had left school. This wasn't the time or the place for the revelation of yet another tragic moment in my life. And after the other night, I wasn't quite ready to open myself up to him again.

"That took some guts."

"And a lot of naïveté," I said, swallowing the rest of my wine. "I didn't have a whole lot of success. I came thinking I was going to take the city by storm. In less than two months I realized that the city was full of young people just like me. It was a sobering experience."

Matt had finished clearing away the table. He carried the candles over to the fireplace and set them on top of the mantel.

"I'll bet you had a lot of interesting parts."

"Oh yes," I said sarcastically. "I got to do Shakespeare again. *King Lear*. I played Regan as a horse. Perhaps you caught it?"

"Nooo," Matt said, feigning serious consideration. "Missed it, I'm afraid to say. Must have been out of town."

"Let's see. There was a lesbian production of Camus's *Caligula* in which all the characters were women. An environmental epic called

The Revolt of the Lemmings. A play called *No Talking,* in which, literally, no one talked. A production of *Waiting for Godot* in which I had the unfortunate honor of playing the title role and never appearing, although I was listed on the playbill. An original piece entitled *Richard Nixon in Hell,* which is where I think he'd have been perfectly happy to be instead of in the theater. A gay production in the village of Sartre's *No Exit* in which all the characters were men."

Matt started to interrupt.

"Don't even ask," I said. "Shall I go on?"

Matt laughed. "I think I get the point. Did you ever think of writing yourself?"

"What? What do you mean?"

"I mean writing a play for yourself. I was thinking about what you said about how you made up all sorts of stories when you were a little girl. That's not so different from the kinds of things I used to do. Except I used to write them down instead of act them out. It's really not that different."

"Oh, I couldn't write. I mean I did write some poems in school. What liberal arts major hasn't? I started a play once—" I waved my hand dismissively. "It wasn't any good."

"I'd like to see it sometime," Matt said, "if you still have it."

"Oh, God no," I said. "I'd be so embarrassed. You're a published writer."

"Let me tell you a secret, Johanna. There are a lot of writers out there. More often than not the only difference between a published one and an unpublished one is greed. If you have a story someone thinks they can make money off of, they'll publish it no matter how lousy a writer you are. Hell, they'll write the damn book for you if necessary. You just need a hook."

"I don't know, Matt."

"Think about it. That's all I'm saying. Now, how about some dessert?"

Matt returned from the kitchen with what he called his specialty: a raspberry chocolate mousse.

"You're quite the gourmet cook," I said, spooning up the dreamy confection of chocolate and raspberry, laced with Kahlúa. "Aren't you having any?"

"The Kahlúa," he said.

"Oh. For someone who doesn't drink, you keep an awful lot of spirits in the house. I hope I didn't give you the impression I'm some kind of lush."

"Will you stop worrying about the impression you're making? You aren't on an audition, you know."

"Sorry," I said, scooping up another spoonful of whatever heaven must taste like. "An old habit I guess. How did you ever scrounge together the ingredients for such an elaborate dinner? I was in the kitchen before. The cupboards are nearly bare."

"Having been a struggling writer as well an incurable romantic has its advantages."

Matt smiled.

The tension I'd seen in his face the last few days seemed to have melted away. He looked relaxed, open, warm. I could feel the heat of the intimacy building between us. He was once again the Matt I had met in New York. It was funny how a few good pages could make such a difference to a writer. I suppose it wasn't a lot different for an actress. For the first time in days Matt was no longer brooding and aloof. Here, at last, was the Matt I felt I could ask anything.

Well, almost anything.

"Matt," I said, "what's our address here?"

"Address?" He laughed. "Out in the forest?"

"You must have an address. Everybody does."

"What would I need an address for?" he quipped, still smiling. "I know where I live."

"Very zen," I replied dryly. "What I mean is, what if someone wants to visit?"

"Visitors!" Matt feigned a shudder. "Perish the thought. I don't plan on entertaining any visitors. If I want to see people, I go to New York. This is where I go to get away from the madding crowd." He looked at me closely. "Why? Are you lonely?"

"No. Not really."

I suddenly yawned, surprising myself.

"Excuse me."

Matt leaned toward me, and put his hand over my wrist. It felt strong and warm. Possessive, in a decidedly masculine way.

"You're not having second thoughts, are you? I mean about being out here alone with me."

"No, nothing like that."

He gave a wink and a mock leer. "Maybe feeling a little like Little Red Riding Hood with the big bad wolf perhaps?"

"That's not a role I'm suited for."

Matt leaned back and laughed. "No. I would say you're definitely not the Little Red Riding Hood type. Listen, the best thing about this place, the very reason I bought the chalet is that it has no address. We aren't even officially part of a town. I have complete and utter isolation here. No disturbances. I can get on with my work in peace and quiet."

I thought back to the magazines upstairs, their labels assiduously peeled off.

"How do you get your mail?"

"Post office box. I go there once a week." Matt pointed to the door behind me. "Weather permitting. But I seldom get any mail. After all, no one knows where I am."

"I see," I said, putting down my spoon, and unsuccessfully trying to stifle another yawn.

"I hope my novel makes for more scintillating entertainment than my after-dinner conversation."

"It's not you, it's just—" I started to explain, but was cut off by another yawn.

"More mousse?"

"No, thank you. I seem to have gotten really tired all of a sudden."

"Tired?" Matt sounded genuinely disappointed. He had gone out of his way to prepare a romantic dinner. He was in an exceptionally good mood. His intentions seemed obvious and I wasn't going to offer any objections, in spite of my resolve a few nights ago. He seemed back to his old self again and I wasn't going to do anything to spoil that. I felt badly about disrupting his plans for us. Unfortunately, I could hardly keep my eyes open.

"I'm terribly sorry, Matt, but I'm going to have to make it an early night."

"That's okay," he said good-naturedly. "There'll be other nights. After all, it doesn't look like we'll be going any place real soon."

"Are you sure you don't mind?"

Matt shook his head and pointed to his desk. "My editor will thank you."

I bent over and kissed him on the forehead. "You're sweet. Good night."

"Good night, my dear Erato."

"Huh?" I turned around drowsily, nearly losing my balance on the high-heeled mules. "What did you say?"

"Nothing, my sweet muse. Just go to sleep."

I slipped off the mules and climbed the stairs barefoot. I barely beat the sandman getting out of my clothes and underneath the covers. I slept deeply and dreamlessly, waking up only once sometime in the middle of the night, and that was to hear Matt arguing loudly on the phone downstairs.

I thought to get up and go out onto the loft to hear what was the matter, but before I could gather up the energy to do so, I fell soundly back to sleep.

25

---•---

I woke up the next morning, feeling awful.

My head was pounding and every joint in my body ached. It took all of my energy just to get out of bed. I shuffled into the bathroom and examined myself in the mirror. I looked exhausted. I splashed some water on my face, patted it dry, and tried to comb my hair, but the effort was more than I could afford to expend. As I passed the bed, it was all I could do to keep from crawling back under the covers.

I broke a light sweat going downstairs, where Matt was standing at the window, looking out at the snow. He turned around when he heard me.

"Good morning," he said cheerfully, but the expression on his face quickly turned to one of concern. "My God, Johanna, you look terrible."

"Thanks," I said feebly, trying my best to smile. I was holding on to the railing for support, afraid that if I let go I'd fall.

Matt put the coffee cup he'd been holding down on the desk and came toward me, taking me by the arms. He led me to the couch and gently sat me down. He laid his hand on my forehead and his brow furrowed.

"I think you have a fever. I'll be right back."

Matt returned shortly with a thermometer, a glass of orange juice, and two aspirin. He had me swallow the aspirin and drink as much of the juice as I could stomach, before popping the thermometer in my mouth. He looked down at his watch until about a minute had passed and then took the thermometer from under my tongue. He turned around and held it up to the light in order to read the slender silver thread of mercury.

"Just as I thought," he said, shaking the thermometer vigorously as he turned back to face me. "You've got a fever all right. One hundred and three. Come on. I'll help you back up to bed."

"Can't I just lie down here?" I protested.

"No. Up to bed."

"I don't think I can make it back up those stairs."

"Then I'll carry you."

Matt scooped me up off the couch as if I were a child. Too sick to feel anything but gratitude, I laid my head against his strong chest and let myself take comfort in his care. He carried me back to my bedroom and laid me on the bed. Sliding a hand under my back, he sat me up, and carefully undid the delicate silk laces of my gown.

"What are you doing?" I asked groggily.

"Ssh," he whispered. "Try not to talk."

Matt eased the gown off my shoulders, baring me to the waist. He went to the bathroom and came back with a damp washcloth and a soft, fluffy towel. He placed the damp washcloth on my forehead and then gently worked his way down the back of my neck, my shoulders, my back, and breasts. My hot skin rebelled against the cool cloth and I started shaking, but Matt insisted.

"We have to get this fever down."

He lifted the gown up over my legs and continued his ministrations, stopping only to rinse out the cloth in the bathroom sink. He managed to remove my gown entirely and pulled out a plain white cotton shift from the antique oak bureau. He worked it over my head and I was grateful for its soft warmth. Matt helped me under the covers and kissed me lightly on the top of my head.

"You shut your eyes and try to get some rest, okay?"

I nodded.

He pulled the curtains across the windows until the room was in semidarkness.

"I'll be up to check on you," he said. "But if you need anything, just call. I'll leave your door open."

"Thank you," I whispered.

Matt left the room and I reluctantly drifted off into a fitful sleep.

It seemed like only five minutes later that I felt Matt gently shaking me awake.

I opened my eyes to a dark room, the only light coming from the bedside lamp. I instantly looked to the windows, but could see only blackness between the drawn curtains.

"How long have I been asleep?"

"About six hours," Matt said. "How do you feel?"

"Weak. A little dizzy."

"That's to be expected. You still have a fever. And you haven't eaten anything all day."

I vaguely remembered Matt coming to check on me throughout the day. He changed my sweat-soaked clothes, sponge bathed me, and forced liquids down my throat. With some embarrassment, I also remembered him helping me walk unsteadily to the bathroom.

"I've brought you some broth," he said, holding a tray with a steaming bowl.

"I don't think I could."

"You really have to eat something."

I looked dubiously at the bowl.

"I'm sorry about all this."

"About what?"

"Getting sick and all."

Matt just smiled. "These things happen."

"But it's got to be a terrible inconvenience. You came up here to work, not to play nursemaid."

"The work can wait. There are more important things than work."

"But I know the pressure you're under."

Matt put his finger to his lips. "Sssh," he said softly. "I don't want to hear any more about it."

"You've been so great. I wish there was something I could do to repay you."

"You can. Have some soup."

"You don't give up, do you?"

"Never."

He pulled up a chair and slowly spoon-fed me the soup. It was surprisingly tasty.

"It's good. What is it?"

"Vegetable broth, with a few special seasonings. It's what my mother used to give me when I had a fever. Of course, she used the more traditional chicken soup, but I modified the recipe a bit, given your sympathy for our animal friends, four-legged and otherwise."

I silently envied the image of Matt's mother making him soup when he was sick and thought back to my own mother. She was always too busy with her own life to tend to me, even when I was sick. Her idea of nursing me was to defrost some frozen fish sticks and scribble some microwave directions before she went out on a date.

Matt proffered another spoonful of the savory soup and I eagerly slurped it down.

"Good girl," he encouraged me.

I finished more than half the bowl before I convinced Matt to put it aside. He seemed pleased and I was happy to please him.

"Matt? Can I ask you a question?"

"Sure," he said, wiping my mouth.

"Why do you lock your bedroom door?"

Matt smiled, but it looked forced. "How do you know I lock my bedroom door?"

"It's not like I tried to go in there or anything," I said quickly, to reassure him. "But I've heard you use a key to open the door and I've heard the lock click shut when you leave."

"I see," he said. "Well, it's no great mystery."

"I didn't think it was."

"But it bothers you anyway?"

"I was just curious is all. Forget it. You don't have to tell me if you don't want."

Matt stood up and walked to the window, his back to me. He pulled back the curtain and stood there for a long time without saying a word.

I wasn't sure I wanted to know what was behind the door. Not now anyway. I was suddenly so tired. And though I didn't want to admit it: I felt incredibly vulnerable. I was sick, barely able to get out of bed, dependent upon him for nearly everything, and now I had risked getting him angry. Still, the locked room had bothered me ever since I had arrived at the chalet. And though it was true I hadn't tried to open the door, I had been sorely tempted to give it a try on more than one occasion.

"Really, Matt," I said, "I don't care."

"No," he said finally. "I want to tell you."

He let go of the curtain and turned from the window. His face was stoic, but not the expression in his eyes.

"You notice I don't go in there much."

"Yes," I said. "I just figured you weren't getting much sleep lately with the book and all. You seem to be working through the night."

"That's true. But the fact is I seldom sleep in there anyway."

"I don't understand."

"Remember when I told you I'd never been married?"

"Yes," I said, my insides twisting, not quite sure I was up for a bombshell revelation.

"Well, I wasn't being completely honest."

"You mean you were married?"

"No, not exactly."

"Matt, I don't understand." I tried to rub away the beginnings of what felt like a dull headache. I wasn't feeling up to a game of emotional cat-and-mouse. "Just what are you trying to tell me?"

"I was engaged to be married. It was right before I sold my first book. We bought the land for this chalet together. Actually, she bought it. Back then, I didn't have two dimes to rub together. She had confidence in me. She was the only one who did at the time. It was to be our own private getaway. They didn't find the cancer until it had spread beyond her uterine wall. It was already too late. It was ironic, really. Instead of the children we'd planned, she'd given birth to her own death. I would have sold the land, burned the plans for the chalet, but she made me promise to build it. So I did. That winter I wrote the first novel I ever sold. She was my inspiration."

"I didn't know, Matt. I'm terribly sorry."

Matt rubbed the material of the lace curtains between his fingers, a faraway look in his eyes.

"It was a long time ago," he said. "Time heals all wounds. Or so they say."

"Why didn't you tell me?"

His eyes snapped back to the present. He looked down at me with an expression of such tenderness it made my heart ache.

"I didn't want you to think I was one of those guys living in the past. It's been a long time. I'm ready to move on. Still, that room was supposed to be ours. I have a hard time sleeping in it. It's stupid, I know. I hope you can somehow understand."

"I think I do," I said, wanting desperately to reach out to him, but somehow feeling he needed to be left alone with his grief.

"Anyway," he said, affecting a sudden levity, "aren't you glad you asked? At least you won't have to go entertaining fantasies that I'm some kind of Bluebeard and have a collection of dead ex-wives in there. Or that I have my stuffed mother in a chair looking out the window."

"The thought had crossed my mind," I feebly joked.

"Come on, let's get that bed changed for the night."

My legs were surprisingly shaky as he led me out of bed and to the old cane-backed rocker against the wall. I sat there with a comforter across my legs while Matt changed the sheets. He then helped me back to the bed after I assured him I could make it to the bathroom under my own power. Safely ensconced in the warmth of the fresh flannel sheets, Matt sat back down in the chair beside the bed and read to me from a book of love poems by Pablo Neruda.

I fell asleep to the soft melody of his voice, only to wake up hours later in the pitch-darkness.

The door was closed, but even so I could hear Matt shouting in the living room. I made my way out of the bed and crossed the room on shaky legs. I cracked the door and crept out onto the loft overlooking the room below. Matt was pacing the floor, the hand-held phone pressed to his ear. I couldn't see the expression on his face, but the short, harsh expletives that peppered his conversation left no doubt as to his emotional state.

"Goddammit," he growled. "You can't fucking do this to me. I'll make you pay if it's the last thing I do, I swear it. That's not a threat, that's a promise. You think I can't touch you? I'll make you wish you never met me. Nobody does this to Matt Lang and gets away with it. Nobody. You're through!"

Matt slammed the phone down on the coffee table so hard I thought it would break. He stood for a moment and then wheeled around, his head down, toward the stairway. I still felt shaky on my feet, but adrenaline spurred me on. I rushed back to my room and jumped back into bed just as Matt came up the stairs. It was only when I pulled the covers up to my chin that I realized I'd forgotten to shut the door.

I closed my eyes tightly, feigning sleep. I could sense Matt standing in the doorway. He stood there for what seemed an eternity, looking in. Then I heard his voice calling softly.

"Johanna? Johanna? Are you awake?"

I didn't move. After another minute or so he shut the door and walked quietly down the hall.

I heard him sigh, take out his keys, and unlock the door of the room he'd designed for himself and his dead fiancée.

The morning sun was streaming through the sheer curtains and I could hear the tinkling sound of melting snow outside the window.

I kicked off the covers and swung my legs over the side of the bed. I was still a little shaky as I made my way to the window but, all in all, I felt better than I had. I pulled back the curtains and saw the welcome sight of a thawing world, the pines surrendering heavy arm-loads of snow, the icicles hanging from the eaves growing shorter, the steady *drip-drop* of water running down the tin gutters. I could even see the green roof and the sun glinting off the windshield from the great white mound that used to be the Jeep.

"I thought I heard you moving around up here. You shouldn't be out of bed."

I turned from the window to see Matt in the doorway. He was holding a wicker breakfast tray.

"But I feel much better," I said. "Besides, have you looked outside? The weather is breaking. Isn't it wonderful?"

"Yes," Matt said, a little glumly I thought. "It does seem to be warming up. No matter, you're still recuperating. You need all the rest you can get. Now you get right back into bed. Here, I've brought you something to eat."

"I'm not really very hungry," I said, eyeing the bowl of hot cereal on the tray.

"Nonsense. You've got to keep your strength up. You'll feel even better after you've eaten some breakfast."

I sighed in mock exasperation and climbed back into bed as Matt set the tray over my thighs.

"Happy?" I asked.

"Yes."

I reluctantly spooned some of the oatmeal into my mouth as Matt busied himself around the room. I watched him for a while, took a sip of orange juice, and decided to take a chance.

"I woke up in the middle of the night. I heard your voice. It sounded like you were arguing with someone."

Matt seemed to freeze for an instant. He took a long time answering. When he did his voice was slow and careful.

"How much did you hear?"

"Not much," I lied. "I was still half-asleep."

Matt turned, looking sheepish.

"I'm sorry I woke you. I guess I got a little carried away."

"It was nothing. Like I said, I was half-asleep. I couldn't even make out what you were saying. But you sounded pretty upset."

"My agent," Matt said. "He's been on me about finishing the final draft of the novel. The publisher moved up the release date at his insistence and without my consent."

"Your agent? I thought you said the only one who knew you were up here was your editor?"

"I meant to say my editor and agent. I guess you might call it a Freudian omission. I try to think of my agent as little as possible."

I thought back to Ruth. "I can understand that. But can he do that?"

"Do what?"

"Push your book forward without asking you?"

Matt shrugged. "He insists it's good for my career. Get another Matt Lang novel out there while the getting is good. He's sure that with the right formula and the right marketing plan I can make the bestseller lists. He's even got the publisher convinced. They've already committed to a big-time ad campaign if I can deliver the goods. They want a rough draft with a killer hook, something really commercial."

"But you're not convinced?"

"I may not be writing the great American novel, but there are still some things that can't be rushed and inspiration is one of them. I'm not working on an assembly line for crissakes. I can't just crank out more novels on demand as if it were merely a matter of typing faster. I don't care how much money they wave at me."

"Okay, okay." I laughed. "Calm down. You don't have to convince me. I'm the one who happens to think your work is pretty terrific, remember? I agree with you one hundred percent."

Matt rubbed his face. "I'm sorry. I guess I'm still pretty worked up about the whole thing. Let's just forget it. Finish your oatmeal. And don't forget to take your aspirin."

Matt took away my breakfast tray and returned a short time later with a couple of books, a portable radio, and a pitcher containing the rest of the orange juice.

"Thank God for frozen concentrate," he said, putting the pitcher on the nightstand. "Do you need anything else?"

"No. I don't think so."

"Okay then. I'm going down to work. See if I can't crank out a novel before noon," he said sarcastically. "I'll come up around lunchtime. Meanwhile, I want you to stay in bed and rest."

"Yes sir," I said and saluted.

Matt shook his head. "I mean it. I want you up and around. I miss you."

With that he returned downstairs. I fiddled with the radio for a while, flipped through the books he'd brought, but my mind was busy running one question over and over: *what kind of an agent calls a client at three in the morning?*

26

———•———

By evening Matt determined that I was well enough to come down for a light dinner.

Afterward I sat in the living room while Matt cleaned up the dishes. He joined me on the couch when he was done and we sat quietly together, looking into the dancing flames of the fire. Every once in a while, Matt got up to put another log on the grate and it was while returning to the couch after doing so that Matt asked me about my past sexual experiences.

"I don't really think . . . I mean—"

Matt just sat there staring at me calmly.

"That's just not the kind of thing lovers talk about," I finally managed to stammer.

"Why not?" Matt asked, nonplussed. "They talk about everything else. Why should their sexual pasts be private?"

"I don't see how it's relevant to anything. What's past is past. It only leads to jealousy."

"I think it can be highly erotic."

"Don't you trust me? I can assure you that I don't sleep around, that I've been careful, that I don't have any diseases."

"You're not hearing me, Johanna. It's okay. I didn't mean to offend you. If you'd rather not talk about it," he said, "I understand. I just thought it would be interesting to get to know you better that way."

"It's not that I don't want to talk about it," I began. "But—"

"But?"

"I don't have anything to hide if that's what you mean."

"That's not what I meant. I'm sorry if that's what it sounded like. Like I said, I just want to know everything about you."

He looked so genuinely contrite that I began to feel guilty.

"I guess you just caught me a little off guard I guess. Maybe I overreacted."

"Let's just forget it, okay?"

"No," I said. "Maybe you're right. Why can't lovers talk about it? I never thought of it that way, but I imagine it can be kind of erotic."

"And you're willing to give me a fair answer this time? No acting?"

"No acting," I promised. I felt myself blush. "God, it's kind of hard getting started."

"How about your first time?"

"My first time? That's not very erotic, I assure you."

Matt grinned. "Why don't you let me be the judge of that?"

"Okay," I said, feeling strangely lightheaded, as if I were more than a little high. "The first time was in the basement of a girlfriend's house. I had just turned fifteen. We were playing Ping-Pong and her brother came down. He challenged us to a game and the loser had to do whatever the winner said. I guess you can see where this one's going?"

"I sure hope so."

"My girlfriend assured me we could beat him, but it quickly became obvious that he was a lot better than she let on. To make matters worse, she suddenly seemed to be purposely flubbing easy shots. Well, we lost pretty badly. I got the feeling it wasn't the first time my friend and her brother had played this game. She was already undressed before I could take off my sneakers. She helped me up onto the Ping-Pong table and kissed me while her brother . . . well, let's just say we both experienced something of the thrill of victory."

Matt laughed. "See? That's what I mean. You didn't think that story was erotic? I found it quite arousing."

"After that there isn't a whole lot to tell. Like I said, I was kind of a late bloomer. There was a time in a cheap motel room after my senior prom. I think you'd call it date rape now. I was stupid to go up there with him. But I was insecure. I wanted to please him. I'm just lucky I didn't get pregnant. I didn't do much of anything sexual after that for a long time. I got involved with a boy in my college drama class. He didn't push me, so not much happened. I think he was as inexperienced as I was. We did it a couple of times. It was pretty nondescript. I think he just did it because he thought he was supposed to. That's what it felt like anyway. Still, he was the first boy I ever really loved."

"What happened to him?"

"Oh," I said, feeling a quick stab of pain at the memory of his death. "We just drifted apart. That's when I came to New York."

"Sin City."

"Yeah. Only I didn't sin too much. I avoided the usual stupid stuff like sleeping with guys who told me they could get me parts and stuff like that. They usually got bored waiting for me to put out and went on to someone easier or more gullible. I had my share of flings, though. I once had sex in an empty theater with one of the cast of *Phantom of the Opera*. He invited me on stage hours after the show. We had just finished, when from somewhere among the darkened seats came the sound of clapping. God, was that embarrassing."

"I'll bet you won't include that performance in the bio of your first playbill," Matt joked. "Although I saw *Phantom* and I would have certainly found that to be the high point of the show."

"Thanks," I said, making a face.

"Any other public performances?"

"Nooo. But I did go to one of those S-M clubs once."

"Really? Did you participate?"

"The guy I was with begged me to, but I was just curious. I have to admit the idea kind of turned me on, but the reality of it all was rather sordid and depressing. It just wasn't my type of scene."

Matt seemed a little disappointed.

"I did have a gay experience once," I said. "One and a half actually."

I had promised Matt I wouldn't act, but I couldn't help but feel that in a way I was putting on the ultimate performance. The truth was my script, and I was determined like any good actress to keep my audience interested.

"It was during that lesbian production of *Caligula* I told you about. She played Caligula's favorite horse, you know, the one he made a senator? Anyway, she took a liking to me. I'd never done anything like that before. I mean I'd kissed girlfriends and stuff, but nothing sexual. In the play there was a scene where I shared a bed with Caligula's horse."

"Bestiality and lesbianism," Matt said, shaking his head. "You'd never know it to look at you."

"I didn't know it either at first. I must have been the only straight chick in the play because I was the only one who didn't realize what was going on. One of the other actresses finally clued me in. I don't know why I did it. I mean, I'm not gay, but she was sweet and sincere. I think she really loved me. We did it a couple of times before she realized that it just wasn't meant to be."

"And the other half?"

"What do you mean?"

"You said you had a gay experience and a half. What was the half?"

"Oh, that. I was going out with this guy. He was an actor, too. He convinced me to go in for a threesome. It was a really dumb idea. But the girl was beautiful, a model, actually, and I was kind of flattered that she was attracted to me. One night we went out together and we all had a little too much to drink. We went back to his place and one thing led to another and we wound up in bed together. We did it a couple of times after that. It was okay, but I was really doing it for him. Like I said, it was a dumb idea. He wound up choosing her. You know, this is really strange."

"How so?" Matt asked.

"I don't know. I just never talked about this to anyone."

The fire crackled on the grate, split a log, and sent a shower of sparks up the chimney. Matt reached out and stroked my hair, his fingers trailing lightly along the side of my neck, down to my shoulder. I felt flushed and strangely excited.

"How does it make you feel?" he said softly.

"Kind of turned on," I admitted.

"Me, too," he said. "Johanna, tell me your fantasy."

"My fantasy? There are so many—"

"No, I mean your deepest darkest fantasy. The one you dare tell no one."

I stared at him for a moment, unable to speak, hypnotized by the two tiny flames dancing in his eyes. I never felt more exposed, more naked, in my entire life. It was as if he knew my fantasy before I told him and yet he wanted to hear it from my own lips. He wanted me to confess to my darkest and most titillating shame.

"Trust me," he said.

"I do," I said.

"Tell me."

"I want to be taken," I said, my voice barely above a whisper, a voice that hardly sounded like my own. "Not just sexually. I want to be consumed body, mind, and soul. I want to be totally annihilated. I want to be a sacrifice. I want to give myself only to the kind of man who can appreciate the incredible beauty of my act of self-destruction."

"What's this man like?" he asked.

"I never see his face. He's like a shadow. He comes to me in the dead of night. I don't know who he is. He may be someone I know very well. Or he may be someone I've never met. But somehow he seems to know all about me. I have no secrets from him. He tells me things about myself that no one else knows. Things I've never told anyone. He never so much as touches me and that makes me want him all the more. I know that if he touches me, I'll die. But I don't care. It's what I want. It's what he wants. But he is waiting. I don't know why he waits. Maybe it's for the right time. All I know is that I live for that moment. The moment when he accepts my sacrifice. Does that sound crazy to you?"

"No. It sounds quite beautiful. Have you ever been tempted to make your fantasy a reality?"

"If fantasies were possible, they wouldn't be fantasies."

"Yes," Matt said, staring off into the fire. "I suppose you're right."

We sat there quietly for some time, watching the fire die down. Under the grate a pile of burning embers slowly collected like molten gold coins.

"Let me ask you a question," I said at last.

Matt turned his head from the fire.

"Are you using me as a resource?"

"That sounds so cold and calculating," he said.

"How would you put it?"

"I'm writing about a woman. I like my books to be as authentic as possible. To do so, I have to get inside a woman's mind. You are my inspiration."

"Is that all?"

Matt shook his head as if I were a child too young to understand.

"That's everything," he whispered.

I wanted him to kiss me, to touch me, to make love to me. Instead, he stood up.

"You look so tired. I shouldn't have kept you up so late."

"I feel fine," I lied.

"No. I think we overdid it tonight. We'd better get you up to bed. Let me get you a pill."

"I'm all right, really."

Matt wasn't listening. He went to the kitchen and returned with a pill and a small cup of water.

"Here," he said.

"What are these pills anyway?" I said.

"Antibiotics. They've been around awhile, so I'm not sure how effective they are, but they'll have to do for the time being. Swallow."

I did as he said. He took the cup and put it on the coffee table. He slid one arm under my thighs and wrapped the other around my chest. He picked me up effortlessly and carried me up the stairs to my room. I was too tired to object anymore.

I sighed and buried my head into his chest. He laid me on the bed, took off my slippers, and pulled the covers up to my chin.

"Won't you stay?" I murmured.

"Sssh," he said. "Go to sleep."

He kissed me gently on my feverish lips, his mouth so soft and warm, but gone so soon.

"Matt," I groaned.

He turned off the light on the night table.

"You're dreaming," he whispered.

The last thing I saw was the dark outline of his body just before he shut the door.

I felt worse the following three days, so bad, in fact, that I spent the entire time in bed. For the first time I was concerned that I might need to see a doctor, but when I brought the matter up with Matt, he tried to allay my fears. Instead, he continued his own brand of nursing, insisting that I would start feeling better any day now.

Meanwhile, the calls continued. They came at all hours, sometimes two or three times a night, and each time the effects on Matt were the same. I could hear his muffled but angry voice even from behind the closed door of my bedroom. His profanity-laced warnings had given way to outright threats so virulent it was becoming increasingly difficult to believe he was telling the truth when he said the calls were coming from his agent. I decided not to bring up the matter again, certain I was unlikely to get an honest answer, even while I noted the weariness etched on his handsome features and wondered if he was getting any sleep at all.

Matt put me to bed every evening. It quickly became the favorite part of my day. He made time for the nightly ritual in spite of the increasing demands and pressure of his work. I appreciated the gesture. The half hour or so before I fell asleep had become the only significant time we had together. On one such night, I was sitting on top of the bed, my bare feet resting in Matt's lap. He had brought up a ceramic bowl of scented oil and he was rubbing the warm oil over my feet.

His strong unhurried hands slowly and patiently kneaded my soles. His fingers slipped between my toes, gently squeezing, pulling, and rubbing them one by one. I lay back on the pillows and closed my eyes, sighing my satisfaction. His expert hands massaged my ankles and then worked their way up my calves. He dipped his hands back into the oil and rubbed my knees and the tender place behind my knees.

Around the room Matt had lit scented candles, the same scent as the oil, a kind of fruity, spicy potpourri. The scent of the candles and oil, the feel of Matt's warm hands, and the soft flickering light put me into a dreamy, melting, half-sleep. Matt had lifted my nightgown and I felt his hands on my thighs now, his slippery hands feeling hotter, as I gave a soft little moan and almost involuntarily opened my legs. He was so close now I was afraid to move, to breathe, to do anything that would cause the delicious sensations rising through my body to stop.

I was naked under the gown and Matt's hand was between my legs, one finger sliding over the center of me, so brief, so fleeting. . . .

"Johanna," he whispered, "are you afraid to die?"

At first I didn't know if I'd heard him correctly. I looked up at him confused, disoriented.

"Are you afraid to die?" he repeated.

I felt as if I'd been slapped.

I sat up in bed, wide awake now, the delicious erotic twilight state I'd experienced only a heartbeat ago vanished like a dream.

"What kind of question is that?"

"A perfectly reasonable one I think," he said. "Everyone reflects on their mortality from time to time."

"Of course," I shot back, angry and frustrated. I suddenly realized that my gown was still up over my thighs, leaving me exposed. I yanked it down. "But what makes you bring it up now?"

"It's been on my mind lately."

"But we were—"

I started to explain what I thought was happening between us before he asked his question, but I realized it was pointless. Matt was looking at me without the least trace of comprehension. Had I somehow misread what he had been doing? No, his hands had been there. The oil, the candles . . .

God, what was he trying to do, drive me insane?

"So?" he said.

"So what?"

"Are you afraid to die?"

"Yes," I said, as steadily as I could.

"What was it like when your father died?"

I regretted now having lied about my father's death. I should never have told Matt my father had died. It made things too complicated. Now, I would be forced to keep lying. If I admitted the truth, Matt would accuse me again of having acted out the whole story of my past. He would feel emotionally manipulated. Worse, he would never believe another word I'd said. Then again, my little lie did make things more interesting. *More dramatic.*

"I'd rather not talk about it," I tried, hoping to avoid lying some more.

As I expected, Matt wouldn't let the matter rest so easily.

"After what you already told me? I just want to know about the funeral. How you felt. What your first experience with death was like. It says a lot about a person."

"But why? What purpose will that serve?"

"Please?" he said. "I think it would really help."

"The book?" I asked. "Is all this about the book?"

"Please," he said again. Only this time it wasn't a question.

Was he testing me? Did he still suspect I wasn't telling the truth? Well, if nothing else, training in acting made you a very good liar. I remembered my classes in method acting from Drake. You learned how to use the emotion from a real-life event to simulate emotion in a fictional event. I thought back to the first funeral I remembered attending. It had been traumatic enough to elicit some real emotions in me then. I let them flood back over me now.

"How old did you say you were when your father died?" Matt asked.

Had I even told Matt how old I was? Was he trying to trick me? No matter. I always told people the same thing.

"Twelve."

She was an aunt on my father's side. I did remember her well. We weren't close. My father had left by then, but my mother thought it important to keep up appearances. We had visited my aunt in the hospital once and once at home. By the time they let her come home, she had little more than a month or so to live. She was lying propped on some pillows, breathing through a plastic mask connected to two green oxygen tanks. She had been diagnosed with inoperable breast cancer only three months earlier. It had spread to her lungs. She was dead before Christmas.

"What was your reaction?" Matt asked.

"I was just a kid. I don't think I even really understood. A part of me did, of course. But a part of me—"

I let the sentence trail off as I remembered the funeral.

My uncle softly sobbing and smelling of booze, my grandmother collapsing in the aisle, wailing with grief, and my father, who had flown in from the West Coast, trying hopelessly to console her. Worst of all, I remember my aunt inside the coffin, wearing a bad wig and overly rouged, looking like a department store mannequin.

"It all seemed matter-of-fact to me, the way even the most terrible things often do to a child. I just accepted it. I guess I must have been in a kind of shock. My mother made me take my turn on the little kneeling bench to pray. My mother had insisted on an open casket. The undertaker had done his best to reconstruct my father's face. He had tried to make it appear lifelike. I jumped up from the bench and tried to run, but my mother forced me back. Whatever was lying in that casket was not my father. The thick makeup barely covered the stitches. For months afterward I woke up in the night in a cold sweat seeing that misshapen, sewn-together face."

I shuddered at the memory of my aunt's wasted, overly rouged face. She had looked like a dead clown.

"It was a bitterly cold day, early December, and we all drove to the cemetery. There was another short ceremony at the gravesite, and then we all walked back to the warmth of our cars. I remember staring out the back window and seeing the coffin, covered with flowers and standing beside the hole dug in the frozen earth. A light snow had begun to fall and I thought of how we were all going to our warm homes and how they were going to put my father in that cold hole in the ground and cover him with earth and how that's where he would stay for the night, all alone beneath the small stars, all alone forever. For the first time the truth of death hit me and I wept. For the first time in my life death had become real."

"How did that make you feel?" Matt said softly.

"Empty," I said. "Like something had been taken out of me, something large and deep, and all that was left was a hole. A hole the size of a coffin. The coffin that held my father."

"Johanna, how are you most afraid to die?"

"Is this for your book, too?"

"That's not fair, Johanna," Matt answered. "The book is not everything."

I stared at his tired face in the candlelight. I had pulled my feet from his hands and curled them up under me. I wanted him to go away right then, but I knew he wouldn't leave without an answer.

"When I was a little girl, my parents always had to check the house for intruders before I went to sleep. In the closets. Under the bed. Behind the curtains. I would watch as they double-checked the locks on the doors and windows. Finally satisfied, I would go to bed."

"That's interesting," Matt said. "Your fantasy . . ."

"People are often attracted to what they fear the most."

"Yes." Matt nodded. "Yes, I suppose that's true. Thank you, Johanna."

I let Matt tuck me under the covers. He blew out the candles and kissed me on the forehead before closing the door to my room and heading downstairs to work.

That night it took me a long time to fall asleep.

27

———•———

I woke up to the low rumbling growl of heavy machinery.

I leaped out of bed and ran to the window. I rubbed my eyes, half expecting what I saw to be a fragment of some feverish dream, but it was true enough all right. I could see the bright yellow plows pushing aside the piles of heavy snow. I threw on a silk robe and ran downstairs like a kid on Christmas morning. Matt was sitting at his computer. He didn't turn from the screen.

"Why didn't you tell me?"

"I wanted it to be a surprise."

"Isn't it great?"

"Yeah," Matt replied, finally turning around in his chair to face me. I could see the bags under his eyes and the deepening lines around his mouth. "Now the whole world can rush in and disturb us."

"Who's going to disturb us?"

Matt didn't answer. I thought of the phone calls he'd been getting in the middle of the night, the ones that were supposedly from his agent. Could that be whom he was talking about? I was tempted to ask him again about the caller, but decided against it. I didn't want anything to put a damper on this glorious morning. Besides, it seemed rather cruel. He seemed genuinely stressed out by the situation. For the first time I noticed the plate beside his mouse pad containing the crushed filters of at least a dozen cigarettes.

"I thought you didn't smoke."

"I don't, usually. Sometimes just when I'm writing. It helps me concentrate, gives my body something to do."

Just then there was a loud knock on the door.

"Mr. Jablonsky? We're just about finished out here."

Matt stared at the door with a startled look on his face, but made no move to answer it.

"Mr. Jablonsky?" The voice came again.

"Matt?" I said.

Matt seemed to snap back to awareness. "Yes, I'm sorry. Look you better wait in the other room. You're still recuperating. And the way you're dressed, you'll catch your death of cold."

Matt waited until I walked back into the kitchen before answering the door. I listened as he and the man from the plowing service made polite small talk. Matt seemed impatient to send him on his way. Finally, he must have thrust a handful of bills in the man's hand because the man abruptly stopped talking and thanked Matt for his generosity. Matt wished him good day and hustled him out the door, bolting it behind him.

I came out of the kitchen to find Matt staring at a pink receipt.

Something was bothering me and it wasn't just the way Matt was acting.

"Why did he call you Mr. Jablonsky?"

"What?"

"Jablonsky. I heard him call you Jablonsky?"

Matt folded the receipt and put it in the front pocket of his corduroy pants.

"Because that's my name."

"What do you mean that's your name? I thought it was Lang."

"That's my pen name. When I'm up here, I use my real name. That way no one knows who I am. If people knew I was Matt Lang the writer, I wouldn't be able to go into town without being asked a hundred questions. You don't know what it's like. 'How do you get your ideas?' 'I've written some haiku, how can I get them published?' 'Are your books autobiographical?' It never ends. It's bad enough on the signing circuit, but here I need the solitude to get down to the business of writing."

"So no one knows Matt Lang lives up here?"

"No one but you."

"Me and your agent."

"Yes," Matt said, looking suddenly annoyed. "You, my editor, and my agent."

Later that same day a man came to fix the radar dish. Matt had me wait upstairs until he was done. I listened again as the man referred to Matt as Mr. Jablonsky, but didn't give much thought to the matter. I pretty much accepted Matt's explanation at face value.

When I came down, Matt was back at his computer, writing. Or rather staring.

From where I was I could see only a half-finished paragraph marking the cerulean-blue void of his screen. He was staring into that void as if looking for answers, the fingers of his left hand tapping silently on his desk. The fingers of his other hand were wrapped around a cigarette, which was already almost burned down to the filter.

I curled up on the couch and grabbed the TV remote. I flipped it at the large-screen set, and was instantly rewarded for the first time in weeks with a splash of sound and color. I didn't realize how much I'd missed the endless variety of mindless diversions television had to offer. Like someone who'd undergone an experiment in sensory deprivation, I found everything interesting, even the advertisements. It was like looking through a window at another world. Seventy-five worlds to be exact as I hit the channel button on the remote.

For the first time in weeks, the time passed quickly. It was already nearly three o'clock and *The Way We Live* was scheduled to come on in minutes. I thought of asking Matt what channel Maine's ABC affiliate broadcast on, but he didn't look as if he'd welcome being disturbed. Instead, I frantically hunted around until I found it myself, missing only the opening segment, and tuning in just in time to see Cindy make an entrance into a posh cocktail party.

She looked stunning. Her hair was swept up, her face expertly made up, her body filling to lush perfection a designer cocktail dress sparkling with sequins. She accepted a drink from a tuxedoed bartender and her glance swept the room until she locked eyes with the man she was there to steal. I watched the show for the next hour, awed by her performance. I guess I should have felt jealous, but it was impossible. She was just too good. Maybe, if I hadn't met Matt and I was still languishing in New York things would have been different. . . .

"That's her," I said after one of the commercial breaks. I figured this was important enough to interrupt Matt for. "That's her."

"That's who?" Matt said, sounding irritated.

"That's my girlfriend. Cindy. Come look."

Matt pushed his chair away from the desk, lit a fresh cigarette, and came over. He stood behind the sofa and watched for a minute or two.

"She's great, isn't she?" I said.

Matt grunted noncommittally and returned to his computer. I was too excited to let his lack of enthusiasm affect me much, though I did feel a twinge of annoyance that he showed so little interest in my field of endeavor. I didn't even wait for the end credits to run before I went to the telephone and dialed Cindy's number.

I got her machine.

"Matt," I called out from the kitchen, "what's the number here?"

"Why do you want to know?"

"I want to leave a message for Cindy."

"The number's unlisted."

"But Matt, it's just one person. It's not like she's going to be giving it out."

"The number's unlisted for a reason. I give it out to one person, I might as well give it out to a hundred. Just tell her you'll call back. I'm sure she'll be in sooner or later. Now please, let me get back to work. See? This is what I meant by the world crashing in on us."

"Crashing in on us?" I laughed. "It's just one call."

"One call now, another call later . . ."

I heard the beep on the other end of the phone and hung up. I walked to the door of the kitchen.

"Matt, this is ridiculous. Give me the number. I'll make her promise not to tell anyone."

"I told you to just call her back. What the hell's the big deal?"

Maybe we'd been cooped up together too long. I didn't like his tone and I didn't like his domineering attitude.

"I don't want to have to keep calling her back," I shot back. "If I give her the number, I just have to call her once and she can call me back when she's home. Get it?"

Matt caught my sarcasm and glared at me.

"What else do you have to do all day, anyway?" he said, mimicking my sarcasm.

I felt the blood go to my face.

"You bring me to this cabin in the middle of nowhere and now you have the nerve to criticize me because I have nothing to do?" I was shouting now, sounding more like a harpy than a muse, but I didn't care. Matt had pushed me too far. "I'd at least like to talk to a human being once in a while since you don't seem to have the time to say so much as boo to me."

"If you're so desperate to talk to her," Matt said smugly, seeming to find satisfaction in getting me angry, "then you shouldn't mind calling her back until you get her."

"That's funny, Matt," I said, trying in vain to control my anger. "Real funny. Are you going to give me the number or not?"

"I should think we already established the answer to that question by now."

"Dammit! Why are you being so pigheaded about this?"

"Because I don't want that goddamn phone ringing at all hours of the day and night."

"I promise you that won't happen."

"I can assure you it won't."

Matt turned back to his computer with an air of finality as if he were dismissing a child or an insignificant subordinate.

"You and your precious privacy!" I shouted. "It's not like you're J. D. Salinger for crissakes."

I had wanted to say something to get back at him, but I didn't expect the violence of his reaction. Matt slammed his fist down on the desk. I flinched, instinctively taking a step back. His anger shocked me. He grit his teeth, as if trying to control himself, and ran a hand over his face.

"I must have my privacy," he said in a low, almost threatening tone. "I will have my privacy."

"Matt," I said, already regretting getting him so upset. "Let's talk this over. . . ."

He stood up from his desk and went to the door. He put on his coat and boots, pulled on his hat and gloves, and wrapped a scarf around the bottom half of his face.

"Where are you going?"

"For a walk," he said tonelessly, as he pulled open the front door.

He slammed the door shut. I stood between the kitchen and the living room feeling the chill from outside, but it was the chill from Matt's sudden change in behavior that touched me to the bone. I had seen a good deal of his eccentricity already, but I had not seen this side of him. His obsession with privacy had always seemed more than a little unreasonable. Now it seemed to border on paranoia. Of course, he was under a lot of pressure. I'd heard him arguing with his agent. Creativity was an elusive, unpredictable thing. It came. It went. If you were lucky, it came again. Maybe the environment in the chalet was the only thing over which he felt he had any control.

I went to the window next to Matt's desk and saw him walking through the snow, lifting his knees out of the thigh-high drifts, as he headed toward a small clearing among the firs.

I rushed back to the kitchen, picked up the phone, and punched the zero button. I'd get the number of the chalet, and Matt wouldn't ever have to know. I waited impatiently for someone to answer.

"May I help you?" said a bored voice.

"Operator assistance, please."

There were a series of clicks and then another voice that almost sounded like a computer, only not as human, came on the other end.

"City please," it said impatiently.

"I'm not sure," I said. "It's somewhere east of a place called Green Hollow. Maybe north."

"You'll have to be more specific than that, ma'am."

"Can you just tell me the number I'm calling from?"

"You don't know what number you're calling from?"

"It's not listed on the phone."

"My records indicate that you're calling from a private residence."

"That's right. I want to find out the number."

"I'm sorry," the voice said, not sounding sorry at all, "but the phone you're calling from has restricted access."

"Restricted access? What does that mean?"

I looked anxiously at the door. Matt could be coming in at any moment. I certainly didn't want him to hear this conversation.

"It means it's an unlisted number."

"Can you tell me what it is?"

"I'm afraid not."

"Why not?"

"That's the privileged information of the owner. We have a duty to protect the privacy of our customers."

Stretching the curls out of the phone cord, I could make it from the kitchen far enough to see out the window by Matt's desk. He was treading through the deep snow, heading back, making slow but inevitable progress toward the front of the chalet.

"But I'm staying at his house," I said. "I'm using his phone."

"Then why don't you ask him for the number?"

For the first time the voice sounded remotely human. I realized why. It was the note of sarcasm.

"I can't ask him. Please, you have to hurry."

"Is this an emergency, ma'am? Is that what you are trying to tell me?"

The sarcasm was not entirely gone, neither was the computerlike monotone, but for the first time there was a slight tone of genuine human concern. "I can notify the police, if you like."

"No, it's not an emergency. Don't call the police."

I could just imagine what Matt would do if suddenly the police came roaring up to the door disturbing his peace and quiet.

"Are you sure?"

"I'm sure. Everything's fine. . . ."

The door swung open and Matt banged his boots against the door-frame before coming inside.

"Having a great time. I'll try to call again. Good-bye."

"Who was that?" Matt said, unwrapping the scarf from around his face and hanging it on a hook by the door.

"Cindy."

"You finally got through?"

"No. But I left a message."

Matt didn't say anything. He took off his coat and gloves and squatted down to unlace his boots.

"I'm sorry, Matt," I said. I still didn't think it was my fault, but one of us had to make the first move. The sooner we got this incident behind us, the better. I couldn't think of anything worse than the two of us bumping around in this chalet, ignoring each other like a resentful old married couple.

Matt looked up, his cheeks red from the cold, his black hair tousled.

"I'm sorry, too," he said. "I didn't mean to be such a bastard about the whole thing. It's just that I can't be distracted. Hell, if I had my way, I wouldn't even have a phone in the place. Unfortunately, my editor and agent insist on being able to contact me. As you've heard . . ."

"I just feel so isolated and alone, Matt."

Matt stood up. "Come here," he said. "I think maybe I can take care of that."

I walked over to him. He put his arms on my shoulders, put a finger under my chin, and lifted my lips to his. His kiss was warm and full and gentle.

"I'll tell you what," he said. "To hell with work this afternoon. We'll spend some time together."

"Okay," I said, snuggling closer in his arms, my mind still restless, trying to figure out some way to get the phone number.

28

The next three days passed uneventfully.

We had settled into a kind of domestic routine that, if not bliss, was certainly comfortable. The illness I had suffered had taken the edge off my boredom and left me relatively content to sit around the chalet, sipping tea, watching television, and reading the occasional book. Matt was working even harder than ever, if that were possible. The calls had stopped coming in the night and he seemed less ill at ease.

I had tried to reach Cindy four times without success. I figured she was either busy on the set, or she was staying over with Brad. I finally left her a short message telling her how great I thought she was on *The Way We Live,* how excited I was for her, and jokingly asked if she wasn't answering her phone because she was already on her way to Hollywood. I told her I'd call her back and hung up. I didn't explain why I couldn't leave a return number. She wouldn't have understood.

This morning I was feeling better than I had since I fell ill. I was munching on some raisin toast and watching one of those morning aerobic exercise shows. I wasn't feeling quite up to following along, but at least the idea wasn't nauseating. I watched the hard-bodied men and women swinging their arms and marching in place and realized that I hadn't been able to exercise in weeks. I never thought I'd say it, but I really missed my Nordic Trak.

"I'm going into town for supplies."

I looked up from the television. I guess I had been so engrossed in the exercise show that I hadn't noticed Matt getting up from his desk.

He was dressed in a plaid jacket, leather gloves, and a pair of Timberland boots. He looked every bit the rugged Maine outdoorsman as he had the successful New York writer only a month or so ago.

"Why didn't you tell me?" I said. "I want to go, too. I just have to find something to wear. Maybe you can lend me one of your coats."

Matt shook his head. "I don't think that's a good idea."

"Why not? I'm feeling a lot better. Honest. Look at this."

I started marching in place with the models on the television, vigorously swinging my arms, lifting my legs in comic exaggeration.

"See?" I said, smiling triumphantly.

Matt didn't seem amused. He shook his head. "You're just getting over a very bad flu. I don't want to risk your having a relapse."

"I won't, I promise. Look, I'll even stay in the Jeep if that'll make you feel better. Keep it running and the heat cranked up. I just want to see some scenery."

"No," Matt said firmly. "There's plenty of time for sightseeing. Right now, it's best if you just stay here and rest. I'm not going to be gone for long. I'm just going to run a few quick errands. Get some groceries and some computer paper. I'll be back before you know it. Really, it's just not worth it. I'll take you out another time when you're a little stronger. I promise."

"But I feel fine," I protested feebly, knowing I was fighting a losing battle.

"You're better. But not fine. Look, just that little bit of fooling around has got you winded."

He was right. I was breathing a little raggedly and a fine sheen of feverish sweat stood out on my forehead.

I sat back down on the sofa, defeated.

"Just relax, Johanna. There's no need to rush things. Believe me, give it a couple of days. It's really for the best. I don't plan on being gone for long anyway. I have to get to work. This isn't a sightseeing trip. It's a necessity. I'll be back before you know it."

"At least make sure to stop at the cleaners and pick up my clothes. I'm getting pretty tired walking around here dressed like some kind of walking lingerie model."

"Funny, I'm not getting tired of it," Matt said and leered good-naturedly.

"I am," I said, not in the mood to be charmed. I almost felt like asking him why if he found my state of undress so exciting it hadn't done anything for our love life, but I held my tongue. Being a bitch wasn't going to help things, though it would have made me feel a whole lot better.

At least temporarily.

Instead I ignored him when he kissed me on top of the head. I picked up the remote and turned the channel to one of those loud and raucous early morning talk shows. I listened petulantly as Matt started up the Jeep, let it warm for a while, and rolled over the crunching ice down the long drive to the highway. As I watched two overweight black women bickering violently over a skinny, bemused-looking guy slouching in a chair with a red bandana around his head, I allowed myself to wallow in self-pity. Sometimes feeling sorry for yourself can be a real luxury.

True to his word, Matt wasn't gone long. No more than an hour or so. He came in with a gust of cold air that almost made me glad I hadn't gone out after all. He was carrying four bags of groceries, two sacks under each arm, and one in each hand. He went out for four more bags and then started taking off his coat and gloves.

"My clothes," I said, surveying the bags, and not seeing a plastic laundry bag among them.

"I've got some bad news," Matt said.

"Bad news?" I said, feeling a queasy sensation in the pit of my stomach.

Matt must have sensed how close to the edge I was because he raised his hands in a calming gesture. "Now don't get upset. It's really no big deal."

"What is it, Matt?" My voice was trembling. "What happened now?"

"Johanna, you're getting upset."

"You're damn right I'm getting upset, and stalling isn't making it any better. Spit it out, Matt."

He sighed. "Okay. But promise me you won't get too mad. It's really kind of funny in a way." Matt smiled nervously. "The laundry lost your clothes."

It took a moment for his words to register, but when they did, I felt the blood drain from my face and my blood pressure skyrocket.

"They lost my clothes?" I said, and then repeated the words, as if trying to believe them. "They lost my clothes?"

"It seems there's been some mix-up—" Matt began.

"What the hell do you mean they lost them?" I shrieked.

"Like I said," Matt started, "there was a mix-up—"

I didn't give him a chance to finish.

"Goddamn it, Matt, I didn't ask you to bring those clothes to the cleaners in the first place. They were the only clothes I had. What the hell am I supposed to do now?"

"Johanna, please," Matt said, a look of genuine concern on his face. "You promised you wouldn't get too mad. You're going to make yourself sick."

"Fuck that!" I hollered. "There's nothing wrong with me. What I want are my goddamn clothes."

"I'm sure they'll turn up. It's not a big deal."

"Not a big deal?" I was so angry I could barely get the words out. "You stupid ass! How can you stand there and say it's no big deal?"

"Johanna, you're getting yourself overly excited."

"If you say that again, Matt, I swear you're going to be sorry. Take me there," I said, already heading for the door, so mad I didn't think about what I would do if I actually got there, dressed as I was in a gown and slippers. "I want to talk to them myself."

Matt stopped me, his hands on my arms.

"Johanna, please calm down. You're trembling."

He was right. I could feel my body shaking in his strong hands. My knees suddenly went weak, and I felt dizzy. Matt guided me back to the sofa and sat me down. He placed his hand on my forehead.

"You're feverish again. Let me get you something to drink."

He went to the kitchen while I tried to clear my head. What the hell was going on here anyway? Matt returned with a glass of water, which I sipped slowly. He sat down across from me on the coffee table and put his hands on my knees. I was still so angry I wanted to push his hands away, but didn't have the strength. I let them stay where they were.

"I know you're upset," he said with a patience I found maddeningly condescending. "But there's really nothing we can do. These things happen. I promise I'll go back into town tomorrow and buy you some clothes you can wear until they find your things. Okay?"

It wasn't okay, but what else could I say?

"Okay," I said.

"Good," Matt said and smiled, looking relieved. He took me in his arms and kissed me, the first real kiss he'd given me in some time. He held me out at arm's length and smiled.

"Okay," he said again, as if more to reassure himself than me.

"I'm sorry," I said, feeling the first pangs of guilt. After all, he had only been trying to do me a favor by taking my clothes to the laundry. "I didn't mean to lose it like that."

"Don't worry about it," Matt said. "You haven't felt well."

Matt leaned forward and I closed my eyes to kiss him again, but he hadn't leaned forward to kiss me. He had merely been rising from the coffee table.

He let me go and headed off to put the groceries away while I sat there with the kiss dying on my lips.

The next day I handed Matt my credit cards before he left for town.

"What's this?" he said, staring down at his hand.

"My credit cards."

"I know what they are," he said. "I don't understand what they're doing in my hand."

"I want you to use them to buy me clothes."

"Nonsense," Matt said, trying to hand the cards back, "I feel responsible for this whole mess. Between the airport and the laundry, you've lost everything. The least I can do is replace your clothes."

I put my hands behind my back, refusing to take back the cards. Instead, I explained my precarious credit situation in as off-handed a way as possible. "I may have missed a few payments on some of the cards. Just keep picking one until it goes through. Let's see, I'll need some jeans, some sweaters—"

"Hold it," Matt said. "This is ridiculous. You're my guest here and I'm not going to let you spend your money replacing clothes you wouldn't have lost if you hadn't come here in the first place. Besides, you can ill afford to be buying all those clothes. Now, take these damn cards back. You're insulting me."

"Look who's insulting who, buster," I said. "I may be an out-of-work actress, but I can afford to pay my way. I'm not asking you to buy me anything fancy. Just a few essentials. I can afford that."

"Okay, okay," Matt said, throwing up his arms, feigning surrender. "I understand. I didn't mean to offend you or to imply you couldn't pay your own way. I just feel responsible, that's all."

"Well, you don't have to feel responsible. Like you said, it was an accident. I can use some new winter stuff anyway."

Matt stuffed my credit cards into the pocket of his flannel shirt and threw on his coat. This time I didn't even try to talk him into letting me go. I knew I wouldn't change his mind and I didn't feel like fighting about it.

"There. It's not so hard to be a good girl, is it?" Matt joked.

"Is that what you want? A good girl?" I shot back, unable to resist.

Maybe I would do as he asked, but I didn't feel like having my face rubbed in it.

"I didn't mean it that way," he said.

"Whatever," I said, turning away to the television.

I could feel the bitchiness from yesterday rising unbidden inside me and it was all I could do to resist its temptation. How much of it was Matt and how much of it was the time of month, it was hard to say.

In any event, Matt seemed to take it good-naturedly, as if making a conscious effort not to respond in kind to my black mood.

"Sorry," I mumbled. "Just feeling a little cranky."

"Nothing to be sorry about," he said. "I understand it can get a little claustrophobic being up here, especially if you're not used to it like I am. But you'll be out and about in no time. I know I've been working hard, not paying you enough attention. Maybe tonight we can . . . I can make it up to you?"

"That sounds great, Matt, but I don't think the next couple of days . . ."

"I understand," Matt said. "That's okay. I'll just take a rain check."

Somehow I got the feeling that he was more relieved than disappointed.

After he left, I didn't feel like watching television and I didn't feel like reading. I poked listlessly at the logs in the fireplace, sending a shower of orange sparks up the flue, until I'd coaxed a pale flicker of yellow flames from the recalcitrant wood. It was while I was bent over working at the logs that I noticed the computer.

I crossed the room, turned it on, and waited for the machine to complete booting up. I was far from an expert at operating a computer. But I did have some experience with the damn things from working as a temp, even if it was mainly limited to word processing, and the occasional browsing of the Internet.

After about thirty seconds I was rewarded with the familiar Microsoft Windows screen. I selected the icon of what looked like a word-processing program and waited for it to load. When it did, I pressed *open,* but was rewarded only with a prompt asking for a password. I hadn't expected that. Matt had his files password protected. I should have guessed he would, given his propensity for secrecy. Still, why would he need a password, living alone out here in the wilderness? Had he installed the system just to keep them from me?

The password prompt blinked impatiently.

"Damn," I muttered.

I typed in Matt's name for want of a better idea and the screen was suddenly filled with lines of randomly ordered characters that was obviously some kind of code. I tried another password, only to get the same results. The third time I was unceremoniously bumped out of the program and returned to the Windows screen.

I tried again and again, but with the same results. I was sitting there compiling a list of possible passwords when the phone rang. I sat there stunned for a moment, as if I'd never heard a phone ring before, wondering whether or not I should answer it.

I shut down the computer, pushed back the desk chair, and slowly went to the kitchen.

The phone was still ringing.

I picked it up gingerly and held it to my ear.

"Hello?"

The woman on the other end sounded older, refined, polite, with the kind of accent that didn't suggest foreign influence, but old money. She introduced herself as Matt's editor. I couldn't imagine this genteel old lady capable of putting pressure on Matt to finish his book. But then again, what did I really know about publishing? I suppose she, too, had a schedule to keep and a job to defend. Such concerns did strange things to otherwise decent people.

"Is Matt in?" she asked.

"No, he isn't. He went into town for a while, but he should be back soon."

"You must be Matt's latest inspiration?"

"What do you mean?"

"Nothing, dear," she said, and even her laugh was controlled, cultivated. "It's just that I've read Matt's latest pages and they're absolutely fabulous. Whatever you're doing, keep it up. This is by far Matt's best work yet. If he can bring this off, he'll make the bestseller list for certain."

"He's not late or anything?"

"Oh my, no. If anything, he's well ahead of schedule. Anyway, please give him my message. I know he's so busy these days, but if he gets the chance, have him give Margaret a call. I'd like to tell him what a fabulous job he's done. I'm really so very proud of him."

She rung off and I stood there staring at the blank computer screen until the dial tone came on. I don't know how long I stood there like that before I heard the sound of Matt's tires crunching up the drive.

Minutes later Matt brought in three large bags bearing the logo of a local clothes store.

"It's not exactly Saks Fifth Avenue," he said, "but it's the best little boutique in the middle of nowhere."

I looked at the receipt stapled to the first bag. There were three digits to the left of the decimal point.

"My God, Matt. I can't afford this."

"Don't worry about it. It's my treat."

"What do you mean?"

"I know this trip hasn't been everything you expected. I'm sorry. I thought maybe I could make it up to you."

"But, Matt," I said, looking at the receipts on the other bags, each higher than the one before, "you must have spent nearly a thousand dollars. It's really very sweet of you. But I can't accept these clothes. I wouldn't even be comfortable in them."

"Nonsense. They were made for you. And, if you're going to be a famous actress someday, you're going to have to get used to dressing like one."

"Please take them back and let me buy something a little more suited to my budget. All I really need are a couple of pairs of blue jeans and some sweaters."

"I'm afraid that's impossible in any event," Matt said.

"What do you mean?"

"Your credit cards were rejected."

"Rejected? All of them? I don't understand. Let me see the cards."

"I can't."

"What do you mean, you can't?"

"The store confiscated them."

"I don't believe this. Did they give a reason why?"

"They never do."

It took awhile for Matt to calm me down, but eventually he was able to persuade me to let the matter go—at least until I got back to New York. There was nothing I could do about it for the time being anyway. I couldn't call the credit card companies because I didn't have the cards with their numbers and I couldn't get the numbers from information because I didn't remember—if I ever even took notice of— the banks through which the cards were financed.

"By the way," I said, casually. "I almost forgot. A woman called for you."

Matt looked alarmed. "A woman?"

"Yes. She said her name was Margaret. She called about a half hour ago. Who is she anyway?"

"She's my editor," Matt said distractedly. Then he added, more pointedly, "Did you talk to her?"

"Of course, silly. The phone rang and I picked it up. Isn't that what you're supposed to do?"

"The answering machine, dammit. That's why I have an answering machine."

"I didn't think you'd mind if I answered the phone."

"You didn't think I'd mind," Matt mimicked my voice. "You didn't think I'd mind. Haven't you been listening to a single goddamn word I've been saying since we got here? I want my privacy!"

"Matt, you're not being fair. I didn't mean anything—"

Matt threw up his hands. "It's done. What's done is done."

He started pacing the room, rubbing his hands together, muttering under his breath.

"Look, there's nothing to worry about," I said, trying to calm him down. "She had nothing but great things to say about your novel. She thinks you might have a bestseller in the making."

He didn't seem to hear me. He continued to pace the floor, moving like a caged animal, his body coiled with tension. I didn't understand what could be upsetting him so badly. The call from his editor had obviously thrown him into a panic. But why?

"Matt, what's wrong?" I tried. "Please tell me."

He was standing at the window now, his forehead placed against the cool glass, his hand resting on the wall. Suddenly he balled up his fist and slammed it against the paneling.

"Damn it!" he shouted.

"Matt, please talk to me," I pleaded. "Don't do this."

He turned from the window with a look of tortured confusion. For a moment he looked completely disoriented.

His eyes refocused as if he suddenly remembered I was in the room.

"You don't understand," he mumbled. He ran his hand through his hair. "You just don't understand."

"I'm trying to understand. Really I am. But you have to help me help you. You've got to trust me, Matt. Come here."

Matt hesitated as if making a decision.

"Come here," I said again softly. "Please."

Matt walked slowly, almost reluctantly, toward me. I reached out and placed my hands on his shoulders, gently pushing him down onto the sofa, where he sat, stiff backed, his legs tensed beneath him, as if he was about to bolt at any moment.

"Let me get you something," I said. "Stay right here."

I went to the kitchen and poured Matt a glass of brandy. I carried it back to the living room and knelt down in front of him.

"Here," I said. "Take a sip. It'll make you feel better."

Matt took the glass and I started to see how badly his hand was shaking. Almost mechanically, he lifted the glass to his mouth and swallowed the entire contents in three hard gulps. I took the empty glass from him and placed it on the table.

Whatever was troubling him, he obviously didn't—or couldn't— trust me enough to share it. In the end, all I could do was comfort him, stroking his hands and face as he sat, pale and trembling with anxiety, on the edge of the sofa.

"There," I tried to sound reassuring. "Does that feel better?"

Matt nodded.

"Now can you tell me what's wrong?"

Matt's lips were pale and drawn thin. "The writing," he said, shaking his head.

"What about the writing?" I said quietly, not wanting to upset him, desperately anxious to know what was wrong.

"It's not going well," he said, his voice sounding small and scared, almost like a little boy's.

"But your editor said—"

"She doesn't know. She has no idea."

"She doesn't know what, Matt?"

"How hard it is."

I knew he wouldn't say anything more and to push him would only be to drive him away. In the end all I could do was comfort him, stroking his trembling hands as he sat rigid and unmoving on the edge of the sofa, his terrified eyes fixed at a faraway spot over my head, as if he were looking at a ghost.

29

"Really, Matt," I said sleepily, "is this your idea of practical clothing for the most brutal Maine winter on record?"

I held up a beaded, white mini dress and a pair of gold high-heeled sandals.

It was nearly noon and I was beat. I hadn't gotten more than four hours of sleep. I'd stayed up with Matt until nearly four a.m. the night before. It had taken two more glasses of brandy before sheer exhaustion finally sent him off to a fitful sleep on the couch. I covered him with a throw and sat on the floor beside him, afraid to go upstairs to bed or even to so much as close my eyes in case I should fall asleep and he should wake up and find himself alone.

So I sat beside the couch and watched as the steely gray light of dawn spread over the pines and slanted through the window next to Matt's desk. I got up to make some coffee and brought a mug back to the living room. I sat down in an armchair by the fireplace and slowly sipped the hot black brew. I remember looking at my watch and seeing it was eight-thirty. I hadn't dared turn the television on before, but then I did, keeping it as low as possible, watching the local news.

Matt had stopped moaning and tossing hours before and was sleeping peacefully. In spite of myself, I must have fallen asleep at some point shortly after that, because the next thing I knew I woke up with the throw pulled up to my chin, bright light streaming through the windows, and Matt typing away at the computer.

"Good morning, sleepyhead," Matt said cheerfully.

"Are you okay?" I asked tentatively.

"Sure," he said. "Never better. Why?"

"Last night—"

Matt looked at me with a puzzled expression.

"What about last night?"

"You were so upset."

Matt waved his hand dismissively. "Forget that. Just a little writer's anxiety. It comes with the territory." He pointed to the unopened bags on the table. "Hey, you never got a chance to look at your new duds."

I decided not to press the issue. If Matt wanted to put the incident behind him, so be it. I figured he was probably embarrassed. Up until then I had seen only the strong, confident author. For the first time I saw behind to the insecure, suffering artist within. It had taken me by surprise, shaken me, even scared me a little, but the fact was that, in a strange way, seeing his vulnerability made me feel closer to him than ever before. He needn't have felt embarrassed. But I knew enough about the male psyche that to tell him so would have been even more embarrassing. So I pretended to buy his explanation and let the matter go. In any event, it was just good to see him back to his old self.

I opened the first of the bags as Matt looked on expectantly. I opened the second and then the third. It was then that I held up the beaded minidress and sandals.

Matt grinned. "What's the matter," he said, "you don't like my taste in clothes?"

"If we were going to an opening at Lincoln Center in the middle of summer this would be perfect," I said, picking up an elegant sheath of black silk, "but hardly for tromping through five feet of snow."

"You can hardly blame me for wanting to see you in these things rather than a flannel shirt and a pair of L. L. Bean hiking boots."

"Yes, but, Matt, I can hardly leave the house dressed in these."

"Let's worry about that later. Why don't you put on the pink taffeta gown for dinner?"

I picked up the dress he had pointed out. It had a tight beaded bodice and a full, but short skirt. It reminded me of the dress I'd worn to my senior prom ten years ago.

"Matt, I don't know. I feel kind of foolish."

"Come on. I'd love to see you in it."

"Well . . ."

I saw the look of playful desire in his laughing eyes. It was a lot better than the look of tortured confusion I had seen only the night before.

* * *

That evening I wore the dress. It pleased him. And to a degree that took me by surprise, pleasing him pleased me, too.

He was back to work on the computer after dinner and I was watching television. I forget exactly what I was watching, some melodrama or other, when Matt jumped up from his desk, his chair skidding behind him.

"Jesus Christ," he yelled. "Ever since that goddamn dish was fixed all you ever do is watch television."

"What do you want me to do? I've been cooped up in this cabin for over a month wearing these ridiculous clothes and watching you write."

"Why don't you pick up a book for chrissakes?"

"I can't read sixteen hours a day."

"Maybe you can try to watch something that isn't an outrage to anyone with half a brain in their head."

"What do you suggest I watch? C-Span? I'm bored enough as it is without listening to some congressman from Kansas talk about housing funds."

"All I hear from the minute you come down in the morning to the minute you go to bed at night are talk shows, soap operas, news magazines, who's sleeping with who, what car can blow up, how a fucking hamburger can kill you, on and on and on. And what's this insipid crap you're watching now? Don't you have any fucking taste whatsoever? Can't you see how hackneyed it is? It's been done a thousand times."

"I thought you were writing. Why are you even listening to it?"

"I can't help it. It's so goddamn stupid it's offensive. How can you stand to watch it?"

I answered before I thought. "This is the kind of stuff you yourself write."

I then ran up to my bedroom and locked the door behind me, but there was little need of that. Matt didn't so much as call up after me.

I was sorry the minute I had let the words slip out of my mouth. The look on his face told the whole story. I remembered how he had told me about his love of serious literature and his youthful attempts at publishing poetry. We all had failed dreams painful to revisit. I had just thrown his up in his face. He had trusted me with what had hurt him the most. And I had impulsively used it against him in a moment of anger. I had revealed him for what he had feared to become in his more idealistic days, something he'd probably sworn to himself never to become: a simple hack writer.

In spite of my own anger over what he'd said to me, I felt so terrible I was tempted to go down and apologize to him immediately. After all, what he'd said was probably only the result of the pressures he was obviously feeling over his novel. It was clear that he was having difficulty writing. He was smoking more, getting less sleep, hardly eating. And on top of that, there were still the strange late-night calls from his agent, and that message from his editor that had so inexplicably disturbed him.

I wish I had gone down. Maybe things would have turned out differently. But I figured that he wouldn't have been ready for an apology anyway, and that it was better to wait until things cooled down. Instead, I took a hot bath and sat on the bed flipping through a magazine. In spite of how tired I was, I knew it would be hopeless to try to go to sleep. I had used the last of my Xanax before leaving New York. Besides, I didn't like taking them anyway. It seemed to me that I was growing way too dependent on them lately. Still, I could have sorely used something to help me unwind. I threw down the magazine in disgust, unable to concentrate.

I got up from the bed and walked to the antique mirror over the dresser. I stared at myself in the glass, wondering how I could have made such a mess of things. It was while I was staring in the mirror that my eye was caught by a small triangle of pink in the heating vent on the ceiling. I turned from the mirror and walked under the vent. The grate was of a design that whatever it was couldn't be seen directly from underneath. I took a few steps from one side to another.

Nothing.

Had I imagined it?

I walked back to the mirror and sure enough, I saw it again. It looked like a folded piece of paper.

Curious, I put the lamp on the floor and climbed onto the night table. I tried to work my finger between the grate in the vent, but the spaces were too small and I couldn't see what I was looking for anyway. I pulled at the vent, but it was screwed tightly into the ceiling. I climbed off the table and looked around for something I could use as a screwdriver. The best I could come up with was the little file on the nail clipper in the bathroom.

Standing under the vent, I fit the edge of the file into the tiny screw. It was difficult work. The fit was far from perfect and the file kept slipping out of the screw's slot. But I kept at it until I'd loosened the screw enough to twist it with my fingers. I pushed the grate to one side. It was still attached to the ceiling by the other screw. I reached up inside for the folded paper and felt it under my fingertips.

I stepped off the night table and sat down on the edge of the bed. I slowly unfolded the paper in my hand. It was dusty from being up in the vent, so worn it was nearly ripped at the creases, either from age or exposure to heat from the furnace. The paper was faded, the kind of rose-colored stationary that only women used, and I could almost smell the faint scent of perfume on it. As if to leave no doubt in my mind, I saw the delicate script of an unmistakably feminine hand carefully drawn in lavender ink across the disintegrating paper. The letters were broken in places, but the words were still legible.

> *Beware the lover*
> *dressed in black*
> *he'll borrow your heart*
> *your soul*
> *your life*
> *he'll make them his own*
> *and won't give them back.*
> *Look for me whenever*
> *green comes to the hills*
> *for all that he's left of me*
> *are the bright daffodils.*
> *—Ariel*

Just then I heard the front door pulled shut. I jumped off the bed and ran out the door of my room to the loft. Outside I heard the engine of the Jeep start and then the tires whining as they spun in the snow before gaining purchase. Through the windows of the darkened living room I saw the headlights sweep over the walls and then slowly recede.

Matt was leaving.

I ran downstairs and over to the front window just in time to see the Jeep disappearing around a bend in the drive concealed by a tall drift of snow.

Dammit, I thought.

I was about to go back upstairs when I saw the computer. It was still on, humming away, the screen saver shooting digitalized stars against the black monitor.

For the time being, I forgot the mystery of the poem in my hand and sat down at Matt's desk. I moved the mouse and the blue screen leaped into view. My heart gave a sympathetic jump. I scrolled up hoping to catch anything of what Matt might have written. Unfortunately, I reached the top of the document only to find it completely empty. I tried the file command and selected "open." There I saw a list of chapters numbered one to seven. I selected the first chapter. The computer buzzed and chirped as I waited anxiously for the screen to pop up. After a few seconds the monitor went black and the same password prompt appeared as before.

I sat in front of the blinking prompt, trying to think of what the password might be. If I only knew the title of the book he was working on. That, it seemed to me, would be the most obvious answer. I tried word after word, getting bounced out of the system, reopening it, and trying again and again without any success. It was hopeless. I was flying in the dark. Still, it kept me occupied longer than I thought because before I knew it, Matt's Jeep was pulling up the drive, headlights sweeping the room.

I froze.

I hadn't thought of how I was going to get the computer back to the screen at which I found it. There was no time to figure that out now. I could only hope that the screen saver would come back on before Matt came in and that he wouldn't notice or remember that he hadn't left the computer at the password prompt.

I grabbed the poem off the desk and hurried upstairs to my bedroom, closed and locked the door, and climbed into bed. I lay there staring at the ceiling, wondering what in the world could be taking Matt so long to walk from the Jeep to the chalet.

30

———•———

Matt was up early the next morning.

When I came downstairs, he had already set the table and was putting the finishing touches on a big breakfast.

"Hope you like country-style French toast," he said, turning from a large cast-iron skillet on the stove. If he was still angry about the night before, he didn't let it show. If anything, he seemed in especially good spirits. Perhaps the writing was going well again. "It's the specialty of the house."

"Sounds great," I said. "Smells even better."

"Grab yourself a cup of coffee and sit down. Breakfast will be up in a minute."

I poured a cup of coffee and sat at the polished oak dining table. Matt carried over a large plate piled high with French toast and a bottle of syrup. I forked a couple of slices of toast onto my plate, cut a pat of butter from the stick, and poured on some syrup. The bread was sliced thick, with a heavy crust fried to a perfect crispiness and sprinkled with powdered sugar.

"How is it?" he asked.

"Delicious."

"I'm glad," he said, looking genuinely happy. "It's been awhile since I've tried to make it. Can I get you some fresh-squeezed orange juice?"

He didn't wait for an answer. He was already halfway out of his chair before I stopped him.

"Matt, we have to talk."

Matt sat back down, a contrite look on his face. "I know what you're going to say, Johanna. I'm sorry. I know I've been saying that a lot lately, but I really am. I had no right to blow up like I did last night. It was inexcusable. It's just the pressure of this book getting to me. I'm afraid I took it out on you again."

I shrugged. His apology and his eagerness to please had unexpectedly taken the edge off my anger.

"It's not all your fault," I said. "I guess I should have known you didn't mean what you said."

"I didn't," he said. "You know I didn't."

"It's just that you made me feel so inferior. And I guess that struck a nerve. I've been feeling like a failure myself lately."

"Johanna, you're not a failure. You're a beautiful, talented, intelligent woman."

I laughed bitterly. "So how come I can't get a decent role anywhere?"

"You've got a starring role in my life," Matt said. "That is, if you want a role in the life of a hack writer."

He said the words as if they pained him, the smile on his face looking forced and sad.

"Matt, you have to know I didn't mean that. It was just anger. I was only trying to get back at you. I said the first thing I thought would hurt you."

"It doesn't matter."

"Yes, it does. I have nothing but respect for your work. You know that."

"No, what you said was true. I am nothing but a hack. But hack or not, my whole future as a writer could well depend on the success or failure of this book."

"You're not a hack. I won't have you talking that way."

"Like I said, it doesn't matter. What's important is that you know how much I love you."

"Matt, I love you, too. But I've been thinking. Maybe we've been cooped up here together too long. I think I'm getting on your nerves. Maybe it would be better if you had some time alone. I think I may be distracting you. You would probably do better work without me."

"No!" Matt reached over and grabbed my wrists and the look in his eyes bordered on desperation. It was there for only a moment, gone so quickly I doubted whether it had ever been there at all, and replaced by a look of such gentleness that I felt something melt inside me.

"I'm just not sure I'm good for you," I said in a small voice.

Matt lifted my right hand and kissed it passionately.

"Don't ever say that. Ever. You're the only thing that's good for me. I've been waiting for you my whole life."

"If only I could be certain," I said hesitantly.

"What can I do to convince you?"

I wasn't sure I wanted to bring it up right now. I wasn't sure how Matt would react. I wasn't even sure how I would react. But I knew I had to clear the air once and for all if things were to get back to even a semblance of what they had been between Matt and me.

"What is it, Johanna?" Matt said gently. "What's troubling you?"

I laid the piece of folded pink paper on the table between us.

"It's this," I said.

Matt looked down at the paper and back up at me, obviously confused.

"What is it?"

"I found it in my room last night. It's a poem."

Matt reached across the table and picked up the paper. He carefully unfolded the delicate paper and began to read. I watched his face closely as his eyes scanned the lines. A small tick formed at the left corner of his mouth and when he looked up, his eyes were glistening.

"Where did you find this?" he said in a tone of almost hushed reverence.

"In one of your books," I said, instinctively lying. There was something about the truth that seemed best left untold. It would have sounded too much like I was snooping around if I told him the lengths I went to in order to retrieve the paper.

"It's one of her poems," Matt said, still staring at the paper. "Just before she died."

"One of whose poems?"

"My fianceé. Ariel."

"You never told me her name."

" 'What's in a name?' Shakespeare asked," Matt mused. "In a name is everything: love, pain, loss, grief, guilt. Ariel. I try not to say it."

"I'm sorry, Matt. If I'd known—"

"There was no way you could know. I just don't know how it could have gotten in one of my books. I thought I'd boxed up all her poems and put them in the upstairs crawl space. After she died, I took them out to burn them, but I couldn't bring myself to do it. So I put them in the crawl space. And still they turn up to haunt me."

He folded the paper carefully, as if afraid it would disappear into a rose-colored mist in his hands, and put it back in his pocket. I felt badly for him, but better about the poem. The fact that it was supposed to be in the crawl space above my room made its appearance in the vent seem far less mysterious. Also the fact that it was written by his long-dead fianceé kept my jealousy in abeyance.

I knew a man like Matt was no virgin, but I had begun to suspect that, contrary to his assertions, perhaps I wasn't the only one by a long shot that he brought to the chalet for inspiration. The one thing that nagged at me was his obviously powerful emotional connection to the dead woman. The locked bedroom and now his reaction to the poem made me wonder if a large part of his problem wasn't his fixation on the object of his original inspiration.

It was a line of thought I didn't feel like pursuing right then.

Instead, I busied myself by helping Matt do the breakfast dishes. To my surprise, Matt declared he was taking a vacation from his novel. We spent the rest of the day together. I put on one of his old trenchcoats, long johns, overalls, and the boots I'd worn up from New York and we went outside for a while and laughed and played in the snow like a couple of kids. We even made a snowman. We had big mugs of hot soup for lunch and afterward Matt even watched *The Way We Live* with me on the couch. When I pointed out Cindy, he complimented her acting. There was only one thing that could have made the day perfect, but for more than one reason, it was not meant to be.

Later that week I finally got ahold of Cindy.

She seemed genuinely glad to hear from me. Until I heard her voice, I had no idea how much I'd really missed her.

"I've been watching you on TV nearly every day," I said. "You're fantastic."

"Oh come on," Cindy said, giggling embarrassedly. "You're just saying that."

"No, I'm not. You're really good. You blow everyone else on the show away. Even Matt said so, and he's not a fan of soaps."

"You know they extended my contract. Remember how they said I was supposed to die after a couple of episodes? Well, they changed the story line. It seems like I'm going to hang on for a while longer."

I felt a small familiar twinge of jealousy. But only for a moment.

"That's fantastic," I said. I'm pretty sure I meant it.

"And speaking of your new boyfriend, how's that going? Is he still a cross between George Clooney and Tom Berenger?"

"Maybe more like George Clooney and Charlie Sheen," I said.

I heard the concern in Cindy's voice. "He's not hitting you is he?"

"No, no, nothing like that," I reassured her. "It just that he's under a lot of pressure to finish this novel he's working on, so he's been a little edgy. To tell you the truth, we haven't really had much quality time together, in spite of being holed up in this chalet like an old married couple. But things will be better when the book is finished."

"You don't sound too sure."

Over the last few days things had returned to normal between Matt and me. Still, I knew that after what had happened, nothing would ever be quite the same between us. Though the fairy-tale aspect of our relationship was lost forever, what remained was something more real, if I had the courage to accept it.

"Don't worry about me. Things are fine. I can't wait until you meet him."

"He really liked my work?"

"Yes."

Cindy laughed. "I guess he can't be all bad."

"This is gonna lead to bigger and better things, I just know it."

"Do you really think so?" she said, her voice betraying her own fantasies of success.

"Definitely."

"I hardly dare let myself dream of such things. I keep telling myself that it's only one gig. But—well—I guess it's okay if I tell you."

"Tell me."

"I've got an audition set up for a new crime drama they're pushing for next fall. It's not a corpse shot either. It's a supporting role."

"Cindy, that's great."

"It's just an audition. I hear I'm up against some pretty big names. But, hey, it's a chance."

"I'll bet you get it."

"Please. You don't know how hard it is not to get your hopes up too high."

Don't I? I thought.

"Listen, Johanna, you've got to come back to New York. There's so much happening here. I just get the feeling that things are shaking loose. There are a lot of opportunities opening up. You could land something, I'm sure of it. Can you imagine that, both of us working?"

Her enthusiasm was infectious; she almost had me convinced.

"I can't, Cindy. I really never had much luck."

"You can't give up, Johanna. You've got so much talent. Don't waste it. You're better than I am."

"No—"

"Really, Johanna. I'm not just saying that. You can do it. I have faith in you."

"I'm just not ready to work yet. Maybe in a few months. But not now."

"All right," Cindy conceded. "But at least come to town for a visit.

We could have a blast for a couple of days. It would be fun. I really have missed you."

"I've missed you, too."

I hadn't realized how much that was true until I said it. But it wasn't just Cindy I missed. It was the city itself, the people, the excitement, the feeling that something was always just about to happen.

Or could happen . . .

"So you'll come?" Cindy sounded so hopeful I could hardly bear to let her down.

"I don't know," I said, chewing my lip. "I'll have to check with Matt."

"Check with Matt? What's that mean?"

"It means I can't just leave at a moment's notice," I snapped. I was being defensive and I knew it. It was a normal question. The fact that I found it so hard to answer only highlighted for me the unusual nature of my relationship with Matt. It was something I couldn't expect Cindy, or anyone else for that matter, to understand. If Cindy noticed my annoyance, she made no mention of it.

"Why not?" she asked, sounding genuinely bewildered.

"Because I made a sort of commitment," I said uncertainly. How else could I put it?

Cindy refused to let the matter go. "What kind of commitment?"

I poked my head out of the kitchen and saw Matt working at the computer. I ducked back into the kitchen, and stood in front of the window, staring out at the snow-covered branches of the firs. I twined the telephone cord between my fingers.

"Johanna?" Cindy's voice said. "Are you there?"

"Yes, yes, I'm sorry."

"What kind of commitment have you made to this guy?" For the first time Cindy sounded worried.

"I'm here to help him," I said, as lightly as I could.

"Help him? Help him do what?"

"Finish his novel."

Cindy sounded incredulous. "How are you going to do that?"

"I don't know exactly."

"Johanna, you're not making any sense."

"I know. Just be patient with me. I'm in love with him, Cindy. Try to understand."

I could hear Cindy sigh on the other end.

"I'm trying, Johanna."

"I'm good," I said, trying to reassure her. "Really."

"Okay," Cindy said reluctantly. "If you say so. But promise me you'll think about coming back to New York for a couple of weeks."

"I promise."

We rung off shortly after that. I was glad she hadn't asked for my number. I had no idea how I was to explain that Matt had forbidden me to give it out.

I broke the possibility of returning to New York that evening during dinner with Matt. He slammed his fork down so hard the dishes on the table rattled.

"What the hell gave you that idea?"

"When I was talking to Cindy today . . ."

"Cindy? That bitch from the soap opera?" He stood up, pushing his chair back so hard it fell to the floor. "What the hell right does she have to interfere with our business?"

"She wasn't interfering, Matt," I said, trying both to quell his temper and keep my own. "She was merely suggesting—"

"I know what she was suggesting. Let me guess. She didn't think you should be up here with me. She thought you were wasting your time. She thought I was holding you back from some bright future. Maybe she thought I was using you?"

"No. Nothing like that."

"Then what?" His cheeks had taken on an unhealthy-looking mottled red color. He had slammed down his fork, but he was still holding a knife in his left hand.

"She just thought it would be nice to get together," I said quietly.

"Yes, and I suppose she wasn't trying to lure you back into acting again."

"She was only looking out for me. But the fact is that I explained I wasn't ready to go back to acting just yet."

"I knew it, dammit!" He threw his hands up in the air and turned from the table. When he whirled back around, his eyes were wild with anger. "I knew I should never have allowed you to call from here."

By now I could feel my own anger rising. "What do you mean 'allowed' me?"

"Just what I said. Don't you understand? This is a sanctuary, a retreat from the outside world. I don't need the interference. I can't have it. That is why I come here."

That was it. I'd heard enough about his precious privacy. I had tried to keep my temper in check, but I'd had enough. I didn't care how mad he got. I didn't care if he didn't want to hear my complaints. I didn't even care about the knife still clutched in his white-knuckled fist or the wild look in his eyes. I picked up a nearly empty bottle of merlot and hurled it in the general direction of his head. He ducked unnecessarily and the bottle tumbled in slow motion toward the fireplace, where it smashed against the bricks. The words came pouring out in a red torrent of long-suppressed rage.

"You keep me cooped up here without any clothes to speak of. You criticize what I watch on television. You forbid me to have any contact with the outside world. You all but completely ignore me, except when it suits you, and you expect me to be happy?"

Matt had turned to follow the path of the bottle and now he turned back toward me. He looked stunned and pale for a moment, but the blood slowly came back to his face. When he spoke he nearly spat the words out.

"Did *she* say that?"

"No, of course not. Do you think I told her how it really is up here? I'd be too embarrassed."

Matt stepped forward and laid the knife down on the table with exaggerated care. He looked up at me, his face still red and swollen, but somehow no longer filled with rage and violence.

"Is it that unbearable to be with me?" he whispered hoarsely. "I treat you that badly?"

"I didn't say that, Matt."

I had calmed down myself, but not so much that I was sorry I'd thrown the bottle. After all, he wasn't the only one who had a right to express his anger. Besides, it had had the desirable effect of snapping him out of what were becoming all-too-common fits of potentially violent temper.

"That's what I'm hearing."

"You don't understand. When was the last time you touched me?"

Matt looked puzzled. "Touched you? I touch you all the time. I kiss you. . . ."

"I mean intimately."

"You said yourself it wasn't a good time."

"That was a week ago."

"I guess I lost track of time."

"What about all the time before that? Ever since we've been up here, we haven't had a real moment of intimacy."

"You don't understand," Matt said, his voice strained.

"You keep saying I don't understand. Why don't you try me out? I'll never understand if you don't even try to explain."

Matt began to speak, but it was as if the emotion were strangling him. He waved me away and turned to the wall. He stood leaning against the wall, his hands clasped behind his head.

I went up behind him, put my hand on his shoulder, and felt it shaking.

"Matt, please . . ."

"Don't!" he said, violently jerking his body away from my hand. He left the room, careful to hide his face, his tears.

He went upstairs, unlocked his room, and slammed the door behind him. I got a broom and dustpan and cleaned up the broken glass by the fireplace. I sat down and turned on the television.

Matt stayed in his room until just before midnight when he walked into the living room, went to the closet, put on his jacket and gloves, and without saying a word, left the chalet.

The next morning I came down to find Matt lying on the couch. He hadn't even bothered to take off his coat and boots. The room was permeated with the stale smell of alcohol.

I walked over and gently shook him. He moaned, mumbled incoherently, and fell back to sleep. I opened the windows a little to let some fresh crisp air into the house. Then I turned the television on low and watched one of those morning news shows for about an hour. Every once in a while Matt would turn and groan and say something I could not quite make out, but he didn't wake up.

I went into the kitchen and brewed a pot of coffee, black and strong. I carried a big mug back to the couch and tried to wake Matt again.

This time he opened his eyes, red rimmed and bloodshot, and swore softly. He used his arm to shield himself from the light and propped himself up on one elbow.

"What time is it?"

"Nearly ten o'clock."

"Ten o'clock. Shit. Why did you let me sleep so long? I have to get to work."

He swung his boots from the couch and tried to sit up. He made it only halfway before grabbing the sides of his head and sinking back.

"Christ. My head."

"Do you want a couple of aspirin?"

Matt nodded.

I went to the medicine cabinet and returned with the aspirin, a small glass of water, and a damp washcloth.

Matt popped the pills into his mouth and swallowed them with the water. He didn't try to get up again, but lay slumped on the couch with his eyes closed. He accepted the washcloth gratefully.

"Here, take this." I handed him the mug of black coffee and he sipped it tentatively. "Matt, what happened?"

"Not now, Johanna," he said softly.

"Don't give me that, Matt," I said. I thought of the brandy I had given him the night his editor called. Had I started something then? Had he lied to me? Was he really a recovering alcoholic? "I think I deserve an explanation. I thought you told me you didn't drink."

"I don't. Usually."

"Then how do you explain this?"

Matt reached up and took the cloth away from his forehead. His eyes opened slowly and he fixed me with a sad, bloodshot gaze.

"It's your fault."

"My fault?"

"Your talk of leaving. Abandoning me right when I need you the most. How could you do that to me, Johanna? I thought we meant something to each other?"

"You can't blame me for this, Matt."

"Can't I? I'm under a tremendous amount of pressure. You can't possibly know the kind of pressure I'm under. I need you, Johanna. Can't you understand that?"

"I don't see how it is I'm helping you. I only seem to be making things worse."

"No, Johanna. That's not true. Everything can be fine if I could only feel certain that you were there for me. Please promise me that. Promise me that you'll stand by me."

I looked deeply into his red, tortured eyes. I felt his pain, his anguish, his desperation as keenly as if they were my own. I knew I was making a big mistake, everything inside me told me so. I should have left right then and there. It would have been so much easier. I couldn't save him from himself. No one can save a person from themselves. I knew that intellectually. But my heart was telling me something else altogether.

Matt looked so lost, so vulnerable, so sad, so alone. I knew all too well what he was feeling. That was the problem. I was afraid of what would happen to him if I left. He needed someone to take care of him, to watch over him, to protect him. *Run,* my brain was screaming. My heart spoke softer, but more powerfully. *Stay,* it said.

In the end the heart always wins.

That is what all tragedy has in common.

"I promise," I said.

31

———————•———————

"Matt, you can't keep drinking like this."

It was the fifth day in a row. Each night he would leave around midnight and he wouldn't come home until around three in the morning. I'd hear him staggering into the chalet, his keys hitting the coffee table with a loud clatter, his body tumbling onto the couch where I'd find him sleeping it off the next morning.

No matter how hard I'd try to wake him, he wouldn't rise until nearly noon. And then only after I'd poured black coffee and aspirin down his throat. Finally making it to his feet, he'd stumble off to the bathroom to undress and take a shower. Then, with hardly a word, he'd go to his computer. On the desk beside him he kept a water glass, and a bottle of bourbon from which he poured liberally, as he more or less just stared at the blue screen, occasionally typing in a sentence or two, usually cursing under his breath and deleting it a few seconds later.

"Matt, did you hear me?"

He was dressed in a terry-cloth bathrobe, his hair spiky and still wet from the shower. His cheeks were dark with growth, accenting the red in his eyes. He hadn't bothered to shave this morning. The cigarette in his right hand sent up a plume of smoke. The water glass was half-filled with copper-colored liquid.

He had been staring at the computer without touching the keyboard so long the screen saver had come on. He didn't seem to notice. He just kept staring at the stars rushing toward him as if he were indeed a million light-years away.

"Matt, are you going to answer me?"

He turned slowly from the screen to face me.

"What is it?"

"Matt, you need help."

"What the hell are you talking about?" he snapped, taking a drag from his cigarette.

"Look at what's happening to you. You're falling apart. You're never going to be able to finish your book if you keep on like this."

"I'm fine. Just get off my back. The last thing I need is someone else putting the screws to me."

"You're an alcoholic, Matt. Aren't you?"

He stabbed his cigarette out angrily in the saucer beside his glass.

"I'm not an alcoholic!" he snapped. "I told you I don't drink."

"Don't drink? You've been doing nothing but for the past week."

"I only drink when I write. It helps me relax."

"I've been watching you and you've hardly written a word in five days. I'd call that relaxed all right."

"So what the fuck are you doing now, monitoring me?"

"No, I'm trying to help. But since you bring it up, I would like to know where it is you've been going every night for the past week."

"Business, goddammit. It's business."

"Business? What kind of business could you have every night from midnight to three in the morning?"

"Research. I'm doing research for the novel. Do you think I can just sit here and have the ideas hatch all by themselves?"

Matt must have seen the look on my face.

"I'm sorry, Johanna. I'm terribly sorry. Look, I know this all seems pretty bad, but I swear it's only for a short while. You've got to believe me. It's going to be okay. I'm just in a rough spot in the novel. It always happens. What comes next? It's a writer's worst nightmare. Once I get over the hump, I'll be okay. I promise."

He took a sip from the tumbler of bourbon.

"I've got to take a little nap now. You don't mind, do you?"

It had become a habit of Matt's to fall asleep in the late afternoon after a half bottle of bourbon finally caught up with him. He shuffled over to the couch and lay down. He was asleep almost immediately.

Needing some support, I tried Cindy. Luckily, she was home.

"Hi, Jo, how are you?" she said, sounding hopelessly upbeat as usual. Even in tough times, she was always unfailingly optimistic, as if success were just around the corner. In her case, she'd been right. Perhaps that was the source of her never-ending faith that I would eventually follow in her footsteps. She just couldn't conceive of an unjust world.

"I'm doing okay," I lied. I looked over at the couch where Matt slept, his mouth hanging open, snoring lightly. "Matt—is . . . working. I guess I just wanted someone to talk to."

"I'm glad I got your call. You know it's a bitch not having your number. Can't you give it to me?"

"I just can't, Cindy. Matt would have a fit. He really doesn't like the phone to ring up here. He has a kind of fetish for privacy."

"I told you writers were weird."

"How are things going?"

"Fantastic, Jo. I went to a closed audition for that cop drama I told you about. It was just me and two other actresses. I mean they handpicked me from my work on *The Way We Live*. No more cattle calls. Anyway, I think I did a pretty good job."

"No Elmer Fudd this time?"

Cindy laughed. "Not this time." Her voice suddenly got serious. "Hey, maybe that's a bad omen. I did pretty well acting like Mr. Fudd last time."

"Cindy, please," I said, "I was just joking."

"I know. But superstition comes with the territory. Actually I think I did pretty well. At least my agent thinks I have a chance. He says they've already contacted him, asking a lot of questions about my background, sniffing around about my terms at *The Way We Live*."

"That sounds pretty promising."

"I didn't tell you I got a new agent, did I?"

"No."

"Alvin Watkins."

"Alvin Watkins!" I said, hardly able to conceal my astonishment. "Doesn't he handle—"

"Yes!" Cindy said. "He's a great guy. Queer as a kangaroo in sandals, but a helluva agent."

"How in the world did you ever land him?"

"He contacted me," Cindy said. "Can you imagine? He said he saw my work and thought I was destined for bigger things."

"God, Cindy," I said, feeling a mixture of awe and hollowness inside, "it really seems you're on your way."

"I'm not counting the Emmys and Oscars just yet. But this show they're talking about? It could be bigger than *NYPD Blue* ever was."

I was standing at the kitchen. Suddenly I felt like I needed a drink. I opened the refrigerator, pulled out a nearly dead bottle of merlot, and poured the contents into a juice glass. I took a long sip.

"By the way," Cindy said, "that's another reason I'm glad you called. There's a walk-on spot being written even as we speak for *The Way We Live*. I already spoke to the director about it. He's not as big a prick as I thought. I told him you would be perfect for it. You'd get to play a character they killed off two seasons ago because the actress playing it decided to move on to sitcoms. Anyway, the character has had extensive plastic surgery to explain the difference in her looks. She's supposed to be some kind of secret agent. The way it's set up now she has a history with my boyfriend. So we'll be nemeses. How's that for a hoot?"

"Ironic," I said.

"Have you been in contact with Ruth? I think she could help get you in for an audition. I mean I did recommend you to the director, but he leaves the casting calls to the casting director. If you could just get in for a reading, you'd already have a leg up on anyone there."

I stared out the window at the snow melting to transparency and sliding down the glass in the sunlight. I took another swallow of the wine.

"I don't think Ruth would enjoy hearing from me," I said. "We didn't exactly leave on good terms."

"Ruth is an agent," Cindy said. "If she thinks bucks are involved, personal differences are all water under the bridge. You know that."

"I just don't think I could work with her again."

"Jo, you're just being pigheaded. Give Ruth a call."

"I have to discuss it with Matt first."

"Discuss it with Matt? What's to discuss?"

"I can't just leave him here."

I looked back to where he was on the couch.

"Why not? This could be what you've been waiting for. Surely he can't be that selfish."

"It's not that, it's just—"

"What?"

"Please, Cindy. Be patient with me. You don't understand."

I looked over at Matt lying passed out. How could anyone understand?

It was nearly ten p.m. and Matt was still passed out on the couch, snoring loudly, a half-empty bottle of bourbon beside him on the coffee table.

In the last few days he had only grown worse. The constant drinking was taking its toll. He now spent most of the day alternating between drinking and sleeping, hardly getting any work done at all. He would usually wake up around midnight, mutter something about business, and leave the chalet, seldom returning before daybreak.

The mysterious calls had stopped coming, but I was certain that whatever "business" Matt had in town had something to do with whoever it was on the other end. I knew better than to ask Matt anymore about either the calls or where he was going at night. His growing paranoia had made him increasingly sensitive and subject to outbursts of irrational rage, which, though he invariably and abjectly apologized for later, I had no intention of provoking.

I should have left him, but somehow I couldn't. I knew he needed help and he needed it badly. What I was seeing wasn't the real Matt. Something—or to be more exact someone—was driving him to this erratic behavior and I suspected the answer lay in wherever he was going and whoever he was meeting at night.

I walked over to the coffee table and saw Matt's pack of cigarettes lying there beside an overflowing saucer of crushed butts. Next to the saucer was a nearly fresh folder of matches. I picked it up and saw that it was inscribed with the name of the Redwood Inn, a bar in a town called Green Hollow. I vaguely remembered passing a sign for the town on our way to the chalet that first day, which now seemed so long ago.

I searched the room for Matt's keys, but couldn't find them anywhere. He usually just dropped them on the coffee table. I looked down at his unconscious form and saw that he was still wearing his clothes from the night before. There was a sinking feeling in my gut. The keys, I suddenly knew, were still in his pocket.

He was lying on his left side, facing the fireplace. Carefully I reached into his pocket. He stirred for a moment, moaned, and I froze. He threw his arm across his eyes and I removed my hand just in time as he rolled over, his face now buried in the back of the couch. I reached into the other pocket and felt the soft leather folder containing the keys. I slowly pulled them out and for the first time in what seemed like minutes let out my breath.

The next problem was finding something to wear.

I thought of the makeshift outfit he had loaned me when we had gone outside to frolic in the snow. Unfortunately Matt had insisted that I remove it immediately upon returning to the chalet as it was wet with snow. He had hung it up to dry in the utility room off the kitchen and had taken it back to his bedroom. I'd thought nothing of it at the time, but now I wondered if he had quickly secreted the clothes away purposely to keep me from putting them on and leaving the chalet on my own.

Suddenly I remembered the keys in my hand.

Surely one of them must open his bedroom door.

I went up to the loft and tried each of the keys.

Once.

Twice.

Right side up and upside down.

Only one even made it into the keyhole, but after a significant amount of jiggling and a scary moment when I thought I'd jammed it in the lock, I realized that none of the keys fit.

Disappointed, I walked back downstairs to the closet by the door. After some searching I found a nylon snowsuit that looked like it went with a pair of old, unused cross-country skis tucked away in the corner. I yanked the snowsuit off its hanger and brought it out into the light. It was electric blue with yellow piping on the sleeves and legs. Well, I couldn't afford to be fussy. I also found a pair of thick woolen socks and heavy insulated gloves. I climbed into the oversize snowsuit and zipped myself up, rolling up the cuffs to a manageable length. Then I went back upstairs to grab my boots.

I looked down at myself in the oversize snowsuit and boots. God, I would never have dreamed of going out in public dressed like this. I looked like a homeless person. But I didn't have much of a choice. I threw Matt's trenchcoat over the whole ensemble, which helped, and as quietly as I could manage, slipped out of the chalet.

I flinched when I started up the engine, half expecting to see Matt charging out the front door to stop me, but as I slipped the Jeep into gear, there was no sign of him. I crept slowly in reverse up the long drive and breathed another sigh of relief as I backed out onto the highway and headed into town.

The Redwood Inn was located on the outskirts of Green Hollow on what passed for the seedy side of a small, neat New England town all but shut down for the night.

I parked the Jeep in the nearly empty parking lot and walked around to the entrance of a long low building fringed with icicles. It was darker inside the bar than outside and it took a moment for my eyes to get used to the lack of light. There was nothing fancy about the Redwood Inn. The walls were paneled with redwood, hence its name, and the bar was built of the same. There were booths with red vinyl seats along the back and a few scattered tables in the center of the main room. There was another room off to the left, better lit, with two pool tables, their bright green felt blazing. You had to look closely toward the ceiling to see the animal heads: deer, moose, bear. The neon light of the beer signs behind the bar shone off their glass eyes.

"Hello," I said to the bartender. "Can you help me?"

"What's the problem?"

He'd been watching me ever since I came in the door. He was a big man who looked like he might have been a logger in his youth, but whose muscles had mostly melted to fat, but the kind of bulky fat that was still intimidating. Behind him, on a shelf next to a row of glasses, was a small color television. I could sense him sizing me up, trying to figure out what the hell to make of me. I must have looked a sight, dressed as I was.

"I was wondering if you could tell me if you know a Matt Jablonsky."

He turned away for a moment, picked up a small bottle of seltzer, and took a sip. He eyed me over the bottom of the bottle, turned back around, and put it down on the exact ring of moisture from which he had taken it. From the next room I could hear the click of pool balls striking together and the thump of a ball finding a pocket. There was a whoop of disbelief from one of the players.

The bartender sighed. "You his wife?"

"His girlfriend."

"Look, lady, whatever you are, I don't drag 'em in here and I don't bolt the door so they can't get out. If you got a problem with your man being in my bar, then settle it at home."

"It's not like that," I said, trying to sound as reassuring as possible. "I just want to know if he comes in here."

"If he's your boyfriend and there's no problem, why don't you just ask him?"

"Please," I said, unable to think of a plausible lie, "I can't explain. I'm not trying to get anyone into trouble. You have to believe me. I don't care if he comes here. I'm really looking for the person he's meeting."

"I'm sorry, lady. I can't help you. Like I said, if you got a problem, settle it between you."

He started to turn away.

"You want to stay out of trouble," I said, desperation spurring me on, "then how about this for trouble? My boyfriend has been leaving here so drunk he can hardly make it through the front door every night for the past week. If he gets into an accident, who do you think is legally responsible for serving him? You don't think the police might be interested in that?"

The bartender glared at me, his face turning red.

"Are you threatening me?"

"I'm just laying out your options," I answered as calmly as I could manage. "You can either tell me what I want or I can go to the cops."

He was so mad his jowls were quivering. He looked like it was all he could do to restrain himself from coming around the bar and throwing me bodily out the door into a snowbank. Instead, he seemed to be weighing the seriousness of my resolve.

Just then a voice came from over my shoulder.

"It's okay, Al. It's me she wants to talk to."

He was no taller than me.

He had the wide face of an ex-boxer and a body to match, his broad shoulders stretching the fabric of a corduroy sports jacket worn to the color of dust. Beneath his heavy, corrugated forehead, a pair of anthracite eyes gleamed with two sharp pinpoints of reflected light that reminded me of those stuffed animals on the walls. He smiled and the long deep lines in his five-o'clock shadow looked like scars.

"How about we take a seat?" he said.

I followed him to one of the booths in the back. He slid in front of a half-drunk mug of beer and I sat across from him. Above us, on a shelf, a stuffed racoon reared back on its hind legs, black lips pulled back baring small, sharp-looking, white teeth.

He stared across the polished wood table with an amused look and slowly refilled his mug from the open bottle standing beside it. He lifted the mug to his lips, drank about a quarter of its contents, and laid it back down on the table. He licked the foam off his lips with a deliberation that struck me as purposefully obscene.

"So," he said at last, "what's this all about?"

"My name is Johanna Brady."

The man stared at me impassively. He obviously had no intention of introducing himself. I began haltingly. "I know Matt. I suppose you do, too?"

"So what?"

"Do you know he's a writer?"

The man smiled crookedly. "Claims to be, don't he?"

I ignored the sarcasm.

"I'm going to get right to the point Mr.—"

He let the question dangle for an uncomfortably long period of time. Just when I thought he wouldn't answer, he smiled again, his teeth small and square and flat and too white for his swarthy skin.

"Clay. The name's Clay."

"Mr. Clay—"

"Just Clay," he corrected me. He reached into the pocket of his flannel shirt and pulled out a short, well-chewed nub of a cigar. He stuck the cigar, unlit, between his teeth.

"Matt's been going through a difficult time with his new book. Someone was calling at all hours of the night. Matt said it was his agent. But I don't believe him. I don't think it was his agent. I think it was you. And I think it's you he's coming to see every night."

"Is that so?" Clay said, looking amused.

"I don't know what business you have with Matt, but he's under a lot of pressure to finish his book and you're not making it any easier for him. He's been extremely upset lately. I'm very worried about him."

"I'm sorry to hear that," Clay said. "Very sorry."

He had taken the cigar from his mouth. He was slowly and silently tapping his fingers on the table. Like everything else about him, they were wide and flat.

"I'm not going to beat around the bush. I want you to stop bothering Matt. If you don't, I'm going to go to the police."

"You wouldn't want to do that, Miss Brady."

"Wouldn't I?"

He leaned forward over the table, the sheer bulk of him making me flinch. His face, in the harsh light of the tin lamp hanging over the table, looked like an angry plain of broken red rock.

"No," he said simply. "You wouldn't. And neither would Matt."

"Are you threatening me?"

"Do I threaten you, Miss Brady?"

"No," I said, trying to sound convincing. "I just want you to leave Matt alone."

"I'm afraid that's impossible."

"Why? What does Matt have to do with you?"

He put the cigar back in his mouth and leaned back in his seat. His fists, like an irregularly shaped stone, were folded on the table.

"He's my collaborator."

"Collaborator? Matt never mentioned working with anyone. I don't believe you."

The man grinned. He put a flat, square finger to his lips and let out a loud *shhh*. "It's a secret," he said.

"I don't believe you," I said again.

He shrugged as if he didn't care whether I believed him or not.

"I'm going to ask him."

"I wouldn't do that, Miss Brady."

"Why not?"

"It wouldn't make Matt very happy. Like I said, it's a secret."

He put the stump of cigar back in the pocket of his flannel shirt and drained the rest of his beer, his tiny black eyes watching me the whole time. He laid the mug back on the table and slid from the booth.

"You'll have to excuse me," he said. "But I have some work of my own to do. It's been a pleasure to meet you at last, Miss Brady. Matt has spoken highly of you. I hope we can work together. After all, we both have a stake in Matt's success, don't we?"

He smiled the way a boxer smiles at his opponent before the opening bell and threw a couple of crumpled bills on the table.

He put his fists on the table and leaned forward toward me again, close enough so that I could smell the beer on his breath.

"And if you ever need a man—a real man—let me know. I imagine it's getting very lonely standing up there on a pedestal."

"Go to hell," I whispered hoarsely.

He straightened up, laughed, and turned away. I watched as his broad frame made its way to the coatrack against the wall. He put on a nondescript black jacket, opened the door, and disappeared into the night. All the way from across the bar I felt the blast of cold air that punctuated his exit.

I sat there trembling with anger, confusion, and outrage. And the worst part was that I didn't even know for sure whom I should be angry with. Was Clay telling the truth? If so, why had Matt kept it from me? Even if he wasn't Matt's collaborator as he claimed, the man clearly had some connection to Matt. But what possible business could Matt have with such a crude and dangerous-looking character? And what was that comment about me being up on a pedestal? How had Clay known anything about my intimate life with Matt? Did Matt talk with him about our life together?

The plot was thickening and I was desperately trying to sort out the tangled strands. I'm not sure how long I sat there before I heard a harsh, impatient voice above me.

"This is a bar, lady, not a bus stop. You want something to drink or not?"

I looked up into the jowly face of the bartender.

"No," I mumbled. "I was just going."

I started to slide out of the booth when I noticed the open matchbook on the table for the first time. Inside it was a phone number.

And a single word.

"Clay."

32

I killed the engine of the Jeep and sat inside a few minutes until the last of the heat dissipated.

I looked up at the chalet. I had carefully made my escape into town, but I had given little thought to how I would explain to Matt my meeting with his "collaborator." Not that I felt the burden of explanation was on me, anyway. If what the man had said was true, Matt had a hell of a lot more to account for than I did. The only thing was how to bring the subject up before Matt heard about it from the man himself. At least, I thought, I had the night to think it over.

I was wrong.

No sooner than I quietly turned the key in the lock and pushed open the door, Matt came charging across the room. He was wearing a parka with the hood up and carrying a bottle of bourbon.

"What the hell is going on?" he bellowed. "Where the hell have you been?"

"Calm down, Matt."

He had come nearly face-to-face with me and I could smell the stench of alcohol on his breath.

"What the fuck do you mean calm down? I wake up and find you and the car gone and you ask me to calm down. How was I supposed to know where you were? You could have left me, for all I knew."

"Do you really think I would do that?" I said, trying not to say anything that would escalate the situation. I could see by his eyes that he was very drunk and very angry.

"You pull something like this, I don't know what you'll do next."

I moved back a step. "Maybe I should just leave for a while until you cool down."

"No!" Matt shouted and lurched toward me awkwardly. I dodged away from his outstretched hand and put the couch between us.

"I'm not a prisoner here, Matt. I have the right to come and go if I want."

"You abandoned me."

"I was only gone a couple of hours."

"Do you know I had an appointment?" he said. "Now you made me miss it."

He pulled back the sleeve of his parka and looked down at his wrist, but there was no watch there.

"I know."

"What the hell time is it?" he mumbled and started looking around for a clock as if he were unfamiliar with the room. He had lifted the bottle to his lips and was taking a long pull of the bourbon when he suddenly stopped. He turned around and looked at me with a look of terror on his face.

"What do you mean, you know?"

"I met him at the Redwood Inn."

He took a stumbling step toward me. "You did what?"

"I met him. I had to find out who's been bothering you. The calls, the late-night meetings. I found the name of the bar on a book of matches. I only wanted to help. You have to believe that."

"You've been spying on me!"

"Matt, I haven't been spying on you."

"What do you think you are? A fucking detective? Is that the role you've decided to play? I'm the one writing this story. Not you!"

"Matt, I don't know what you're talking about."

Suddenly, with an agility that belied his drunken state, Matt leaped up on the couch, planted his foot on the back, and flipped it over. I jumped back with a shout as he stepped off the back of the overturned couch and staggered toward me.

"So you don't know what I'm talking about, do you?" he said, mockingly. "Poor, poor Johanna has no idea what I'm talking about."

My back was nearly against the bookcase now.

"Matt, you're scaring me."

"Am I, Johanna?" he said. "Maybe you should have thought of that when you were stabbing me in the back." He put his face so close to mine I almost thought he was going to kiss me. "Am I scaring you now?"

"Matt, I wasn't stabbing you in the back. I was just trying to—"

"Answer the question," he said sharply. Then he lowered his voice. "Am I scaring you now?"

"Yes," I said quietly. "Does that make you happy? Does that make you feel like a man?"

Matt didn't say anything. He just stared at me, our faces nearly touching, our eyes locked.

"Matt, please—"

"Boo!" he shouted.

I jumped in spite of myself.

"You look so beautiful when you're scared," Matt said, his bleary, bloodshot eyes examining my face with a cold fascination. He was really scaring me now. We had argued before, but I had never seen this side of Matt. The man in front of me now was a complete stranger. I had to get the old Matt back. Under the alcohol, the anger, and the fear, I knew he was there. I knew he needed me.

"Matt, we can work this out together. Who is this guy? He says he's your collaborator."

Matt seemed to snap out of his trance. "Is that what he said? Is that the exact word he used? 'Collaborator?' "

"Yes. He said it was a secret."

Matt stumbled back a step, for which I was grateful, and hugged himself with laughter.

"A secret collaborator, huh?" he said, coughing until his face had turned an unhealthy red.

"Is it true?"

Matt wiped his mouth with the back of his hand. He ignored my question. "What else did he say?"

"Nothing."

The laughter was gone and Matt's eyes were cold as ice. "Do you swear?"

"I swear. Matt, what's going on?"

He lifted the bottle, its contents sloshing around, and took a long pull.

"Matt, you've had enough of that. Please put the bottle down."

"Don't tell me what to do," he slurred.

"Matt, you need help." I reached out for the bottle. "Please let me help you."

Matt snatched his arm away. "I don't need anyone's help, goddammit."

"You're killing yourself, can't you see that? You need to trust someone. You need to trust me. We can get this straightened out."

"I *did* trust you," he growled. "I trusted you and you betrayed me."

I saw Matt's hand on the other side of my face before I felt the burning blow of his palm across my left cheek. He hadn't hit me hard; the blow hurt my pride more than anything else, but I'd long ago sworn to myself that I would never let a man lay a hand on me in anger. My words were calm, neutral, but left no room for argument. "Matt, I want to leave."

"Okay," he said quietly. "You can leave tomorrow."

I would have preferred to leave right then, but I knew that it was impractical.

"Can I please have my car keys?" he asked.

I handed them to him. I knew he shouldn't be going out in the condition he was in, but after what had just happened, I decided it was no longer any concern of mine.

"Thank you," he said. He left the chalet, still clutching the bottle of bourbon and drove off into the night.

The sound of the Jeep's engine hadn't faded five minutes down the trail to the main road when the phone rang.

I picked it up.

"So did you tell Matt of our little meeting?"

"What do you want, Clay?"

"I told you he wouldn't be too happy about you knowing."

"Look, this is between you and Matt. I'm leaving tomorrow."

"That's for the best, Miss Brady. That's for the best."

The phone went dead before I could tell him to go to hell.

True to Matt's word, I was on a flight back to New York by three o'clock the following afternoon.

Matt had woken up early, stone-cold sober for the first time in weeks, and set about preparing for my departure. The first thing he did was to drive into town and buy me an outfit of suitable traveling clothes. Then he was on the phone with the airport arranging for a ticket. Through it all, he was silent and unemotional. I had expected the usual round of abject apologies and desperate pleas for forgiveness for his irrational behavior the night before. I was certain he would beg me to stay. Instead, he seemed almost anxious to have me on my way.

I had already called Cindy the night before. She was gracious as always, even though I hadn't called her until nearly three in the morning.

"Jo, hi," she said, her voice sounding tired and somewhat disappointed in spite of her attempt to sound upbeat. "This is a surprise."

"I'm terribly sorry. I hope I didn't wake you."

"No," Cindy said. "In fact I just got home from a date with Sal. I just met him a couple of days ago. I didn't get a chance to tell you about Brad and I. We're through."

"Cindy, I'm coming home."

"What?"

"I'm coming back to New York."

"When?"

"Tomorrow."

Cindy could tell something was wrong from the sound of my voice.

"What happened?"

"I can't go into it all right now. Let's just say he's gone Jack Nicholson on me. Like in *The Shining*."

I tried to laugh, but I felt the tears coming down my cheeks. My breath caught.

"Oh God, Jo. I'm so sorry. You know I thought it was a mistake for you to go up there in the first place, but I still hoped everything would work out for your sake."

"I know, Cindy. I appreciate that, I really do. I guess it just wasn't meant to be."

"You'll put it behind you, Jo. You always do."

"I guess so," I said. "But this is going to be a little harder than usual. I sublet my old apartment. I've got no place to stay. On top of that, there's some problem with my credit cards I have to straighten out. I don't even have enough money to get home from the airport. If Matt weren't buying my ticket home—"

I felt like I was going to cry again. Jesus, how did I let myself get into this situation?

"Jo, don't say anything else. I'll take care of everything. I'll arrange to have you picked up at the airport. Just call me again tomorrow when you know the exact time. I have to go to the studio, but I'll keep checking my messages. When you get here, you can stay with me until you get back on your feet."

"Cindy, I couldn't," I started, knowing damn well I didn't have any other choice.

"Nonsense," Cindy said. "You're my best friend. I would have been hurt if you asked anyone else."

"Thank you, Cindy," I said. "I don't know what I'd do without you."

"I owe you one, Jo, you know that. Whatever you need . . . "

"I've really got to go now," I said. "I think Matt may be coming back and I want to get up to my room. I don't want to see him again tonight."

It was a lie, but suddenly I desperately wanted to get off the phone, to be alone. What Cindy had said about owing me one had struck a nerve. I was afraid she would bring it all up again. She had always wanted to explain, to talk it out, but I didn't, wouldn't, couldn't bear to hear her out. It was over and done with as far as I was concerned.

"You'll be okay?" she said.

"Yes. I just don't want to see him."

"Okay," Cindy said, hardly sounding convinced. "But if you need anything . . ."

"Cindy, I really have to go. Thank you so much. For everything. I'll see you tomorrow."

I hung up the phone before her reply. I sat up for another two hours and then went upstairs to my bedroom to pull together what few personal belongings I'd managed to keep with me in my carry-on. I didn't take any of the clothes Matt had bought me. And the last thing I did was place the copy of the paperback I'd read on the plane carefully on the night table. Then I sat in the rocker and waited for him to return, which he did, an hour after dawn.

Matt drove all the way to the airport in silence. I didn't feel any need to talk either. There was nothing left to say. When we arrived at the ticket window, I saw Matt had booked me for first-class.

"I'll pay you back once I get settled," I said.

"Forget it."

"No, I mean it. I just need your address."

"I said forget it. Come on, I'll walk you to your gate."

"You don't have to. I can find it from here."

Matt didn't answer. He had already started walking away, with my ticket in his hand.

It was all too easy. I still expected some kind of emotional display. Right up until he handed me the ticket and I took my place in line to go through the metal detector, I thought he would ask me to stay. Not that I would have stayed, even had he begged me. What he had done, how he had behaved, it was unforgiveable. Yet there was something deep inside me, something I hardly dared admit even to myself that still cared for him, that still needed some kind of closure. Even as I walked down the corridor to board the plane, I listened for his voice calling me back.

"Good-bye Matt," was all I said.

"Good-bye," was all he said.

I put out my hand and he took it, holding it briefly before letting it go.

What had I expected?

In spite of the fact that I had been dreading some kind of last-minute scene, I had certainly expected something more than a handshake and a cool farewell. In spite of the fact that things didn't work out, hadn't we meant more to each other than this?

"So this is the way it ends?" I said, unable to play it cool any longer.

"Evidently."

Tears came to my eyes.

Damn him.

I walked quickly and determinedly down the corridor to the plane. I told myself I wouldn't turn around. But halfway down the corridor I did anyway.

Matt was already gone.

33

It had been almost a week since I returned to New York and I was still getting used to the hustle and bustle of the city that never sleeps.

After my voluntary exile in the Maine winter, it felt great to be back among the shops, the restaurants, the theaters, and even the crowds. The cold weather was hanging on, crusts of dirty snow still survived in dark corners, but every couple of days or so there was a hint of spring in the air. If you looked closely, there were even buds on some of the sticklike trees that grew from out of the small plots of unpaved earth spaced regularly along the sidewalks.

Cindy did her best to show me a good time and take my mind off Matt. She was fighting a losing battle. I tried to deny it, but the fact was that I missed him terribly. Even as bad as things got toward the end, I couldn't help feeling an aching nostalgia over the good times we had shared together and for the first heady days of our romance that seemed so promising, so perfect, so fated for better things. I knew that leaving had been the right decision. So why was I second-guessing myself? Maybe there was something I could have done to help him? Maybe we could have worked it out?

"That's nonsense," Cindy said. "You can't help people like that by yourself. They're sick. They need professional help."

We were sitting in the living room of her new apartment in the upper eighties. She had moved in shortly after signing the contract extension that guaranteed her two more years on *The Way We Live*. The place had three bedrooms and two full baths and overlooked Central Park. She hadn't had a chance to buy new furniture yet and the slightly shabby furnishings were all that remained as a reminder of the days when we were both struggling actresses.

"Maybe if I'd stayed," I said, staring out the window at the bare branches of the park, "I might have been able to convince him to get help."

"No one can talk someone into getting help if they're not ready," Cindy said, taking a drag from a fashionably long and impossibly slender brown cigarette. Since when had she taken up smoking? She blew out a stream of white smoke. "They have to hit rock bottom before they're willing to pick themselves up. And no one can convince them otherwise."

"But he was so different when I met him."

"He wasn't drinking when you met him, was he?"

"No. But then he wasn't writing either."

Cindy crushed out the cigarette after taking only three puffs.

"Don't torture yourself like this," she said. "Just forget him."

"It's not that easy, Cindy."

I was about to say "for me," but caught myself. After all, she was only trying to help. Cindy tried on and discarded men like a woman trying on evening gowns. She had told me about her breakup with Brad and I had already met her new boyfriend, Sal, whom Cindy had described as an up-and-coming independent producer. He struck me as little more than a hustler. Another streetwise guy from the neighborhood who was banking on his slick, dark-haired good looks and wisecracking confidence to escape a life of petty crime, or worse, a job in a pizzeria. Still, I didn't feel the need to express my concerns to Cindy. I knew from experience that she could take care of herself. My guess was that Sal would be back behind a counter in Little Italy faster than you could say "extra cheese please."

"How about we make it easier with dinner at Sardi's?"

"Sardi's?" I said. "Couldn't we just go to the Peking Duck? I haven't been there since I left for Maine. It'll be like old times."

Cindy made a face. "I can't eat there anymore. The place is a sty. And the food is full of cornstarch and grease. But if you're in the mood for Chinese, we could go to a place the cast all goes to after shooting. It's called Dish of Salt over on Forty-seventh Street."

Since when had Cindy become such a connoisseur of fine restaurants? At what point had she decided the Peking Duck was no longer good enough for her?

"No," I said dully. "Sardi's will be fine."

I no longer bothered to remind Cindy that I couldn't afford such luxuries as dinner at Sardi's. She just took it for granted that it would be her treat. In the beginning I had protested, but Cindy would hear none of it. She said I was just being silly. That I would do the same for her. That we were friends. She said all the stuff you're supposed to say. In the end, her persistence and my dependence wore me down.

Without saying as much, she let me know that she had plenty of money and she enjoyed sharing it with her best friend. It was a mortifying experience for me. But, like I said, I had little choice. I went along with her on one condition: I insisted that I would pay her back once I got a job. She just laughed, said it wasn't necessary, but that if it would make me feel better, I could pay her back. Maybe I was just being sensitive, but I couldn't help but feel that she was just amusing me.

I had no job, no savings, and my credit was still suspended. I had tried to straighten out the credit card situation, only to be informed that they had been maxed so far beyond the limit the company had assumed either fraud or theft. I didn't understand. I knew the cards were at the limit, but the totals the company were claiming I owed were absurd. I remembered the expensive clothes Matt had bought me, but he had used cash. I had seen the receipts on the bags.

Unable to convince the customer service representative that I had not made the purchases, I asked to be transferred to their legal department. The woman's false cheerfulness, which had changed to irritability during the course of our conversation, suddenly turned cheerful again at the prospect of passing me along to someone else. I waited several long minutes, listening to a Muzak version of "Yellow Submarine" before someone answered. The legal representative made no attempt to sound friendly. His job was to protect the company from deadbeats trying to get out of paying their bills. He brusquely informed me that whether I had made the purchases or not I was still responsible for the balance.

I argued, threatened to call a lawyer, take them to court, but the representative didn't seem impressed. He must have heard it all before. He coolly replied that legal action was certainly within my rights. I felt like telling him to go to hell. Instead, I asked him to forward a copy of the statement detailing the charges against my account, which he condescendingly assured me he would do within the week. He said he sincerely hoped we could work the matter out, as they valued me as a customer. Then he wished me a good day in a tone of voice that made it clear our business was finished and hung up. My hand was trembling so much I could hardly fit the receiver of the phone back in its cradle.

And so I let myself be carried along on the wave of Cindy's newfound success. I went with her to a seemingly endless round of restaurants and shows, openings and cocktail parties. She introduced me to everyone she knew. It was humiliating. They would talk to me just long enough to find out that I was no one who could further their careers and quickly move on to someone else. I usually wound up standing in a corner somewhere pretending to sip a drink. Cindy, attracting attention wherever she turned, never seemed to notice.

That evening at Sardi's Cindy once again brought the subject around to my career.

"You should really give Ruth a call."

"I don't know," I said, sipping a six-dollar glass of mineral water. "I really don't think she wants to hear from me. Are you forgetting the Sol Silverstein incident?"

"She can't blame you for that."

"She was pretty damn upset."

"I'd call her anyway," Cindy said, cutting a small veal cutlet whose cost could have bought me groceries for a week. "She's a businesswoman. What's more, she's an agent. You could kick her mother down the stairs and she'd get over it if she thought there was a chance of getting fifteen percent."

"I don't know. . . ."

"Call her," Cindy said, holding the veal poised before her mouth. "Promise."

"I promise."

"Tomorrow?"

"Tomorrow."

Just then two fiftyish women dressed in expensive-looking tailored suits and wearing lots of flashy jewelry came to the table. Each was holding a pen and a playbill from the show *Ragtime* in her hand.

"Excuse me," one of the women said, "but don't you play Sasha on *The Way We Live?*"

"Yes," Cindy said, "I do."

"I knew it," the other woman squealed. "You're just terrific. We never miss a program. The way you treat Cole. It's terrible. You're such a, such a—"

"Bitch," her friend chimed in enthusiastically.

"Why, thank you," Cindy said and laughed.

"You and Susan Lucci are just the best," the woman continued. "Do you know her?"

"I've met her briefly."

"I really hope they give her an Emmy soon. She really deserves it."

"Yes," Cindy said, "she does."

"And you, too . . ."

"Well, I wouldn't go that far—"

"We just went to see *Ragtime*," the first woman said. "Would you please sign our programs? It would be the highlight of our night."

"Sure," Cindy said.

"See," one of the women observed. "I knew she would." She turned back to Cindy. "Our husbands—they're over there"—she pointed a well-manicured finger at two well-dressed older men sitting at a table against the wall and talking through a haze of cigar smoke—"they said not to bother you, that you'd be mad, but I can tell you're really a nice person, even if you are so bad on television."

Cindy signed the programs and handed them back to the women.

The two women thanked Cindy profusely and one of them turned to me.

"Are you somebody?" she asked.

"No," I said quietly, feeling an intense anger rising inside me against these two harmless older women.

They shrugged, turned back to Cindy to thank her again, and finally they were gone.

"God," Cindy said under her breath, "I never thought I'd say it, but this is getting to be kind of a drag."

It wasn't the first time someone had come up to Cindy. It seemed everywhere we went, someone knew her or recognized her from the show. She always acted embarrassed or annoyed afterward, but I could tell from the excitement in her eyes that she relished the attention.

I speared at my salad, no longer hungry.

"So you promise you're going to call Ruth tomorrow?"

"Yes," I said and stuffed my mouth with salad to put an end to the conversation.

I waited until Cindy was out of the apartment the next morning on her way to the studio before trying Ruth. I was hoping she wouldn't answer, my hope that I would get her machine after three rings, but on the fourth, a voice answered.

"Good as Gold Agency."

This time the voice on the other end really was Ruth's niece.

"Is Ruth in?" I asked. "It's Johanna Brady."

"I'll see. Can you hold please?"

See? If anything, Ruth was sitting in the room right next to her.

After a short pause, the girl came back on the line.

"I'm sorry, but Ms. Gold is on another line right now. Can she call you back?"

"Sure," I said and gave her Cindy's number.

I waited until nearly four-thirty that afternoon. I had all but given up hope, convinced that I'd been right, and that Ruth had written me off when the phone rang. I picked it up and heard her familiar cigarette-cracked voice.

"Johanna," Ruth said. "Sorry I couldn't get back to you sooner, but I have some interesting projects cooking. What can I do for you?"

"I just wanted to let you know that I was back in town. You know, back in the business."

"Good, good," Ruth said, noncommittally.

"The fact is that I wanted to know if you would still represent me."

There was a long pause on the other end and the sound of smoke exhaling across the receiver.

"I'm kind of busy right now," Ruth said. "I've taken on a lot of new clients."

"I know we left things on kind of a sour note," I said, desperation creeping into my voice. "But I think we can work things out. Come to some kind of common agreement."

I remembered what Cindy had told me. For an agent, and especially a struggling one, Ruth didn't seem so eager to have me back.

"The fact is, Johanna—"

I could hear the rejection in her voice. I knew the sound all too well and I was determined to stop it at any cost.

"Look," I said, deciding to play my trump, "I'm not coming empty-handed. I have a friend who's got a role on *The Way We Live*. They just gave her a two-year contract extension. Anyway, there's a part opening up and she's already put in a good word for me with the director."

"Really?" Ruth said. I could almost hear the *ka-ching* of her mental cash register. Cindy was right, after all. Agents would sell their souls for a fifteen-percent commission.

"I have an audition next week. I'd like you to represent me."

"That puts a whole new spin on things, Johanna. I'd be glad to represent you."

"Thank you, Ruth."

"What are friends for?" she replied.

Yes, I thought. What are they for?

34

The audition was the following Thursday and I was determined to give it my best shot.

I felt a sense of urgency I'd never quite felt before. Sure, I was always nervous, but this time it was somehow different. I knew that I wasn't likely to get another chance this good. On top of that, I felt the expectations of two people who'd put their faith in me. Cindy had personally gone out on a limb and recommended me for the part, something I couldn't expect her to do again for fear of looking foolish. And Ruth, as reluctant and opportunistic as her motives were, had nonetheless agreed to grant me renewed legitimacy by representing me. I was used to dealing with my own disappointment. I had become something of an expert at it. But I couldn't bear the thought of dealing with the disappointment my failure would cause these two women.

It was with that motivation that I decided to visit the Actor's Studio that Saturday. I had sworn I wouldn't go back after the way Drake had treated me the last time I was there, but I needed a place where I could brush up on my skills and he was one of the best teachers in the business. I dressed in sweats and sneakers and told Cindy I was going for a jog in the park. Cindy hated jogging—preferring a well-planned program of aerobics classes and bulimia to maintain her perfect figure— so I knew there was no chance of her asking to come along. If she knew I was going to the studio, she would have insisted on paying my dues and she had done enough for me already.

"Have a good run," Cindy said, tucked into a robe, having just gotten up after a long evening with Sal.

"Thanks," I said, feeling a little guilty.

I took the elevator downstairs, jogged to the automated teller on the corner so as not to be a complete liar, and withdrew fifty of the last two hundred dollars in my account. Then I took a subway to the studio.

Class was already in session by the time I got there. I slipped in quietly and sat down in the back, crosslegged on the cold bare floor. Off to the right, near the front, I spotted Harry Krinkle or whatever his name really was.

Drake was up in front, giving a fire-and-brimstone sermon on one of his favorite topics: the degeneration of acting into nothing more than a cult of celebrity. His current target was Leonardo DiCaprio. He insisted we review that "dreadful" *Titanic* movie and notice how the "pipsqueak" was dwarfed by virtually every other actor in the film.

"Nonetheless," Drake said disdainfully, "the teenage girls love him and the Hollywood star makers have put their golden finger on him. Now we will be forced to see him in movie after movie, no matter how inappropriate he is for the role. *That,*" he spat out the word, "is what acting is today."

Drake's eyes passed over me only once as he spoke without so much as pausing, as if I'd been to class every Saturday for the months I'd been gone.

When he was done with his lecture, he began the day's improvisational exercises.

He called three people up to the front of the class to discuss an arbitrary sports score he had pulled out of the morning paper. Drake let them go with it for about ten minutes before growing impatient and telling them to sit down. Then he called on a handsome nervous-looking young man I'd never seen before and told him to reveal that he was gay. The guy was so nervous—stuttering and blushing—he actually did a fairly credible job. Drake seemed to enjoy the man's discomfort, especially as he was exactly the kind of typical pretty-faced actor Drake had just got done railing against. He dismissed the young man with a slow sarcastic clap of his hands, which was as close as Drake ever came to complimenting anyone. The good-looking guy hurried back to his place with a look of mortification, relief, and triumph.

As usual, I was filled with anxiety and anticipation. On the one hand, I dreaded the possibility of being called upon and subjected to Drake's humiliation. On the other hand, I was here to get some work. He called several other actors up front and I was beginning to feel sure that he was purposely ignoring me, perhaps as punishment for missing so many classes, when he dragged two metal folding chairs to the front of the room. I looked up at the shriek of the chairs' legs against the wooden floor and saw him pointing directly at me.

"You," he said and turned to a woman next to Harry Krinkle. "And you."

I walked up to the front of the class, feeling everyone's eyes on me, like the victim of a sacrifice. If there was one good thing about being called in front of one of Drake's classes, it sure made going to an audition seem like a piece of cake by comparison.

The two metal chairs were positioned side by side.

Drake pointed to one.

"Sit down," he said.

I sat down. The other woman, a nondescript, slightly overweight woman with a passing resemblance to Kathy Bates, sat in the other.

"All right," Drake said. "You are in a commercial airplane. It is clear that it is going down. In a matter of minutes you will both be killed. Go."

I was still trying to process the scene in my mind when the woman beside me grabbed my arm, her fingers digging into my flesh.

"Ouch," I said, startled. "Jesus."

"What's happening?" she said, her eyes wild with fear. "What's going on? What's that sound?"

"I—I don't know," I answered, trying to recover.

"Oh my God, what was that?" the woman suddenly shouted. "Stewardess. Where are the stewardesses?"

"I don't know—" I started, playing catch up. The woman had gotten the jump on me and was completely running away with the scene.

"We're going to crash," she wailed. "We're going to die!"

I stared at her in astonishment. Tears were running down her face, her fists were clenched in her hair.

I didn't even think.

I slapped her, hard, across the face.

I wanted her to shut up. I was angry that she was upstaging me and I used that anger in the scene. Unfortunately, the moment I slapped her, my mind was snapped back to that last night in the chalet when Matt had hit me. In that instant, I lost my concentration.

The woman beside me was now screaming at the top of her lungs. The plane was going down. We were only moments away from dying. What would one feel in such a situation? What would I feel?

Confusion. Anger. Panic.

I was thinking too much and I knew it.

Drake came right up beside me.

"You're going to die!" he shouted right in my ear, his voice the words to the demented tune of my screaming classmate. "You're going to die!"

I started screaming, too. I screamed as loud as I could.

Now Drake was shouting even louder. "No! No! You're going to die! You're going to die!"

Confused, I raised the pitch of my scream.

Drake was now screaming like a madman. "No! Goddamn it! No! You don't understand! You're going to die! It's like an orgasm, dammit! It's like an orgasm! You have to let go!"

I bolted from the seat, tipping it backward, its metal clang echoing through the loft. I ran toward the door, sweat and tears streaming down my face. I didn't stop running until I had exited the old warehouse and was halfway up the street. I slowed down and came to a stop, feeling the hot tears still coursing down my cheeks in the cool morning air.

"Damn him," I muttered, thinking of Drake. What kind of a sadist was he, anyway? Why did he seem to have it in for me? Why did he turn everything I did back to the subject of orgasm? Was he playing some kind of perverse sexual game with me?

I should never have gone to the studio. I thought I would get a quick brushup on my skills and maybe gain some confidence going into next week's audition. Instead, Drake had succeeded in completely crushing me.

"Johanna?"

I heard the voice behind me just as I felt the touch of a finger on my shoulder.

I caught my breath and wheeled around.

"I didn't mean to scare you."

Harry Krinkle's face creased in that imitation DeNiro style. He jerked a thumb over his shoulder.

"What he did back there, I wouldn't let it bother you. He's just busting your chops. Like he busts mine. It's because you have a gift. You notice how he never calls me up? It's all a test. He wants to see if you really have what it takes."

"Thanks. That's nice of you to say."

He just stood there, smiling, watching me, waiting for me to say something else.

"I really should be going."

"Going where? I'll walk with you."

He had pulled out a cigarette and was trying to shield a match from the breeze. He took a drag, stared at the cigarette in disgust, and threw it on the ground, grinding it into the pavement with a worn leather workboot.

"Filthy habit," he said, more to himself than to me. "All around you someone is trying to take advantage of human weakness. The only way to defeat them is to discipline yourself. You have to make yourself stronger than them."

He looked up at me. "You're strong. You're a survivor. I can tell."

"Look," I said, "I don't want to seem rude, but I'd rather be alone right now."

"I understand," he said. "Solitude can be like a medicine. It cleanses the mind and soul. I spend a lot of time alone."

He smiled again. In spite of myself, I couldn't help but find him interesting.

"I should be going," I said.

"If you ever want to talk, you know," he started, stumbling awkwardly over the words, "just about things. Anything. Call me."

He handed me a card that read "Ace Taxi Service."

"I don't have a phone in my apartment. But you can always reach me there in the evenings."

"You're still driving a cab?"

"Yeah," he said and smiled. "It pays the bills and keeps life interesting."

He watched me put the card in my pocket and smiled again as if we had just exchanged some kind of intimacy. Then he turned and walked back in the direction of the studio.

I headed for the subway.

When I got back to the apartment, Cindy was gone. She left me a note on the kitchen table saying that she was spending the day with Sal and would probably stay over at his place for the night. It was just as well. Harry Krinkle—or whoever he was—was right. Sometimes solitude could be like a medicine. I thought about Matt up in Maine all by himself. I wondered if the solitude he had so passionately craved was curing him.

If it was inspiring him.

Or if it was killing him.

35

I was startled awake on the morning of the audition.

I lay in bed, staring at the ceiling, feeling my heart hammering in my chest. I looked over at the clock and saw the luminous display reading three-thirty a.m. I looked instinctively at the doorway, but the door was closed, and there was no stranger standing in the darkness. I lay back down on the pillow, but knew that it would be hopeless to try to get back to sleep.

I threw on one of Cindy's satin robes and padded barefoot to the kitchen. I poured myself a glass of water and sat on the couch. I turned on the television and flipped aimlessly through the channels. I could feel my stomach churning as if something alive were trapped in there and trying desperately to escape. I leaned back against the sofa cushions and tried to relax, my mind running on fast-forward.

I decided to make myself some toast, figuring it might calm my stomach. I went to the kitchen and began searching the cabinets for Cindy's toaster. Jesus Christ, I thought, she couldn't have hidden the damn thing any better if she had tried. I had looked through all the cabinets and was beginning a second search when I heard Cindy behind me.

"What in the world is all the racket?" she asked.

She was leaning against the doorjamb, holding her robe closed across her chest. Even half-asleep she looked sultry and sexy.

"I'm sorry," I said sheepishly, a large pot in my right hand. "Was I making a lot of noise?"

"Noise?" Cindy said. "I thought it was either the world's clumsiest burglar or the biggest damn mouse in Manhattan."

"I was looking for the toaster," I said lamely.

Cindy pointed to the four-slice, stainless-steel toaster in plain view next to the Oster blender on the counter just below the bread box.

"Oh," I said. "I didn't see it."

"How long have you been staying here? What's the matter anyway?" Cindy looked up at the clock on the wall behind me. It was one of those clocks shaped liked Felix the Cat with a tail that wagged the seconds. "It's four o'clock in the morning for crissakes."

"Nerves."

"The audition. I nearly forgot."

I had resumed my search through the cabinets.

"What are you looking for now?" Cindy asked.

"The bread."

"Did you try the bread box?"

I stared at the bread box as if it were an object left behind by UFOs. Cindy laughed.

"I'm glad they're not asking you to play a detective. Why don't you go sit down. I'll make you some toast."

"No," I said. "Forget it. I don't really think I'm hungry. Do you have any Pepto Bismol?"

"I think so. Check the cabinet next to the sink. Behind the vitamins."

"Thanks."

Cindy made herself a bowl of cereal and put a pot of coffee on to brew. She followed me into the living room and stayed up with me the rest of the night. She tried to calm my nerves and bolster my confidence, but nothing she could say was doing any good.

"Could we please talk about something else?" I said. "Anything else besides the audition?"

"Okay. How about Sal?"

I made a face. "I did say anything, didn't I?"

Cindy regaled me with the details of her latest real-life leading man: the irresistible Sal, whom she generously described as one part Al Pacino and two parts Andy Garcia. I just sat back and listened. If I didn't know her so well, I would be convinced that Sal was the One. The trouble was that I knew Cindy all too well. And I could spot Sal's type from a mile away. To me, he was like one of those characters straight out of central casting. Nevertheless, her version of the love story of the century was distracting enough to keep me from spending the morning in the bathroom, throwing up from sheer anxiety.

As the morning sun came up, we began searching the closets, looking for something for me to wear. Of course, it had only become painfully obvious on the morning of the audition that the outfit I had planned to wear all along was completely wrong. We spent nearly two hours looking through my clothes for an alternative. We then looked through Cindy's things, despite the difference in our sizes, for something that might work. In the end, we both decided that the original outfit was perfect after all.

I had chosen the black dress I was originally going to wear to the first audition before I'd changed my mind and gone with the beige outfit. This time, I thought, black would work. After all, I was supposed to have a past involvement with international espionage. Not to mention I was supposed to be dead for the past two years. I figured it would make me look both sexy and mysterious. Cindy helped me dress and fix my makeup. She lent me a pair of earrings and a sexy gold anklet Brad had given her. My black heels were kind of worn, so Cindy fetched a beautiful pair of Ferragamo's from her closet. Naturally they were too big, so she stuffed the front of them with toilet paper until they fit reasonably well. I couldn't walk to the audition with them, so I put on my own pumps, put her shoes in my bag, and figured I'd change into them when I got to the studio.

"Let me look at you," Cindy said and stood back.

"Well?" I said nervously.

"You look just like a female spy returned from the dead to steal away my adulterous lover. It'll be a pleasure dishing dirt with you, bitch."

I managed a weak smile and went to the bathroom to touch up my makeup.

"Good luck," Cindy said and kissed me on the cheek. "Not that you'll need it," she added hurriedly.

"Thanks," I said.

"Just relax. You have this in the bag."

Over my objections, Cindy had ordered a car to take me to the studio. It arrived right on time at ten sharp. She threw on a pair of jeans and a coat and walked me downstairs.

"Call me as soon as you're done," she said. "I want to be the first to hear the good news."

I slid into the backseat and the car pulled away from the curb. The driver's eyes flicked to the rearview mirror. He was a big man, his shoulders taking up half the front seat. His large head was covered with a mass of graying leonine curls. He looked like a bodyguard—or a hitman.

"Good morning," he said. "Name's Al. You an actress?"

"What makes you ask?"

"Pretty lady going to a television studio. Just a wild guess."

I could only see the side of his face, the long clean line of his well-defined jaw, his salt-and-pepper sideburn, and the blue eye flicking occasionally in the mirror.

"So, are you an actress or what?" he repeated.

"Not yet," I said.

"Going on an audition?"

"Yes."

"Saving up the dialogue, I see."

"I'm sorry," I said. "I'm just a little nervous."

"No big deal. You know I've had a couple of actors sitting right where you are. Even had Kim Basinger in here once. Of course, that was before she won an Academy Award. She was just a joke back then. Did that movie with that nut Mickey Rourke. *Nine and a Half Weeks*. Lost a girlfriend to that movie. Don't ask. Still, you could tell she had something. By the way, what's your name?"

"My name?"

"Yeah. In case you ever become famous. I can say I drove you to an audition."

"Tia Garbo."

"Garbo? Are you a relation—?"

"Grand-niece," I said.

"Wow," he said, "that in itself is something worth telling people."

He took the turn at Fifty-seventh Street, blew his horn at a cutting cabbie, and turned his head slightly back.

"Did you ever meet her? Greta Garbo, I mean."

"Yes," I said.

"What was she like?"

"Quiet. Very quiet."

He sped up through a red light, ignoring a well-dressed businessman giving us the finger.

"Did she ever tell you she wanted to be left alone?" He laughed.

"No," I said, feeling the butterflies fluttering as we neared the studio. "I hope you don't mind, but I don't feel much like talking now. I'm a little nervous."

"Okay," he said and laughed again. "No offense taken. I guess it runs in the family."

We pulled up outside the studio about ten minutes later. Somehow Al had maneuvered his considerable bulk out of the driver's seat and around the car before I could get out. He opened the door and offered me one of his large, meaty paws, decorated with a star sapphire pinky ring. I felt rather foolish, but I took his hand and stepped onto the sidewalk.

"Good luck, Miss Garbo," he said.

I held out the ten I'd fumbled from my purse. It was part of the fifty dollars I had intended to use as dues for a month at the Actor's Studio.

"Keep it," the driver said, smiling. "Your friend already took care of it. Maybe you can consider hiring me as your personal driver if you hit it big."

He handed me his card.

"Thanks," I said.

"Ah," he said, waving his hand, and grinning. "I told Ms. Basinger the same thing."

He ambled back to the car and pulled away.

Unlike the last audition, this was no cattle call. There was no waiting room full of nervous actresses chomping at the bit like high-strung racehorses at the starting gate. No preening and posturing and jostling for position. No sizing each other up like prizefighters. No hostile stares of superiority that served as compensation for a growing sense of insecurity. Instead, I was handed a script by a young woman who didn't bother to identify herself and quickly ushered through a maze of doors and halls directly to the soundstage where they filmed *The Way We Live.*

The set was only partially assembled, but I recognized the living room of what was supposed to be Cindy's character's house. I walked slowly to center stage, the script in my hand as if it were a map to an unfamiliar part of town, and squinted into the lights.

"Who's this?" I heard an impatient voice grumble.

"Johanna Brady," a woman answered.

"Brady?" the voice said, as if it were a word he'd never heard before.

My eyes grew accustomed to the light and I recognized the director. He looked like he had gained a little weight and gone a little balder since last time, but he still had the same carefully cultivated half-growth of beard. Someone should really have told him that the *Miami Vice* look had gone out almost two decades ago. I remembered the woman sitting on the left from last time. She was the one I took to be the casting director. But the man sitting on the right I didn't remember. Even sitting down, he was tall. He wore his blond hair parted in the middle, framing his delicately handsome face in perfectly feathered bangs.

I saw him lean over to the director, and whisper something in his ear. The director nodded and the blond man-boy straightened up in his chair.

"I'm sorry, Miss Brady. You're not right for this part."

I felt like someone had pulled the rug out from under my feet.
"What—"

"I'm sorry for wasting your time," he snapped. "You're not what we're looking for."

I held up the script in my hand as if it were some kind of bill of rights. "But I didn't even get a chance to read. . . ."

"Just a minute," the woman said. She smiled and tried to sound reassuring, but I could hear the tension in her voice. She turned to the director and started speaking low and fast. I heard her mention Cindy's name and the words "recommended" and "friend."

The director was shaking his head "no."

"At least give her the courtesy of a reading," she made one last plea.

"She's too damn old for the part," he said, not even bothering to lower his voice. "She's not attractive enough. If someone were going to go through the trouble to get plastic surgery to conceal their looks, they would certainly make sure they came out better than that."

The blond at his side looked like the cat who ate the canary.

"Neil . . ." the woman said. She turned to me. "I'm sorry—"

"I don't give a damn," the director said. "No one is going to buy her as Cindy's rival."

"Ms. Brady," the woman said. "Please wait."

I heard her words drifting up to the empty stage. I was already through the door and into the hallway. I staggered through the maze of halls, tears blinding me, as I desperately searched for the way out. It was like a bad dream. In front of my eyes people floated in and out of view. I saw the look of alarm on their faces as they stepped out of my way to let me pass. I must have looked as sick as I felt. It was as if the shame I'd just experienced had been stamped on my face like a scarlet "A" and everyone could see. I knew if I didn't get out of there and fast, I was going to lose it.

From out of nowhere a young woman came up to me. She was dressed in what looked like some kind of uniform. I guessed she must be a page of some kind.

"Can I help you, ma'am?" she said. Her young, fresh-faced, girl-next-door good looks showed concern.

She put her hand gently on my shoulder and tilted her head. For the first time I realized that I was walking nearly doubled over. I forced myself to straighten up.

"The way out," I said. "Please. I just need to find the way out."

"Are you okay?" she asked. "Do you need a doctor? I can call security."

"No," I said, trying my best to smile, my whole body shaking as if it were going to come apart at any minute. "I'm okay. I just need some fresh air."

The girl looked somewhat unsure, as if she were going to call security anyway, for my own good. It took the last of what little strength I had to convince her to show me the way out. I felt her eyes on me as I left the studio and walked down the street, the corner seeming a thousand miles away.

There was a bus stop there and fortunately a bus was just pulling up. I ran on rubbery legs to reach it in time.

I had somehow managed to retrieve my belongings on my way out of the studio, how I don't even remember, and now I rummaged through my handbag for my change purse. I dropped the exact change into the meter and found a seat near the back. I slid into it and felt the tears running down my cheeks. I squeezed my eyes closed, hid my face behind my hand, and made myself invisible.

I had no idea where the bus was going.

I had no idea where I was going.

I got off the bus, lost in a crowd of other passengers, about two hours later. I steered myself through the streets without any direction whatsoever, not caring where I was going, going nowhere. For no reason at all I turned into a small Irish pub sandwiched between a discount five-and-dime and one of those quickie photocopy places. I didn't want a drink, but I sat at the bar and ordered a beer. The bartender slid it under my chin without so much as a word.

There was a map of Ireland on the wall. A handcarved wooden sign that read GOD BLESS THE IRISH hung above the rows of bottles. And to my right there was another sign that read IF YOU CAN WALK OUT OF HERE, YOU'RE NOT IRISH. There were also about a dozen or so signed and framed black-and-white photos of now ancient or dead celebrities looking impossibly young. I looked around the place. The corkboard ceiling was blotchy with rust-colored spots and in one place bulged perilously close to bursting as it fed a bucket perched on a chair just beneath it with a sporadic *drip-drop* of water. I wondered how long ago it must have been that this place was considered a hot spot. There wasn't a face in the photographs that was younger than Frank Sinatra's.

I don't know how long I sat there, but the place was beginning to fill up with young guys in suits. I figured it must have been after five. I looked down at my beer. The head had disappeared long ago. The yellow liquid was flat and warm and looked like urine. I could hear the excited chatter of the newcomers and decided to leave before anyone decided to talk to me. I reached into my bag, pulled out a five, and left it on the bar underneath the glass. It was my way of thanking the bartender for letting me rent the seat for so long without disturbing me. As I headed for the door, it occurred to me it was that kind of discretion that had kept the place in business for so long.

The sun was beginning to set and the streets were crowded with people heading for the subways on their way home. I found my way to Washington Square Park and sat on a bench. The place used to be swarming with drug dealers until Mayor Rudy Giuliani had instituted the controversial idea of mounting surveillance cameras monitored by nearby police vans. The American Civil Liberties Union and related groups were screaming Big Brother and invasion of privacy, but at least you could sit in the park without being propositioned every ten seconds.

I looked around and spotted one of the cameras. I wondered if I was being watched. I looked at the other people in the park: sitting and eating hot dogs, walking their dogs, jogging, talking to each other. It was all one big movie. A movie of real life. And there was no one to say that you weren't right for a part in it. For the first time since I left the studio I thought about what had happened. What the director had said. I felt my hands shaking again, only this time it wasn't shame or even hurt, it was anger. I was angry at him, angry at myself, and angry at Cindy. How could she have put me through that? Didn't she have any idea what kind of person they were looking for? She should have known. She had said I was perfect for the part. How could she have been so wrong? Had it just been innocent enthusiasm on her part? Or was it something less palatable?

I forced the last thought from my mind. It was beginning to get cold out. The last thing I wanted to do right then was go back to the apartment and answer a lot of questions. I couldn't face Cindy. I couldn't face anyone.

Except—

I opened my bag and pulled out my wallet. I hoped I hadn't thrown it away. My heart gave a little leap when I saw the card. I pulled it out and saw it was the one the driver had given me this morning. I had only kept it out of courtesy, intending to toss it the first chance I got. Now I crumpled it up and threw it on the ground, hoping the surveillance cameras were trained on something more interesting for the time being.

Damn, I thought, I lost it.

I found it in the side pocket I almost always forgot about. There beside an old book of outdated twenty-five-cent stamps was what I was looking for.

I pulled it out and stared at it in the light from the lamppost beside my bench. On the white card in simple black lettering was the name and number for Ace Taxi Service.

The voice on the other end was gruff and to the point.

"I'd like to speak to Harry Krinkle, please."

"Krinkle? Lady, this is a business line. You want to talk to Krinkle, call him at home."

"I don't have his number."

"That's the breaks."

He had a short fit of violent coughing, which is probably what prevented him from slamming down the phone.

"Look," I said, "this isn't a personal call. I want a taxi."

"Yeah?" he said, clearing his throat. "From where to where?"

"Washington Square Park to—" I hesitated. "To Queens."

"All right. I'll have a driver there in twenty minutes."

"No," I said. "You don't understand. I want Harry Krinkle to drive me."

"This isn't a freaking dating service. You want a cab or not?"

"I want a cab. Harry's cab."

I could hear the man on the other end breathing heavily into the line as if thinking over this unparalleled request. Finally he sighed.

"Krinkle has the midnight shift. He won't be in until eleven-thirty."

"I'll wait."

"Fine. It's your dime. What's your name?"

"Just tell him it's Cybill."

I hung up the phone and searched out a coffee shop to escape the cold. It was already a quarter to nine. I sat at a yellowing Formica table and slowly drained cup after cup of black coffee. The waitress serving me didn't give me a hassle. She had the face of someone hardened to seeing people in trouble. I figured she took me for an uptown call girl fallen on bad times or a well-dressed professional woman dragged down by drugs. I stared at her skinny white arm, no more than bone with a thin layer of blanched skin stretched over it, as she poured my coffee. On the inside of her wrist was a crude tattoo in the likeness of Christ's weeping face. I drank half the cup and headed for the door, leaving behind me a ten-dollar tip.

I saw Harry's cab waiting for me at the curb in front of the park, smoke puffing softly from the tailpipe.

I slipped inside onto the backseat and his black eyes flicked in the rearview.

"Hi," he said. "How did you know?"

"I was watching *Taxi Driver* on video. I caught the scene with the Secret Service agent. Very clever. If you're not paying attention, it's easy to miss."

I could see the corner of his right eye in the rearview crinkle as he smiled.

"But you didn't."

"No."

"That's what makes you different."

He turned the cab onto a sidestreet and cruised slowly past a series of crumbling buildings. The people on the street looked up to stare as we passed. On the corner, a man looking like he was just completing a drug deal pocketed something and gave us the finger. Harry turned his head to watch him, his face expressionless.

"So if you're Travis Bickle and I'm Cybill Shepherd, what are you trying to save me from?"

"The rest of them."

"The rest of who?"

"The liars, the cheats, the fakes, the fucking parasites. This whole stinking city. You don't belong here."

We had stopped at a light. Harry was staring out the driver's side window at a fight between a black man and a drunken white woman. The woman was screaming the same words over and over, although it was impossible to hear what they were through the windows of the cab. Harry was staring at them and drumming his fingers on the steering wheel, the muscles in his jaw working as if he were chewing gum.

"Where do I belong, Harry?"

He took his eyes away from the arguing couple. The light changed and he eased the cab forward.

"Some place safe. Some place where there's grass and tall trees and clean air. Some place far from here."

"Do you know a place like that?"

"Sure," he said.

"Why don't you go there? Why do you stay here if you hate it so much?"

"This is where I belong."

We drove in silence, up and down the city streets, viewing the squalor that was so carefully hidden in the daytime, as if the entire city were a kitchen where the roaches only came out after the lights were turned off.

"Harry," I said. "Do you always carry a gun?"

"When I'm out at night."

"Have you ever shot anyone?"

He didn't answer, but once again his eyes flicked in the rearview.

"Have you?" I repeated.

"No."

"Do you think you would? I mean, like DeNiro. To clean up the streets. To save people."

"That would depend on the circumstances."

We drove past a group of prostitutes huddling together, looking cold under a street lamp.

"Harry?"

"What?"

"Have you ever been inside my apartment?"

"What the fuck kind of question is that?" he said, putting his arm across the front seat and turning around.

"I just wanted to know if you've ever been there. You know, feeling like you need to protect me."

He stopped short in the middle of the street.

"You think I'm some kind of thief? Some kind of pervert?"

"No," I said quickly. "Not at all. I was just wondering if you had ever thought of visiting me. I have these dreams. At least they might be dreams—"

Harry started the car forward again, but I could tell from his silence that I had disappointed him.

"Harry?"

"What is it?"

"What is your real name?"

"That's not a question I should answer."

"Do you mean it's off base?" I asked, trying to trap him.

"I mean it's not important."

"I see."

"Where are we going anyway?" he asked.

"How about back to your place?"

Harry smiled, stopped the meter on the cab, and made a sharp turn, doubling back in the direction from which we had come.

I didn't return to Cindy's until sometime just before dawn. I turned the key in the lock as quietly as I could, but it was unnecessary. Cindy was waiting, looking about as haggard as a beauty like she could be, dressed in an expensive silk kimono and holding a large mug of coffee in her hands.

"Where the hell have you been!" she hollered, her voice strained to the breaking point between the extremes of anger and relief.

"I was out," I said simply.

"Out!" Cindy said, anger suddenly winning the tug-of-war. "I've been worried sick to death about you."

"I'm sorry," I said without emotion.

"I called the studio. They had no idea where you were. You've been gone since ten this morning!"

I shook off my coat and threw it on the sofa. "I said I was sorry."

"But you didn't tell me where you were."

I spun around, glaring fiercely at her.

"What am I, a goddamn teenager? Do I have to check in with you when I want to go somewhere? What are you going to do now," I said mockingly, "give me the old 'when you're under my roof' speech? Save it! I'm out of here tomorrow."

"Jo," Cindy said, her voice small and quiet, "I was just worried, that's all. This just wasn't like you—"

"Maybe I'm not like me!" I shouted, feeling as much like a teenager as I sounded. "Do you know who I really am? Maybe it's all just an act!"

"Please," Cindy said. "Tell me what happened at the studio."

"I don't feel like it," I said. "I'm going to go to bed."

"Jo—"

I didn't wait for her to finish. I walked quickly down the hall and punctuated my exit from the scene with the slam of my bedroom door.

36

I stayed in my room the following morning until I heard Cindy leave for the studio.

She tried only once to talk to me. I heard her knock softly on the door about ten minutes before she finally left. She called out my name, waited, and called again. Then I heard her sigh, walk down the hall, and leave the apartment. I waited another ten minutes before I figured it was safe enough to come out.

I wandered out to the kitchen where Cindy had made a fresh pot of coffee. I grabbed a mug, poured out some coffee, and took a sip before seeing the note on the table.

> *Dear Jo,*
> *I'm sorry I jumped on you last night. I was just worried. Whatever happened yesterday, let's talk about it. I'm sure it's not as bad as you think. How about we do dinner at Ruth's Chris? Ooops. Sorry. Forgot about the meat. That's Sal's favorite place. How about Patsy's?*
> *Love, Cindy*

I crumpled the note and threw it in the trash. I knew Cindy was only trying to be nice. But somehow I couldn't help but sense there was pity behind her charity. Pity and guilt. She had won and I had lost and now she was feeling sorry for me. She would never admit it, probably not even to herself. She was just trying to be a good friend. She would never understand how she was humiliating me.

I left the apartment and wandered around the city. Fortunately, it was a decent enough day, cool and breezy, but sunny. I had to carefully ration what little money I still had left, but I nevertheless decided to treat myself to a movie. I found a theater playing a quiet little foreign film that had created quite a buzz for its quirky depiction of an erotic triangle. I bought a bucket of popcorn, a Coke, and took a seat in the back of the nearly empty theater. Two hours later I emerged into the bright afternoon sunlight, squinting and feeling disoriented.

I never grew tired of that feeling. I'd experienced it on other occasions, but I always associated it with the movies. It was as if you had been transported out of your body into another time and place. For the space of a couple of hours you lived in a world far more intense, far more real than the one that waited for you outside the theater. When it was over, it was like waking from a dream. In the real world the colors, the sounds, the scenery all seemed somehow smaller and faded. Life was a movie in which the dialogue was tedious, the plot tenuous, and the characters trite.

By four-thirty it was beginning to get chillier. I knew I couldn't avoid facing Cindy forever. I waited until the bulk of the rush-hour traffic thinned out and then I took the subway back to the apartment. Cindy was already home, dressed in a silk kimono, her bare feet propped up on the coffee table. She was sipping a glass of white wine and watching herself on a videotape of *The Way We Live*.

She pressed a button on the remote and turned the tape off as I shut the door.

"Hi," she said tentatively.

"Hi," I said, trying to sound as casual as I could. "You didn't have to turn that off."

"Oh," she said, waving the remote dismissively at the television, "it's embarrassing. I can't possibly look at that when someone else is in the room." She laughed self-consciously. "I can barely stand it even when I'm alone."

"I'm sorry for the way I acted last night," I said.

"No," Cindy said. "You don't need to apologize. I—"

She looked flustered and I knew what she was going to say next. She was trying to decide whether to go on or not. I wished she wouldn't.

"Jo, I heard what happened at the audition."

"It's all right, Cindy."

"No," she said. "It isn't. I already had it out with the casting director. She's completely hopeless. I tried to get in to talk with his almighty majesty after the shoot, but his new secretary—that blond guy who seems to be joined at his hip—said the great man was in a meeting with the producers. I'm going to bring it up on the set tomorrow—"

"I really wish you wouldn't."

"Jo, it was totally unprofessional. Besides, you are right for that part. I know it."

I shrugged. "Not if he doesn't think so. Besides, you don't need to jeopardize your job because of me."

"To hell with that. You're my friend."

"Friend or not, you know how hard you worked to get this break. Don't blow it on account of me—"

"They aren't going to get rid of me—"

"Don't even risk it," I said. "It's not worth it. There are other jobs out there. Don't worry about me."

Cindy seemed to ponder for a moment what I said. "Are you sure?" she said tentatively.

"Yeah. Besides, I sure as hell wouldn't risk my job for you."

I faked a smile convincing enough to fool Cindy into letting the topic drop.

"So what about Patsy's tonight?" she asked. "Are you up for it?"

"Nah," I said. "I had a whole tub of movie popcorn and one of those Cokes that look like a missile silo. I'm not hungry. I think I'll just change into something comfortable and have a glass of that wine you're drinking."

"Okay," Cindy said. Did I hear a tone of relief in her voice or had I just imagined it? "Do you mind if I go with Sal?" she said, almost apologetically. "I've already made the reservations and I haven't eaten all day. I'm famished."

"Go ahead," I said from the kitchen. I poured myself a water glass of wine. "I'll be fine."

For the next week I let Cindy console, pamper, and encourage me. Meanwhile, I started to look realistically at the options available to me. I contacted the temp agency I had worked with before leaving New York. They were still sore about how I'd skipped out on them without giving notice. I tried several other agencies, but none had any immediate openings. They took my name and number and said they'd get back to me. I knew they never would. I figured I'd just wait ten days and call them again.

I bought the *Times* and scanned the wanted ads for secretaries. I used Cindy's computer to type up my resume and sent about thirty copies out. I got only three responses. Of the three, only one granted me an interview. I hadn't heard in a week and so I called back the temp agencies. They still weren't hiring. I couldn't believe getting a lousy secretarial job in New York was turning out to be so hard. It was almost as bad as trying to land an acting role.

Cindy didn't know it, but I overheard her and Sal talking about moving in together. Sal was pushing the issue, but he didn't seem to have to push too hard. Though Cindy tried her best not to let on, I could tell she was anxious to get on with her life. I started talking about reclaiming my old apartment. The sublet was nearly up. But Cindy wouldn't hear of it, not until I'd gotten a job. How, she argued, would I support myself? I'd find a way, I said. I didn't convince her or myself. So I stayed on with her.

I started applying for waitress jobs. I finally got one at a small coffee house down in the Village. I lasted about three days. I got another one that Sal himself had set up at a fancy restaurant in Little Italy. I lasted almost a week.

What turned out to be the last snow of winter fell in the middle of March. After that, the weather turned warmer. The green buds came out on the skinny trees. The birds returned to the city.

I was growing desperate.

Something had to give and soon.

It did.

Cindy had been out for the evening on a date with Sal so I had the apartment to myself. I spent the night curled up on the couch watching television, flipping through a few magazines, pigging out on a pint of chocolate Häagen Daz to forget my troubles. I planned to wait up for Cindy, but got tired sometime after one a.m.

The next morning I woke up late. I went to the kitchen and feeling guilty, I had a cup of tea and a grapefruit for breakfast as compensation for the Häagen Daz of the night before. I passed Cindy's room on the way to the shower and saw that the door was open. I looked inside. Her bed was made. I didn't think anything of it. She often spent the night at Sal's. It was just one more reminder of how I was in the way.

I wondered how long it would be before Cindy agreed with Sal that it would just be easier to share a place. Surely, it could only be a matter of time. Guilt, pity, even friendship, only went so far, especially where a man was concerned. That much I knew from experience.

It wasn't until the studio called at eleven o'clock that I began to suspect something was wrong. I figured it was Cindy calling to tell me that she'd gone to work directly from Sal's place. Instead, I got the worried voice of one of the assistant directors. They were already an hour late for the shoot and Cindy had neither shown up nor called in to explain her absence. I could hear the fear in the voice of the young man on the phone. He clearly didn't want to report any bad news to his tyrannical boss. From my experience of him, the egotistical and mecurial director of *The Way We Live* was not a man who bothered to separate the messenger from the message.

"Do you have any idea where she might be?" he asked pleadingly.

"She was at her boyfriend's last night. Maybe she's still there," I offered, feeling sorry for him.

"Thanks," he said, sounding overly hopeful.

I gave him Sal's number, which I'd seen enough times on the caller ID to know by heart, and rung off. It wasn't like Cindy not to show up for an appointment, but I didn't give it much thought until twenty minutes later when the phone rang again.

It was Sal.

"Is Cindy there?" he said, sounding breathless.

"No. I thought she might be with you."

"She left last night. I put her in a cab around one. She said she had to get up early for a shoot. Jeezus, where could she be?"

He sounded genuinely worried.

"I don't know, Sal," I said.

"This isn't like her."

"I know."

"I'm going to call the police."

"Don't bother," I said, a little more abruptly than I intended. "I'll take care of it. I've known her longer than you have. I'll be able to give them a better idea of where she might be."

"All right," he said, sounding reluctant. "But call me right back and let me know what they said."

I promised I would and rung off.

Then I called the police.

When they learned that Cindy had been missing less than twelve hours, they told me there was nothing they could do just yet. Procedure, they said, and the way they said it let me know that no amount of arguing could change procedure. The rest of the day the calls alternated between the studio and Sal until I stopped answering the phone altogether. I slept very little that night.

The next day Cindy still hadn't shown up. Sal came over that evening. He looked tired and disheveled. His usually flawless slicked-back hair looked merely hand-combed and the normally clean sharp angles of his pretty face were shadowed with a growth of beard and etched with lines of worry. When he walked past me into the apartment, I caught the faint whiff of body odor rising from his wrinkled designer jacket.

"I'm worried, Jo," he said. He'd picked up the nickname from Cindy. I hated it. I hated when Cindy called me that. My father used to call me Jo. But I never mentioned it. I just let it quietly gnaw at me. "I'm really worried."

I'd fixed Sal a drink and he sat on the edge of the sofa. I sat in an armchair off to the side.

"I'm worried, too, Sal."

"What about the police? Surely they can do something by now?"

"I called them again. They said they'd start looking. But it's a big city and they have a lot of cases. She's a television personality, so that should help get her some kind of priority treatment. Frankly, they didn't seem very enthusiastic."

"She should have shown up by now. If there wasn't something wrong . . ." Sal let the sentence trail off. He downed the drink I'd given him in one gulp, his Adam's apple pumping like a piston. He put the glass down and ran his fingers through his oily hair. "There must be something we can do."

"We?"

"I know you don't like me very much," Sal said. "But Cindy means everything to me. This is killing me."

Yeah, I thought, rather unkindly. I bet it's killing you. Your meal ticket has just disappeared and you're looking at a life of filling cannolis or, if you're really lucky, maybe driving a car for some obscure mob lieutenant.

Sal looked up at me pleadingly. Suddenly he put his face in his hands and started sobbing.

Before I quite knew what was happening I found myself on the couch beside him. For some reason my antagonism toward him had instantly vanished. I rubbed his shoulders, narrow but well-muscled under his sports coat, and tried to say something to soothe him. It was tough to find anything to say. I could hardly keep myself from fearing the worst.

Finally he seemed to get ahold of himself and looked up at me. Tears clung to the long dark lashes that ringed his eyes. In spite of myself, I had to admit that he really wasn't so bad after all.

"Will you help me find her?" he said in a small voice. "Please?"

"Yes," I found myself saying. "Of course."

Two days passed and there was still no sign of Cindy. Sal and I had gone to every restaurant, shop, and newsstand in the area surrounding both his apartment and Cindy's. Sal couldn't remember which cab company Cindy had used so we called every one in the book but with no luck. We talked to anyone and everyone we could find that might have seen Cindy that night, but without any results. We made a xerox poster with a picture of Cindy, a description, some information, and even offered a reward. We put them in store windows, taped them to walls, tacked them to trees, tied them around lampposts. Between us, we must have put up at least a couple of hundred posters. We were just giving ourselves something to do while we waited. It was the waiting that was hardest of all.

I decided it was up to me to call Cindy's parents. Her father took the call. At first he seemed unable or unwilling to comprehend what I was saying.

"What do you mean she's missing?" he said.

I told him the whole story, although there wasn't much to tell.

"Have you called the police?"

I assured him I had. Then I told him how I'd put up posters all around the areas where Cindy had last been. He didn't seem pleased and I felt a desperate need to please him. I had descended like a bomb in his life and I wanted somehow to help him clean up the ruins. His questions came out in a torrent and then dwindled to an impotent trickle. I could hear the anger in his voice turn to fear, then to guilt, and finally there was nothing but a silence louder than any cry of grief.

"Are you there, sir? Hello?"

"I'm sorry," he said. His voice caught. There was another silence, this one shorter, and when he spoke again, I could hear the calm rationality of the successful businessman he'd once been. "I don't want to tell my wife just yet. We didn't want to trouble Cindy, but her mother hasn't been well lately. I don't suppose there's much I can do in New York and I can't leave Mrs. Dresner by herself. I'll call you periodically throughout the day to find out if there is any new information. And please call here immediately if you hear anything"—he paused for a moment and I could hear him trying to retain control of his voice—"if you hear anything. Anything at all."

"I will."

"Just do me one favor, please," he said. "I'll try to answer all calls. But if my wife picks up first, ask for me. There's no need to upset her unless—"

He didn't finish the sentence.

"I understand. But I'm sure everything will be all right."

"Yes," he said woodenly. "I'm sure it will."

"I'll be in touch."

"Thank you. And thank you for all you've done. Cindy is lucky to have a friend like you."

"I'm the lucky one," I said. "Cindy has done so much for me. I just wish I could do more."

We said good-bye and I placed the phone down on the receiver.

I'm the lucky one.

This was an ironic plot twist. Only three short days ago I would never have dreamed I'd ever say such a thing.

37

It had been nearly a week since Cindy's disappearance.

Sal and I had spent another day tacking up posters, talking to shopkeepers, and bugging the cops.

All to no avail.

No one had seen a thing.

Neither of us wanted to admit it, but the situation did not look good. We knew that the longer she remained missing, the slimmer the chances were that we'd ever see her alive again. Still, we clung to the most improbable of hopes. Perhaps Cindy had been attacked, but was still alive and wandering around the city in an amnesiac daze. Maybe she'd been abducted by some obsessively smitten if misguided fan of *The Way We Live* and was just waiting for the chance to escape. When your hopes were that low, you knew you were in trouble.

Sal had left only a half hour earlier and I was talking to my mother in Florida. I didn't tell her about Cindy. She worried enough about me living alone in the city without giving her concrete evidence supporting her conviction that my life was in a constant state of mortal danger. Besides, I was certain that she probably didn't remember who Cindy was and it would have required more energy than I had to remind her. As it was, my mother was at that stage in life when her circle of attention had grown smaller and smaller, encompassing only the most immediate events in her own life, no matter how insignificant.

"You know," she complained, "you could have told me you left town. I called your apartment and a strange woman kept answering the phone. I didn't know who she was so I hung up."

"Why did you hang up on her?" I said, feeling my tolerance level rapidly falling. "Didn't you wonder who she was?"

"I thought maybe I had the wrong number."

"How many times did you call?"

She hesitated on the other end, as if actually trying to count the times she'd called. "Twenty-five times I think."

"And you thought you dialled the wrong number twenty-five times? Mom, that doesn't make any sense."

"Don't be mad, Johanna. I guess I wasn't thinking."

"I'm not mad, Mother," I said, my voice strained to the breaking point. If there was one thing that annoyed me more than my mother's self-absorption, it was her self-deprecation.

"I was just worried," she said. "You know how I worry."

"Yes," I said, kicking myself for calling her. I had enough on my mind as it was. "You don't have to worry."

"I'm your mother. I can't help it. So who was he?" she asked tentatively.

"Just some guy I met."

"Some guy?" That old irritating note of concern crept into her voice. "How long did you know him?"

"Mother, is that really important?"

"I just don't think you should go running off with someone at the drop of a hat—"

"See," I said, as if I were an attorney driving home a key point. "That's why I didn't tell you in the first place."

"Where did you go?"

"Is that really important?"

"I was just curious."

"Cape Cod," I snapped. I don't know why I lied. It was stupid. There was no reason not to tell her the truth. For some reason talking to my mother still brought out the rebellious teenager in me. I couldn't help but feel that her concern and curiosity about my life was an invasion of my privacy.

"What does he do?" she said, ignoring my waning patience, seemingly determined to forge ahead before I completely slammed the door.

"He's a writer."

"A writer," she said to herself. "That sounds nice. What does he write?"

"Books."

"Okay," she said, her voice rising to that suffering-mother pitch. "I guess I'm asking too many questions."

"It's not that, Mother," I said, suddenly feeling exhausted. "It's just that the whole conversation is irrelevant. The relationship is over. Things didn't work out."

"Oh," she said. "I'm sorry Johanna. I didn't mean to—"

"It's all right." I sighed. "I know you didn't."

Why was it so difficult to talk to her?

"Why don't you tell me what's going on with you?" I suggested reluctantly, but desperate for anything to change the subject.

For the next hour or so she gave me a detailed rundown on the living soap opera going on behind the pink stucco walls of the Whispering-Pines-by-the-Sea adult community. Who was talking to whom. Who wasn't talking to whom. Who had died. Who was about to die. Who was going to bed with whom. Who had broken up with whom. I never heard my mother talk about her life at Whispering-Pines without feeling incredibly depressed. Life, it seemed, never changed, no matter how old you got. We were still caught up in the same old round of feuds, affairs, and gossip.

When I finally hung up the phone, I needed a glass of wine. I went to the kitchen, poured myself a glass, and headed for the shower. I turned on the water, stepped out of my clothes, and sipped my wine until the bathroom grew warm and steamy. I finished the wine, set the glass on the sink, and stepped into the shower. I lathered up my hair and thought of the day behind me and the day ahead. How much longer could this go on? How much longer could I take it? I guess it was the phone conversation with my mother that made me think of Matt. I hadn't thought of him since Cindy's disappearance. I wondered if he was still at the cabin. If things were still the same with him or if they'd gotten worse. If perhaps he'd somehow pulled himself together. But most of all I wondered what would have happened if I had stayed. Were things really as bad as I had made them out to be?

If only Cindy were here now, she would set me straight.

If only she were here. . . .

I had just turned off the shower when I heard the doorbell ringing. It must have been ringing for quite some time and whoever was at the door must have grown impatient, because they were holding the button down so that the buzzer was sounding steadily. I hadn't been able to hear it with the bathroom door closed and the sound of the water.

"Wait a minute," I shouted, throwing on one of Cindy's bathrobes and wrapping my wet hair in a towel.

I ran through the living room leaving a trail of wet bare footprints on the carpet. My heart was beating double time. The doorbell had all the urgency and insistence of an alarm.

"Who is it?" I tried to shout over the sound of the bell.

There was no answer.

I undid the locks and threw open the door to find the landlord and a pair of men in trenchcoats standing outside in the hall. The one without the hat introduced himself.

"I'm Detective Weld," he said, flipping open a leather billfold to show me a badge and card I hardly looked at. "This is Detective Deegan."

"What's this about?" I asked, my speeding heart suddenly seeming to stop mid-thump. It was like the script to a television drama. I knew exactly what he was going to say. I knew exactly what my role was to be.

"Are you Johanna Brady?"

"Yes."

"I'm afraid we have some bad news."

"What is it?" I said, my voice steadier than my hands.

"Do you know Cynthia Lynn Dresner?"

"Yes," I whispered.

"I'm sorry," the detective said. "She's dead."

"Dead?" I repeated, just like they always do on every cop show you ever watched. "How?"

"She's been murdered."

My eyes must have rolled up, because I was suddenly staring at the ceiling. The room started spinning quickly to the left and the floor seemed to disappear beneath my feet. I reached out to grab the door, hoping to stop the room from turning, but the door suddenly seemed twenty yards away. I felt my knees buckle as if someone had cut the strings holding me upright and the next thing I knew I was staring up into the concerned faces of the two detectives, who were kneeling at my side.

The good looking blond one—Weld, I think—told the other detective to go to the kitchen to get me a glass of water.

"Are you okay?" the blond detective asked.

"I think so," I stammered. "I—"

I never finished the sentence. Instead, I broke down sobbing, reaching instinctively for the detective, who pulled away.

"Here," he said. "Drink this. It'll make you feel better."

I took the glass gratefully, even though I wasn't thirsty.

"Why?" I asked numbly. "Why?"

"I think it's better if we went to the station, Miss Brady," he said. "We can talk there."

The rest of the evening is still a blur. They took me to an office at precinct headquarters and asked me some questions about Cindy: her job, her habits, her acquaintances. The blond detective did most of the talking. He sat on the edge of the desk, talking in a low, quiet voice. The other detective stood in the corner, nervously fingering a cigarette, as if he couldn't wait to get out into the hall to smoke it. He was short and bald, a belly of hard fat protruding from his cheap sports coat. He seemed to be making a point of looking everywhere in the room but at me.

The blonde detective—he turned out to be Weld after all—asked me about Cindy's latest boyfriends. I told them about Brad and Sal. He seemed very interested in both of them. He especially asked me about the particulars of Cindy's breakup with Brad. She had told me enough to make it clear that Brad had not taken it well. Detective Weld took down notes of everything I said.

"Do you think he could have done it?" I asked, shocked. I couldn't imagine the pale, sulky, Ed Begley-lookalike insurance executive involved in a crime of passion.

"We're just getting as much background information as we can," the detective explained matter-of-factly. He asked some more questions before closing his notebook.

"We need someone to identify the body," he said as gently as he could. "Do you know who we can call?"

"I'll do it."

He seemed shocked. "I don't think you understand how it is. Considering your reaction before—"

"I understand perfectly," I said.

"I really would advise against it," the other detective objected from the corner. "It's not pretty. She's been dead for about a week. Gunshot."

"She was my best friend," I stated, with a conviction that stopped all further argument. "Unless you want to wait until her parents fly in to make a positive ID, I'm the closest thing she has to family right now. I won't have anyone else looking at her. Especially not someone who may be a suspect in her murder, regardless of what you say. I owe it to her."

The two detectives exchanged a glance.

The fat one in the corner shrugged.

"Okay," Detective Weld said. "Let's go."

It was a hallway of gray concrete. At the end, there was a swinging door that looked like the door to a restaurant kitchen. You'd think there would be guards or something, but there weren't. The room was brightly lit, as sparsely furnished as a zen temple, and smelled of disinfectant. A man in green scrubs greeted us. He led us to a gurney covered with a sheet that bore the unmistakable outline of a human body.

"Are you ready?" he asked.

I nodded.

He pulled back the sheet to her pale, bluish shoulders.

I must have still been in shock. I didn't even flinch.

Cindy lay on the gurney, one side of her face bruised and grotesquely swollen, her eye bulging from its socket.

I just stood there, staring down at her, speechless.

"Is that her?"

The voice came from so far away I hardly heard it.

"Ms. Brady. Is that her?"

I heard another voice answer. It was a voice I didn't recognize.

"Yes," I whispered. "That's her."

38

Two days later Detectives Weld and Deegan returned to the apartment.

Only about an hour earlier Sal had stormed out, angry, claiming that I had implicated him in Cindy's murder. I tried to calm him down, telling him that I had done nothing but give the police the facts, but he would hear nothing of it.

"I'm warning you," he said, pointing a finger in my face, "if you make me trouble, you'll be fucking sorry."

"Are you threatening me?" I said, too angry to be scared.

"I don't threaten," he answered, trying on his best wiseguy impersonation. I'd seen better in high school drama class. "I give people options."

"Well, maybe the police would be interested in the options you're giving me."

He was dressed in Little Italy street-thug chic: a red shirt and pegged black pants topped with a leather sports coat. Still, his face looked haggard and pale, dark circles ringing his eyes, his cheeks sporting two days' growth of beard.

"Listen, you bitch," he growled, backing me up to the wall. "I know what kind of game you're playing and you don't even know the rules."

He was no taller than I was, his face nose to nose with mine, so close I could smell the alcohol and tobacco on his breath, but I kept my eyes locked firmly on his.

"Maybe you can tell me the rules," I said calmly.

"The rules are simple. You fuck with me and you're dead. You hear me? You're fucking dead!"

"Is that what happened to Cindy?"

"Shut the fuck up!"

He grabbed me around the throat with one hand and reached back with his other to hit me, but something stopped him.

"Go ahead," I mocked. "Hit me. The cops will just eat that up. Go ahead and hit me, I dare you."

We stood there for what seemed like minutes, staring at each other like two poker players. His eyes were wild, desperate. Mine were cold and steady. I knew I was holding the winning hand.

"You don't have the balls," I said.

He was trembling with rage and frustration. He dropped his hand and let go of my throat. I'd called his bluff. He was helpless.

"You fucking whore," he muttered.

"That's the best you can do?" I laughed. "You're fucking pitiful. I never knew what Cindy ever saw in you. Get the hell out of here before I call the police right now. I suspect they'll be coming for you soon anyway."

He didn't say another word. He just turned for the door and left.

Like I said, as chance would have it, the detectives came less than an hour later.

"Good afternoon, Ms. Brady," Detective Weld said. "Sorry to bother you. But could we have a few moments of your time?"

"Sure," I said. "Have you found out who killed Cindy?"

"No," the blond detective said. He reminded me a little of a cross between a thin Nick Nolte and a young Robert Redford. I thought of Cindy—how we would never play that game again—and felt a terrible sadness wash over me. "Are you okay, Ms. Brady?"

"Yes," I muttered. "Yes. I was just thinking—"

"Detective Deegan and I just wanted to ask you a few more questions," the blond detective said. "May we come in?"

"Sure," I said woodenly, stepping out of the way to make room for the two big detectives. "But I'm not sure I can tell you any more than I already have."

It had been like that a lot these past two days. In spite of the fact that I had identified her body in the morgue, seen the evidence of her brutal murder, there was another part of me that kept thinking of her in the present tense. I was so used to confiding in her, to telling her everything, it was impossible to believe she was gone.

The most bizarre part of it all was when I found myself planning to tell Cindy all about the surreal sequence of events that began with her disappearance and ended with me being brought to the police morgue only to realize that it was really her I'd seen on the gurney.

This wasn't a dream or a story. She was dead. She would never be there to share my secrets, my fears, my insecurities, my triumphs. We would never gossip, laugh, or cry together like we'd done so many times before.

Not again.

Not ever.

It was like what they said about having a limb amputated. You still dreamed you had it, could still see yourself using it, could even feel pain in it, even though it was no longer there.

The reality of Cindy's death was taking a long time catching up with me.

Maybe it was better that way. Maybe it was the mind's way of easing the shock.

"Can I get you anything?" I asked. It seemed like a dumb question, but what did people say to cops who came to their homes investigating the murder of a friend?

"No thank you," Detective Weld said.

"You got grapefruit juice," the fat, bald cop said. It didn't sound like a question. More like an accusation. He had stationed himself in the corner of the room. He seemed to like the corners of rooms.

"No—I don't think so. . . . I can check. . . ." I said hesitantly.

He just grunted, looking pissed off.

The blond detective shot him a glance.

"What?" Deegan said gruffly. "The doc said it was good for my prostate."

"Please sit down," Detective Weld said softly, keeping his eyes on his partner for a moment before turning them on me. His eyes were blue and kind. I wondered if he was married.

I sat down on the couch and he pulled an armchair around to face me.

"There are just a couple of things we'd like to clear up for the record and then we'll leave you alone, Ms. Brady."

"Johanna."

He smiled. "Johanna. We know this is a difficult time for you and the last thing we want to do is cause any undue stress."

"The funeral is tomorrow," I said.

"Is it? I wasn't aware." He produced a small pad from somewhere and flipped it open. "Anyway, we checked Ms. Dresner's past boyfriend out, Brad Netzger. It seems he was in Vancouver that week on business. In fact, he seems to have bounced back pretty well from the rejection of being dumped. He was with a woman who can vouch for his whereabouts on the night of the murder."

He looked up at me for a reaction, got none, and flipped the page.

"As for Salvatore Lero, aka Salvatore Meola, Salvatore Spina, and Dino Scala, he sticks to his story that he put Ms. Dresner in a cab about midnight on the night of her murder. We're trying to run down the cab company, but we haven't had any luck so far. It seems she called for the car. He says he personally told the driver her address, kissed Ms. Dresner good night, and that was the last he ever saw of her."

"And you believe him?"

Detective Weld looked up from his pad.

"You don't?"

"I think he's a creep. He was here not more than an hour ago, threatening me because he thought I might have said something to you guys that made him look bad."

"But you worked together trying to find Ms. Dresner after her disappearance."

"He seemed sincerely distraught. I thought maybe I'd misjudged him. Now I realize I was right all along. He's nothing but a two-bit petty hustler. He's got a record doesn't he? I'm right?"

Detective Weld nodded. "He's done some time for some relatively minor offenses. But, yes, he does have a record."

"I knew it."

"Ms. Brady—Johanna—that doesn't necessarily make him a murderer."

"He was using her," I said. "She was probably going to dump him and he got mad and killed her."

The detective shook his head. "I don't know. According to Mr. Lero, the two were thinking of moving in together. Were you aware of that?"

"I overheard them talking. . . ."

"So it's true?"

"It wasn't going to happen," I said. "I know it. Cindy had too much sense. Besides, she could never settle down with one man. She moved from one to another like a hummingbird sipping nectar. That was the way she was." I realized how that sounded only after I'd said it. They didn't know Cindy like I did. They would no doubt take it the wrong way. "What I meant to say was . . ."

Detective Weld wasn't listening. He was writing down something on his pad—or pretending to when he looked up.

"Mr. Lero told us you seduced him."

"He what?"

I straightened on the sofa, gripping the armrest with my left hand until my nails dug into the fabric.

"He told us that during the week you were looking for Ms. Dresner, the two of you became intimate and that you initiated the relationship."

"That's bullshit!" I shouted, leaping up. "He's lying. He's lying about everything! Can't you see what he's doing?"

"Please calm down, Johanna."

"How can I calm down? That bastard probably killed my best friend and now he's got the nerve to say I slept with him?"

"Sit down, please," he said, motioning with his hand. "I know you're upset. But we have to get through this."

I sat down, my whole body trembling.

"So you're denying Mr. Lero's statement?"

"Yes," I said. "You're goddamn right I am."

The detective scribbled in his pad again.

"Johanna," he said and looked up with a pained expression on his face, "I'm going to have to ask you a difficult question."

"What is it?" I said, feeling slightly queasy.

"You once dated a man named"—he looked at his pad and up at me—"Stephen Kiley."

"Yes," I said woodenly.

I knew what was coming.

"Is it true that the relationship ended after you caught Ms. Dresner and Mr. Kiley together in a compromising position?"

"Where did you hear that?" I snapped.

"That's not important. Is it true?"

It was no use denying it. They could have checked with Stephen. They probably already had.

I nodded.

The detective cocked his head, as if this were one of the most interesting things he'd ever heard. From the corner I felt the intense stare of the short, fat, bald cop.

"And you still remained friends?" the blond detective asked softly.

"Yes," I said. "Stephen was a first-class asshole. Cindy was just one of the people he was cheating on me with. She made a mistake. She apologized. I forgave her and we went on. We both realized Stephen wasn't worth ruining a friendship over."

"I see," he said gently. "Johanna, I need to ask you where you were the night of the murder."

"What do you mean?"

"The night of the murder," Detective Weld said, his eyes no longer so gentle or so friendly. "Where were you?"

"Am I a suspect?" I said, feeling a mixture of outrage and disbelief. It had never occurred to me that they'd think I might be involved.

"Please don't be upset."

"Don't be upset? My best friend is murdered and you're asking me where I was the night she was killed. How am I supposed to react?"

Detective Weld smiled sympathetically. "I'm sorry. It's just a formality. We have to tie up all the loose ends," he explained.

"Do I need a lawyer?" I felt myself blush. I sounded so young and childish.

"I can't give you legal advice, Johanna," the blond detective said gently. "But this isn't an interrogation. I just want to know where you were the night Cindy was killed."

He was so kind and patient. He had such gentle eyes. For some reason I couldn't quite explain, I trusted him implicitly. I couldn't imagine him ever being harsh or brutal. I was thankful that it was him asking the questions and not his partner, who was now absently picking up and examining various objects in the room.

"Does he have to do that?" I asked.

Detective Weld turned. "Deegan," he said, a slight trace of conciliatory humor in his voice, "how many times do I have to tell you not to touch anything. You might drop something."

Deegan grunted. "I'm going out in the hall for a butt," he said impatiently.

The blond detective laughed. He waited until his partner went outside.

"Don't mind him," he said. "He gets like that when his blood-sugar level is low. Now, if you'll just tell me where you were the night of Cindy's death, we'll be on our way."

"I was here," I said. "In the apartment."

"All night?"

"Yes. I was watching television."

"Is there anyone who can verify your whereabouts? Did you call anyone, talk to anyone, anything like that?"

"No," I said.

"I see," the detective said. "Well, that just about wraps things up, Johanna. Thank you for your time." He flipped his pad shut, put it in the pocket of his jacket, and stood up.

I stood up with him. "You'll let me know if you learn anything," I said.

He smiled. "Yes, I will. I promise."

"Do you think you'll catch who did this?"

"I certainly hope so, Johanna."

*   *   *

That evening it was difficult getting to sleep. The funeral was scheduled for ten the next morning. It made me feel sick to even think about it. I hadn't eaten all day and finally forced myself to have a cup of tea and a bowl of cornflakes. I sat down to watch television, but couldn't concentrate. The cornflakes and the tea sat untouched on the table. I laid out my clothes for the funeral. I must have changed my mind at least a dozen times before I finally settled on an outfit. How stupid and self-centered. But then that's the way people are at funerals. You'd think they were going to a cocktail party or some swanky social event. They paid more attention to each other than the person they were supposedly mourning. Afterward, they would all be talking about who looked good and who didn't, who'd come with whom, who said what to whom, who'd shown up and who hadn't. What was the matter with people anyway?

It was after two in the morning before I decided I'd better get to bed.

It was useless.

I was never going to get to sleep.

I turned to the clock on the nightstand.

Two-thirty.

Three.

Three-thirty.

I looked up and he was standing in the doorway. It took me a while to pick out his dark form from the surrounding darkness, but when I did, my heart skipped a beat.

"You scared me," I said.

"You don't look scared."

"What are you doing here? How did you find me?"

He chuckled softly. "Those are two very different questions."

"I really don't want to play this game. Not tonight."

"Death is part of the drama. You have to expect it."

I felt the cold sweat on my body. I hardly had the breath to force out the words.

"Did you kill her?"

"That question is off base."

"Who are you?" I reached for the light.

"Don't!"

I heard the threat in his voice and for the first time since the night I'd called the police, I felt afraid he might hurt me. My voice was barely a whisper, barely a breath in the darkness.

"Please tell me who you are."

He chuckled again. "You really don't want to play tonight, do you?"

"Do I know you?"

"That's better," he said. "Now you're catching on."

"Do I? Know you?"

"You know me better than you think."

"Then why can't you tell me who you are?"

He shook his dark head. "That would ruin it."

"Ruin what?"

"Why the story, silly."

I felt all the frustration and exhaustion building inside me. "What is it that you want from me?"

"Just to play your part."

"And what am I supposed to be playing?"

"Yourself. It's what you do best."

"And you? What part are you playing?"

"You're getting very clever. I knew you had it in you. You are beginning to learn to improvise. But I'm afraid that question is still off-base."

"Can you tell me anything then?"

"Yes. You're almost ready."

"Ready for what?"

"The performance of your life."

He turned and walked quietly out of the apartment. I lay there in the dark, the sweat drying on my flesh, my heart pounding. What did he mean by "the performance of my life"? And what was the role I was supposed to be playing? Even more disturbing, he claimed that I knew him better than I thought. I remembered with a shudder that I had asked him if he had killed Cindy. What would have happened if he had answered that question instead of claiming it was off base? Would he have had to kill me, too? Was that why it was off base?

I got out of bed and walked to the front door.

As usual, it was locked.

So were the windows.

I sat on the sofa in the dark and waited for the dawn to come.

I was almost ready, he'd said. Ready for the performance of my life.

But first I had a funeral to attend.

39

Cindy looked like a princess.

She was wearing a white satin gown cut low in the front, her cleavage modestly covered with some kind of thin iridescent material. Her delicate hands were crossed beneath her bosom, her long, shapely fingers perfectly manicured. I idly wondered who had done them. Someone had placed a bouquet of white roses with a spray of baby's breath against her chest to make it look as if she were holding them.

I knelt by the side of her shiny white casket with its glimmering golden handles and looked into the face of my friend for the last time.

Her head was resting on a small white satin pillow. Her fine hair was expertly pinned up in back, a few stray tendrils curling over her white shoulders. They had done a magnificent job with the makeup. Whoever it was should have gotten an Academy Award. The Dresners must have spared no expense to ensure that the last time they would see their daughter she would look as she always had. I wouldn't have believed it possible if I hadn't seen it myself. The swelling that had so grotesquely distorted her face had miraculously disappeared and there was no trace of the abrasions I had seen at the morgue. The side of her head that had been shattered by the bullet was, mercifully, facing the other way.

Yet in spite of all the expert work, the illusion was not quite complete. It was like getting too close to an aging film siren whose best days were behind her. On the screen she still looked flawless, as if age had been unable to touch her. Yet if you looked close enough, you could see the cracks in the facade, the seams, the patches. Looking closely at Cindy, I could see the bluish pallor beneath the white makeup, the tension around the mouth set to look peaceful, the flesh pulling back from around the slightly sunken eyes.

I closed my eyes tightly, fighting a terrible wave of dizziness that hit me from out of nowhere. I folded my hands tightly, placed them against my forehead, and tried to pray, but the words just wouldn't come.

Why.

The word repeated itself again and again inside my head.

Why.

That question, his voice answered, is *off base.*

I rose from the bench beside the coffin and returned to my seat. I didn't hear a word of the service. I never even shed a tear.

Cindy's mother and father had flown in from Phoenix. They were seated in the front row. I had never met them, though Cindy often talked about them with a great deal of affection. They always insisted that she visit them on the holidays and many times sent her tickets out of the blue with a note explaining how they'd missed her. I couldn't help but envy her relationship with her parents and even then wondered how my own parents would have acted if it were me lying in that coffin. Could my mother keep from making a spectacle of herself? Would my father bring his new wife and kids, even though I had never met them?

The Dresners had been married over forty years. Mr. Dresner was still a good-looking man. On the downhill side of sixty, he was tall and slender with a full head of steel-gray hair and the deeply tanned face of a man who spent a lot of his free time golfing under the Southwestern sun. Mrs. Dresner was shorter than Cindy, plump, her hair dyed an improbable blond, her face jowly with age, the pale skin freckled and unhealthy looking. Even though she was younger than her husband, she had not aged nearly as well, and whatever illness she was suffering from was clearly taking its toll. I wondered if she would long survive this terrible news. She was weeping into a powder-blue handkerchief and leaning against Mr. Dresner, who stared unblinking toward the coffin with a grim and stoic look. Cindy had been their only child.

I stole a glance at Cindy's boyfriend. Sal was seated on the other side of the aisle. He was wearing a dark suit, his face looking haggard, sleepless. Even from across the room I could see the places where he'd cut himself shaving that morning. He was passable straight on, but from where I sat, I could see by his profile that he had a large nose and a receding chin. Cindy could have done a whole lot better.

He was clearly avoiding looking my way. No doubt he was embarrassed at what he had told the police. I suppose he figured that it was every dog for himself. I should have trusted my instincts. I was right about him from the start. He was a low-life gutter rat and that's what he'd always be. He had been the last person to see Cindy alive. He claimed she had left his apartment sometime around midnight. She was found the next morning in a park in Chinatown by some old Chinese guys practicing t'ai chi. She had laid unidentified in a morgue drawer for a week before someone going through a routine check of the missing persons' reports matched her description with the body.

The detectives had no doubt questioned Sal. I wondered if that was partly why he looked so haggard. He was their prime suspect. He wouldn't slide his way out of this one so easily. But what was his motive? Perhaps I had supplied one when I told Detective Weld about the long trail of broken hearts Cindy had left in her wake. It was true that Cindy didn't seem nearly ready to dump Sal any time soon. But had he seen the writing on the wall? Had she said something that made him realize she had no intention of being his meal ticket after all?

The priest said a few things, and a couple of her colleagues from *The Way We Live* talked about what a wonderful person Cindy was, but they were all just acting. The priest hadn't known her at all and the people from the show had only known her for a few months. They didn't know the real Cindy. I knew her better than anyone. Yet no one had thought to ask me to speak. If they had wanted a performance, I would have given them a performance to remember. There wouldn't have been a dry eye in the house. But, like I said, no one gave me a chance.

Sorry, Cindy.

They passed me over again.

After the service, I ran into Stephen on the steps of the church. He looked tanned and buff, as if he'd been working out. Gym muscles, not the real thing. He was talking to a tall, dewy-eyed anorectic-looking brunette, who looked like she belonged in a Calvin Klein ad, except she looked like she showered and she was older than thirteen. From the proprietary way she was eyeballing me, I knew they were lovers.

"Hello, Johanna," he said. "This is Cat."

I didn't know if the name was short for something else, like Kate or Katerina, or if the woman used it as a one-word moniker, like Cher or Madonna. By the looks of her, I would have guessed the latter.

"Pleased," the woman said, holding out a limp hand for me to shake. "I'm going to mingle, Stevie," she said, as if bored to death.

"I'll see you at the car." She turned to me. "Nice to meet you," she said and the smile on her face told me she had dismissed me as serious competition. She walked toward a group of actors from *The Way We Live.*

"Well, this is a little awkward," Stephen said and grinned boyishly, shoving his hands in his pockets and looking perfectly comfortable. "I haven't seen you since—well—since . . ."

"I remember," I said dryly.

"Of course. So what have you been up to lately? I heard you were out of town for a while."

"I was up in Maine. Doing some writing," I lied.

"Writing? Really? That sounds interesting. I didn't know you wrote."

"There's a lot of things you don't know about me, Stephen."

"I suppose there are," he said, pushing his hand through his mop of dark-blond hair, and grinning that young Harrison Ford grin.

He was still the handsomest man I'd ever met.

"What's up with you?"

"I've been doing the modeling thing for a while," he said. "J. Crew, etc. I've got an audition set up in L.A. a few weeks from now. A new action picture Bruce Willis is interested in. Could be a go."

"Good luck."

"Thanks. Hey, are you going to the reception? The producers of *The Way We Live* are going to be there. And so is someone from that cop show Cindy was close to landing."

"No, Stephen," I said. "I think I'll skip it. I didn't come here looking for a job. But don't let me hold you up."

If he got the insult, he showed no sign of it.

Or maybe he just thought it was a form of show business humor.

"It was nice seeing you again, Johanna," he said. "Even under the circumstances. I'll call you."

He always said that.

He never did.

Cindy's parents were taking Cindy's body back to Phoenix. I remembered my aunt's funeral, the one I had pretended was my father's when Matt had pressed me for details. This time there would be no gathering at the cemetery, no raw hole in the ground, no leaving of the casket to be buried all alone under the vast starry sky.

Well, there would be, of course.

But I wouldn't be there to see it.

* * *

For the next two weeks I existed in a surrealistic daze.

I could hardly sleep. Each night I stayed awake until nearly three in the morning, watching infomercials and old reruns on the classic movie channel until I fell asleep on the couch. I didn't wake up until nearly noon and could hardly find the strength to get dressed without downing half a pot of coffee.

When I did manage to get dressed and out, I mainly wandered the streets, sometimes buying a subway token, and letting the trains hurtle me back and forth under the streets of the city. I watched the men and women going to and from their way to work or to business lunches or meetings with important clients. I watched young men and women, fresh faced, hopeful, attractive, clutching portfolios they dreamed in vain might somehow distinguish them from the tens of thousands just like them. I felt a sharp pang of sadness over my own lost youth. I, too, was once as naive as them.

And yet it was possible.

Look at Cindy. She had made it.

Lightning had struck so close, but, like they said, it didn't strike twice in the same place. I guess it was the conviction that, one of us having bucked the astronomical odds against success to make it, the chances of me making it, too, were reduced to zero.

I considered the fact that she'd been killed, the gift snatched away from her, and it might be bestowed upon me. It was a selfish wish. But I'm sure Cindy would have understood.

The detectives had been to the apartment again. They had some more questions. I answered them the best I could, but I didn't really have much to say. I asked them if they had any leads. They were pretty tight-lipped. All Detective Weld would say was that they were working on it. I assumed that meant they had no idea who killed Cindy and would likely never find out.

The murder had made the papers. Granted, it wasn't front page news, but because of the television connection, it appeared rather prominently with pictures and everything. One article was pretty good. It called Cindy one of television's up-and-coming actresses. That might have been stretching it for effect a bit. After all, she was only in a soap opera. Still, soap opera fans were fanatics. The picture wasn't one of Cindy's best but, hell, she made the second page with two columns of type. It had even earned a short spot on the local New York television stations. But Cindy's fifteen minutes of fame didn't even last that long. Her story was supplanted the very next day by the murder of a newborn by two Long Island high-school sweethearts.

As for me, I knew I was going to have to leave the apartment soon. I had no money for the next month's rent and still no job. I thought of calling my mother for help, maybe asking if I could move in with her for a while until I got back on my feet, but even I had to laugh. She was probably down in Miami spending some rich, retired wholesaler's money. The last thing she would want was to have me around. My father, of course, was out of the question.

I had no idea what to do.

And that's when the phone rang.

It was Matt.

"I'll understand if you don't want to talk to me," he said. "But I just had to try. You're all I've been thinking about."

I listened closely to his voice. He didn't sound drunk.

"How did you get my number?" I asked.

"From my phone bill. Since I never talk on the phone while I'm up here, this was just about the only number on there."

I told him about Cindy's murder. He said he had heard about it. It was one of the reasons he was calling.

"I know I said some bad things about her," he said. "But I didn't mean them. I couldn't have. I didn't even know the woman. But she seemed to have your best interests at heart and I can't fault her for that."

"What do you want, Matt?"

"I want you to come back to Maine with me."

"I don't know if that's a good idea."

"Things have changed, Johanna. I've changed. I'm not the same man I was when you left. I've straightened things out. I'm writing again. I just need you with me. I miss you."

"How do I know things won't just be the same?"

"I promise you. I'll buy you a round-trip ticket. You can leave anytime you want. Okay?"

I let him keep talking, trying to convince me to come. Of course, in the end I agreed. I knew I would go back the minute I heard his voice on the other end. I really had no other choice. Little did Matt know, he had become my last and only option.

40

True to his word, Matt was a changed man.

Or rather the man I had first fallen in love with from the moment he spoke with me in the bookstore.

Over the past week, he had seemed looser, happier, and more at ease with himself than I had ever seen him before. He no longer seemed beset by worry over his book. In fact, I hadn't seen him turn on his computer so much as once in the last seven days. He was up every morning before dawn, dressed in sweats and running shoes, and jogged three miles along the highway. He was always back by the time I came downstairs, his complexion ruddy, his eyes sparkling. The abuses he had visited on his body only a short time ago had fortunately left no long-lasting effects. He had clearly regained the youthful vigor of a man twenty years his junior. Not being a morning person myself, I grumbled amazement at his early morning stamina. He merely laughed. He had insisted on making breakfast and I didn't argue.

The chalet itself had been restored to immaculate order. There were no signs of the empty bourbon bottles and overflowing ashtrays that had littered the place in the days before I'd returned to New York. A cozy fire burned on the grate, warm smells of cooking emanated from the kitchen, soft music played on the stereo. Everything was as perfect as it had been the first time I came to the chalet.

Even the weather had lightened.

There was still about a foot of snow on the ground, though it had retreated from the warmth around the house, revealing dark brown earth, a few spindly azaleas, and even some ambitious crocuses, whose purple flowers braved the evening frosts. It was great to go outdoors and crunch around in the melting snow, watching for signs of spring, and breathe in the fresh, pine-scented Maine air.

I had returned to my old apartment in Queens before I left New York and packed the clothes I thought I'd need in four large suitcases I'd borrowed from Cindy. I hadn't asked her family, who would be coming for Cindy's personal effects in a few days, for permission to take the suitcases, but I really didn't think Cindy would mind. What would her family want with a few worn pieces of luggage?

While I was back at my old apartment I asked my sublet a few veiled questions about how things were going. She seemed nervous that perhaps I had come to ask for the place back, but when I assured her that I had no plan to return, and that I was going out of town in a few days, she lightened up. She said she liked the apartment just fine. She didn't mention anything about any break-ins or any nocturnal visits from a man in black. Somehow I felt a strange satisfaction.

He had kept his word.

There was no trouble with the suitcases this time around. To make sure, I kept a carry-on of clothes in the overhead rack above my seat. When I got to the chalet that evening, I was surprised to find the closet in my bedroom empty. Matt had removed the flimsy gowns, diaphanous robes, and impractical slippers to make room for my own wardrobe.

"What's this," I joked, "you don't want me to dress like a harem girl anymore?"

"Of course I do. But only when the mood strikes you, if you know what I mean."

"I think I do. And I think it will. Soon."

Matt grinned. "Good. It's more exciting that way."

That first night was a time of tender reconciliation, of heartfelt apologies for past transgressions, and whispered promises of a happier future. I sipped cognac on the couch in front of the fire. Matt kissed me gently, sweetly on the lips. He stroked my face with his fingers, as if trying to trace my likeness in his memory. I felt his urgency, barely suppressed, in the tension of his body, but he didn't press himself upon me, perhaps sensing my wariness. The fact was that I was exhausted both physically and emotionally: from the hastily planned trip back to Maine, from the events surrounding Cindy's murder, and from the anticipation of being with Matt once again.

I had waited so long for the rekindling of the physical intimacy we had known in New York. Yet I was not quite ready. Not yet. Matt seemed to understand without a word spoken between us. I appreciated his perceptiveness. I don't think I could have explained the storm of conflicting emotions I felt at that moment.

Matt sat back against the arm of the sofa and looked at me with tears in his eyes.

"Thank you so much for coming back. You don't know what this means to me."

"I'm glad to be back," I whispered.

"Do you really mean that?"

"Yes," I said. "I do."

"You know, you're still my inspiration."

"When I saw you'd emptied my closet, I thought perhaps you'd found another inspiration."

"Not a chance. In fact"—Matt smiled boyishly—"would you do me one favor?"

"I guess I owe you one favor."

"Would you dye your hair blond for me?"

"Dye my hair?" I said, as if trying to confirm what I'd heard. The request had come out of the blue and though I couldn't say exactly why, it made me feel vaguely uneasy. "But why?"

"I don't know," Matt said casually. "I just thought it might be something different."

"I guess I could," I said uncertainly, fingering my hair, looking at the soft, brown strands between my fingers. My sense of uneasiness was giving way to curiosity. Besides, Matt was a changed man. I'd already seen that. To my surprise I was actually beginning to warm to the idea. But one nagging suspicion remained.

"What is it?" Matt said, catching the look on my face.

"I don't know," I said. "It's just that . . . Oh, never mind."

"No, please," Matt persisted. "Something's bothering you. What is it?"

"It's silly," I protested, just weakly enough not to convince him.

"You're insulted, aren't you?" he said. He smacked his palm against his forehead. "I'm such a dolt. It never occurred to me. Believe me, Johanna, I love you exactly the way you are. If you don't want to do this, you don't have to."

"I thought maybe you wanted me to be . . ."

"Who?" Matt said gently.

"Somebody else."

Matt laughed so spontaneously as to leave no doubt in my mind.

"Just the opposite," he said. "I want as much of you as I can get."

"Good," I said. "Because that's what I intend to give you."

"So you'll do it?"

"Will I have more fun as a blonde?"

"You bet."

"Sure, why not?" I agreed. It would be fun and it would symbolize the beginning of a whole new chapter in my life. "We could go into town tomorrow and get the stuff."

"No need for that," Matt said, smiling. "I already bought everything we need."

"I guess you were pretty sure I'd say yes," I said wryly. "About everything. Including coming back here. You have a lot of confidence in your ability to get your way, Mr. Lang."

Matt shrugged and grinned. "As a writer you get used to having your way. After all, the characters have to do what you say."

"Yes," I said, reaching out to play with a button on his shirt. "But I've heard authors say that sometimes the characters take on a life of their own and do things they never expected."

Matt pulled me close, his body strong and warm.

"Is that a promise?" he whispered huskily.

"You bet."

He bent his head to kiss me, but I pushed him back playfully.

"Not yet Vidal Sassoon," I said. "The next time you kiss me, I'll be blond."

Matt insisted on helping me with my hair. He lit a half dozen scented candles and gently washed my hair in the kitchen sink. Then he applied the bleach, wrapped my head in a thick towel, and set the timer on the stove to count down the proper number of minutes before the bleach was to be removed. We sat in the living room and watched television in the meantime. I had carried the box of hair color in with me and read the name of the color printed next to the photograph of a shiny cascade of light golden hair.

"Angelblonde? Oh please," I said.

"What better color for my muse?" Matt said, sounding very pleased with himself.

A half hour later the stove's timer went off and I went upstairs to shower the preparation out of my hair. I stood for a long time under the hot water, letting it cascade over my body, as I washed and conditioned my now treated hair. I stepped out of the shower and dried myself, careful not to catch a glimpse of myself in the mirror. I sat in the bedroom with my hair once again wrapped inside a towel until it was dry enough to comb. I went to the closet and found the sexiest nightie I had brought: a red silk teddie with the thinnest of spaghetti straps. I slipped the nightie over my head and let the cool, sleek material slide over the curves of my body. Then I walked over to the mirror on the bureau with my eyes closed. When I opened them, my breath caught involuntarily in my throat.

I hardly recognized my reflection. I looked like a completely different woman.

I decided not to go back downstairs that night. Let Matt wait and wonder, I thought. He had said he wanted his characters to take on a life of their own. I wasn't going to disappoint him. He wanted inspiration? I'd drive him mad with inspiration. He thought he could control his passion? I'd drive him to distraction with desire. He had called me his muse often enough, but it had always seemed vaguely embarrassing to me. Not tonight. He had wanted me to play his muse all along. I had never felt up to the role. I didn't think I had it in me. The woman looking back at me in the mirror convinced me otherwise. She showed me the power all women had to inspire, bemuse, and bewitch. She showed me what Matt had known all along.

I wasn't just capable of playing his muse.

I *was* his muse.

Needless to say, I rather liked being a blonde.

In fact, for the first couple of days, I could hardly take my eyes off myself. I should have made the change a lot earlier. Not that I hadn't thought of it. But somehow I didn't think I could pull it off. Besides, Cindy was a blonde and it would have looked too much as if I were trying to be her. Maybe—deep inside—I would have been. The fact was that I never felt like I could ever measure up to her. Any attempt to do so would have just been humiliating. It sounds terribly selfish to say, but now that Cindy was dead, I felt strangely liberated to truly be my own person.

Matt seemed to really enjoy the change in me as well. He didn't seem able to take his eyes—or his hands, for that matter—off me. I caught him looking at me all the time, staring really, as if he were seeing me for the first time.

"What is it?" I finally asked.

"You are just so beautiful," he said. "So terribly beautiful."

I just laughed.

Things had really changed. He'd been taking me to town almost every day for the past couple of weeks: restaurants, shops, movies. There wasn't a lot to do in the isolated corner of Maine in which he'd decided to make his sanctuary, but what there was to do, we did.

One day we took a long drive into the upper mountains. Matt seemed in an exceptionally good mood.

"What do you say we go skiing?"

"Skiing?" I said uncertainly.

It was almost officially spring on the calendar, but there was still some leftover snow on the ground at the upper elevations and some of the resorts were still making their own snow.

"The weather's perfect. And the slopes should be clear of most of the tourists," he added.

"I don't know. I've never gone skiing before."

"So, neither did I the first time I went."

"Very funny."

"Really, it's not that hard," he said. "I'll teach you."

"But we don't have any equipment. Or the proper clothes."

"We'll get what we need at the resort."

The matter seemed to be decided. Matt drove us through a mountain forest to a rustic-looking lodge tucked away at the foot of a series of snowy hills and dense stands of fir. He made arrangements for a room while I explored the huge lobby. The interior was constructed entirely of varnished timber, except for one wall, in which a massive fireplace had been built of natural stone. The central ceiling soared as high as the trees that surrounded the lodge and the rooms were ranged on four floors overlooking the lobby. Here and there dark armchairs and sofas were placed to create cozy nooks for talking or simply sitting and sipping a hot toddy in front of one of the several smaller fireplaces that filled the room with a soft amber light. I wandered over to a glass display case in front of a large window overlooking a magnificent view of the surrounding mountains. Inside the case there was a recreation of the entire resort.

Matt came up behind me.

"It's all set," he said. "Let's hit the slopes."

We made our way to the ski shop, where Matt bought me the works: a blinding white ski suit, gloves, boots, scarf, hat, and special metallic, UV-protection wraparound goggles to match.

"Really, Matt this is all too much," I said, feeling like Picabo Street getting ready for an Olympic downhill run. "I'm just going to be inching my way down the bunny slope. I don't need all this."

"Nonsense," he said, looking pleased as punch. "You look terrific."

After renting skis and poles, we took the lift up the side of the mountain. As I watched the ground disappearing beneath my new boots, I grew more and more apprehensive. "I'm not so sure this is a good idea, Matt."

"You'll be fine," he said, slipping on his leather gloves and a red knit cap decorated with big white snowflakes which he had bought at the lodge. Otherwise, he was dressed as he had come, in a pair of blue jeans, a heavy sweater, and a lightweight goose-down coat.

"Matt, this doesn't look like a beginner's slope to me," I said, my unease growing as the lift moved higher among the snow-covered mountains.

"It's not a beginner's slope," Matt said calmly. "It's something a little more challenging."

"But, Matt—" I started to protest.

"Ease off the chair now," he said. "Just drop your feet and slide off it on your skis."

"Matt, I—"

"Hurry. If you wait any longer, we'll wind up on an even steeper slope."

"Damn you," I said, letting my skis touch the snow beneath me and, to my surprise, gently sliding off the chair.

Matt came off behind me. "See, that wasn't so hard."

We pushed our way to the start of the trail. The slope was nearly completely deserted. Just a few other skiiers cutting crisscross paths farther down the side of the mountain. I stared at the steep trail in front of me and turned back to Matt.

"You've got to be kidding. There's no way I'm going down there unless I crawl down."

"It's really not as hard as it looks," he explained. "I'll show you." He pushed off with his poles and zigzagged expertly about thirty yards down the slope before stopping and climbing back up to where I was standing. "See? The mountain does most of the work. You just follow its lead and try not to fall."

"Or run into a tree."

Matt ignored me. "It's a lot like dancing."

"Which I wouldn't mind doing right about now. How about we go to the lodge and see if they have a piano bar?"

"Come on," Matt said. "Don't be afraid."

"Famous last words . . . right before they carry you off at the bottom with a broken leg."

"You're not going to break your leg, I promise."

"How can you be so sure?"

"Don't you trust me?"

I stared down at the hill. "Matt, I'm standing on the brink of what looks like the edge of Mount Everest covered with a sheet of ice, with nothing but a pair of six-foot-long aluminum runners and a pair of flimsy poles. Trust has nothing to do with it. I'm terrified."

"Terror," he said, sounding even more cryptic behind his dark glasses, "is the closest thing we can experience to union with the divine."

"I thought that was sex."

Matt smiled broadly. "We'll just have to compare the two, won't we?"

With that, he pushed himself off the edge of the slope and began to go downhill. Against my better judgment, I followed. True to my word, I inched my way down the first few yards of mountain, digging my poles deep into the snow for support. Matt was already about fifty yards ahead of me. He shushed to a stop, turned, and shouted back. "Come on!"

"I'm doing the best I can," I protested.

"No, you're not. Just let it go."

He continued skiing and soon I lost sight of him. I had made my way far down the slope enough that the way back up seemed almost as arduous a task as going the rest of the way down. The sun was already beginning to sink behind the mountain at my back and the snow was turning blue.

"Matt!" I called out, hearing my voice echo down the slope. "Matt!"

There was no answer.

Damn him!

In spite of my outfit, I was growing cold. I was also growing angry. Out of frustration and desperation, I pushed the poles into the blue snow, which was beginning to freeze over and straightened out my skis. I moved forward shakily, but I didn't fall. I tried it again, turning slightly from the waist, as Matt had told me, and using the poles for balance. Little by little, I grew more confident. I pushed hard, twisting my waist first one way, and now the other, eventually straightening out my skis to pick up more downhill speed. I fell two or three times, but by now I had overcome my general fear of falling. So long as I didn't try anything stupid, it seemed that the worst that could happen was that I would get a little wet.

I turned a difficult corner on the trail and there was Matt, leaning against one of his ski poles, grinning from ear to ear.

"What did I tell you," he said, his voice coming out in little clouds of frosted breath. "It's not so hard, is it?"

"You bastard!" I shouted back playfully and took off after him.

We were three quarters of the way down the slope by now and the bottom was in sight. Matt waited for me to move ahead before pushing off himself. He pulled even with me for several seconds and then leapt ahead, his arms pumping rhythmically as he sped down the slope. I threw all remaining caution to the winds. I felt the exhilaration of the cold air whipping my face, the intoxicating sensation of speed as my skis slid over the glazed snow, and the indescribable feeling of freedom as I did my best to catch him, but it was hopeless. He waited for me at the bottom as I skidded on the seat of my pants to a stop about ten feet in front of him.

He ran over, laughing, and helped me up.

"See, that wasn't so bad after all, was it?" he said, beaming.

"No," I said, panting, trying to catch my breath.

It wasn't until that moment that I realized that somewhere on that mountain I'd left my fear behind.

It was by far the best day we had shared together since the time we'd spent in New York.

Later, we sat in the cozy lodge and warmed up with a couple of large hot cocoas. Matt looked at me from across the table.

"I've never been so happy in my whole life," he said.

He was looking deeply into my eyes, which made me a little uncomfortable, as I had lost one of my contacts the first morning back in Maine.

Yes, I wore contacts.

Colored contacts.

Aquamarine.

Like the color of nothing else on this earth.

It was my deepest and darkest secret. I had put them in their little cups to clean for the night and the next morning found the plastic holder on the floor. Somehow I must have put it too close to the edge of the sink. On hands and knees, I frantically searched the entire bathroom from top to bottom, putting off an increasingly alarmed Matt until I had no choice but to tell him the humiliating truth.

Now he sat across the table from me, staring into a perfectly ordinary pair of brown eyes framed by nondescript glasses.

I had remembered what he wrote in my book and I was afraid he would no longer see me the same way. I remembered how I had stood there in my bathrobe, ready for his shock, and worse, his anger at my betrayal.

Instead, he had taken me, sobbing and embarrassed, into his arms.

When I stopped crying, he pulled back and with one strong finger lifted my trembling chin and waited patiently until I finally found the courage to lift my tear-filled eyes to his.

"It was never the color," he whispered. "It was the spark of life I saw inside them. The spark of life I see now. You still have the most beautiful eyes in the world."

He was looking into my eyes now with a look of tenderness and passion that made me feel foolish for ever having doubted his love for me. I was no longer ashamed to look at him with my "ordinary" eyes. In spite of everything, he seemed to see the extraordinary in me. He'd seen it right from the beginning. I was the star of his drama.

Our room was rustic but elegant and furnished with a pair of twin beds.

Neither of us seemed to mind.

I, for one, was exhausted, both physically and emotionally, from my first day on the slope. I was barely awake when Matt kissed me good night. My last thought was about how he'd said that terror was the closest thing we can experience to union with the divine. I had argued that it was sex. After the rush I'd experienced on the slope that afternoon, I wondered if he was right after all.

41

Matt had suggested the day trip because of the weather: a sunny, almost balmy sixty degrees.

There was no doubt that spring had finally arrived in Maine. The last of the snow was running off into the crystal-clear streams and the trees were decorated with brilliant green buds. There was even the occasional shock of ambitious wildflowers pushing up through the black muck of the forest floor. I sat back and enjoyed the scenery along the winding mountain roads as classical music played on the Jeep's excellent CD system.

"It must be absolutely breathtaking here in the fall," I said, hoping not to sound too obvious.

Would I still be in Matt's life come autumn?

"Yes, it is," Matt said, inscrutable behind his Ray-Ban sunglasses. "Though I don't get up here much. I usually return to the city by the end of summer."

We ate a picnic lunch Matt had prepared at a scenic overlook. We sat at a wooden table carved with initials of past loves and stared down the fir-lined slope of the mountains into a slowly greening valley dotted with white houses. It was really still a little chilly for a picnic, but Matt brought out a thermos of hot cider and we took turns sipping from the plastic cup as he gathered me into the warmth of his arms. We kissed a little, breathed in the fresh cool air, and let our flesh drink in the sunlight. Matt took out a penknife and dug our initials into the weathered wood of the picnic table. He carved a crooked little heart around the letters and we kissed again.

Just then a deer stepped out of the trees at the edge of the clearing. She was lithe and beautiful, her legs as long and delicate as a young dancer's. She stared at us with large, liquid eyes, her ears twitching, as if hearing some far-off hunter. We stared at each other for a magical moment, perfectly still, perfectly quiet, and then she was gone, bounding through the underbrush with a flash of white tail.

I let out my breath, unaware I'd been holding it the whole time, and turned to Matt.

He was staring off into the forest where the deer had disappeared. "Do you believe in signs?" he asked.

"Yes," I said. "I do."

That evening we ate dinner in a town about two hundred miles north of Bangor and about fifty miles south of the chalet. Matt had ordered sirloin tips and I had fettucine alfredo. I drank merlot. Matt had seltzer. The food was delicious, even by Manhattan standards, and a lot more plentiful. We ate nearly in silence, but not a bad silence, the kind of silence two people share who almost don't need to talk to communicate. As if in proof, Matt looked up at me through the flickering candlelight.

"What's wrong?" he said.

"Nothing," I lied.

"Something is wrong. I know it."

I considered denying it, but the knowing look in Matt's eyes convinced me it would be useless.

"Okay, I'll tell you," I said. "It's just that—well—it's been nearly two months since I've been back and I haven't seen you at your computer once. Shouldn't you be working on your novel?"

Matt laughed. "My novel? Isn't that what caused all our problems the first time around?"

"It's different now, Matt. You're different."

He shook his head. "There are more important things than writing. You, for instance."

"But writing is what you do. It's your life."

"That has always been the problem. I think it's time for me to stop writing about living for a while. I need to recharge my batteries. I need to live life for real. I need to be inspired. You're doing that for me."

"Just promise me you won't give up writing for me. You'll regret it, Matt."

Matt reached over and laid his hand over mine. "I promise."

* * *

That evening back at the chalet, Matt built a fire and poured me a glass of wine. We sat close together on the couch, so close as to be almost touching, a pleasure made more delicious with anticipation than touching itself. I had already decided that I would no longer put Matt off. He had suffered enough. He had passed every test. He had proved himself. I was convinced beyond a shadow of a doubt that whatever had happened the last time I was here was merely an aberration. The man I had spent the last few weeks with was the real Matt. This was the man I had fallen quickly and madly in love with back in New York.

I put down my glass of wine and turned to say something to him, only to find he had turned toward me at the same time, our lips nearly brushing together.

"Matt, I—"

"Johanna . . ."

There was nothing left to say. We had said all we could. Some things cannot be expressed with words. Our mouths found each other and spoke the silent, desperate, hungry language of a passion that had been shut up far too long. His hands were at the front of my blouse, fumbling with the impossibly small buttons, his hot mouth already on the side of my throat and working its way down.

"Tear it," I managed to gasp.

He didn't hesitate. The flimsy blouse came apart in his strong hands, buttons flying everywhere. He reached behind me and undid my bra, my breasts rising as I caught my breath, nipples erect and aching for the touch of his soft burning lips, which were not long in coming. I arched backward against the sofa and groaned as I felt the heat building, my own hands running through his thick dark hair and over his broad shoulders. He took his hands and mouth from my breasts only long enough to straighten up and remove his dark turtleneck, but it felt like an eternity.

I pulled him down and felt his bare flesh against mine, our frenzied breaths coming in unison. He was pulling up my skirt, his hand on my panties, grunting in appreciation when he felt the warmth and moisture there. My own fingers were working at his belt, the button on his jeans, the zipper that barely contained the bulge of his throbbing penis. He slid his hands underneath me and lifted my bottom off the sofa, pulling my panties down around my thighs, his mouth sucking my left nipple. I had managed to push his jeans down past his buttocks, which I now grabbed, pushing them toward me until I could feel the rock-hard flesh of his penis between my thighs.

"Do it," I muttered. "Do it now. Fuck me."

He groaned and slid his body up until our mouths were sealed together, our breaths becoming one breath, our lives one life. He took me by the shoulders and quickly and easily shifted my body so that I was lying full-length on the sofa. He covered my body with his and I felt him poised to enter me. I tore my mouth away from his, gasping for breath, moaning as he pushed himself slowly inside me, his own breath escaping in a mumbled glossalia of passion, obscenity, and devotion.

He was nearly all the way inside me when the phone rang.

Suddenly, he stopped.

"No," I moaned. "Let it . . . let it . . . ."

He started moving again, but I could already feel him shrinking inside me.

"Matt—"

He was sitting up on the sofa between my legs, his eyes narrowed to two dark slits, staring in the direction of the phone.

The phone stopped ringing and the answering machine picked up the call. After about ten seconds the tone sounded and the loud, crude voice of Clay came through the other end of the machine.

"What the fuck gives, Matt old boy? You forget about your old writing partner or what?" Clay laughed sarcastically. "Too busy playing Romeo I suppose. Well, I can't say as I can blame you for wanting to soak your dick, but I'm getting goddamn sick and tired sitting around with my thumb up my asshole waiting for you to produce. Your deadline is coming up and I ain't seen so much as page fucking one from you yet. So what gives? You ain't trying to give me the old butt-screw are you, Matt? I always figured you for more intelligent than that. You've written enough books to know what happens to folks who butt-screw characters like me. So you get your dick in your pants and your ass in gear old friend. They don't call it a deadline for nothing. You miss it and you could wind up dead."

There was another bark of laughter, and then silence, and then the sound of the phone hanging up.

I was sitting up on the couch. I had pulled together what remained of my ripped blouse and smoothed down my skirt. Matt had already yanked up his jeans and walked over to the answering machine. He was staring down at the blinking red light as if hypnotized by it. What had only moments ago seemed so beautiful and erotic had somehow been rendered dirty and shameful by Clay's profanity-laced message. No doubt that was exactly what Clay had intended. His timing couldn't have been more perfect.

I stared at Matt's back as he stared at the blinking light. I didn't know whether to be mad at him, at Clay, or at both of them.

"Matt, I want an explanation."

He didn't even seem to hear me. I stood up from the sofa and took a step toward him. "Matt, I'm talking to you."

He turned around, looking startled.

"What is it?"

"Matt, I thought we had an understanding."

He turned and stared back at the answering machine.

"Maybe you should go upstairs to bed Johanna," he said mechanically. "I'm sorry."

"Sorry?" I said. I put my hand on his shoulder. He had not put his sweater back on and his skin felt impossibly cold. "You've got to tell me what's going on, Matt. Maybe I can help."

He pushed my hand away. "Nobody can help."

"Don't say that. Between the two of us we can work this out, whatever it is."

"You wouldn't understand."

"Why don't you try me?"

Matt turned around and looked at me, trying to decide whether to tell me or not. For the first time, I noticed the small tic which had developed between his eyes.

"Please, Matt," I said. "Don't shut me out again. It'll be the end of us. I swear it will. I'm willing to go through anything with you, but I won't go through being pushed away. Not ever again."

He broke eye contact and turned away. He walked to his desk, yanked open the top drawer, and pulled out a pack of cigarettes. He fumbled with a match, his hands trembling, and took a deep drag. My heart was thumping in my chest as I watched him struggle with what he was about to say—or not say. I had already laid down my ultimatum. If he decided not to talk, I'd have no choice but to leave.

"Okay," he said finally, "I'll tell you. But you may want to leave me, even after I tell you."

"Trust me."

Matt took another deep drag on his cigarette. His hands were no longer trembling, but the tic between his eyes had grown more pronounced.

"Clay helps me with my work."

"So he was telling me the truth. He's your collaborator."

"No," Matt said violently, stabbing out his cigarette directly on his desk. "He's not a collaborator. He's a resource."

"What do you mean?"

Matt sighed, letting the last of the gray smoke escape from his lips.

"He gives me insights that make my work more authentic. You see, he's an ex-con. He served three years on a rape conviction and another eight for kidnapping and aggravated manslaughter. I'd read about his case in the newspaper and decided to visit him. It was when I was still struggling as a writer. I realized that part of my problem was that I didn't really know what drove a man to acts of extreme violence. I needed first-hand knowledge about how the criminal mind worked. I needed access to the mind of a killer. I met him while he was still in prison. He helped me. Shortly afterward my first novel was published. I was so grateful I gave him twenty percent of the advance. I even went to his parole hearing to plead on his behalf as a rehabilitated man. My recommendation helped get him released."

"So you helped him get out of prison. You must have believed he was reformed."

Matt didn't answer.

"You did think he had changed, didn't you?"

"I don't, Johanna," Matt said, his face a road map of agony. "I honestly don't. I wanted to believe it. I really did."

I heard the pines rustling in the wind outside the chalet. In the fireplace, the flames trembled.

"You're not the first writer to be fooled by a con," I said, recalling a book I'd read in college written by a murderer. "Remember Norman Mailer and Jack Abbot?"

Matt walked to his desk, opened a drawer at the bottom, and pulled out a half full bottle of bourbon.

"No, Matt," I said, rushing over to him, grabbing his wrist before he could bring the bottle to his lips. "Don't do it. Drinking isn't going to help."

Matt stared at the bottle with a look of reluctant obligation, as if it were a despised long-lost family member who had just shown up at his door.

"Three days after you left, I stopped drinking," he said, staring into the coppery depths of the bottle. "I swore I'd never drink again. I've kept that promise."

"And you are going to continue to keep it," I said. "Look at me, Matt."

He reluctantly turned his eyes from the bottle.

"What does he want? You got him out of prison. He should be grateful to you."

"He wants money."

"Money? Why should you give him money? You paid him for his help on your book. It's more than he deserved."

"It's more complicated than that." Matt set the bottle down on the desk and walked slowly across the room toward the answering machine. He stared down again at the blinking red light. He spoke slowly and with great difficulty. "Since he's been released from prison, he's been helping me."

"Helping you? I don't understand. Helping you how?"

"He's been helping me write. At first I thought they were just fantasies. Or stories he heard from other inmates in prison. At worst, I tried to believe they were crimes he had committed before he'd been incarcerated. I was just fooling myself. I didn't want to believe the truth. But I can't deny it any longer. I can't lie to myself. The truth is, he hasn't stopped."

"Hasn't stopped what?"

Matt looked up, tears in his eyes. "Killing, Johanna," he whispered, as if we might be overheard. "I swear I didn't know it. I never would have gotten involved with him. He's a serial killer, Johanna."

I stood there for a moment too shocked to speak. I was hoping I hadn't heard right, hoping there might be some mistake. The tortured expression in Matt's eyes told me there was no mistake.

"My God, Matt," I managed at last. "Are you sure?"

Matt nodded.

"How do you know?"

"He's told me. It gives him some kind of perverse pleasure I think. He travels around the country and then comes back to tell me what he's done. He gets a kick out of knowing that I'm writing about his crimes."

"You mean your books . . . they're based on what he's—"

"Yes," Matt said, cutting me off, as if he couldn't bear to hear the words aloud.

I had pleaded with him to trust me. But I had never expected anything like what he had just told me. I had sworn to stand by him no matter what. Now I wasn't so certain. There was one thing I had to know before I went any further.

"How long have you known, Matt?" I said, trying to keep my voice even.

"Shortly after we first came up here. Just as I was starting this book . . ."

"So that explains it," I said. Everything suddenly made sense. The phone calls, the drinking, the erratic behavior. "No wonder you haven't been able to write."

Matt seemed to sag from weariness, as if an unbearable weight had just been lifted from him.

"It's all been true. Every murder. Every victim—"

"Matt," I said, trying to control the panic I felt rising inside me, "You've got to go to the police." What he had said stunned me and yet I knew I had to be strong. Strong for both of us.

Matt shook his head emphatically. "I can't."

"Why not?"

"He's threatened to implicate me in his murders."

"That's ludicrous," I exclaimed, trying to sound a lot more sure than I felt. The way Matt was acting wasn't helping matters any. "No one will believe him."

Matt didn't answer the question in my voice, not directly, anyway. "I can't take that chance, Johanna."

"But he's blackmailing you!" I argued.

"Yes," Matt said resignedly, rubbing his face with his hands. "But I don't have a choice. Either I keep quiet, or he brings me down with him."

I calmly picked up the bottle and without a word turned to the fireplace. I wasn't going to take the chance that he'd start drinking again. I poured the liquor out onto the burning logs. They hissed and sizzled their protest before bursting into a bright flame that brought a sweat to my face and throat. Matt didn't protest. When I turned from the fireplace, I saw that he had pressed a button on the answering machine and the tape rewound, erasing Clay's message.

"What are you doing!" I shouted. "We could have used that message. You've got him on tape threatening you."

Matt shook his head sadly. "It's hopeless, Johanna."

"No, it isn't. Dammit, Matt," I said, feeling an unexpected surge of anger coursing through me, "there must be something we can do. Are you going to let some ignorant backwoods cretin get the better of you? Or are you going to stand up for yourself and act like a man for crissakes!"

Matt took a step back. He looked stunned. But whether it was the force of my outburst or the words I had used, I couldn't tell. I only hoped that I hadn't gone too far.

"I'm sorry," he said abjectly. "Maybe you should just get out now. Get out of this whole mess while you can."

"Sorry isn't going to cut it," I said, deciding that I had nothing left to lose. It was now or never. "And I'm not going anywhere. I didn't come all this way with you, go through all we've gone through together, to lose you like this. I'm sticking by you, Matt, because I love you and

I'm not going to let anyone hurt you. We'll get out of this somehow and we'll get out of it together."

"But what can we do?" he said in a weak voice.

Somehow the idea must have germinated in a dark corner of my brain while we were talking. Now that I had turned my attention to it and brought the full light of concentration to the matter, it seemed the most logical course of action.

"Invite him over for dinner, Matt. We'll offer to pay him off once and for all."

Matt shook his head. "It won't work, Johanna."

"Yes, it will. We just have to find his price. A man like him always has a price."

42

Matt had to wait an hour before Clay showed up.

Matt had gone into town to pick him up at the Redwood Inn. It would have been nearly impossible—even with the most detailed directions—for anyone to find the chalet otherwise. Even though Matt assured me Clay had never been to his home before, he walked in like he owned the place. He was wearing a cheap-looking, imitation-leather jacket over a plaid shirt open down the front, and a pair of maroon polyester pants. In the wiry hair of his chest shone some kind of gold medallion. He made himself comfortable on the couch and propped a pair of worn black boots on the coffee table. I saw Matt's jaw tighten, as if he were biting back the words.

"What have you got to drink?" Clay asked.

"I've got some burgundy," I said, quickly, trying to diffuse the situation.

"I guess you didn't hear me. I said what have you got to *drink?*"

"Listen, Clay don't talk to her—" Matt said, but I interrupted him, laughing it off as if it were all a joke.

"I think I know what you mean," I offered. "We have some decent bourbon."

"Figured you might. That's your poison, ain't it, Matthew?"

"Not anymore," I jumped in. "Matt hasn't had a drink in months."

"Is that so?" Clay said, grinning at Matt. "Something else oiling up the old creative wheels? She is one fine-looking piece, if I say so myself."

Again the color rose in Matt's face, but again I decided the best course of action was to try to treat the comment like a joke.

"Why, thank you," I said, with just enough playful sarcasm. "I'll take that as a compliment."

Clay removed the ever-present stub of cigar from his lips and blew me a kiss. He took the glass of bourbon from my hand and downed half of it in one gulp. He shoved the bitten cigar back into his mouth.

"Hardly seems fair, Matthew. I do half the work and you get all the ass. Does that seem fair to you, sweetheart?"

"I'm sure you do okay, Mr. Clay," I said.

"You're sure of that, are you?" Clay grinned again. His eyes locked on mine and I felt myself shudder inside. This man seated so casually on our living-room couch was a killer.

"If you'll excuse me," I said, shaken, "I think dinner is about ready."

Clay was the only one who really ate. Matt, looking dreadfully pale and nervous, barely touched his food and I pretty much just sipped my wine, watching the man across from me with a mixture of curiosity and horror. Clay either didn't notice or he didn't care. He ate with an off-putting gusto, cutting his meat in large chunks and eating it right off the end of the knife. He sopped up the blood pooling around the edge of his plate with one dinner roll after another. The silence between us was broken only by his frequent and uninhibited belches.

He and Matt returned to the living room while I cleaned up the remains of dinner. I returned with a tray of coffee and pastries and set them down on the table. Clay reached forward and grabbed four of the fancy confections, pushing one into his mouth before settling back on the couch.

"So," Clay said, his mouth full, sugar dusting his lips, "why did you invite me to this cozy get-together anyway?"

"We have a business proposition for you," Matt said tightly.

"A business proposition," Clay said, pushing another pastry into his mouth. "What kind of proposition?"

"I want to buy you out."

Clay laughed so hard he spit out part of his pastry onto his lap. He brushed the crumbs off onto the floor.

"Buy me out?" he said, incredulity stretched across his broad face. "You've got to be kidding me, Matthew. Do you think I was born yesterday? Why would I let you buy me out, just when you're about to hit it big?"

"There's no guarantee of that," I said, cutting in. "It's a long shot in the book business at best. But we figured we'd give you the full advance, plus all the royalties for Matt's next book. His editor already thinks it's the best he's written so far. And if Matt does hit it big, the book will continue making money for you. So, you see, it's really a good deal for all of us."

"All of us? Since when are you involved, sister? This is between Matthew and me."

"Matt and I just thought—"

"Is this what it's come to, Matthew?" Clay said, turning to Matt, his face twisted in an ugly, mocking sneer. "You're letting some cunt make your decisions for you?"

"Shut the hell up, Clay. I won't have you talk to her that way."

Clay laughed. "So that's it. My, you've grown chivalrous."

"Shut up, Clay," Matt growled. "I'm warning you."

"Warning me?" Clay said, casually leaning forward for another pastry. "I think you've confused yourself with one of the heroes in your books. What are you going to do, beat me up?"

"I'll tell you what I'm going to do," Matt said, his voice trembling as badly as his hand, which laid his chattering cup and saucer down on the mantel. "I won't write anymore. That's what I'll do."

"You'll write," Clay said calmly. "You'll write because you have to write."

"I don't have to write," Matt said, looking at me. "Not anymore."

"If you don't write," Clay said with the same disturbing calm, "I'll go to the police."

"Go to the police then," Matt said. "I'll take my damn chances."

"My, my. You've suddenly grown a set of real balls on you, Matthew." Clay turned to me. "Is that your doing, sister? If so, you must be some woman. You know, Matthew," he said, not taking his hard, dark eyes off me, "I think I'm getting shortchanged with the present arrangement. I think it's high time we shared all the fruits of our labor."

He stood up and came toward me. I started to back away just as he reached out his hand. Matt leaped from where he was standing by the fireplace and wrapped his arm around Clay's throat, dragging him backward, knocking the coffee table on its side.

They staggered to their feet and grabbed hold of each other. Matt was taller by at least five inches, but Clay was wider and heavily built. He drove his shoulder into Matt's solar plexus and shoved him back against the wall. I heard the breath go out of Matt as Clay hit him with his thick fists. Matt put his own hands up in defense, but was barely able to ward off the attack. I saw his face twisted in pain and screamed at Clay to stop the beating. He turned around only long enough to grin at me before he hit Matt again. Then he came toward me.

It was then I became aware of the hot pot of coffee in my hand. Without thinking, I flung my arm forward, the lid coming off the pot, the scalding coffee flying out in a black wave toward Clay's twisted, brutal face.

He flung his hands up, but it was too late.

Screaming obscenities, he staggered sideways, as Matt jumped him from behind. He used his elbows to back Matt off him. He was wild with pain, but still partially blinded. Matt was able to hold his own. They scuffled violently when, suddenly, a heavy object hit the floor and skittered toward the hearth.

Matt and I froze. We looked up at each other.

It was Clay who broke the spell. He swore and lurched toward the revolver on the floor, but it was Matt who got there first.

Clay let out a shout of rage. He threw himself at Matt, who staggered backward. They groped at each other in a macabre dance as I watched from across the room, still unable to move. I heard Matt cry out and then Clay swore again and then there was the explosion of a gunshot that rattled the glass of the windows.

For a second the two of them stood as if surprised and then Clay fell backward onto the floor, his head striking the edge of the overturned coffee table on the way down.

He lay on the rug faceup, a look of profound disbelief distorting his brutal features, a wet hole in the center of his splintered chest, hissing blood and air.

"Oh my God," Matt stammered. "What have I done?"

He was hunched over, holding his bruised ribs, looking as though he was going to be sick. His gaze fell on the gun still in his hand and he dropped it as if it had burned his fingers. He backed up, stared at the body on the floor, and began crying. A moment later I felt the hot trail of tears streaming down my own cheeks as well. It had taken awhile for the impact of what had just happened so quickly and so violently to fully register.

"It wasn't your fault, Matt," I said, my voice catching on the words. "You did what you had to do. It was self-defense."

"This is bad. This is very bad."

"No, it's not bad. Don't you see? Now you can go to the police. He had a record. He threatened you. I'm a witness."

"We can't go to the police," Matt said.

"Why not?"

"How am I going to explain why he was here? There'll be too many questions. They'll conduct an investigation. Who knows what will turn up? Even dead, he'll implicate me in his crimes."

"So what do we do?"

Neither of us were crying any longer. The problem of the logistics of the situation had momentarily overtaken our emotions.

"We've got to get rid of his body," Matt said matter-of-factly. "Then I'll go into town. He has a room there. I'll make sure nothing is left behind to tie me to him. As far as I know, he has no family connections anymore. No one to miss him. He'll have just disappeared off the face of the earth."

"I don't know, Matt—"

"It's the best possible solution. You know, it's strange the way things turn out. If he had accepted our offer, he would still be on the loose. By killing him, we've actually done the world a favor. Who knows how many lives we've saved?"

"I suppose you're right," I said quietly, more because I wanted to believe it than because I did.

Matt went down the hall and came back with a white bedsheet. He laid it on the floor next to Clay's body.

"Help me roll him over, would you?"

"You've got to be kidding."

"Come on," he said, kneeling down. "He's dead for crissakes."

"I can't, Matt," I said, suddenly panicking. All at once, the full implications of what was happening were crashing down on me. I was involved with a murder. Yes, it was justified. I had seen that Matt was only acting in self-defense, but what he was suggesting now was clearly wrong. We would never get away with it. We would get caught. I wanted no part of any of this and yet there was no way I could get myself out of it now. I was as deeply involved as Matt. Accidentally or not, he had made me an accessory to murder.

"Damn you, damn you, damn you!" I screamed at him. "Why the hell did you have to shoot him? Why couldn't you just go to the police like I told you? You dumb pigheaded bastard! Now look at what you got us involved in."

"I had no choice, Johanna. You said so yourself. Now let's go," he said impatiently.

"I won't do it, Matt," I said, my voice trembling. "I'm not going to touch him."

"All right then, dammit," he snapped. "Then you can at least grab that lantern on the mantel and light it. We're going to bury him in the shed."

I retrieved the old-fashioned oil lantern and struck a long fireplace match. My hand was trembling so badly it took me three matches before I finally got the wick lit.

I turned just in time to see Matt pulling the sheet around Clay's body. The dreadful hissing had long since ceased from the hole in the dead man's chest. His eyelids were closed enough to cover his eyes, but there was still a disconcerting rim of white peeking out from below. Even worse, his lips were peeled back into a sneering grimace of pain and defiance as if somehow he expected to get the last laugh.

Matt bent down and with great effort hoisted the heavy bundled body, first to his knees and then onto his shoulder. Grunting under the weight, he slowly stood up.

"Come on," he said, grimacing. "Let's get this over with."

Carrying the lantern, I led the way through the darkness to the large aluminum tool shed at the edge of the woods.

Matt shifted, rebalancing the body on his shoulders, and reached into his pocket for his keys. He separated a small silver one and handed the ring to me.

"Open it," he said, barely able to catch his breath.

The keys on the ring made a jingling sound in my still-shaking hand. I stabbed the tiny key toward the tiny lock again and again, unable to fit it inside.

"Jesus Christ, Johanna," Matt swore. "Hurry up."

"I can't get it—"

Matt let the bundled body fall off his shoulder. It made a terrible thud on the ground behind him.

"Give me those," he said, snatching the keys from me.

He unlocked the shed and threw open the door.

"Get inside with the lantern," he said.

I walked into the shed. It looked smaller inside than it did from the outside. It had a sloping roof, but it was high enough over the main area to easily stand upright. From the light of the lantern I could see the shapes of various tools, machinery, and other outdoor supplies neatly arranged along the walls, hung up on a pegboard of hooks, or stacked on what looked like metal bookshelves. There was a riding mower, hedge clippers, rakes, chainsaws, leaf blowers and the like, as well as bags of fertilizer and topsoil, the latter probably giving the shed the almost overpowering earthy, fertile smell I had immediately noticed upon entering.

Matt hadn't bothered picking the body back up. Instead, he dragged it to the middle of the dirt floor of the shed. Wrapped up, it was almost possible to forget what was inside, except for the large red carnations of blood that had formed on the front of the white sheet.

Grabbing a shovel, Matt began to dig into the hard-packed earth. He grunted and cursed as he worked. Every once in a while, he stopped to straighten up, rub his lower back, and wipe the sweat and dirt from his face. It was taking too long, impossibly long, for him to dig. I kept switching the lantern from one tired arm to the other.

"Will you stop shaking the damn light?" Matt snapped.

"I'm trying," I said, holding one arm with the other, both arms shaking.

The shadows from the light of the burning wick were making weird shapes on the tin walls of the shed. I was trembling worse than ever. The shadows on the walls grew ever more wilder. The sound of the shovel scraping against the earth was becoming unbearable. Suddenly, out of the corner of my eye, I thought I saw him, his shadow standing just inside the doorway.

I wheeled around wildly.

"What are you doing here?" I shouted.

I thrust the lantern forward and in the glare of the light I saw what I had mistaken for my dark visitor. It was an old ragged coat hanging from a hoe propped in the corner.

"What the fuck is wrong with you?" Matt screamed. He was standing in a narrow pit that was barely up to his knees.

I looked at him in amazement and suddenly started laughing. I was doubled over, my stomach aching, unable to catch my breath. There were tears burning down my face, but the laughter continued.

"Stop it," Matt said sharply. "Stop it right now."

His seriousness struck me as even funnier. I tried to hold it back, but it was impossible. I was laughing wildly now, the sound echoing off the tin walls of the shed, making me laugh harder still. I stared at the white bundle on the floor with its red carnations and could no longer control myself. I sank to my knees, placing the lantern on the ground beside me, and crawled over to the corner of the shed.

It was there that Matt grabbed me and forced me to my feet. He pulled me close, shaking me, his face an angry hollow mask in the diffused light.

"Johanna!" he was shouting, his voice seeming to come from far away. "Johanna, stop it! Stop it, goddamn it!"

He was shaking me so hard I could feel my teeth knocking together and then he was holding me and I broke down sobbing against his shoulder. I don't know how long we stayed like that, but when he finally pushed me away, I had stopped crying. He used his muddy finger to brush away some dirt smudged on my cheek and realized he had only made it worse.

"Johanna, I'm sorry. But if this is going to work, we have to remain calm. Now I have to get this body buried. Will you help me?"

I nodded, choking back a sob.

"Good. Then let's get finished."

Matt finished digging the makeshift grave and rolled Clay's body inside. Then he started throwing dirt back into the hole. The lantern had long since guttered out and I was sitting on the seat of the riding mower, hugging myself against the morning chill. By the time we left the shed, the sky was already lightening in the east. I trudged beside Matt along the path to the chalet. Matt stripped off his clothes and had me hose the mud off his body. He shivered beneath the spray of the cold water, but insisted I get him thoroughly clean. I was so exhausted I was barely able to hold up the hose. Finally, he decided he was clean enough and I went inside to fetch him a towel.

Matt padded barefoot to the table on which sat the bottle of bourbon we had served Clay only hours before.

I didn't object when he poured out two tumblers.

We sat down on the couch without a word and stared into the ashes of the fireplace. We both knew that sleep was out of the question. I wondered if I would ever sleep again. Matt refilled our glasses. We emptied them again. I don't know how I even found the strength to lift the glass to my lips.

Sometime later, Matt lit a fire.

We sat closer together on the couch.

It was nearly April and not cold at all.

Yet no matter how close we sat, no matter how much bourbon we drank, or how many logs Matt threw on the fire, I could not stop shaking.

The first few days after the shooting were the worst. We lived in almost constant dread of a knock on the door. As planned, Matt had gone into town and searched through Clay's room, making sure there was nothing left behind that could tie them together. According to Matt, Clay lived the Spartan existence of most transitory people. The landlord would find little more than a toothbrush, a razor and shaving cream, a cheap suitcase, and a change of clothes or two. Most likely, he would just assume that his tenant had skipped out on his rent. It would not be an unprecedented event, given the kind of dive in which Clay had chosen to hang his hat.

Still, there was always that vague "what-if" hanging over our heads. The more I thought about it, the more possibilities I could come up with for something going wrong. What if Clay had mentioned his connection to Matt to a third party? What if there was a formal investigation into Clay's disappearance? What if the bartender at the Redwood Inn connected the two? What if Clay had left behind some kind of confession in a safe-deposit box somewhere as insurance against Matt betraying him? We spent a lot of time reassuring each other, trying to give logical answers to increasingly far-fetched scenarios of disaster, but in the end it was all more wishful thinking than real conviction.

We still lived in dread of a knock on the door.

But as the days passed and the knock didn't come, the hydra-headed "what-ifs" began to grow more slowly. And, finally, not at all.

We no longer talked about that dreadful night. It was as if it were just a bad dream. I tried not to look at the shed where Matt had buried Clay, though once in a while my eyes would betray me and catch a glimpse of it just at the edge of the forest, the lush, rapidly growing leaves of the secondary growth of brambles all but hiding the shed from view.

Things had returned to normal.

Matt went back to his writing. He was now working steadily on his novel. The writing was coming quickly and easily. Matt's spirits seemed to soar. Even though he was writing again, there was no more moodiness or drinking or smoking. And, best of all, there were no more calls in the dead of night.

He made a conscientious effort to make time for me, even though he often had to tear himself away from the novel. We went to restaurants and movies, and even on the occasional day trip, whenever Matt felt he could spare a whole day away from the computer.

After lunch, before Matt returned to work, we often took long drives in the surrounding mountains, now vibrant green with the full flowering of spring. The book, according to Matt, was almost finished and he was certain that it was his best yet. We still hadn't slept together since we had left New York, but I realized now that Matt was saving all his strength for his writing and I had every confidence that that part of our relationship would also resume soon.

One evening, after a romantic afternoon picnic by one of upstate Maine's most scenic lakes, Matt went to his computer and quickly typed in a page. The printer hummed and I watched curiously as Matt stood by the machine with barely suppressed excitement.

He walked over to me with the page trembling in his hand.

"What is it, Matt?" I asked, taking the piece of paper.

"I couldn't have done it without you," he said. "You truly are my inspiration. My muse. I'm dedicating this book to you."

I looked down at the paper and saw the simple words that carried more meaning than anyone could ever guess. A simple dedication that meant more to me than anything:

for johanna

43

Matt had gone out for his morning run.

I shuffled sleepily into the kitchen where, as usual, he had made a pot of coffee for me before leaving. As I took down a mug from the cabinet and poured the coffee, I stared out the little kitchen window. On a bough of green buds a robin was tilting its head from side to side. I put the coffeepot back on the burner and reached over the sink to open the window. A soft breeze blew in, carrying with it the faint smell of flowers. I stood there for a moment, basking in the sunlight and the scent of spring, thinking how good life could be.

I glanced up at the clock.

Matt wouldn't be back for another hour. I wished he was there to share the moment with me.

Lately I had grown so used to his presence that I could hardly bear to be parted from him. It was silly, really. After all, we were together virtually all the time. Still, I found myself overcome with loneliness whenever we were apart. The depth of my feelings for him surprised and sometimes even frightened me. I tried not to think about what I would do without him. Yet the thought that he might abandon me crept up unbidden from time to time.

He had never given me a single reason to doubt his love. If anything, these last few weeks had been the sweetest of all. I guess I was thinking that it all seemed too good to be true. I tried to conceal my insecurities from him as best I could, but I couldn't help but be afraid. What if his book was a success? What if he became famous? Would he still want me? Or would he cast me aside and seek his inspiration somewhere else?

Would someone else be his muse?

I chased the thoughts from my mind. It was too beautiful a day to worry.

I carried my coffee into the living room, picked up the remote and turned on the television.

It was then that I saw it.

I don't know how I could possibly have missed it.

I must have been over that section of rug a hundred times, but there it was: a dark rust-red stain about the size of a quarter.

Blood.

Clay's blood.

I felt my heart skip a beat and a shudder passed through my body as if a window had been thrown open in my conscience, letting in the cold wind of guilt I'd so successfully blocked out the past few weeks. It was like something out of Poe or Macbeth: the stain of sin that kept reappearing, no matter how thoroughly you tried to wash it away.

I checked the clock on the VCR. Matt wasn't due back for another forty-five minutes. I hoped it was time enough to get the stain up before he returned. I had already decided not to tell him about it. Not when things were going so well. Besides, there was no point in both of us being upset.

I retrieved a pail of hot water and bleach from the kitchen and, along with a stiff brush, knelt down and proceeded to scrub away at the spot on the floor. It was tough going. The stain was as stubborn as the man who'd left it. I had to cut away some of the rough fibers with a scissors and pour bleach directly on the remainder of the spot.

In the end I was certain that only I could see the faint discoloration and then only because I knew where it was. The rug was just a bit lighter where the blood had been, the nap just an eighth of an inch shorter. I moved the coffee table a little farther from the couch so that one of the legs hid the spot entirely. Still, sooner or later, I would have to suggest to Matt that we get a new rug.

It was as I was picking up the scissors that I saw the billfold lying under the sofa. My first thought was that it must have been Matt's, but then a dark fear clutched at my heart. I reached under the sofa and pulled out the billfold. I knelt there, staring at it for a few moments, the leather scarred, stained, and worn, and I had no doubt whose it was. It must have fallen out of his jacket in the scuffle and somehow got kicked under the sofa.

My fingers, still shriveled from the hot water, trembled as I opened the wallet. The intimacy of actually holding something that belonged to the man we killed and buried was unnerving. For the first time since that fateful night, Clay became a real human being and not just an abstraction.

Mercifully, there were no photographs inside. How much harder it would have been if there were pictures of loved ones, a woman maybe, or even worse, children. Instead the plastic sleeves held only his driver's license, insurance card, and the like. There was about sixty dollars in twenties, tens, and fives and an assortment of credit cards, some—I noticed—with different names.

I was flipping through these when a half dozen business cards slipped out onto the floor. I picked one up and read a terse no-nonsense message printed on the cheap stock:

Travis Clay
Private Investigator

There was a number that I took to be for a pager, though I didn't recall seeing him wearing one. The card offered no more information.

I stared at the card as if it were written in hieroglyphics. Could the man we had killed really have been a private investigator? Matt had said he was an ex-con. But ex-cons couldn't become private investigators, could they? Maybe Clay was a private investigator before he went to prison. Maybe the card was fake. After all, he had a collection of credit cards bearing different names. Were they aliases or were the cards simply stolen?

I looked at the card declaring him to be a private investigator again. Maybe he used it to lure his victims into his trust before he killed them. I quickly thumbed through the other business cards. None of them bore his name. If Clay was even his name. I remembered the night I had met him at the Redwood Inn. He had left me the matchbook with his number. I remembered how later that same night he had called the chalet and seemed glad when I told him I was leaving. At the time I just figured he wanted me out of the way so he could torment Matt. But what if he had been trying to protect me?

All I knew about the man was what Matt had told me. Was it possible that Matt had been lying?

No—

I couldn't allow myself to think that.

I wouldn't.

I don't know how long I knelt there. Long enough for Matt to return. I heard the sound of his keys jingling as he ran up the drive. I gathered the cards, shoved the billfold back under the sofa, and returned the pail and scrub brush to the kitchen just as Matt put his key in the lock of the front door.

"Johanna?" he called out. "Are you up?"

I came out of the kitchen and saw him closing the door. He was wearing an old gray sweatshirt cut off at the sleeves and a pair of red cotton running shorts that showed off his lean, muscular legs. His dark hair fell boyishly over his forehead and the outdoors had brought the color up in his cheeks. He looked strong and young and impossibly handsome. He smiled so happily that my heart ached. How could I possibly have suspected him?

"There you are," he said cheerfully. "Look what I've brought you." He held out his hand. "I found them blooming out back. I thought you might like them."

I stared at the yellow daffodils and felt my knees go weak. I put my hand up to the doorjamb to steady myself.

Act natural, I told myself. *This doesn't prove anything.*

"Johanna?" Matt asked curiously.

He took a step forward.

I forced myself to smile. "They're beautiful."

I took the flowers and Matt circled a powerful arm behind me, pulling me toward him. He kissed me and there was something different in his kiss. It was harder, fiercer, more demanding. I could feel him beneath his shorts, his strength and his arousal frightening me.

"What's the matter?" he asked, a look of hurt on his face. "You're so stiff and cold."

"Am I?" I answered, suddenly aware of the tension in my body.

"Yes."

"I'm sorry," I said softly.

I tried to remember every acting lesson I'd ever taken. I always had trouble with love scenes. To me there was nothing more difficult than to kiss a complete stranger with passion, to melt in his arms and blend your breath with his, to dissolve into that state of oneness where you lost yourself totally to another. It was the moment of greatest vulnerability and it demanded the greatest act of trust. There was no greater challenge for an actress.

Yet I knew I had to summon up the ability to meet that challenge now or everything would be lost. The director would yell "cut," the lights would come up, the scene would be over. I would have lost the part again. I drew on the energy from all the auditions I'd ever gone on, all the workshops I'd ever taken, all the parts I'd ever lost—all the disappointment, pain, and rejection I'd suffered and concentrated them into one last desperate act of passion upon which everything depended.

I threw my arms softly around Matt's neck. "Is this better?" I murmured.

When our lips finally parted, I could tell by the look on Matt's face that I had won the part once and for all.

"Much better." He grinned.

"Good. Now why don't you run upstairs and take a quick shower." I held up the daffodils. "Meanwhile, I'll put these in some water."

I gave Matt a playful pat on his backside as he turned and headed up the stairs.

I walked stiffly into the kitchen, feeling the smile dying on my face. Mechanically, I set about looking through the cabinets for something in which to put the flowers. I found an old wine carafe, its label long removed, under the sink and filled it with water. I placed the bright yellow flowers inside and arranged them prettily before bringing them out to the living room.

Matt had come down by then. He was wearing a light blue pullover and a pair of jeans. His hair was still wet from the shower and stood in tiny spiky curls all over his head like a dark halo.

"They look nice," he said, pointing to the daffodils on the dining room table. "Really liven up the place."

He was eating a bowl of cereal and I was sipping anxiously at a cup of black coffee.

"I thought maybe I'd take the day off," he announced between spoonfuls of Cheerios. "We could drive up to the lake. It must be beautiful today. There's a field of wildflowers usually in bloom around this time of year. It's quite a sight."

"No," I said, a little too quickly. Matt looked at me quizzically. "What I mean is maybe you should push forward on your novel the next couple of days. It's almost done, right? Why not finish it and get it over with? Then we can take all the time we want."

Matt seemed amused. "I don't believe it," he said. "You're actually asking me to write?" He feigned suspicion. "Have you been talking to my editor? Are you two in cahoots or something?"

"No, nothing like that. I just think that since you're so close to the end and the writing is going so well—it is going well, isn't it?"

"Better than it ever has," he said, looking at me over his glass of orange juice.

"Then why not just go through with it?"

"Maybe you're right," he said, putting down his glass. "You know, if I were the suspicious type I might think you just wanted to get away from me for a while."

"Don't be silly." I laughed a little too shrilly. "I only want you all to myself—no novel in the way. The wildflowers can wait for a couple of days."

"Okay," Matt said enthusiastically, clinking his spoon against his bowl. "So be it. On to the finish."

I cleaned up while Matt settled down behind his computer. I brought him a fresh cup of coffee, careful not to appear to be looking at the screen.

"Where are you going?" he said, turning around in his seat before I'd gotten halfway to the door.

"Just outside for a bit," I said, trying hard to sound natural. "I want to take a walk. It's such a beautiful day."

I expected him to object. Instead, he just smiled.

"Okay. Have fun."

I opened the front door, cringing at the telltale *swoosh* it made, certain that would be his cue for calling me back. I heard only the *clickety-clack* of his keyboard. I stepped outside, hardly believing I'd gotten so far, ready at any moment to hear him say my name. I closed the door softly behind me and leaned against it, my heart thumping wildly in my chest. I could hardly believe my luck. I'd made it out.

I took a couple of deep breaths.

Then I headed for the shed.

I didn't have any time to lose.

I had slipped the little key off of Matt's key ring while he was writing. Now I worked it into the lock on the shed. I stepped inside and smelled the fertile, oily darkness. I hadn't been in here since that awful night we had buried Clay. I tried not to look at the spot in the middle of the shed where the earth still looked newly tamped down. I walked close to the walls, as if Clay's hand might thrust itself through the soil and grab me by the ankle.

I found the long-handled shovel where Matt had left it, standing against some stacked bags of peat moss.

I grabbed it quickly and hurried out of the shed, closing the door behind me.

The words of her poem were singing eerily through my head as I walked toward the place where the woods rose about twenty yards from the back of the chalet.

Look for me whenever
green comes to the hills
for all that he's left of me
are the bright daffodils

I found the spot easily. The daffodils were crowded in a dense patch in a clearing among the trees at the top of a little bluff. They wagged their heads merrily in the sunlight as if glad to see me. As I stepped among them, they seemed to step out of my way, welcoming me among them. I saw the place where Matt had cut away the flowers he had brought me that morning. I could almost hear the other flowers bemoaning the rape of their friends.

"I'm sorry," I said to them. "But I have to know."

The wind rose again and the flowers nodded sympathetically.

I lifted the spade and plunged it into the soil.

I dug until my back ached and my arms and legs were sore. I had grown somewhat out of shape in the last several months and I had to take several breaks to catch my breath and rest my protesting muscles. During one such break I stared at my hands and saw two angry red blisters opening up between both of my thumbs and forefingers. This was insane, I thought, as I dumped each shovelful of earth out of the deepening hole. What was I looking for? And what would I do if I even found it? There was nothing here. I was just letting my imagination get the better of me. Still, I forced myself back to the work. I don't know how long I was out there—several hours at least—when I heard Matt's voice calling from a distance.

I threw the shovel down, cleaned myself off as best I could, and took a circular route through the woods so that I approached the chalet from another direction.

I saw Matt standing by a small rock garden, looking the other way. He called my name again.

"Matt!" I shouted.

He turned around and I waved.

"There you are," he said. "I've been calling for the last five minutes. God, look at you. Where in the world were you?"

"Just rambling around in the woods."

Matt took hold of my wrists and turned my hands over.

"What happened here?" he asked, holding my hands up and examining the raw blisters peppered with dirt.

"I . . . was climbing a tree," I said, my mind frantically trying to come up with some kind of plausible excuse for the wounds. "I guess I'm out of practice."

"Climbing a tree?" he said incredulously. "I never knew you were such a tomboy. Well, no matter. You better get them washed before they get infected."

As we walked back to the chalet, Matt apologized for losing track of the time.

"That's okay," I said. "I guess I kind of lost track of time myself."

"Yes," he said simply. "I suppose we both did."

When we got back to the chalet, I went upstairs to clean up and Matt started fixing dinner. It was still a little early for dinner, but we had both missed lunch and Matt said he was famished. After a shower and change of clothes, Matt carefully cleaned my blistered hands with peroxide and applied fresh, cool Band-aids to the now-burning wounds.

"There," he said, satisfied with his handiwork. "That should do the trick."

That night at dinner Matt's spirits were unusually high. He talked enthusiastically about the book, returning to New York, maybe even taking a vacation some place warm. I tried to match his enthusiasm, but it was difficult, and sure enough, Matt eventually sensed my uneasiness.

Matt glanced up at me. "That's odd," he said.

"What?"

"I would think you would be hungry." He swirled fettucine around his fork and popped it into his mouth as if to emphasize his point.

"I guess it was all the activity today. I must have overdone it."

"Did you have fun out there?" he asked. "Climbing trees, and all?"

"Yes." I was anxious to change the subject. "How did the writing go today?"

"Very well. I can see the end coming up at last. Just a few more twists and turns and I should be there. It's been a long, strange trip. But definitely worth it."

"That's good," I said, as convincing as I could.

"What's wrong, Johanna?" Matt asked, his brow furrowing. "You don't seem quite yourself. You seem—I don't know—preoccupied."

"I'm sorry," I said, lifting a forkful of fettucine to my lips as if to eat it and then putting it back down on my plate. "I think I'm getting a migraine."

"A migraine? I didn't know you got migraines. You've never mentioned it."

"I don't very often, but when I do, it's usually pretty awful."

Matt pushed his chair back. "I'll go get you some aspirin."

"We're all out," I said. I'd flushed a half bottle of aspirin down the toilet, leaving two or three for authenticity, while Matt was boiling the pasta. "And, they don't usually work. I need prescription medication. I have an empty bottle in my room. I don't have any refills on it, but you can usually persuade the pharmacist to give you a couple of extra pills to tide you over until you can get a new prescription."

Matt looked at his watch.

"There's a drugstore in town," Matt said, almost to himself. He looked up at me. "It'll take awhile to get there and like everything else, it closes rather early. If I hurry I can probably make it."

"Would you, Matt, please?" I said, putting my hand up to shield my eyes, as much to pretend the light hurt them as to conceal the desperation I was sure was showing in them. Anything, I thought, anything. Just get him out of the house for a while longer.

"No problem, sweetheart," he said, already up, and leaning over to kiss me on the top of the head. He grabbed a light coat from the hook by the door and fished his keys from his pocket. "I'll be back as soon as I can."

I hardly waited for his Jeep to clear the long gravel drive before I ran out the door to the back of the house and up the little hill to where the bed of daffodils lay in ruins.

I picked up the shovel and ignored the pain in my ruined hands, digging furiously in the hole I had started earlier. I scooped out shovelful after shovelful of soft dark earth, the sweat beading on my brow, when finally I heard the metal edge of the blade strike something with a sharp clang. I dug around the smooth object, trying to loosen it enough to pry it up. It was tough going, but finally I was able to wedge the shovel underneath what looked like a large white stone stained yellow with dirt and age. I stood on the shovel blade and felt it sink deep into the earth. Then I used the handle to lever up whatever was buried inside the hole. The object gave a satisfying lurch, and with one final effort it came free from the surrounding earth with a deep sucking sound.

I leaned forward and stared into the hole to see what I'd unearthed.

The smooth object had rolled over and the yellowed stone looked back at me from the bottom of the hole.

It gazed up mournfully through large empty eye sockets, but its jaw of broken teeth, filled with earth and worms, was opened wide in a silent guffaw.

I stared in terrified fascination at the skull. My mind screamed at me to run, but I couldn't move. I knelt instead at the edge of the hole and reached down to remove a delicate glittering charm from around the separated vertebrae that had once been a woman's neck. The thin chain broke easily and the charm came away in my hand. I stared down at the single name scripted on it elegantly in gold.

Melpomene.

44

The password.

I knew the password to Matt's computer.

Or, to be more accurate, I knew exactly where to find it.

I dropped the charm in the hole and started running for the chalet as quickly as I could. I stumbled twice before reaching the door, nearly throwing myself against it. I slammed the door shut behind me, not bothering to take the time to lock it. Matt had the key anyway. Gasping for breath, I went directly to the wall of books, my eyes desperately scanning the dozens of titles lined neatly on the shelves.

Where was it?

There were too many books, goddamn it.

I was never going to find it.

I forced myself to slow down. He must have them in some kind of order.

No, dammit. No.

They were shelved randomly.

How did he find anything?

I could feel my heart beating at the back of my throat.

Please, please let me find it.

I must have passed over it at least three times before it registered.

There, on the second shelf from the bottom, I found what I was looking for. A dictionary of Greek mythology.

Sitting at Matt's desk, I turned on the computer and thumbed through the index while I waited for the password prompt to flash onto the screen. I looked in the index under the muses and flipped the pages until I found the entry.

Matt had already written four books. He had told me that Ariel was his dead fiancée. He had lied. She was his fourth muse: Melpomene. He was now working on his fifth book. I counted across the list of names until I came to the fifth muse.

Erato. The muse of erotic poetry.

I typed in the name.

Sure enough, the light on the hard drive lit up and the machine made a satisfied buzzing sound. A moment later the screen flashed sky blue and I was staring at a white scroll box with a list of chapter numbers.

I picked one at random and felt the bottom fall out of my world.

It was all there.

I opened file after file, glancing only briefly at each, enough to confirm my worst fears.

He had called me his inspiration, his Muse. Sure enough, everything that had happened up to now had been faithfully recorded in the pages of his "novel." It wasn't as if he'd only used me as a resource. My life had become the story itself. Every word, every emotion, every intimacy. A wave of nausea crashed over me. His violation of me had been calculated, obscene, and absolute.

Was this all our relationship had been to him: material for a novel?

I remembered his words to me only a couple of days before: *I am dedicating this book to you.*

On instinct I reached above the computer to the shelf containing his other novels. I looked at the dedication pages. Funny, I had never noticed them before. I suppose not many people do, unless you know you are mentioned beforehand.

Marsha.

Diane.

Sandy.

Ariel.

Each book was dedicated to a different woman.

Frantically, I scrolled down the list of chapters until I came toward the end. I called the files up one after another until I found what I was looking for. The one in which Clay's death was described. It, too, was all there. The argument, the scuffle, the shooting, the burial. He had recorded it all faithfully, right down to the letter.

Was he mad?

How did he expect to get away with this?

I was still staring in disbelief at the screen when I heard the front door close softly behind me.

"Not bad, huh?"

I swung around in the desk chair to see Matt standing in the doorway, a big grin plastered across his face. He stepped inside the chalet and gently closed the door behind him. He nonchalantly threw his keys on the little table under the mirror, shucked off his coat, and hung it up on the hook by the door. Under his arm was something wrapped in a brown paper bag.

He had not been gone long enough to drive to town, never mind go to the pharmacy.

"Matt, what the hell's the meaning of this?"

"Oh, I think it's painfully obvious by now, Johanna. Don't you? If not, I'm in big trouble. If you don't get it at this point, the readers certainly won't."

I didn't like the look in his eyes. He was watching me as if I were an actress in a play, watching with a critic's eye every gesture, every nuance of voice and expression.

"This is all some kind of sick game to you, isn't it?"

"Not a game, Johanna," he said. "Art."

"You call this art?" I asked, pointing back to the computer. "You've stolen my life. Our life."

"I'm sure you've heard the expression at one time or another that 'life imitates art.' " He frowned. "Or is it 'art imitates life'?"

I had gotten up from the desk and moved to where I had a clear line to the door. Either Matt didn't notice or—even scarier—he didn't care.

"This isn't art," I said. I figured the longer I could engage him in conversation, the more chance I had of distracting him and giving myself an opportunity to escape. It was my only hope.

Matt laughed. "Everyone's a critic. You know, I was wondering how long it would take you to figure out the password. I certainly gave you enough hints with all that talk about inspiration and muses. I like to keep my novels under five hundred pages, so I couldn't wait around forever. I hoped finding Clay's wallet under the couch would help jar you enough to put two and two together."

He pulled up the sleeve of his shirt, revealing the bandage on his left forearm.

"The blood on the carpet was mine, incidentally. The only thing is the place reeked of bleach when I came back. Didn't you think I'd smell it? Oh well, that's the kind of detail most readers don't pick up on anyway."

Matt shrugged. He walked to the table and pulled a bottle of champagne out of the paper bag. I hadn't seen the two elegant champagne flutes or the corkscrew until that moment.

"A little celebratory bubbly," he said, twisting off the foil wrapper, and inserting the corkscrew. The bottle gave a soft pop and Matt expertly guided the foaming champagne into the flutes. "Courtesy of the Redwood Inn."

"And Clay?" I asked. It was already too late to hope that Matt would let me live. I already knew too much. I might as well know it all. And Matt seemed more than eager to satisfy my curiosity. "He wasn't a serial killer after all. He was a private investigator. He was on to you, wasn't he? You killed an innocent man."

My eyes took a quick inventory of the room, looking for a possible weapon. I saw nothing that might serve the purpose but the fireplace poker and the heavy champagne bottle. To get to either of them, I would have to get past Matt.

"He really wasn't innocent," Matt said. He seemed to be relishing the chance to explain the dark secrets of his craft. "He was a private investigator all right, but a crooked one. A seedy bastard. A real bottom feeder." He laughed. "You see, it's true he was blackmailing me, but not for my knowledge of what he was doing. Rather for what I was doing. I've been trying to kill him off for the past three books."

"You killed them, didn't you?" I said, knowing perfectly well the answer. Could I make it up the stairs to my room, lock the door, climb out the window—and then . . . what? "The names in the books. The dedications. You killed them all."

"Every last one of them," Matt said. "I pride myself on my research, you know. Marsha was my first. She was a runaway I picked up in Times Square. She was a sweet little thing, but altogether too easy. All she wanted was to get off the streets. She got me out of bussing tables at the rib joint though. Sold my first novel after I left her strangled in a flophouse down in the Bowery. Then there was Diane. She was just the opposite. A cold-hearted call girl with dollar signs in her eyes. Six-foot-three, she made a grand a night. Can you believe that? She had a secret passion for rough sex, though. I told her exactly what I was going to do to her from the start, but she thought it was just part of the game. They'll never find all of her body."

Matt gazed off into the distance, a bemused look on his face. I leaned my weight toward the door and his eyes snapped back to the present.

"Sandy. Now there was a real bitch. She was a concert cellist with the Philharmonic. She nearly drove me crazy. She was fucking around on me—on me—of all people. Still, there was something about her that kept me coming back. I guess you could say I was obsessed with her." Matt reached into his pocket and pulled out what looked like a piece of small bone. "In fact I keep a piece of her with me to this day.

"And then, of course, there was Ariel. I met her in an Internet chatroom. A prim and proper society woman, married to one of the richest men in New York. She wrote poetry. Haiku, of all things. Perfectly horrible. On top of that she was old. Almost fifty. But she didn't ask for much. Just someone to pay her a little attention. Read her dreadful poems, fuck her tired cunt. In return she took me to the finest restaurants, bought me the most expensive clothes, put me up in the poshest of hotels. She paid me well to keep quiet about our affair. By the time I was through with her, I must have earned over three hundred thousand dollars.

"I sank most of it into this place. Our secret love nest. Then I told her I was going to her husband anyway. She committed suicide right upstairs in your bathroom. A truly poetic gesture. The most poetic thing about her, I'm afraid. Such devotion. I couldn't let it go unrewarded. So I buried her right here on the property. Under the daffodils she wrote about in that wretched piece of doggerel. Poetic justice, don't you think?"

Keep him talking, I told myself desperately. No matter what, no matter how horrible, keep him talking.

"I think she deserved more than that," I said. "I think they all did."

Matt feigned shock. "Why I preserved the best part of each of them. Their stories. As they say, everyone has a novel in them. Or at least a part to play."

We were coming to the end of this story. There was only one last thing to ask. I had to know the truth.

"And what part did Cindy play?"

"Simple." Matt shrugged. "She was a convenient plot point. I needed someone to die at that point in the book to keep the reader's interest. I had a serial-killer novel going and nobody was getting murdered. It was a real problem. So I drove back to New York, rented a room, and started calling her. I told her I needed to meet with her. About you. She was reluctant, of course, but I finally convinced her that I would leave you alone for good if she'd only agree to hear my side of the story. If not, I would start calling you directly. She was afraid if that happened you'd go back to me for certain.

"She was the one that told the cab driver to stop at that park in Chinatown. That's where I told her to meet me. I would have liked to come up with something a little more imaginative than a simple gunshot to the side of the head, but I was pressed for time. Besides, it would have thrown off the whole balance of the book if I'd killed her in too unique a way. Still and all, I would have liked to do something special with her. She would have made a great sixth muse."

Matt waved his hand in the air. "Aah, what's written is written. Anyway, it was the perfect device to get you to come back. I'm afraid nothing else would have been emotionally powerful enough. Putting your personal feeling aside for a moment and looking at the dramatic aesthetics of the situation, it really worked out great, don't you think? Got you to come back and put a murder smack dab in the middle of the story. Two birds with one stone. It seldom happens. I'm really proud of that twist. Pure inspiration."

For a blinding instant I forgot the danger I was in, I forgot about escaping, I forgot about everything. In that instant I knew nothing but sheer hatred and rage for the monster in front of me. I felt my hands curl into fists and my body tense to throw itself at him. I had come around the sofa and was walking toward him. What he said next stopped me in my tracks.

"And I have you to thank for her," Matt said.

Just as suddenly as it came over me the rage drained from my body.

He was right. If it wasn't for me, Cindy would never have been murdered. It was me who had brought this monster into my life.

Into hers.

She had tried to protect me from him and she had paid with her life.

"So that's all Cindy was to you," I said, fighting against the urge to give in, to surrender to the inevitable. "A plot point?"

"Don't underestimate a plot point," Matt said, lifting his finger as if giving a seminar on the structure of the popular novel. "It's the hinge upon which the whole story opens up. Have you ever read Syd Field's guides to screenwriting? Absolutely brilliant. I owe everything I've done to him."

"Now I suppose it's my turn," I said, my voice sounding surprisingly steady, even to my own ears. "You're going to kill me, too."

"Oh God, no," Matt said. "Not yet anyway. We still have the most important part to go. You have to help me with the ending. Endings are funny things. I never plan them. Or if I do, they also change, take on a life of their own. They almost seem to write themselves and more often than not they come as a complete surprise, even to me. I love a surprise ending. I think most readers do. What about you? Come on, Johanna. How is this story going to end? I'm depending on you. Even more important, my readers are depending on you. Surprise me."

"You can't get away with this," I said, feeling my resolve to survive return. His arrogance had blown the last spark of defiance into a full-scale firestorm. "You must know that."

Matt looked amused. "And why not?"

"Because people know I'm up here, that's why. If I disappear, there'll be inquiries. The police will come looking for me."

He had made a big mistake not taking me a moment ago. I was going to fight him every step of the way. I was not going to die. I would escape, not only for myself, but for the others.

For Marsha.

For Diane.

For Sandy.

For Ariel.

For Cindy.

And for all the other women who would become victims in his future books. I would not be just another one of his stories. There would be no more stories. I was going to be his end.

"I don't think there's much chance of that. I doubt if you told very many people where you were going. You pretty much just picked up and left on a whim. The few people you did tell were given the vaguest of descriptions. My guess is that you told them you were going to stay with a writer who lived somewhere in upstate Maine. If you used my name at all, chances are they forgot it as soon as you said it. On top of that, the chalet is in a rural area with no official name. Even if you did mention the surrounding towns, which I doubt, do you think anyone will remember?"

He was right, I thought. Dammit, he was right.

Still, there must be a weak point somewhere in his well-orchestrated plot. There always was. If I could only find it, maybe I could get him to alter the story just enough to give me a chance.

"But since I came back," I argued, hoping to prick his smug self-confidence, to plant just one tiny seed of doubt, "you've been taking me all over town. Surely someone will remember me with you."

"Have you taken a good look at yourself lately, Johanna? Have you forgotten? If the police somehow traced you here, they would be looking for a brown-haired woman with aquamarine eyes. You are now a blonde, with brown eyes and glasses. Johanna Brady never came back. It didn't work out. She wasn't my muse after all. I found another woman, a woman no one is reporting missing because she doesn't exist.

That's you, Johanna, the woman who no longer exists. And everyone in town who saw me with another woman bearing no resemblance to Johanna Brady will back me up."

"You bastard," I muttered. "You rotten bastard."

"But not to worry. The chance that you will be traced back here at all is highly unlikely. You see, no one even knows I live here. I've kept it very secret, as you've no doubt found out by now. I don't ever use my literary name here. No mail, no credit cards, no phone numbers, no banking is ever done under the name of Matthew Lang. I conduct all my business strictly in the city. To the folks around here I'm just Matt Jablonsky. You might say that my real name is the perfect alias."

Suddenly it hit me like a bolt of lightning.

I had him.

Dammit, I had him.

"What about your editor?" I said, not bothering to hide the triumph in my voice. "She called. I talked to her. She knows you live here."

Matt laughed so long and hard I thought it must be an act.

It wasn't.

His eyes were twinkling with genuine amusement.

"That wasn't my editor. That was my mother. I told her you might be the one. I told her that I wanted to impress you. So she called with a little white lie about how great my novel was, how successful I was bound to be. You can't really blame Mother. She truly does believe I'm destined for greatness. She just loves everything I do."

Oh my God, I thought. That was it. That was my last chance.

I had nothing left.

I could feel myself sag under the weight of his story. I never had a chance.

Matt was smiling, a look of pride on his face, like a little boy who had done good.

"I don't believe this," I said dully. "You had this all planned from the beginning."

Matt picked up the champagne flutes and handed one to me.

I took it.

"It's important to have a good outline," he explained. "Sure, you have to improvise some along the way, but you have to know the general direction of the story or things can get really messy. In the end, it all must seem predetermined, even if you didn't see the end coming. Well, I guess that just about ties up all the loose ends, don't you think? Unless you can think of something else. If there's one thing I've learned over the years: readers hate loose ends."

"You're not an artist," I said. "You're insane."

Matt raised his eyebrows.

"Insane? Why, Johanna, every artist is insane." He raised his glass. "Now, will you please join me in a glass of champagne to toast my new novel? After all, you're the star. My success is your success. I've given the title a lot of consideration. Come, let's drink to *Muse.*"

45

———•———

I lifted the flute halfway to my mouth as if to drink, rolled my eyes back in their sockets, and let my knees buckle.

Matt leaned down to grab me under the arm and that's when I brought the glass around and smashed it into his left eye. He yelped with pain, dropping his own flute, his hand reaching automatically for his wounded eye. He was still half crouched from trying to catch me, and staggered blindly forward, trying to pick the thin shards of glass from around his eye.

I didn't so much as think. I lifted my knee and caught him right on the bridge of the nose. He grunted and fell heavily to his knees, both hands covering his face now, blood spurting between his fingers. I pushed past him, grabbed the heavy magnum bottle of champagne from the table, and swung it at the side of his head. The bottle didn't break, but it had hit Matt squarely. He toppled over sideways onto the floor. He tried to right himself, his hands slipping on the wet floor, and fell over a second time.

I didn't waste any more time watching him. I ran for the door, grabbing the keys from the table, and fumbled with the lock.

I didn't dare turn back. My heart was already fluttering out of control. I expected to feel him grab me at any moment. After what seemed like an eternity, my hopelessly trembling hands were able to turn the simple dead bolt and I pulled the door open. I was hyperventilating, fighting to catch my breath, but the cool spring air instantly cleared my head and gave me a second wind.

I hadn't even felt the pain in my knee from where I'd struck Matt, but I felt it as I half stumbled down the stairs, limped down the path, and lost my balance on the loose stones of the driveway. The keys flew from my hand as I tried to break my fall. I searched frantically on the ground for them, losing precious seconds. Luckily the automatic floodlamps mounted around the chalet were blazing and I spotted the keys about a foot away at the base of a small ornamental shrub at the side of the walkway. Grabbing the key ring, I climbed painfully to my feet and staggered to the Jeep only twenty feet away.

I was no more than halfway there when the floodlamps suddenly went out, leaving me temporarily blinded. Behind me, I heard Matt's voice calling from the front door.

"That's it, Johanna," he cheered hoarsely. "You're doing just fine. Keep it up."

I turned to see him outlined in the doorway. He was standing crookedly, one hand still covering his eye, the other propped on the handle of an ax, which appeared to be all that was holding him upright.

It wasn't the sight of him standing there that terrified me so much, as his eerie, unrushed calm. He seemed far more in control of the situation than he should have been. What the hell did he know that I didn't?

I wasn't about to stand there and find out.

The Jeep was close enough now that I could see its dark shape highlighted by the lights shining from inside the house. The driver's side door was unlocked and I slid in the front seat even as I heard Matt's unsteady footsteps crunching across the gravel.

It took me three attempts, but on my fourth try I finally managed to stab the key into the ignition. I twisted it hard to the right. The engine made a harsh clicking sound, but did not turn over.

Turn over goddammit, I swore. Turn over!

I looked out the driver's side window. Matt was already halfway to the car, the ax cradled across his chest, limping steadily but unhurriedly down the drive.

I stamped on the accelerator and twisted the key again.

Nothing.

I looked out the driver's side window again, my heart pounding against my breastbone, and saw Matt about ten feet away. I slammed my palm down on the door console and felt around for the lock. I found it just as Matt yanked on the handle from outside.

I turned the key again and then again.

I felt the tears of frustration pouring down my cheeks and heard a gentle tap on the window.

Matt was standing outside. He mouthed the words *"open the door."*

Then I saw him lift the ax to his shoulder.

I flinched, threw my hands up, and shrank back in the seat as the ax hit the window. The glass bowed inward, frosted green and white, but didn't shatter. I couldn't see through it any longer, but I knew Matt would hit it again and the next blow would surely smash it to bits. I scrambled right across the console and prepared for the ax to strike when I saw the fire extinguisher mounted to the side of the door.

I reached back and yanked it free, fumbling with the pin, as the ax hit the window for the second time. A fine dust of sparkling glass covered me as Matt's arm reached through the empty window frame and undid the lock.

He leaned down and stuck his face in the window.

"A predictable scene, but obligatory nonetheless," Matt said amiably. "The first thing the heroine always does is run for the car. Of course, the antagonist has already disabled it. At this point he usually pulls the distributor cap or something from his pocket with a dramatic flourish. But to tell you the truth, I couldn't tell a distributor cap from an electric toothbrush. I just disconnected the battery cables.

"I hope you're not disappointed. But I need the car for later and I can't take the risk of doing it permanent harm. Now why don't you come back inside and let's have that celebratory champagne? It's all over, Johanna."

"Not yet, you sonofabitch." I squeezed the trigger of the fire extinguisher and sent a jet of white foam directly into his eyes. Matt dropped the ax and grabbed his face as if it were on fire. He was screaming with pain, weaving wildly up the path, and disappeared into the darkness.

I climbed back over the console, glass dust embedding itself in the palms of my hand. I jumped from the Jeep. I peered into the darkness for a moment, but could see no sign of Matt. I kept my eyes on the dark as I bent down to pick up the ax he had dropped and ran back to the chalet.

The first thing I did was grab the phone in the living room.

There was no dial tone.

I flicked at the receiver button and put the phone back to my ear. It was dead.

I ran to the kitchen, and tried pressing 911.

Nothing.

"Shit!" I screamed, and banged the receiver into the cradle so hard the whole phone came off the wall.

"Johanna, Johanna . . ." I heard Matt's voice coming up the path to the front door. "Wherefore art thou, Johanna?"

I felt my blood freeze. He was so close now that I could hear his labored breathing. I ran out of the kitchen and headed up the stairs to the loft. Matt was inside the chalet by now. I heard him slam the door shut behind him. I turned right and hobbled down the short hall to the locked door of Matt's bedroom. I lifted the ax and brought it down just above the doorknob. The wood splintered. I hit it again. My arms were aching in their sockets. I raised the ax one last time and nearly fell forward with the weight of it.

The door, half demolished, fell partially off its hinges.

I staggered inside.

The room was lit entirely by candles. Their flickering light gave the windowless walls a strange almost insubstantial quality. There was no furniture in the room at all, except for what looked like a plain wooden table at the far end, upon which a stick of incense burned before a primitive statue of a large-breasted woman standing with her legs spread, giving birth to what looked like a full-grown man in a state of exaggerated erotic arousal.

Above the makeshift altar was a framed portrait of a woman with flowing blond hair, deathly pale skin, and bloodred lips. Her large blue eyes were both inviting and merciless.

But the weirdness of the scene gave way to the horror of the photographs to either side of the painting. There, in black and white, were the pictures of four women, their faces captured forever in death, their names engraved in fanciful script on tiny brass plates screwed into the wall beneath the photographs. And, beside them, there was a single empty frame. The brass plate beneath was engraved with the name *Johanna*.

"Come on," Matt whispered in my ear. "It's time."

He took the ax from my hand, let it fall to the floor, and led me unprotestingly back downstairs.

I sat on the couch, numbed by what I had seen, yet some small part of my brain still worked in overdrive, trying to think of a way out of this.

Matt's nose looked as if it might be broken. It was swollen, red, and bent ever so slightly to one side. Dried blood rimmed his left nostril. His left eye was completely closed, a golf-ball-sized mass of raw tissue. I wondered idly if I'd blinded him. The net result was that it distorted his otherwise handsome face into a grotesquely comical caricature.

Matt had retrieved two new champagne flutes from somewhere. He picked up the bottle from the floor and poured what was left into our glasses. He handed me a flute. I watched the bubbles clinging to the side of the glass, then let go and hurry toward the top.

Matt touched his flute to mine.

"No tricks this time," he said softly. "That was all very clever before, but I won't put up with that again." He delicately touched his eye and winced at the pain. "I can't afford to lose my eyesight." He nodded his head toward me and lifted his glass. "To my Muse."

I wasn't certain whether he meant me or the novel.

I watched him sip his champagne. I didn't move.

"Drink," he said. "For luck."

"You don't have to do this," I said. "You're a talented man. It doesn't have to end like this."

Matt shook his head. "That's the beauty of it, Johanna. I don't know how it's going to end. Do you?"

"I think I should survive. No one likes to read a novel where the heroine dies at the end. They'll feel cheated."

Matt threw his head back and laughed heartily. I can't say I wasn't glad to see that it caused him no small amount of pain.

"Very good, Johanna. Very good. Though I'm not sure I wholeheartedly agree. Remember *Looking for Mr. Goodbar* for example?"

I had never read the novel. I only knew the movie version. I still remembered the shock I'd felt during that final scene.

"You see," he said, "readers expect the heroine to live. They can be a little disappointed if she dies. But the emotional impact of her death can be so disturbing that the image of it stays with the reader for a long time. It becomes almost mythic."

He reached into his pocket and pulled out a small vial of pills. He undid the top and shook two out into his palm.

"Here," he said, "I want you to take these. For your migraine."

"Thank you, but my headache is gone. I must have been mistaken. It wasn't a migraine after all."

"Really?" he said. "Well, I think you should take them, just in case."

I looked at the two plain white pills in the palm of his hand. "What are they anyway?"

"They're what I gave you when you were sick. In fact, they *made* you sick. At this dosage, they will put you out completely. I have to admit those scenes when you were ill were a little slow. But it was kind of my homage to *The Collector*. Have you ever read it?"

"No," I said.

"A great novel. By the way, the heroine dies at the end of that one, too."

"I'm not taking them," I said.

"Yes, you will," he said calmly. He reached into the cushion of his chair and pulled out Clay's gun.

"I thought you had buried that with the body," I said dumbly.

"Evidently not. I had a feeling it might come in handy. Now take the pills."

He laid them on the coffee table.

I knew my chances of getting out of this situation were slim. I also knew they were virtually none if I didn't mantain all my faculties. I had to be ready to take advantage of the least opportunity.

"You won't shoot," I said, playing a gamble. "It wouldn't make very interesting reading."

"Not to kill," he said, lowering the gun to my right leg. "But a wounded heroine can be very appealing. Not only does it ratchet up the odds against her surviving, but it plays into the reader's growing thirst for sadistic violence. Unfortunately for you, Johanna, the audience has become awfully jaded. They need even more pain and suffering to get that vicarious thrill."

"I don't believe you," I said. But a look into his eyes convinced me otherwise.

He cocked the gun. "Do you notice how in these situations they always cock the gun or dramatically flick the safety off?" Matt asked. "If you're going to shoot someone, why would you have the safety on? Of course, it's done for dramatic effect. It gives readers that one last moment to anticipate what's to come. It also allows the potential victim one last chance to be defiant. In real life, you wouldn't stand a chance. The person holding the gun would have it ready to fire from the very start. But I'd advise all fictional characters to rush the guy or gal with the gun. They always have the safety on during that first exchange. Unfortunately, this is real life. Now, I'm telling you for the last time. Take the pills."

I picked the pills up off the table and held them between my finger-tips. Whatever they would do to incapacitate me, it couldn't be worse than being shot in the legs.

I put the pills in my mouth.

"Use the champagne to wash them down," Matt said.

I took a sip of champagne, swallowed, and put the glass down.

"Very good," Matt said. "Now do it again. And this time swallow the pills. I'm not having any of that nonsense where you pretend to take the pills. It's been done a thousand times. No one will fall for it. Every reader worth his or her salt will guess you did that right off."

I had no choice. I took another sip of the champagne and washed the pills down.

"There," Matt said. "That's better."

"Now what?" I said.

"Now we wait. We just see what happens. Let the end surprise us."

"You're crazy," I said, already feeling a little woozy.

"Yes, yes," Matt said. "We've covered that already."

He sat back in his chair and watched me as he sipped his champagne. I considered rushing him while I still felt relatively strong, but figured my odds of surprising him weren't very good. I could feel whatever was in the pills begin to loosen my muscles, dull my nerves. My coordination seemed to be lost. The thoughts in my head were becoming disjointed. Even my sense of panic was receding.

The next thing I knew, Matt was carrying me up the stairs to my bedroom.

He laid me on the bed and began undressing me. I offered no resistance. He went to the closet and returned with a long white satin gown. With some difficulty, he was able to get the gown on my now completely unresponsive body. He was smoothing the cool fabric over my legs when, out of the corner of my eye, I caught sight of the gun on the night table where he'd put it down.

He stood up and I thought I'd lost my opportunity. But he turned to my dresser, where he stood for a moment, apparently choosing a bottle of perfume.

My arm felt like rubber lying next to me and it took every ounce of my will power to get it to respond. I watched Matt at the dresser. There was a mirror above his bent head. All he had to do was lift it and he'd see me. He was spraying perfume onto his wrist and sniffing it when my hand reached the butt of the gun.

My whole arm was so numb, I could barely feel it. My hand was at an awkward angle and I was afraid I would drop the gun. The damned thing felt like it weighed a hundred pounds. Ever so slowly I commanded my arm to lift the gun. The sheer effort had me soaking with sweat. I slipped my cold, unfeeling finger around the trigger just as Matt turned.

He was smiling as he came toward me, a purple bottle of Poison in his hand.

Fighting to regain consciousness, I knew I had no time left.

I wasn't sure of my aim, of my strength, of anything, except my will to survive.

"Die, you bastard," I growled.

I closed my eyes with the strain.

With all the strength I had left, I squeezed the trigger.

Matt took the gun from my hand.

"Too easy, Johanna," he said. "It would have been too easy."

He put the barrel an inch from my forehead and pulled the trigger.

The hammer clacked on an empty chamber.

"The gun's empty."

He started spritzing perfume over my body.

"Now," he said, "I'm going to give you what you've been waiting for."

He stood up and started undressing. The naked flesh of his lean, muscular body glowed in the light from the window.

He came toward me, holding something in his hands.

I caught the glitter of gold.

It was a necklace.

He gently lifted my head and worked the delicate clasp closed before settling me back on the pillow.

I felt the scripted golden charm against my chest as he bent to kiss me.

"Erato," he murmured.

And then there was nothing but darkness.

46

He came sometime in the night.

He appeared as he always did, dressed all in black, no more than a silhouette blacklit by the open door.

"So you've come, after all," I said softly. I was squinting into the darkness, the light behind him spreading out from behind his squared shoulders like wings. I hardly dared to trust my eyes. How could he have found me? Was it possible that I was only hallucinating his presence under the influence of the drug that Matt had given me?

No. No, he had come as he had always come. The one person who'd never abandoned me. I felt a flutter of hope come alive behind my breastbone, where my heart had missed a beat.

"Why do you seem so surprised?"

My voice was small in the darkness. "Everyone else has failed me."

"I'm not everyone else."

It was not just his voice, but the way he said it.

I lifted myself up on my elbows to get a better view and realized my mistake. The shoulders—I should have known from them alone—the shoulders were all wrong. Too broad and heavy. And the way he stood in the doorway, it was as if he was barring the exit. There was nothing ambiguous about the way he blocked the light: his dark form was brooding and malevolent.

My head started throbbing and I felt like weeping but I was too tired to weep. "I made a big mistake telling you what I feared the most."

"And what you most desired," Matt said.

He stepped inside the door and I lost him in the darkness.

"It was wrong," I said quickly.

"Is it wrong to be honest?"

I turned in the direction from which his voice had come. I strained my eyes, but could see nothing.

"It's dangerous."

"Yes, it's dangerous to reveal oneself," he said, sounding sympathetic. "But to live is dangerous."

"It doesn't have to be."

"It does if you want the starring role."

My eyes were growing accustomed to the darkness. I thought I could make out his form by the bureau. It seemed important to keep my eyes on him.

"Maybe I don't want the starring role," I said.

He chuckled.

It came from the other side of the room.

"It's a little too late for that now."

I turned my head quickly, the dull pain growing to a peak before subsiding.

"Can't we go back and rewrite the script?"

"In life, you don't get a chance to make revisions."

"But this is a story," I said hopefully. "Surely we can make some changes."

He sighed. "I'm afraid even a story has its own inevitable momentum. You can keep writing, but at a certain point the ending is inescapable."

I was squinting into the darkness now, trying to find him, his voice coming first from one direction and then the other, as if he were gliding around the room like a shadow, like a ghost.

"I wish we had more time," I pleaded.

"All stories must come to an end."

There was an unmistakable finality in his voice.

And a certain sadness.

"Still—"

"No, no, no," he cut me off, as if afraid he might be persuaded otherwise, in spite of himself. "It would be only filler. Too many lives— too many stories—are spoiled simply because their authors don't know when to let go. They fall in love with the characters they create. They know that a part of them will die when they stop writing."

"Do you love me?"

His voice was barely a whisper in the darkness. "Isn't it obvious?"

I no longer felt any fear.

I no longer felt anything.

"Are you going to kill me now?"

"Don't be silly. You're the last suspect."

"What are you talking about?"

"Isn't it obvious?" he said. "You were jealous of Cindy. She had everything you wanted: money, beauty, success. It wasn't fair. And, to top it all off, she had to go and sleep with Stephen. It was you who killed her in the park using Harry Krinkle's gun, which you stole from his apartment the night he took you home. Matt's invitation to return here was the perfect excuse to disappear before the police could figure it out. If they ever did."

"That's ridiculous," I said breathlessly, hardly able to comprehend the depth of his depravity, even after all I had learned him capable of—a depravity that would enable him to so grotesquely twist the truth. But why should I have been surprised? He was a murderer and a psychopath. He wasn't a writer. He was a liar. I could never do the things he said. Never. I wouldn't have hurt Cindy for anything in the world. Was this the way he intended to end this story? It wasn't enough that he would kill me, but he would write that I had killed Cindy. "You bastard! That's the most cockeyed thing I ever heard."

"Is it? It was your idea to change your looks, your identity. The one thing you didn't figure on was Clay. He wasn't fooled. He was Matt's friend and he knew there was something fishy about you. He kept track of you after you left Maine and followed you to New York. He checked into your background. He learned that what Sal had said was true. You did seduce him. He found out how you sabotaged the computer records at the investment firm, where you attemped to get Ms. Parker fired and wire over two million dollars to yourself in a double-blind account. The only problem was you couldn't touch the money until you had some excuse for having come into it.

"That's where Matt comes in. You were hoping his novel would be a success. Matt wasn't exactly wordly-wise in the ways of women. Most of his living and loving was done through his fiction. You would see to it that he fell madly, desperately in love with you. You drove him to distraction with your on and off again sexual advances. Your sad stories—the best acting you'd ever done—touched his heart. Your imagination inspired his writing. You would marry him, stay with him long enough to collect a fortune, and then leave.

"Clay was the only one who knew the truth. And he was going to tell Matt. So you arranged to meet him, hoping to buy him off. Unfortunately for you, he was an honest man. You got angry and dared him to come to the chalet. It would be your word against Matt's. You sent Matt out of the chalet on some errand or other. By the time he got there, you had already told Matt that Clay had tried to rape you, that a scuffle ensued and his gun had gone off, accidentally killing him.

"Matt wanted to report the incident, but you told him it could only destroy the both of you. You convinced him to bury Clay in the shed. But Matt couldn't live with it any longer. He was going to the police. So you had no choice but to get rid of Matt. The poem, the bones beneath the daffodils, the dead women, you made it all up yourself. You were going to blackmail him into silence. But Matt was an honorable man. He wouldn't be blackmailed. So you killed him."

The pounding in my head had stopped. I found myself almost hypnotized by the tale Matt was weaving, as if I was sitting on a chair in front of a fire, a cup of tea on the table beside me, lost in the climax of some hair-raising bestseller. I couldn't believe what I was hearing, and yet I couldn't stop listening. The way he had explained it no longer seemed so preposterous. After the initial shock of it, I had to admit it had even begun to make sense. Was it possible that I could have done the things he said? Could it have been me all along? Or were the aftereffects of the drug Matt had given me distorting my critical faculties?

"No one's ever going to believe that," I said uncertainly. "It's too far-fetched. The critics will say you copped out. Your readers will laugh at you."

Matt didn't say anything for a long time, as if seriously considering the merit of my argument.

"You're right," he agreed, surprising me. "No one will believe it."

He stepped back into the doorway, his body once again a one-dimensional silhouette in the light.

"Get out of bed," he said.

"I don't think I can."

"Of course you can."

"But the pills—"

"Have long worn off by now. Get up," he said firmly, but not unpleasantly.

As if in a dream, I pulled back the covers. He was right. My strength had returned. I swung my legs over the side of the bed and felt the floor under my bare feet. I was strangely calm. He reached out and I laid my naked hand in his black leather gloved one.

"Where are we going?" I asked.

"Come. I have a surprise for you."

We went down the stairs into the living room. It was dark except for the soft glow of Matt's computer screen. A sickeningly sweet smell filled the room that I couldn't identify. And then I knew what it was. There, slumped over in front of the computer, was . . . Matt.

I felt the room give a quick half-turn to the left and thought for sure I would pass out. I grabbed the table for support and forced myself to look again at the body in the chair. He looked as if he had fallen asleep while writing. Except for the fact that his eyes, visible from the way his head was turned, were wide open and staring. The blood that had splashed over his keyboard and screen had already begun to congeal.

My brain was working in overdrive, firing thoughts in every direction at once, each one missing its mark. What was going on here? What kind of game was this? Jesus, I had to remember, remember everything I did. Okay, maybe there were times when I blacked things out— unpleasant things, painful things—but that hadn't happened for years. That was all in the past now. I was in control of things. There was no way I could have killed Matt. And yet there he was—dead. Just like Cindy. And I was the link between the two.

I had loved Matt so much, had trusted him, had dedicated my life to him. And in the space of a few short hours that love had turned into a nightmare of hatred and terror that had forced me into a desperate struggle for survival. Could I have been pushed over the edge? Could I have killed him and blocked the whole thing from my consciousness?

"No, no, no!" I shouted the words, closing my eyes and holding my hands over my ears, barely able to listen to my own denial, afraid it might be a lie. "I didn't do it! I know I didn't do it."

I felt his gloved hands on my wrists, gently pulling my hands away. The soft leather caressed my cheeks, his thumbs massaging my temples, coaxing my eyes open as he stepped back into the shadows.

"Of course, you didn't," he said calmly. "Like you said, no one would believe it."

"What do you mean? I thought you said—"

He pointed to the coffee table upon which I could see a handwritten sheet of paper.

"Read it," he said.

I didn't want to go back to the computer desk and the body slumped in the chair. "Can I turn on the light?" I asked.

"No," he said sharply. He pointed to the coffee table.

There was a single candle in an elegant silver holder. As I walked closer, I saw a book of matches.

I lit the candle and held the letter close to the flickering light.

I cannot go on any longer. I am a fraud. The inspiration has died. I have nothing left. Everything I have written is false. My only regret is that I cannot erase its indelible mark from the world. The only act of contrition left in my power is to erase myself. For forty-plus years all I have managed to do is to disturb the peace and quiet. I will do so no longer.

—Matthew Lang

"My God," I said, staring in disbelief at the suicide note.

"It would be nice to believe that that's the way it ends, wouldn't it? A mad writer offs himself and the heroine lives happily ever after. But I'm afraid it's not that simple. There's still me. I've been the one big problem all along, haven't I?"

It was true. I hadn't thought of that. If Matt was dead, if he wasn't the man in black, who was behind the mask?

"Enough games," I said, throwing the letter down. "Who are you? And don't tell me that that question is off base."

"Nothing is off-base now," he said.

He took a step into the ring of light created by the flickering candle flame.

"Then you'll tell me who you are?" I said, wondering if this was just another of his tricks.

"No."

"What do you mean? I thought you said nothing was off base."

He beckoned me forward.

"Come look for yourself."

I took a step toward him. The figure in black did not move. I took another step. He stood there as if carved out of darkness. I expected him to turn, to run, to somehow stop me. I almost wished he would. That would have made it easier. Then I would have had an excuse not to know. But he wasn't going to make it easy for me.

I was close enough to touch him now. I could feel the raw animal strength radiating from his body. I was certain he could feel the excitement radiating from mine.

He was taller than I, solidly and powerfully built, and I had the unnerving and thrilling sense that he could destroy me as easily as a child pulls apart a flower.

I raised a trembling hand to his mask.

And let it fall.

My fingertips brushed the leather as if in a caress.

Shockingly, something stronger than my own will caused me to lean forward to kiss his lips.

For the first time I was close enough to see the eyes inside the mask. They shone warmly in the glow of the candle, the amusement dancing in their depths, sickening in its familiarity. They were the eyes of a friend, a confidante, a lover. The eyes of someone who knew the deepest secret locked inside your soul.

The word came in a whisper so intimate it might have been used after making love.

"Surprise . . ."

I stumbled back in horror.

He reached up and pulled the mask off. He was grinning from ear to ear, his eyes dancing with a mischievous merriment. He was bald, just a ring of dark curls circling his head, but there was no mistaking who it was.

"How?" I barely choked out the word. I pointed back to the body slumped at the computer, not daring to take my eyes away. My voice was rising to a pitch of hysteria. This couldn't be happening. "You're dead!" I said, nearly screaming the words. "You're sitting right there at the computer. I saw you myself."

"No," Matt said matter-of-factly. "I'm not dead."

I could feel myself losing it. I struggled to keep the blackness from claiming me, but it was rising swift and cold around the last vestiges of my sanity. I knew I wouldn't be able to hold on for long.

"How . . . I don't understand," I stammered. "Who . . . who is that?"

Matt walked past me to the computer, dropping the leather mask on the coffee table.

"Some guy I found jogging along the road. A tourist, I think. I killed him a couple of days ago, and he's getting kind of rank. I was hoping we could get this all over with soon. I've had him in the root cellar in a trunk packed with ice. Still, he's already started attracting flies."

He grabbed the dark curls and they came away easily in his hand. Underneath, the dead man's blond locks spilled in a wet tangle across his forehead. I realized now that the man looked nothing like Matt. The wig, the dim light, and my shock had contributed to the illusion.

Matt put the wig back on his own bald head. It lay crookedly on it like a curly beret.

"You see, Johanna," Matt said. "There never was a man in black. He was all a figment of your imagination. He's the bogeyman who crouched in the closet, the wicked witch who scratched at a little girl's window, the man with the hook-hand, lying under your bed. It's at the root of all our fears and our most potent stories. I suspect the very first storyteller told it to his fellow hunters as they sat huddled around the circle of light cast by the fire outside their cave. I imagine the shadows in the forests around that fire were filled with dark phantoms of one kind or another.

"As a defense, you turned him into something of a romantic figure, blending thanatos and eros, concocting the fantasy of a dark lover who would destroy you at the height of passion. It was that fantasy that I played upon, the fantasy you so carelessly revealed to me. Remember?"

"You're wrong," I said, "he's not a figment of my imagination. He exists. I've seen him. Not just here. He came to me before I even met you. He warned me about you, but I wouldn't listen."

Matt raised his eyebrows knowingly.

"If you say so," he said condescendingly.

His attitude angered me. Even more so did his belittling explanation of my dark visitor. Whoever it was who had come to me was not just some childhood fantasy or an atavastic fear of the dark. I was as sure of his reality as I was sure of mine, or Matt's, or anybody's. And suddenly I was seized with a strange sense of calm. For I was certain that whoever—or whatever—he was would not abandon me even now. If only he could find me. . . .

"So now what?" I said.

"You become my muse."

"Your what?"

"My muse," he repeated. "My inspiration." He had walked over to the table and placed the edge of his phony suicide note to the candle. As it burned toward his fingers, he threw it in the fireplace, contemplating it as it curled into a thin film of blackened ash. He turned back to me. "After all, that was the plan all along, wasn't it? Nothing has changed."

I felt a chill deep in my bones. The look on his face was calm and composed. I had seen that look some place before. It was the look of someone who had already made up his mind about something that would change my life forever and wouldn't hear another word. *It's for your own good, Johanna,* a voice inside my head repeated. *It's all for your own good.*

"No!" I shouted suddenly to silence the echo in my head. Matt looked startled and then somehow pleased.

He'd never get away with this. Never. "You can't keep me locked up here forever," I said defiantly. The fact that he apparently had no intention of killing me gave me the courage to threaten him. Even more, the smug way he assumed he could keep me a prisoner for the rest of my life enraged me. "Sooner or later I'll get away."

Matt shook his head wonderingly. "Johanna, you'll be free to come and go. Within limits, of course."

I stared at him, confused. What did he mean? I felt a kind of relief and yet under it an even greater terror. This man was even crazier than I'd thought. I probably should have left well enough alone. But I couldn't. I had to know what I was up against. It would help me in the long run, and I had a feeling that Matt would never be so open about his plans again.

"But aren't you afraid I'll go to the police?"

Matt dug his hand in the pocket of his pants and pulled out a brown vial. He shook his hand, the pills rattling.

"Do these look familiar?"

"Where did you get those?"

"In one of your bags after I claimed they were lost. They aren't Xanax, are they, Johanna? They aren't even a migraine medication. They are a powerful antipsychotic commonly prescribed for people suffering from bouts of severe depression, hallucination, and paranoid delusions. As long as you take it, you're fine. But if you don't—" Matt shrugged his shoulders.

"In short, given your history of mental instability, no one will believe you."

I stared at him speechless for a moment, too stunned to even move. Of all the intrusions he had made into my life, this one was by far the most devastating. I felt humiliated, dirtied, defeated.

"How—" I managed to mutter. "How did you find out?"

Matt seemed to be almost expecting the question. He turned and walked to the television, reaching to the shelves above to pull out a video I had never bothered watching. It was labeled with the title of some PBS science special or other. He put the tape in the television, picked up the remote, and turned on the VCR.

"Come here so you can see."

I walked in front of the television. The picture warped sideways and the soundtrack momentarily wavered, but then my face came into focus, looking the picture of vibrant American health, as I scrubbed my teeth with a zeal and passion that, taken out of context, seemed completely insane. At the end, in freeze-frame, the camera caught me on the arm of some gorgeous dark-haired hunk, my hair tossed by the bounce in my step, as I flashed my best and most brilliant Electrify! smile.

"I caught this one night while flipping through the channels. I knew at that instant you were the one I was looking for."

The commercial was no sooner over, then it came on again, and then again.

He seemed to read my mind.

"That advertisement came on a lot for a month or so. It wasn't that hard to fill up twenty minutes of tape. In fact, it seemed they'd air it at around the same time on the same channels every day. Is that something they do on purpose?"

I didn't answer. I could only stare mesmerized in horror at the thought of him obsessively videotaping that commercial over and over again.

"So that's how you chose me," I finally said.

"Well, I had to do a little research first. That's always an important part of successful writing. It adds authenticity. You can't fake that. Well, some can, if they're good enough. Anyway, I called Electrify! and tracked you down from there. They gave me the name of the advertising folks that shot the spot, and they gave me the name of your agent, and your agent gave me your name. I have to tell you that Ruth is not very careful about screening for potential psychos. It strikes me she'll do anything if there's a whiff of money in the air."

Matt turned the television off, ejected the tape, put it back in its cardboard sleeve, and replaced it on the shelf.

"Anyway, I did some checking up on you and learned about your past history."

"But that information is confidential," I said.

"Nothing in this world is confidential," Matt said, "at least not to an author. You see, people love talking to us. A book is a magical thing, Johanna. Either everyone wants to write one, or they want to be mentioned in one. It's like a little piece of immortality. What people will tell you in exchange for a promise that they'll see their names printed on the acknowledgments page. The doctors at the hospitals you stayed at were very accommodating when I told them I was researching a novel about a woman who'd suffered a series of severe psychotic breaks since childhood. Of course, I didn't tell them my real name. I had a fake ID made and bought some books by some hack author to prove who I was.

"I have to say the complexity of your case exceeded even my wildest hopes. The killing of those kittens when you were barely five, the elaborate lies you told of sexual molestation at such a precocious age, the half-successful attempt at clitoral self-mutilation, the midnight attacks on your father, the rumors surrounding the death of your boyfriend—well, the list goes on and on."

"It isn't true," I said numbly. "None of it is true. Besides, it was a long time ago. I'm better now. I'm not insane."

Matt acted as if he hadn't heard me.

"I've been looking for someone like you for a long time, Johanna. We're alike, we two. Kindred souls. Your fears, paranoias, and morbid fantasies will give me a lifetime of material. You'll be my caged bird and what tales of madness you will sing. Together, we will frighten the pants off readers. You even frighten me. And that's a good thing. It'll keep me on my toes. The true muse is both desire and death. She makes a man's hair stand on end. It's like writing with death herself in the room. That's Robert Graves, remember?"

"But the book," I said, falling back onto the couch, my mind reeling. "It's all in the book. That's my proof."

Matt laughed.

"It's fiction, Johanna. Nobody believes a work of fiction."

I thought for a moment. Maybe he was right. Even if I went to the police, who would believe me? I'd probably wind up in some mental institution again. This time for good. I'd spent enough time in them throughout my life to know I didn't want to go back. I'd rather die. I remembered the endless rounds of tests, the lousy food, the straitjackets, the needles, the confinement. I remembered the other patients, the truly crazy ones, plotting against me, planning to kill me in the night.

I remembered the guards stripping me, hosing me down with ice water, attaching electrodes to my nipples and clitoris, watching me writhe and spasm on the cold concrete floor, laughing when I lost control of my bodily functions. I remember the pain and the humiliation as I begged them not to rape me, the duty nurses who listened with bored indifference when I tried to tell them what was going on, my parents' pained expression of worry, guilt, and pity, the bored doctors who scribbled it all into their folders, before prescribing higher doses of medication. And through it all that constant refrain—I remembered now where I heard it—*It's for your own good, Johanna, it's all for your own good.* I remembered what it was like when no one believed you.

No, I would never go back there again.

Never.

Besides, there could be worse things than being the partner of a rich and successful writer. Only one thing still bothered me.

"Would we have to kill anymore?"

"With you around to provide the inspiration," Matt said, "never."

"You know," I said, "it's too bad there isn't any more champagne in the house. I could go for that celebratory drink about now."

Matt beamed. "I took the liberty of buying two bottles. There's one chilling in the fridge right now. Why don't you go get it while I light a fire?"

Matt bent down in front of the fireplace and started sweeping away the old ashes and stacking wood on the grate. He had just finished crumpling up the newspaper he used for starter and was placing it between the larger logs when he called up. "Johanna? Johanna, darling, where are you?"

He half turned and I saw the terror in his eyes.

"No!" he screamed, throwing up his hands, as the ax fell.

For Marsha.

His broken arms fell uselessly at his side.

For Diane.

Blood welled up from a huge gash at the top of his head.

For Sandy.

His neck was severed.

For Ariel.

The base of his skull shattered.

For Cindy.

The left side of his face caved inward.

And for Johanna!

The ax made a dull *thunk* in the wooden floor and Matt's head rolled free of his body.

epilogue

It took me three days to clean up the mess and dispose of the bodies.

I called Harry to help me. He listened to my story over a cup of coffee and just nodded. He was still doing the DeNiro thing—if it even was a thing anymore. He looked more like DeNiro than DeNiro with that half-knowing, half are-you-putting-me-on DeNiro smile.

He didn't ask any questions. In return, I didn't ask him any questions.

I figured we all had our little parts to play in this world and our reasons for playing them. What was important was that he was there for me.

He had driven all night up from the city in his taxi cab. He needed a shower and a meal. I gave him both. I knew I could trust him. He knew the ways of the world and the kind of people in it. How they could hurt you. He had warned me. Still, he had the grace not to say "I told you so." He just shook his head as if I was too naive to know better and it was his job to watch out for me. And that's just the way it was.

Matt's obsession with secrecy worked to my advantage. No one knew about the chalet. The only person left who knew the phone number was his mother. She called once. We had a nice chat. I told her Matt was out getting ready for our trip to Europe. She sounded very happy and said how she couldn't wait to meet me, but not in a pushy way. I liked her. As soon as I hung up I had the phone number changed. I haven't heard from her since, but I imagine there are ways of tracking phone numbers and such. I won't be able to stay here for long.

Hopefully just long enough.

My mother, on the other hand, was not so easy to get rid of.

I called her in Florida.

She was as annoying as ever.

"Where are you?" she said plaintively. "I've been worried sick."

"I'm staying at a chalet in Maine," I explained.

"A what? Where?"

I repeated what I'd said.

"I don't understand."

I sighed. "It's a long story, Mother."

"Well what are you doing there?"

"I'm going to become a writer."

"A writer? First it was an actress, now a writer? What do you know about writing?"

I felt a surge of anger. Why did she always have to bring me down? Was it some genetic thing programmed into mothers in general, or just mine in particular?

"I'll have you know I've already finished a novel," I said self-righteously.

"Really?" she said, sounding both surprised and interested. "Is it any good?"

"I think so," I said honestly. "I really do. I've sent it off to an agent. She says she thinks it could be a bestseller."

"Really?" She seemed guardedly impressed, as if she wanted to believe me, but was afraid to. "Well, good luck," she said. There was a long pause. "I know you don't like me asking but—"

"Yes, Mother," I said, "I'm taking my medicine."

"You don't know how I worry, Johanna. Sometimes you forget. You remember what happened the last time. . . ."

"I'm taking it, all right?"

"I just wanted to make sure. It's tough having children. You'll find out." There was a flicker of hope in her voice. The same undying flicker that would arise whenever I came home from the hospital. You had to admire her optimism. "You never stop worrying about them."

"You mean you never stop thinking about how much you sacrificed, don't you?"

"I didn't say that."

"But that's what you meant. Dad, for instance."

"You shouldn't blame your father," she said. "He just couldn't handle your being sick and all. You really should call him sometime. He always asks about you."

I didn't answer. I was about to hang up in disgust. She must have sensed it.

"Johanna? Are you there?"

"Yeah, I'm here," I said. "But not for long. Can't you just be happy for me for a change, instead of dredging up all this bullshit?"

"You're right, darling. I'm sorry. By the way, when are you coming down to Florida? Your grandmother really wants to see you. Her ninety-fourth birthday's coming up. I think it would be really nice if you could pay us a visit."

"Gee," I said, "I'm kind of busy. I'm just starting a new book."

She sighed. "I understand. But maybe someday. Soon? I'm not getting any younger you know."

I rung off and sat looking out the window by the desk.

I thought about the story I'd told Matt about my mother and grandmother in the concentration camp. He was right. I did have a lot of good material. If Matt had taught me one thing, it was that novel writing wasn't very hard. It was a lot like acting. Except you got to give yourself all the best lines. The most important thing was to be a good liar. The best thing about writing novels is that no one could see you lie. And that made all the difference in the world.

Nothing was off base now.

The only other thing you needed was inspiration.

I stared at the blank screen of the computer and let my fingers rest lightly on the keyboard. On an impulse I picked up the phone.

He picked up, as usual, on the third ring.

"Hi," I said.

"Johanna?" he answered, sounding a little uncertain, and even a little hopeful.

"Listen," I said, "I know it's been awhile and I know things got a little unpleasant, but seeing you at Cindy's funeral, I don't know, it just kind of got me to thinking. . . ."

"Me, too," he said.

"Maybe we could get together again?"

"I'd like that," he said. "I really would."

"I've written a novel," I said.

"I heard. A couple of producers for the USA network were talking about it at a party I went to uptown. It seems your agent is trying to option it for a television movie. Congratulations."

"Thanks," I said, trying to sound off-handed about the whole thing. "But you know how these things are. Nothing's final until the money changes hands."

"Still—" I could almost hear his mind working.

"Anyway, the reason I called. I was kind of wondering what your schedule was like. If you had any time off."

"As a matter of fact," he said, "I'm kind of in between projects." He laughed. "Which is to say I'm out of work." He laughed again, but this time not quite so convincingly.

"Well I was thinking that if you'd like to take a break you can come up to Maine with me. I've bought a chalet."

"Really?" His tone of voice gave him away. I could hear he was impressed, even a little jealous. My heart pounded a little harder.

"Oh, it's just a secluded little place in the woods. I come here mainly to escape the city. You know how it is there. It could be a great getaway for the both of us. A chance to get reacquainted. Besides, I could use the inspiration."

"That sounds fantastic," he said.

"Great. I'm flying in to New York next week. I'll give you a call then. We can get together and make plans. Just you and me. Like old times."

"I can hardly wait, Johanna."

I hung up the phone, smiling.

I stared again at the blank computer screen for only a second before the inspiration came. My fingers seemed to move over the keyboard all by themselves.

I sat back and read what I'd written and then I asked him what he thought. He wasn't there, of course, not really. Although he was always there in his own way, watching out for me. Not like Harry, but like some kind of dark angel who could only love me from a distance lest he destroy me with a single touch.

"Well," I said again, "what do you think?"

"Perfect," he said.

I stared for a long time at what I'd written and decided he was right.

It was the perfect beginning.

for stephen